The Wonder of Lost Causes

Also by Nick Trout

Tell Me Where It Hurts
Love Is the Best Medicine
Ever By My Side: A Memoir in Eight Pets
The Patron Saint of Lost Dogs
Dog Gone, Back Soon

The Wonder of Lost Causes

A Novel

Nick Trout

WILLIAM MORROW
An Imprint of HarperCollinsPublishers

P.S.™ is a trademark of HarperCollins Publishers.

THE WONDER OF LOST CAUSES. Copyright © 2019 by Nicholas Trout. All rights reserved. Printed in the United States of America. No part of this book may be used or reproduced in any manner whatsoever without written permission except in the case of brief quotations embodied in critical articles and reviews. For information, address HarperCollins Publishers, 195 Broadway, New York, NY 10007.

HarperCollins books may be purchased for educational, business, or sales promotional use. For information, please email the Special Markets Department at SPsales@harpercollins.com.

FIRST EDITION

Designed by Diahann Sturge

Title page and part title illustration © James Weston/Shutterstock, Inc.
Chapter opener illustration © Maria Bell/Shutterstock, Inc.

Library of Congress Cataloging-in-Publication Data has been applied for.

ISBN 978-0-06-274794-5

19 20 21 22 23 LSC 10 9 8 7 6 5 4 3 2 1

For Kathy, and inspirational, selfless,
and brave CF mamas everywhere

Part I

Never be ashamed of a scar. It simply means you were stronger than whatever tried to hurt you.

—Unknown

1

Jasper

MY NAME IS Jasper Blunt, and I'm always hungry. Not for food. I'm always hungry for air, as in breathing, as in the stuff your lungs are supposed to process without having to think. Only sometimes, like right now, it feels as though I'm about to starve.

Last time I was in the hospital, like three months back, Mom bought me the *Guinness World Records* book from the gift shop in the lobby. Did you know the record for most people jammed inside a MINI Cooper is twenty-eight? Imagine you're squished in the back seat when the last person climbs in. That's the kind of tightness that can take over my chest.

This time is nowhere near that bad, but something's definitely wrong. My heart has shifted to a place between my ears, there's a boa constrictor where my stomach used to be, and the double hit on my puffer did absolutely nothing. I close my eyelids, pretend to be calm, focus on slow deep breaths, and hope I'm not dying.

Normally Mrs. Katz, the school bus driver, would ask me how I'm doing. But yesterday, when I spotted her new ID badge clipped beside her seat, I made the mistake of telling her I liked it.

"Thanks," she had said, surprised but pleased, showing me her best gray-toothed smile. "Hated the old one. But why is it photos always make you look fat?"

I thought about this and replied, "Fat makes you look fat, Mrs. Katz."

Now she acts like she hates me, even though I'm the only kid who ever sits up front. It's October and it's still hot, like someone forgot about fall and won't let summer end. Fortunately, the windows are open and if I angle my head just right, my lungs can grab some of the salty air coming off the ocean. Eyes scrunched shut, with only five more minutes to go, I pretend I'm a free diver preparing to go deep, ignoring the scary belly knot twisting tighter and tighter the closer I get to my stop.

2

Kate

"I GOT HIM, Dr. Blunt," says Martha. She's holding tight to the handle of a steel rabies pole.

Martha is my most experienced technician, überpierced and, for this week only, sporting Slurpee-blue hair gelled into stiff peaks. The wings of the bald eagle tattooed across her inner bicep flutter as proof of her muscular restraint.

We're standing on the loading dock around the back of the shelter. The creature on the wrong end of the pole braces himself against the braided steel noose cinched around his neck. He appears riveted to the concrete, head down, chin in chest, refusing to make eye contact.

In my particular version of canine matchmaking—a significant part of my job—first impressions are everything, but this dog makes you stare for all the wrong reasons. By any definition he is an immeasurable mutt, a Heinz 57 with so many varieties in the mix it is impossible to pick out all the ingredients. Loose mastiff jowls; oversized silly shepherd ears; outstretched Dober-man neck; legs of a Dane; and the broad, beaver tail of an En-glish Labrador. I could probably start over and find a dozen new breeds the second time around. The best I can do is to label him as a predominantly black, neutered male; and big, somewhere in the order of one hundred pounds.

Yet the dog's grab bag of breeds is nothing compared to the scars, a history of previous troubled lives written in permanent aberrations on his poor body. Impossible to ignore, they hold you up, make you stumble, force you to wonder what happened, and why, and—sadly—for how long.

Beside the huge Antarctica-shaped scar on his flank, the other skin lesions may seem minor, but the dog's entire body is peppered with sizable nicks and dings, a used car with way too many miles on the clock to merit a makeover. He's missing two toes from his left back paw, the amputation crude, more butchery than surgery, leaving the remaining nubs gnarled and unsightly. And then there's the trauma to his head. The dog's upper and lower incisor teeth are gone, causing the tip of his tongue to protrude beyond his lips when he isn't panting. His right ear looks as if it was nibbled by a shark and his right upper eyelid droops, making his blink on that side languid and teary.

But my biggest concern lies with the hairless zebra stripes of scar tissue across the bridge of his nose—irregular, thick, al-most rubbery. I've seen them before, just once, in a photograph from a scientific journal, an image I'd hoped to forget. In the version I recall, damage was caused by layer upon layer of duct tape wrapped jaw-clenchingly tight around a dog's muzzle. The intent was not to maim or brand. The intent was to silence—a cheap, crude, heartless binding meant to quiet any dog that barked too much, especially a dog that might give anything to be somewhere else.

I inch into a potential strike zone, my "magic wand" microchip scanner in hand. "Good boy," I say. The dog's posture is confusing. He's guarded and suspicious, yet not overtly aggressive, afraid, or submissive.

If I didn't know better, I'd think he was on the verge of giving up, resigned to his fate.

"That's a good boy."

I stretch forward, waving the scanner back and forth across his hunched shoulder blades. Jackpot—the digital screen lights up and there's an audible ping.

"We have a winner," says Martha, maintaining her solid grip on the rabies pole.

A serial number stretches across the display. This is the best possible outcome—a dog too flawed, too peculiar to be adopted, already has a home.

"You okay while I find out who he belongs to?"

I'm gone before Martha can reply, heading up front to call the tracking company. I'm almost too distracted to catch the sound of the throaty diesel engine, the distinctive crunch of a school bus gearbox slowing for a stop.

3

Jasper

ONE TIME A doctor suggested I learn how to meditate, saying it would help me breathe in stressful situations. What a plonker. *You* try to relax and "open your mind" when it feels like you ran a hundred-meter sprint with your nose pinched shut and a plastic straw duct-taped to your lips.

"Hey."

I look up to find Mrs. Katz towering over me.

"It's your stop."

I check out the window (in case she's lying), mumble sorry, grab my backpack, and scramble off the bus. I try to run, but it makes the nervous tightness in my chest worse. Even at a slog—a slow jog—my backpack feels like it's full of rocks, making me sloth down the white shell driveway to the shelter.

The closer I get to the main building, the more anxious I get. And it's not my usual, "Mom, I think we need to go to the ER."

It's different. More like I'm totally stressed out, and for no good reason. I crash through the front doors, into the empty lobby.

Mom's behind the reception desk, staring at a computer screen, reaching for a phone. She looks up as I come in.

"I feel funny," I say, ditching the pack and shuffling toward her.

Before my stack of textbooks and tracker files can even hit the floor, she's on me.

"You tight? Coughing? Chest hurt?"

If Mom wanted to play poker, she'd have to do it online. She gets this twitchy flicker around her left eye and I know she doesn't want me to notice and I don't want to make her feel bad, but it happens every time she starts to panic.

I fake a smile. "I'm okay. It's just . . . it's like I've done something wrong. Inside. That's what it feels like. Like I'm in trouble. But I haven't, I promise."

Mom crouches down so our eyes are level. Slowly, the twitch fizzles out. "Bad report card coming my way?"

I shake my head.

"But you're afraid of something?"

Under other circumstances, this might be a good time to mention how I bought something I shouldn't on Amazon, but I murmur, "I guess."

The weird feeling scrunches up inside my belly again, and my answer has made her twitch spark back to life, so I reach out and put my fingers on it. I smooth the soft skin, making it disappear, whispering, "It's okay, Mom," quiet enough so that no one else can hear.

4

Kate

HIS LIPS ARE their usual pale lavender—only so much oxygen can permeate his bloodstream—but, paradoxically, the way he speaks settles my nerves. Jasper's voice always has a subtle, smoky timbre, thanks to years of caustic inhaled medications abrading his tiny vocal cords. It's not the sound that matters, nor the pitch. It's the rhythm. How his sentences fit between his breaths. When Jasper isn't being forced to rush, to squeeze words or split syllables around inhalations, that's always a good sign.

I make a joke about a report card but he doesn't laugh. He's either worried or scared, I can't tell. Eleven-year-old boys shouldn't have to worry about anything, least of all about staying alive.

His worry makes me worry. And that's when he gets to me— this sick little boy brushing away *my* concern. The sincerity written in those eyes fells me, my little boy trying to appear carefree, intent on offering me comfort and reassurance.

At work I try to be Dr. Blunt, not Mom, but I bend forward and plant a quick dry kiss on his forehead.

"Drop your stuff in my office and change. We're on the loading dock."

Jasper nods and shuffles down the corridor. He's wearing his favorite "7 Beckham" England soccer shirt for the second day in a row. I stifle a smile. For a split second I almost sweated the small stuff of a normal parent.

Out back, the standoff between Martha and my defiant canine remains unchanged.

"He's another Lucky," I say as I walk through the door.

"How original," says Martha, sounding bored, adjusting her grip on the pole.

"The microchip guy says he'll call me back as soon as he's reached the owner. Meantime, let's try to get our friend into isolation. Lucky, you ready to behave?"

"Lucky," says Martha, with renewed determination, "come on, Lucky. Let's go."

As Martha tugs on the pole, the dog jerks forward, nails scraping across the concrete; but with his front and back legs extended and locked underneath him, Lucky barely budges.

"Lucky," I snap. Lucky doesn't even blink.

"Maybe he's deaf," says Martha.

Or stubborn, I think to myself.

I slink closer, chanting "Lucky" to an animal that looks as though he wants to fold into himself, over and over, until he's so small he disappears. I stretch out my hand and it floats toward the most prominent scar, as if drawn to it. Head bowed, the dog cannot possibly see the gesture, yet he shimmies sideways, twisting out of range.

"No, Lucky," barks Martha, yanking on the noose, making the dog flinch. She meets my glare of disapproval with her own huffy grimace of defiance. I'm certain biting is the last thing on his mind. "You want to grab a sedative or shall I?"

To be fair, she's got a point. We're getting nowhere. But do I want an owner collecting a dog that looks as though he's been binge drinking at a frat party?

"Just hang on." I take the pole from Martha, opting for one more attempt at total dominance, booming out a masterful "Lucky, come," trying to muscle this dogged dog toward the open door.

Nothing. Just dead weight.

Then, without warning, the tension in the rabies pole vanishes, the dog's head rises with regal deliberation, muscles relax, loosen up, and finally, after all our previous efforts, the animal makes his first genuine eye contact.

But not with me.

I follow Lucky's line of sight and there, mesmerized and frozen in the doorway, stands my son.

Seconds crawl by and nobody moves. I'm holding my breath. Immediately, it's clear that this is more than just a boy and a dog sizing each other up, more than simple curiosity or mutual appraisal. The two appear equally starstruck. An odd connectivity burns in their eyes—they're not just looking at each other, they're looking inside each other. If I had to nail down Jasper's expression, I'd go with a flash of confusion, quickly overwhelmed by something approaching—and I know it makes absolutely no sense—the pleasure of recognition.

"Lucky, come," I repeat, trying to take advantage of the dog's dropped guard. The animal stumbles a few steps forward until the trance fractures and once more, the joints of this tin dog rust up solid.

"I'm getting the drugs," says Martha, heading for the pharmacy. I let up on the pole as a small hand tugs on my sleeve.

"Mom, his name's not Lucky."

"Not now, Jasper."

"But Dr. Blunt," insists my son, "it's not."

"Jasper, the dog is microchipped. Don't ask me how but he's twenty miles from his home in Wellfleet, and, according to the tracking data, his name is Lucky."

Jasper shakes his head. More than adamant, he's deadly serious. "His name's Whistler."

And just like flipping a switch, I divine a sea change through the pole, the dog transformed by the sound of two new syllables, as if instantly suffused with relief. His tail toggles in a slow, appreciative wag.

"Whistler," I repeat, and saying the name again only fires up his wag, windshield wiper set to high, making it easy to guide a different, entirely malleable dog through an open door and directly into the isolation ward, with its harsh austerity, fresh antiseptic smell, and ominous echo of distant barking. Straight into a run, I slip off the redundant noose of the rabies pole, lock the metal gate, and turn to my son.

"Tell me the truth," I say. "Have you seen this dog before?"

Jasper shakes his head, but the way he bites down on his lower lip makes him appear either ashamed or afraid.

"Then how did you know his name?"

My only child studies the floor, winces through painful deliberation, takes the deepest breath his diseased little lungs can muster, and says:

"Because he told me."

5

Jasper

I KNOW THIS is going to make me sound a little creepy or screwy or wacked, but for a while I've been getting these . . . weird feelings, around certain dogs. Like a few days ago during visiting hours when I was standing outside Mr. Tibbles's cage—he's this snippy three-legged Pomeranian that seems to like me even if Martha has him marked down as "absolutely no kids, period." This family walked past and, don't ask me how, but the dog might as well have screamed in my ear that he was fine with boys, just not girls, especially girls with pigtails like the one holding on to her mom and dad. And I remember that I suddenly got this pain in my arm, brief but shooting, and at precisely the same time my stomach lurched like on a roller coaster (I'm guessing because I've never been allowed on one). It only lasted seconds, but later Martha told me the Pomeranian lost its leg after it was broken and the original owners couldn't afford to fix it. She thought it probably involved falling from high up. I kept my mouth shut—usually best around Martha—but after my experience today, I would bet money, if I had any, that Mr. Tibbles broke his leg by being accidentally dropped from a height by a little girl with pigtails.

Okay, maybe not a great example, but I swear the moment I set eyes on this dog called Whistler, it was as if this weirdness might actually make some sense. What if I wasn't tuning into *my* nervousness on the school bus, but the *dog's*? And maybe it's more than just realizing something in my head. What if I can actually *feel* the changes inside of a dog myself? What if the boa constrictor swallowing *my* stomach was caused by a scared dog in a scary place, trapped on the wrong end of a scary rabies pole?

I never meant to freak Mom out with the name Whistler. It just kind of popped into my brain. The dog didn't actually speak like in some dumb *Dr. Dolittle* movie. It was more like the name was already there, hiding, but wanting to be found. I knew the name Whistler was right, even if the only voice I heard was mine.

6

Kate

I KNOW THE answers by heart.

Question: What percentage of pet owners speak to their pet?

Answer: One hundred percent.

Fair enough. Nothing to be ashamed of here.

Question: What percentage of pet owners believe they know what their pet is saying?

Answer: Ninety-seven percent.

What Jasper is implying, on the other hand, is more troubling. *"Because he told me."*

I hope this is simply Jasper being cute. Adding auditory hallucinations to his ever-growing list of health problems might throw me over the edge.

From somewhere up front Martha cracks my reverie with a thunderous "Hey, Doc, phone."

With the dog formerly known as Lucky secured in a run, I

follow her summons to the reception desk. It seems that the microchip company has called back.

"What did you find?" I ask.

"Sadly, Dr. Blunt, our records have proven inaccurate," says the same guy as before, audibly embarrassed. I can hear chatter in the background and imagine insipid cubicles, hands-free headsets, and faraway time zones—nighttime in an Indian call center. "Apparently the dog no longer resides with the gentleman on file."

"I don't follow," I say. "You told me the dog's name is Lucky."

"As far as the gentleman knows, it still is. It certainly was. However, he says the dog was given up for adoption over two years ago and this is the fifth time he's been contacted about a dog he no longer owns."

"Wait. This dog has run away from five other homes?"

The line goes silent for several seconds.

"Correct, madam. I assured him that I have made the necessary corrections to the file and this time we've definitely deleted his contact name, number, and address." The man pauses. "But he was very . . . descriptive . . . about what he'd like to do with the microchip."

This makes no sense. You chip your dog because you're worried he or she will run away, get stolen, or get lost. You chip because you are a responsible dog owner.

"Five times, you said."

"Correct, madam."

What prompted this original owner to abandon a dog he

must, at one time, have cared about? More importantly, why would this dog keep bouncing from one new owner to the next? Shelters like ours are really careful about placing the right dog in the right home. We interview and assess to ensure a safe and loving environment for every dog we adopt. What would make this particular dog keep running away?

"You mentioned the town of Wellfleet, Massachusetts. Don't suppose you can give me this guy's phone number? I'd love to find out more about Lucky's history."

"Sorry, madam. The gentleman even spoke to my supervisor."

I feel a boulder of frustration rolling unevenly toward the back of my head.

"Okay, let me ask, are you an animal lover?"

"Of course. I love *All Creatures Great and Small.*"

"Wonderful. Me too. So what I'm trying to do here is save the life of an animal that is, between you and me, unlikely to get adopted. He's older, to be honest he's kind of ugly, and from what you're telling me, he'd rather be a fugitive than a family pet. Please, for Lucky's sake, is there anything you can share that might help me understand this dog so that I can try to place him in the right home?"

Nails tap-dance across a faraway keyboard.

"AKC number left blank," he says. "Breed: mixed. Ah, that makes sense. Sex: male and neutered. Age . . . just says 'mature.' Wait, there's a note about something called a 'Panhandle Canine Railroad.'"

I scratch the name on a scrap of paper. *Panhandle Canine*

Railroad. Never heard of it. Presumably a rescue organization shipping dogs from America's dust bowl to the Northeast, including here on Cape Cod?

"Oh, and here's one more thing: the dog originated in the state of Oklahoma."

"What? Oklahoma?"

There's a pause, and then he adds, "Like Rodgers and Hammerstein."

"I'm not with you," I say.

"*Oklahoma*. It's a show, a musical. 'Where the wind comes whistlin' down the plain,' yes?"

I'm treated to a throaty chuckle, while I'm thinking, *Not possible.*

Whistling down the plain.

Whistler?

7

Jasper

CONFINED BY CHIPPED metal bars, Whistler looks more like a prisoner than a dog.

"Thirsty, hungry, or both?"

His head falls to one side but his chocolate eyes never move, locked on me.

"I'll take that as a yes."

Shiny metal bowls and all sorts of different dog food sit in a cabinet under a sink. Pouring him some cold water is easy. But what would he like to eat?

"Help me out," I say, removing bags and cans and showing them off, hoping for a woof when I point to something he might like. Nothing, but Whistler's stare never lets up.

"Okay, then I'll choose."

I reach for a bag of chicken and rice, but something makes me keep going, fingers walking, eyes sliding, toward, of all things, a bag of lamb and garden peas. One time Grandma tried to feed me sheep for Easter—it's about half past not happening, Grandma—and I pretty much avoid anything green on my dinner plate, but for some reason this choice feels right.

Over my shoulder, I check in, and I'm still in the crosshairs of his focus. Is it possible that, even without a blink or a bark, the dog is *making* me choose for him?

"Lamb and garden peas it is," I say, kibble tinkling on metal. Balancing both bowls, I slide them under the gate.

Whistler shows no interest in either. Perhaps he's distracted by the sound of approaching footsteps.

"You okay?" says Mom. "Or has that dog got you in a spell?"

"Lookit," I say, scrambling to my feet, pointing to the Whistler card I made and hung on his run.

"Ah, so you're feeling better?"

"Much. Soon as I saw Whistler I felt fine."

Her eyes go slitty before she sniffs down so much air she grows into her five feet ten inches. It hurts my neck to look up that far.

"Really?" she says, holding back a half-smile. "Is this what it's come to? A psychic connection between you and a dog in need of adoption?" Mom reaches into the back pocket of her green scrubs, pulls out and applies ChapStick to her dry lips like they might shatter any second if she doesn't. She's addicted. She never wears lipstick. Only in photos from before I was born. "We've been over this a thousand times and the answer's still the same."

I make a face—hurt, with a tiny bit of begging. It's meant to be irresistible. It's meant to make Mom give in. Whistler appears to have followed my lead, delivering a fantastically sad face of his own. Nice.

"Please, Jasper, don't."

Not so long ago I might have started to cry, or stomped off, or hit her with a whiny "But, Mom. . . ." Now that I'm eleven, we've entered a new phase in our relationship—arguing.

"Fine," I say, "but I know you believe dogs can predict when their owner is coming home from work, right?"

"Jasper."

"And we watched that show about the way animals know when a tsunami is coming and service dogs can tell you if you're about to have a seizure. I bet Andrew Peach wished he had a service dog."

"Who's Andrew Peach?"

"Kid in the year below me. Bit of a plonker."

"Jasper. I've told you about that kind of language."

"Mom, it's not a curse word in England, so it can't be a curse word over here."

Mom hates that I've become an Anglophile, which means a person who loves all things English. I've started with slang and soccer, or should I say "football," because the history of the British royal family and the rules of cricket are way too boring. Anyway, I'm thinking long term, because being more English than American might be a game changer.

"Andrew Peach has epilepsy. Seizured in class last week. If a service dog had been there, he might not have peed his pants."

I ignore Mom slowly shaking her head.

"You keep telling me to have an open mind. So I'm just saying that sometimes people and animals can talk without actually speaking and, like, maybe it can go both ways."

Fluttering my "pretty please" eyelashes hasn't worked for years, so I bring the crook of my elbow up to my mouth and toss in a soggy, deep, and what my doctor describes as a "meaty" cough.

"Don't," says Mom, ready to pounce, like I've played the sick card. "You use your puffer?"

"End of class."

Suddenly Martha's detached head floats around the doorway. "Any chance you can take a look at Olive? The pit bull in thirteen. I'm worried she might be going into heat."

Mom tells her she'll be right there, as soon as she's drawn blood and taken chest X-rays on our "new admission." Why doesn't she just say Whistler? And why does Martha look annoyed?

"Let me tell you how this is going to go down," says Mom, clamping my arms to the sides of my chest like a toy soldier at attention. "I was trying to admit a stray dog, a dog who keeps running away from every new home that adopts him. He's a repeat offender. It's no wonder he hates animal control and rabies poles, but the thing is, for some reason, he loves kids. When you walk in he's a totally new dog."

"But what about me knowing his name?"

Wet air sucks between her clenched teeth.

"How can you possibly *know*?" She shakes her head. "Don't answer that. Look, the name can stay. Probably sounds like one of a dozen other names he's had in his past lives."

"But don't you think—"

"No, Jasper. No more. I know what you're doing. *We—cannot—have—a—dog*. Period."

"Service dogs are allowed. I asked the landlord."

"But he's not a service dog and you don't need a service dog. You're not in a wheelchair. You're not autistic. You don't have . . . PTSD."

My shoulders go all watery. I give up.

Mom tickles her fingers between the bars of the run. Whistler looks like he's not buying this as a greeting, so he slides closer to me.

"At least he likes kids," she says. "That's a plus."

I don't get it. She makes it sound like he might be hard to adopt. Gray hairs don't make him old, unless you want a puppy. And Martha's lying when she talks about Black Dog Syndrome—big black dogs being harder to adopt—because smarter people on the Internet proved it was a myth. Anyway, who wants cute when you can have cool? Who wants a dog that humans have made to order when you can get an animal like this?

"What d'you think happened?" I ask, sliding my wrist through the gap between the bars, heading for the biggest hairless scar.

Mom's on me like a secret service agent spotting a gun in a crowd, lunging, snatching me by the shoulder, my wrist clanging against the metal even as Whistler tries to arch into a touch. "Not until he's evaluated. You know better than that."

I'm too stunned to reply, and finally us not speaking gets really awkward.

8

Kate

I RETURN TO the isolation ward ready to start Lucky's admission process—get a body weight, a blood sample, perform a physical exam—but end up waylaid by a son convinced he's found an incontrovertible reason for why we need to adopt this particular dog.

It's not that I don't appreciate Jasper's love for all our waifs and strays, but claiming to have been suddenly and, apparently, divinely blessed with a talent for direct canine communication troubles me deeply. Given all that he goes through, of course I want him to feel special, but not like this. This smacks of desperation, and instead of being cute, I feel as though I'm being played.

For as long as Jasper could talk, he's made enforcing our dogless existence no easy task for me, not least since I'm a veterinarian. My stance has been fraught with second guesses and regret. So many times I have just wanted to cave, as if the decision were that simple, that inconsequential. I have imagined and replayed the look of astonished joy on Jasper's face if I ever were to give in. The thing is, in my world, acts of carefree spontaneity can be as reckless as they are perilous. Mothers like me shouldn't have to defend their actions, but the guilt of denying Jasper a dog pales in comparison to the negative impact such a creature could have on Jasper's health.

If asked, I might play up the lukewarm legitimacy of the apartment's no pets policy, but that's not it. Occasionally I'll push the unfairness of foisting a dog on strangers, at a moment's notice, for God knows how long, every time Jasper gets admitted to the hospital. But the simple, honest answer—control—stays with me. Sure, I'll hide behind words like *structure* and *boundaries*, but *pet-less-ness* simply works best. Why? Because when you live my version of a high-wire life, permanently swaying between fear and futility, who needs the responsibility of one more willful variable, one more dangerous distraction (i.e., a dog) guaranteed to throw you off balance and ensure you fall.

Not that this hard-line stance stops my badgering son. If Jasper were a dog—and we've played this game—he'd be a terrier: smart, relentless, and most of all, fearless. Though you'd never guess to look at him.

People say it's not fair, the good-looking kid being so sickly. Others whisper about the whimsy of God, something to offset the blow: the unruly mop of thick blond hair and those celestial blue eyes, the least any reasonable higher power could do. But spend any time around him, and you quickly realize the angelic features are a facade. Serious imperfections lurk deep inside the pale and stunted brittle twig of his body. It makes him look much younger than his peers in sixth grade. As time passes it's harder to mask these fatal flaws, but easier, as a parent, to be dazzled by both his bravery and his light. I'll catch a glint in something as small as a crooked smile, or be blinded by it when he lets loose a breathless belly laugh, and each time he shines, he snuffs out every silent curse I will ever make over how things turned out. He is my force of nature, forced to defy the will of nature. He is not disabled. Jasper is just different.

In regard to the man who gave my son the other half of his DNA, he is just that. Calling him Jasper's "genetic" father is the best I can do; he has never come close to deserving the "Dad" label. His name was, is, Simon Swift, randomly assigned as my anatomy partner in our first class at the Royal Veterinary College, London. Not that I jumped his bones on day one. It took a while for our anatomical education to go extracurricular, but still, at the time our union seemed fated, almost arranged, a tale to tell the children.

By our final year we were living together, graduation around the corner, weighed down by finals and the uncertainty of what was next.

"Stop worrying," he insisted, his smile slick with self-confidence, hooking a finger under my chin, forcing my eyes upward to meet his. "We'll find a practice where we can both work. I'll do the horses; you can do the cats and dogs. It'll be perfect. I promise." And like a fool I bought into a future with Simon, the two of us landing jobs together in some idyllic English village, strolling down to the local pub at night, our kids destined to dress like extras in *Harry Potter*.

Now, forced to think about Simon, all I see is a nauseating fake incredulity as he asserts, "It can't be mine," and the painful realization that he was only ever in love with *his* version of me, the one in which everything went according to his plan, not mine. Thank God I see nothing of him in Jasper, and believe me, I'm constantly looking.

For the first eight years of Jasper's life I withheld the truth. He didn't ask (not in so many words), so I didn't tell. Now he knows his father comes from England—home of bad dentition, bad food, and, for my son, a national sport that kindles fanaticism. He knows his father's name, knows we graduated in the same class. My conscience is clear. No one can say I denied him his birthright. But knowing is one thing, the need to look is another, because what does that say about his relationship to me? How long before Jasper thinks we should make a pilgrimage across the pond, that he will have so much in common with the father who once practically boasted, "It was never my intention to breed." Is it any wonder I'm upset by my son's burgeoning vocabulary of English slang?

When I look at Whistler (and it's "sweepin' down the plain," not "whistlin'"), I see too much of a past and little chance of finding a future. And yet, somewhere behind those maple syrup eyes, in the places where it counts, Jasper may be right. This dog *does* have a presence. I'm not one for adjectives like *soulful* or *wise*, not least because Whistler's stare can be a little unnerving, but there is something, perhaps more different than special, but something, dancing around back there, holding my interest.

I'm running through all of this as Jasper brings his elbow up to his mouth and unleashes a cough. Most of the time I never even notice. These small clearances are normal, like white noise—the fan in a room, the rattle of a train down the tracks. Jasper's cough has become the soundtrack to my life, virtually inaudible, until he lets out one of his sonic booms.

"What d'you think happened?" asks Jasper, and suddenly he's squeezing his entire arm between the bars, reaching for the dog's largest scar.

An animal that's been tortured may seek an opportunity for revenge. Normally I'm hyperalert to keeping Jasper safe around new arrivals, but I'm distracted by our argument, and slow to react to Jasper's arm in the cage. Instead of calm intervention I wrench on my son's boney, weightless shoulder, the force too much, too shocking. Dog and boy are unified by looks of horror, leaving me to stew in a marinade of guilty silence.

"Sorry," I offer. "I didn't mean to hurt you. It's just . . . this dog may be unpredictable, what with all his . . . injuries."

"You think he was hit by a car? Dragged?"

"Maybe," I say, not wanting to get into the likely origin of certain scars. Safer to change tack and sniff the air. "You smell that?"

Jasper snaps his head to one side and berates me with upward-glancing eyes that say, "Really?" Thanks to fourteen—yes, I'm counting—bouts of severe sinus infections, smell is one of his weakest senses.

"I smell cigarette smoke," I say. "He's going to need a bath, maybe two. You okay helping with his blood draw or shall I get Martha?"

And with that, my rubber ball son bounces back.

"No, I'm good. Cool. Let me get everything." He begins pulling out drawers. "I can't find the purple-top tubes," he says, sounding a little panicky, not wanting to fail me.

"Go check in the storage room," I say. "Third shelf up on the left. I'll get the clippers." He disappears as I mutter, "And a muzzle, just in case."

Rooting around inside a cabinet behind the isolation ward door I hear the familiar wet hacking cough over my shoulder.

"That was quick."

But when I spin around, the room is empty. Empty, except for the dog staring back from behind the bars, his eyes on me, chest heaving with the exertion of clearing his lungs, his tail wagging ever so slowly back and forth. Is this dog a parrot in disguise, perfectly capable of mimicking my son's cough? Forget similar, it's like I just listened to a digital recording.

"Got it," says Jasper, marching into the room, triumphant, beaming, and waving the glass vial with the purple top over-head. Until he sees my face.

"Mom, what's wrong?"

9

Jasper

FOR KIDS LIKE me, having a cough is a total no-win situation. If I'm not coughing at night, Mom freaks out, creeping around with a flashlight, checking to see if I'm dead or alive. When I am coughing at night, Mom freaks out (lots of left eye twitching), because unlike a fever or throwing up or crapping your pants, the sound of a cough is a constant reminder of a sickness in need of a fix.

According to Mom there is only one situation where my cough would come in handy, and that's if I got lost in a crowd, or if someone ever tried to kidnap me, because it's like having my own personal siren, a ping you can follow, what she calls "the LoJack in my lungs." But she's forgetting the time we took the Amtrak from Boston to Washington, DC, to visit the Air and Space Museum, and the train was crowded with men in business suits and pretty women in high heels, and I had this major coughing fit and everyone looked at me like I had Ebola. We got to sit together all by ourselves.

When I get sick, my doctor says I get a Tupac-a-Day cough, which makes no sense because Tupac was a rapper and he died from a gunshot wound not from a lung infection. My Tupac cough can get big and crazy, and sometimes it makes people nearby offer me a glass of water like I'm choking, or pat me on the back. I know they mean well, but sometimes I just want to be left alone.

The other thing about coughing is it makes you really tired. I sleep propped up on at least three huge pillows, and it helps, but it's been years since I've been able to fall asleep lying on my back. Sometimes I dream about falling asleep lying flat, like a baby in a crib, peaceful and safe.

Dog coughing is different. Okay, people like Mom stare, but other dogs are polite enough to ignore it. No dog would give another dog a hard time. They're not nosy about how you're doing or ready to yank their puppies in the opposite direction. When dogs cough, it is what it is, let it go. If it's not bothering me, why let it bother you? Dogs are cool like that. Especially Whistler. And what are the chances that Whistler's cough sounds identical to mine? That has to be more than coincidence. Like he was totally meant to find me. I just hope the reason for his cough is different. I hope it will go away. For his sake, it *has* to go away.

10

Kate

LATER, MUCH LATER, I would look back on that first day and smile, as if it all made sense. But when I lived it, when I saw the X-ray image on the screen, that angry swarm of black-and-white pixels melding into specific shades of gray, it was like a startling déjà vu.

"Is it bad?" asks Jasper.

I'm speechless staring at Whistler's chest. It's not that I don't know what to say, I just don't know where to begin.

Two pictures of the dog's thorax—side on and front to back— heart, lungs, and airways. Life on four legs makes the fundamentals of the canine chest very different from a human's, but where it counts, in the architecture of the tissues, the similarities can be uncanny.

As a mother and a doctor, I've become wholly acquainted with my son's lung pathology. Fluent in the language of Jasper's disease, I stay abreast of the latest FDA trials, yearning for the "breakthrough," make-believing in it because . . . well . . . it's what you do.

"Mom, what is it?"

Protecting our offspring is innate, as instinctual as breathing, but the truth is, I have failed him from the day he was born. Who knew my DNA harbored a fatal genetic disease? I was—am—a perfectly healthy woman. Carrying a mutated gene never crossed my mind. Of course I couldn't know that his sickness began the moment he took his first breath, but sometimes that's no consolation. Forget fate, bad luck, and long odds, Jasper was my choice, my responsibility and mine alone. As my son transitioned from a world of fluid to a world of air it was just the two of us, a stranger squeezing my ringless finger. No, when guilt wants its way, Jasper's disease is my fault.

Whistler drives his scuffed and pointy snout between the bars, as if trying for a better view of his X-ray, as if demanding to know what the fuss is about.

"You're scaring *us*," says Jasper, tugging at my sleeve.

The freaky *us* reference should get my attention, but the X-ray has me in its grip, reliving the early days, Jasper as a sickly two-year-old, struggling to gain weight, asthmatic and prone to debilitating colds and croup. When the doctors finally made a diagnosis, they pulled me aside, their tone somber, sympathetic, phrases interspersed by pained expressions and the open palms of the helpless and impotent. Only two specific words floated to the surface, bobbing around in a strange calm before finally settling. They were meaningless. They sounded foreign, like they had lost their way and needed to get back to some sort of a pathology report. Or maybe the last line from a dictated post-mortem. *Cystic fibrosis*. Whatever happened to good old child-hood diseases like mumps or whooping cough? And shortening this epithet from five syllables to two letters—CF—didn't help. I blanked on the bit about CF being the number one genetic killer of children. I'd switched off long before they got to the phrase "incurable."

Whistler begins to whine.

Dogs do not suffer from cystic fibrosis. Yes, they can get pneumonia, asthma, pulmonary hypertension, and catastrophic changes in the heart, similar to CF, but not all together, not seam-lessly coupled as a total package. The balm of rational thought says that this is simply a dog with chronic, irreversible lung damage, likely from secondhand cigarette smoke inhalation.

But then the same logic snags in an emotional recess of my brain. Here is a dog I would normally write off as a lost cause, too old, unadoptable, denied a second (or however many) chance due to the severity of his lung disease. But now, seeing the shock-ing detail in these X-rays, how can I possibly deny this dog when the image of his chest bears such a striking resemblance to my son's? How would an argument for Whistler's humane eutha-nasia sound in Jasper's ears?

I still haven't answered Jasper's question, and he's staring at me expectantly, a worried frown on his face. "Sorry, Jasper," I say, coming back, "Whistler's chest X-rays look a little . . . kooky, is all."

Jasper meets my eyes, like he wants to measure "kooky." Over the years he's learned my lexicon of holding back. Like that time when an ENT surgeon shoved a massive scope up his nose and I swore it wouldn't hurt a bit. Or when they wanted to check out his stomach and made him swallow a special pill with a camera inside, and I failed to mention it would be like swallowing an iPhone.

"Worse than mine?" he asks.

Unbelievable. In this direct comparison of who has the most ill-fated X-rays, my son is more worried about this alien dog than himself.

"Different," I say, determined not to give anything away, hitting the *X* in the corner of the screen, making the images vanish. How I wish it were that easy. "Go set up for a bath."

He shoots me a killer smile, finishing me off.

"And Jasper—"

He stops in his tracks.

"Make sure that dog doesn't steal your puffer."

11

Jasper

Turns out, in the state of Massachusetts, you have to be four feet nine to stop needing a dumb booster seat. Most kids ditch theirs by third grade. Not me. Every time Mom makes me chug another disgusting high-calorie shake, she reminds me of the impossible "two more inches" I'm lacking. That's why I'm in the back seat, "riding high" for the short trip home.

Mom keeps eyeing me in the mirror. Not that we're talking. I'm too busy working on a secret plan to save Whistler. This is what I've got so far:

1. Try to find out if me and Whistler really do have a special way of communicating.

2. If the answer is yes, it *might* be a good idea to tell Mom, because maybe then she'll let me keep him.

3. If the answer is yes, it might *not* be a good idea to tell Mom because she'll think I'm wacked.

4. Either way, try to fix Whistler's broken lungs in less than fourteen days.

5. Point number four may sound strange, but dogs can only stay in the shelter for two weeks, and if I can't keep him, I have to make sure someone else adopts him, and that's probably only going to be possible if he loses his Tupac cough.

6. Try not to think about what happens if he's not adopted after two weeks.

"You okay?" asks Mom, which is code for "Are you okay even though we're not bringing home the perfect dog, once again?" I hope Mom thinks my lazy "uh-huh" is code for "not really," because at this precise moment I remember the possibility that there might be a package on our doorstep, the result of clicking on a "proceed to checkout" button. This is definitely on me—my bad, my fear of getting caught. If there's a package sitting there, it needs to get to my bedroom ASAP, before Mom sees it.

Sure enough, there's a smiling cardboard box when we pull up. I'm first out of the 4Runner, slogging for the door, key at the ready, but the box is so big and my hands are so small I'm barely across the kitchen before I'm busted.

"Wrong address?" says Mom, pointing to the Amazon logo.

If I were like the cool kids in class, I'd have a lightning-fast comeback, a lie on the fly. But I've got nothing. That's why Mom says honesty will always be my only way out.

"It's for me," I say, not sure why the purchase had seemed like such a good idea at the time. "You said think about a birthday present . . . and it was on sale, but only for a limited time, so—"

"How?"

Amazing—old people and the Internet.

"With a credit card. Your account and card number came up automatically."

"And what exactly did you buy with *my* credit card?"

Here goes nothing.

"It's a tent, a two-man tent. The lightest, most compact, most portable two-man tent in the world."

Mom looks at the size of the box, looks at me, and arches her eyebrows. "Since when have you wanted to go on a camping trip?"

Best to check out my sneakers. I don't want Mom to feel hurt.

"Tell me," she says, softer and closer.

"It's just that . . . with all my meds and treatments, I never get to do sleepovers, and that's why I never go to stuff like summer camp, and why friends never get to stay over here because I cough in my sleep and they'd hate my guts. I just thought . . . maybe we could try camping, somewhere, sometime. You and me. Do something different?"

Now I get to watch her decision in real time, and as she hesitates, I try to nail it.

"Hey, I got free shipping."

The wrong answer buzzer rings inside my head.

"We've been over this, Jasper. It's . . . it's . . . it's like a choice between staying healthy or spending a sleepless night getting eaten by mosquitoes and choking on campfire smoke."

"How come you never make staying healthy sound like fun?"

Mom gives me the slow, stretching giraffe-neck treatment, combined with the flared nostrils and deep intake of breath.

"Go wash your hands and do your vest. Dinner will be in twenty minutes. And while you're at it, fire up your laptop. Let UPS know there's a package they need to ship back to Amazon."

I grab my meds from the fridge, and let Mom see my best mope—grumpy pout, sad eyes, heavy zombie steps—back to my bedroom. I could make my point by slamming the door shut, but my brain has other ideas. What if I've lost the tracking number?

12

Kate

Aside from the occasional cough—the normal speed bumps of Jasper's life—I spend most of the ride home questioning my resolve and selfishness over him wanting another dog. Then I discover my son was secretly sweating over an ill-chosen purchase. The kid has a pathological inability to lie. "Just like a dog," he's quick to remind me.

I'm floored both by the notion of a tent (and based on the unruly package how "light" or "portable" can it possibly be?) and the intensity of his sales pitch.

Most mothers, or should I say most regular mothers, might give up, wipe away a wayward tear, and hand over a blank check. But Jasper's frustration is his reality as much as it is mine, the baseline of *our* lives. Endless restrictions, considerations, and limitations are our normal. The bigger question is: What will Jasper learn if I capitulate?

I hate always having to play the bad cop, the heavy who lays down the law of sensible choices. And it kills me to see Jasper fold so easily, as if he knows there's no point in fighting. Sure, a dumb tent is no big deal, but what other, more dangerous boundaries might he push? How long before he skips a treatment or forgets to take a vital medication because it interferes with something as fickle, as meaningless, as a camping trip? Like it or not, I have to be the trainer bent on keeping my son in the fight, no matter how hard he's hit, no matter how many times he gets knocked down. It's my life's work. There can be no towel to throw into the ring.

Mothers like me cling to the possibility of a scientific breakthrough that will change everything, happily brainwashed by the promise of a cure within reach—aching, full-extension, tickling fingertip close. Right now that cure doesn't exist, but when you're desperate, and this is your sick child, tell me you wouldn't sell your soul for the possibility of hope. "Five years, ten at the most. No more." That's what they keep telling me. What kind of mother would I be if my son were not around to see some version of a healthy future?

When I nix the purchase, he lets loose his loudest, pro tennis player grunt (as angry as Jasper ever gets), opens the fridge, grabs his meds, and mopes off to his bedroom.

The apartment is compact, but it's perfect, possessing several must-have features for a mother in my situation. No previous smoking tenants; two bedrooms, each with its own bathroom; unusually high ceilings and an open-plan style to offset limited square footage; and a ban on pets. I know this last requirement doesn't sit well, but according to Jasper's pulmonologist, cat dander can be a potent trigger for his cough. Hardwood floors throughout mean no rugs to gather dust or dirt, so I can run this place like a surgical operating room. Better the faint tang of antiseptic than festering colonies of dangerous bacteria.

"You think Whistler's doing okay?" Jasper shouts from his bedroom.

Ah, forgiveness—swift and unconditional. He can't see me smile.

"I'm sure he's fine," I shout back.

Pulling open the fridge door, thinking about what to make for dinner, I'm greeted by a perfectly chilled bottle of sauvignon blanc. Right now a glass is tempting, but not irresistible. Unfortunately, out of necessity, my true vice lies elsewhere.

"Mom, d'you think he's called Whistler 'cause he's lost all his front teeth?"

Clearly the kid can move on but he can't let go.

"Stubborn little—" I catch myself, grateful to be blessed with a fighter and not a quitter. I imagine him loading the nebulizer, the transparent liquid medicine transforming into a fine mist, soothing the furthest reaches of his damaged lungs.

Filling a pan with cold water, I grab a box of ziti, a tin of anchovies, and jarred red sauce from a cabinet, together with capers and olives. I think I make a pretty good puttanesca, but for Jasper, this meal is all about one thing—salt.

One ion of sodium, one ion of chlorine; one of the most ubiquitous compounds in life; yet, when it comes to salt, a meticulous balancing act exists within the cells of our bodies, with disastrous consequences if we lose this perfect equilibrium. One mutation on one gene and a sequence of amino acids gets out of synch, a protein coils and folds a little off kilter, and a chlorine ion gets stuck on the wrong side of a cell membrane. It seems so inconsequential, so ridiculously, painfully small; but the cellular rhythm, the passive flow of water drawn by the natural shift of the body's salt will grind to a sticky and tenacious halt, turning every slick, moist secretion into a lethal sludge of molasses. The effect on the liver, pancreas, and intestines can be bad enough, but nowhere is more vulnerable than the delicate airways of a child's lungs.

From down the hall, the sound of Jasper's vest reaches me. Essentially a straitjacket hooked up to an air compressor, it sounds like a prop plane firing up. When he was younger I used to perform so-called percussion on his lungs, as if his tiny translucent bird chest were a perverse instrument in an orchestra from hell. It was legal child abuse, smacking a cupped hand across the front and back of his ribs, trying to disrupt the clogs and pockets of bacteria-laden mucus that refused to budge. For the past few years Jasper has switched to the vest, which oscillates air and literally shakes the gunk out of him and his airways.

With the sauce complete and the water coming to a boil, I check my phone for email. There's a reminder from one of the mothers that it is my turn to bring oranges to the soccer game this weekend. Laura, from my book club, wants to bitch about *The Goldfinch*, claiming that it is way too serious, and when are we going to get back to something smutty? My boss, Katrina Goddard-Brown—chief operating officer for our chain of non-profit animal shelters across Massachusetts, better known to her peons as "KGB"—insists I rustle up the names of a dozen or so local "prospects" that she can lure to her next black-tie fundraiser in Boston. And there is an email from Martha with the phone number for the Panhandle Canine Railroad. Huh. Martha's unusual efficiency makes me question her motivation.

There are four voice mails—an urgent request to call my health insurance provider (no doubt another fight for essential drugs not normally covered by their program); medications waiting for pickup at our local pharmacy (a weekly occurrence); my sister, Gwen, wanting to discuss Thanksgiving and seeing if I'm free on Saturday to give her daughter a ride to ballet; and a request from Jasper's school nurse, Mrs. Fisher, asking if I could swing by after class with refills.

Dirty laundry cascades over the sides of the hamper. That pile of receptionist job applications flounders on my desk. A fluffy, feel-good article for the monthly shelter newsletter lurks unfinished on my computer. Another busy night stretches before me and I'm grateful for the ordinariness of a purpose, a chance to avoid my reality. It will catch up soon enough. It always does. These mundane distractions can offer a survival strategy, but not a solution.

I grab my pocketbook, reach inside for the bottle of Advil. One pill left. Herein lies my vice, my sneaky panacea, the witchcraft that makes the impossible possible. This pill is not ibuprofen and has nothing to do with alleviating headaches. I'm tempted to take the last one, what with all the work that's still ahead of me tonight, but sometimes restraint can be just as appealing, proof that I'm still the one in control.

Poking my head around Jasper's door, I peer into his newly decorated soccer shrine, walls plastered with posters of athletic young men with ugly tattoos and designer stubble, volleying, heading, or dribbling a magical white ball. I love to see him fired up about any activity that might rattle free the toxic junk lodged inside his lungs.

Propped up on his bed, cocooned and convulsing in his vest, Jasper sucks on his nebulizer like a corncob pipe, a trail of white mist drifting around the room. On the side table by the bed slumps Henry, the only canine permitted in the apartment—blind, threadbare, and periodically resurrected with fresh stuffing and stitches. Henry is a nine-year veteran of many a hospital stay. He never complains, weathers weekly waltzes in the washing machine, and, despite the barrage of rejections along the lines of "stupid" or "for babies," manages to crawl into Jasper's bed at night and curl up beside him.

My boy wonder glances up from the screen of his laptop and gives me a thumbs-up. Maybe he is sorting things out with Amazon. Maybe he's playing that annoyingly addictive game Fortnite. Or maybe he's surfing through all those lost dog and adoption sites I found littering his history. If I cross the threshold and he slams it shut, I'll have my answer. Instead I parry with an "I'm watching you" finger gesture and disappear.

With six minutes before the ziti is al dente, I have time to call that Panhandle phone number Martha sent me.

"Yeah, I remember the dog," says a shrill, effervescent woman named Cindy. "Not exactly a looker and beat up real bad. Some folks felt sorry, but still, tough bugger to place. Wonder why he keeps running away?"

"No idea. And it's not the first time. You keep records?" It's a stretch, but I have to ask on the off chance a group of unpaid, overworked, dog-loving volunteers could unmask Whistler's provenance.

"We try," says Cindy, sounding a little too defensive, "but it depends on the specific shelter he came from. If their records are bad—and most of them are—then so are ours. We're dealing with some of the poorest areas of Texas, Oklahoma, Kansas, and New Mexico. Paperwork's low down on our list of priorities."

Hearing Oklahoma nudges me into asking a ridiculous question.

"Does the name Whistler ring a bell?"

"Nope," she says, emphatically. "Reckon I'd remember that one. But if this is the dog I'm thinking of, this was years back. I'm happy to see what I can dig up, but no promises."

Tactfully, I dance around the real reason for my call—would Cindy's group try adopting out Whistler one more time?

"Sorry, no. We get a new shipment every week. We don't have a physical building. We foster, adopt out, and start again. There's no option for taking a dog back." Into my silence she adds, "But you're open, right?"

Open. She's asking the question that should remain unsaid. Is our shelter *open* adoption, as opposed to *limited* adoption?

Mixing a cocktail of bluster and flattery, I manage to change the subject, praising Cindy on her work, hoping to hear from her should she uncover anything on Whistler's background, and hang up.

Somehow I avoided the truth, a truth that constantly motivates my son, and weighs on me more than I care to admit. Limited means, limited space, limited funding, limited time, and for Whistler, our latest, most distorted, peculiar, and sickly canine arrival, let's forget this politically correct term preferred by those in the know for the more realistic, painful, yet honest adjective for my shelter. Yes, our shelter is limited, and like it or not, limited means *kill*.

Perhaps it sounds strange—mother of a sick child, opting for a job awash with compassion fatigue—but I love what I do, even when others suggest I ditch the daily moral stress and make some emotional space for my son to have a dog of his own. If only it were that simple. Back when I started, a naive part of me prayed these encounters with loss might help ease my pain by toughening me up, coating my heart with a thick, impenetrable callus. Ridiculous. They haven't, but here's the thing: every so often an animal will find a home, against the odds, and that high of distorting destiny and sustaining a life, where the alternative was both unnecessary and unfair, feels disproportionately wonderful.

Of course I've considered working at a regular vet practice where I can find flexible hours, but there's always a downside—late nights, rigid office managers, an obligation to take certain weekends and holidays. Yes, I answer to Katrina Goddard-Brown, but I get to make my own schedule, able to handle the

KGB's tyrannical reign—former Wall Street corporate raider, retired before she was fifty, desperate to earn some good karma by offering twenty hours a week of her business skills pro bono—because she works remotely from a fancy Beacon Hill brownstone. Via text and email, she constantly pesters, scrutinizes, and micromanages, but in the eighteen months since she took over, she's visited the shelter just once. And so, aside from the easy commute, I never need permission to leave when Jasper's sick, and I always know he's safe after school.

There's just one catch—and I haven't told Jasper—but I'm seriously worried about job security. More and more people *don't* want to throw money at a shelter forced to kill, and the switch from "limited" to "open" requires a ton of capital. With a slump in private donations, strained budgets, and the constant influx of animals in need, I'm not sure how long we can survive. KGB already shut down a shelter on Nantucket and they were limited.

As it is, every new animal gets just two weeks to make a connection, lock eyes, steal a heart, and find a new life. Poor Whistler's odds of getting adopted were bad enough, but if, in fourteen short days, the right paths don't cross, if he's overlooked or unnoticed, then for the sake of all those newcomers who deserve their chance, I must shut down my feelings, silence my screams against the injustice, and humanely put this sad, mistreated creature to sleep.

13

Jasper

A DAY LATER and I'm back on the exact same bus, sitting in the exact same seat, same salty breeze in my face, waiting for the Whistler connection to happen again. Last time it came out of nowhere, but now I concentrate, try to will it, to kind of reach out with my mind. But by the time the shelter and the bay come into sight I've still got nothing except sadness that belongs to me.

That's why this . . . thing . . . I don't know what to call it . . . has to be a secret, at least until I figure it out. Before soccer, I was into Marvel Comics, mainly Spider-Man; but if I'm Peter Parker, this has to be the worst superpower ever. I don't know how to turn it on or whether it's on all the time. I don't know if it has a range or if the connection only works over a certain distance. I do know that, compared to Mr. Tibbles the Pomeranian, it's never been as strong or clear as it is with Whistler. So how come I'm at my bus stop and I don't feel a thing?

Whoa, wait a minute . . .

No, no, no. If I've got nothing then maybe Whistler has gone. Mr. Boa Constrictor is back, slithering around inside my belly. Please be gone adopted, and not gone, gone.

Coughing and panting, I bolt off the bus, run around back, and stretch my arm out to reach for the door handle, when something over my shoulder stops me. Something feels wrong, out of place, making me spin around to stare off toward the ocean and the sandy scrub and beach plum bushes out where the other volunteers walk the dogs.

In the distance, I spy a familiar silhouette, bent like a shepherd's crook from a manger scene. He's a tall upside down *J* on the horizon.

"Burt!" I shout.

There's a delay—the distance, the offshore breeze, his hearing aids—followed by a half-wave like he's not sure who's calling, and then the old man's shadow, stretched long and flat by the afternoon sun, morphs into the shape of a dancing dog.

It's him.

Burt's too far away to catch my grin, but the situation makes perfect sense now. Instead of a bark—too easy, too confusing— Whistler caused the weird feeling inside of me, like a tap on my shoulder or a whisper in my ear. Our special way of communicating, our secret vibe, it has to be real. And don't call this telepathy because that's like saying it's magic, and then no one will believe me. Thing is, one minute I'm totally "normal" inside my body and inside my head and then, boom, maybe I've got a tummy ache, or, boom, I'm frightened. It's all about feeling the change. It's physical, fast, and so crazy different, it can't belong to me. This time Whistler probably thought I'd abandoned him, but now that he knows I'm back, that sketchy sensation has totally melted away, swapped for a buzz like Christmas morning, like the one when you find the biggest pile of presents under the tree and the hardest decision you have to make is which one to open last.

Shrugging off the backpack, instantly weightless, I rush over to say hello.

"Easy," says Burt, his knotty arthritic hands struggling with the leash as I close the gap. "Don't scare him. It's his first day."

Stopping short, the sensation inside me has flipped, like how the choking panic of losing Mom in the mall turns to a big sigh of relief when I find her. Definitely relief. But is it mine or the dog's?

Whistler quits pulling, transferring the pent-up energy to his tail, the wag dialed up to max. Nothing can stop me reaching out with the back of my hand.

"Might be too soon to . . ."

Burt never finishes his warning. He's been around dogs for seventy-seven years and one of the first lessons he taught me was "Greet with the back of the hand, fingers safely tucked inside the palm. Best not offer a soft target for a bite, if you've misjudged."

Well, I haven't. Burt looks on, more confused than worried because Whistler's greeting is friendly, if a little strange. Rather than an attack from a wild, saliva dripping tongue, Whistler delivers what Burt later describes as a "lazy lick," the dog's tongue rasping across my salty skin in ultra-slow motion.

Squatting down, I dive right in, fluffing up the furry remnants of his damaged neck and shoulders. Though Whistler keeps all four feet on the ground, he bows his head and drives it into my chest, under my chin. He's closed his eyes like he's happy or safe. Maybe this is his version of hugging back.

"You two know each other?"

Then his hair gets up my nose, tickling, and I laugh, but the laughter gets stuck, lodging in my chest until it fights its way out on a whirlwind of a cough.

I'm doubled over, and 'cause I'm wearing my burgundy Portugal soccer shirt, when I come up for air, Burt's lips mouth "Ronaldo" (it's stitched across my back), as if it might be my name tag.

"We met yesterday," I explain once I catch my breath.

"Oh. When I got in this morning I heard a cough coming from isolation. Could have sworn it was you. Found the dog instead."

I panic, and thanks to CF, my gasps are loud and really impressive. "You tell anyone?"

Burt shakes his head, frowning, like I should know him better than that. Even though I hang out with a few kids at school—Jack, even more obsessed with Fortnite than me; Mandy, wants to be a nurse, always bugging me about CF; and Diego, diabetic, we see a lot of each other in the school sick room—Burt is my best friend. He's cool. In fact, Burt's worth one of the best

English compliments there is—*brilliant*. He never mentions my illness, not because he doesn't care, 'cause I can tell he does, but because it has nothing to do with what we share together at the shelter. Other volunteers make fun. They laugh at his saggy pants (so what if he wears a diaper), point out how he forgets things, or seems confused, and one time Martha swore to Mom that she thinks he has Alzheimer's. But they're wrong, because when it comes to dogs, Burt is really smart, notices everything about them, and never forgets. That's why he knows so many neat tricks. Like how you can hypnotize a dog by scratching in his armpits because it's one of the few places on their body that's impossible for them to reach. And how massaging a dog's paws gets them used to playing with their feet, which makes it a whole lot easier when it's time to clip their nails. I love it when Burt talks about dogs and how to read them. Burt's eyes may be sad and brown and tangled in a spiderweb of wrinkles, but I reckon he's lived my version of a perfect life—a life full of dogs. I'm pretty sure no person with CF has ever grown up to be as old as Burt. That's why I always pay special attention to people who have lived a long time and done lots of interesting stuff. When you have CF it makes sense. If I can't get there myself, why not find out what it might have been like?

"This is our third walk today," says Burt. "No one's mentioned a cough to me."

This is good, but how long before Whistler's sucky lungs slip up in public? I mean his cough sounds just like me and let me tell you, people look at you funny and back way off, which is a total disaster for any dog that needs to get adopted. And trying to hold in a cough so that strangers think you are normal can be much harder than holding in a sneeze.

"And he's shown no real interest in me, or other dogs, or people. 'Til you show up."

Whistler nudges his snout under my ribs, the tickling dig makes me giggle. I stumble back and stare into his good eye. He's smiling, like he knows we're talking about him.

"Careful," says Burt, driving a "behind me" thumb into his chest.

I recognize Martha's shape in the distance, hands on big pear-shaped hips, screaming something I can't quite make out.

"What's she mad about?"

"Ah, she's just doing her job. Best to step away from the dog," says Burt before turning and raising a hand in surrender.

In the distance Martha does a one-eighty, shaking her head as she stomps off.

"Reckon your mom might be getting an earful," says Burt. "You getting too close too soon with a dog nobody really knows."

I suppose he's right. When Mom gets back from seeing the school nurse, Martha will snitch and, like Burt says, "Dr. Blunt will have to rip you a new one." "*All new arrivals must pass their behavioral tests before they meet the public, and that includes volunteers.*"

"Sorry, Burt. My bad, not yours."

A seagull glides overhead and the two of us watch as Whistler follows its shadow. I squish a clump of dandelions under my sneaker.

"It's just . . . this dog . . . there's something special about him."

Burt grunts, cracks his knuckles, slow, one at time, which means he's thinking or waiting for more, or both.

"Every dog is special," he says, "to someone. It's our job to help them find that someone."

"But this is more than that. This is totally different. And it's not just about the way we cough. You know how I am around dogs and how much I love dogs. Well, this particular feeling, this has never happened to me before now, before Whistler, at least not properly, at least not so as I understood, and I'm telling you this is so much bigger. It's off the charts bigger."

Burt takes a slow sniff, a long sigh, and nods, just once.

"I get it," he says. "I've known a few Whistlers in my time, but only a few. You're lucky. They're rare."

Burt says he tries to read dogs using clues from their body language, because the better he knows a dog, the better he can place him or her with the right human. Like Match.com, only for a pet. It's what causes Burt and Martha to butt heads the most. The thing is, Burt's a much better judge of which dog goes best with which human and maybe that's because, like me, they "speak" and he "listens."

"Burt, be honest, what are the chances that Whistler will get adopted in the next two weeks?"

Burt narrows his eyes, crinkles his wrinkles, studying the dog who stares at my face like he's watching the best YouTube video ever and doesn't want to miss a minute.

"You mean will someone else want him more than you?"

See, Burt's brain works just fine. But he's not answering my question.

"Seriously, how do I convince my mom to let me keep him? If I even mention adopting a dog she freaks out."

"Here's what I know," says Burt. "Around you, this dog is happy. Around the rest of us, he's got the social skills of a rabid fox. And he looks, well, kind of beat up."

"What do you think happened?"

Burt points to the big hairless patch on Whistler's flank. "Could have been a fire. Could have been a car accident."

"What about the zebra stripes?" I ask.

Burt shrugs, flashes his little yellow teeth. "I should get him back to isolation. Come on, Whistler, let's go."

Why do grown-ups think kids never notice when they try to dodge a difficult question? Fortunately, Whistler is on my side. He refuses to budge.

"I'm thinking something bad happened. Something huge and dark and totally awesome, and not in a good way," I say.

Burt looks like a suspect in an episode of *Law & Order*. He's definitely got something to say, but he'd rather call a lawyer.

"Whatever it was," I continue, "it made Whistler stop barking."

Burt told me dogs sometimes lick their nose as a sign of distress. Burt does something similar, working two fingers into the bridge of his nose when he gets worried. By connecting the zebra stripes with Burt beginning to fret, I realize I must be on the right track.

"What if I can't adopt him? What if no one else will?"

Burt's silence is not the answer I'm looking for. I reach forward, make sure Whistler sees my smile, and gently run my hand along his snout scars. Different doesn't mean abnormal. No one needs to feel embarrassed about being different. I should know. But people get hung up on different. Sometimes it's all they see. What if Whistler's too sick? How long will it take his lungs to get better? What if it takes *more* than two weeks? Does Mom even have a cure? I noticed the look on her face when she first heard his cough and saw his X-rays. My dad never stuck around when I was born. Why would a total stranger take on a dog as sick as me?

Remembering that Whistler might be reading my mind, I say, "Not that he can't bark. It's just that he chooses not to. Right?"

And without needing to think about it, I reach out, touch his mangy right ear, nod toward the shelter, and Whistler, like he's my competitive obedience dog, happily trots on.

14

Kate

I SHOULD HAVE realized it was an ambush the moment Mrs. Fisher, the school nurse, suggested we might be more comfortable in a conference room.

"Hope you don't mind," says Mrs. Fisher, holding open the door and gesturing toward the man and woman waiting in chairs, getting to their feet. "Coach Taft and Ms. Sexton heard you were dropping by and wanted to have a word."

Mrs. Fisher is a big, bosomy woman, with wild bushy eyebrows worthy of a cold war Russian president. After thirty years on the job she can spot at fifty yards the difference between genuine sickness and an attempt to cut class. She plays favorites with her chronically ill children, those she affectionately refers to as her "repeat offenders." Fortunately, among a handful of autistics, epileptics, and diabetics, Jasper has made the cut.

I'm forced to squeeze rather than step past her, and shake hands with my son's teacher and coach.

Ms. Sexton, fresh out of college, possesses the perfect, perky figure and attitude of a woman starting her career. Prone to wearing flip-flops whenever it isn't snowing outside, she combines the fresh, animated enthusiasm of a newbie with a soft-spoken, tactile kindness. Her kids lap it up. In fact she's probably the subject of nocturnal fantasies among the more precocious boys in the class. Jasper, however, loves Ms. Sexton because she cuts him some slack. I can't tell whether his plight upsets or frightens her, but I'm grateful for a young woman who seems sensitive and receptive where it counts.

Coach "Daft," as he is referred to by some of the more aggressively sporty parents who unrelentingly challenge his lineups, tactics, and plays, is a lean, balding man in his late forties. He's wearing his favorite Framingham State sweatshirt—a reminder of his days as a Division III college basketball star.

I am ushered toward a chair, facing, or rather surrounded by, the other three—definitely an ambush. I sit, instinctively employing my best Catholic school girl posture, stiff-backed, angling my chin ever so slightly upward, less out of defiance, more out of a readiness for them to bring it on.

"So," says Ms. Sexton, bright and breezy, adjusting her short skirt, crossing her legs, and leaning forward. "I've been meaning to touch base about Jasper and this seemed like too good an opportunity to miss."

Some parents might have been expecting praise, news of awards, academic acceleration, or advancement to higher classes. Not me. Don't get me wrong, Jasper is a bright, imaginative kid, but it doesn't matter how smart he is if you mix in enough doctor's visits, sick days, and hospitalizations. No, in my world, "touch base" means "address a problem."

"Jasper's cough has become a bit more . . . disruptive for the past few weeks, but—"

"Why did no one let me know?" It's away from me before I can stop it, a reflex, and in the pause that follows, I command my tongue to shut up and lay low.

"Jasper has been dropping by for extra albuterol puffers," says the matronly nurse, totally unruffled. "Sometimes every two hours. He's going through it faster than usual, which is why I called asking for refills."

I'm aware of the way I knead my right index finger, work it like a worry bead, as though it might somehow pump up my composure.

"But," resumes Ms. Sexton, "and I'm no expert, this seems to be about more than just his . . ." She seems torn, uncertain as to which word will be the most politically correct—condition, disease, disability. She finally goes with, "his CF. It's like, sometimes, in class, he's there but not there. And I'm not talking about his ADD."

"He never misses his noon dose of Adderall," says Mrs. Fisher, quick to chime in, as though anticipating another of my impulsive tetchy comebacks.

"I mean," says Ms. Sexton, "is it possible that Jasper might be going deaf?"

As the question registers in my brain, I think how overwhelming and impossibly cruel, to add the loss of hearing to what Jasper already suffers, and for a moment, my mind snags on the prospect of lip reading, sign language, and cochlear implants. But then I sit up, letting the seat back dig into my spine, letting the discomfort bolster my poise. Ms. Sexton must be mistaken.

"As far as I know deafness is not part of his underlying disease. My son's sense of smell is not great, and I've been wondering if he needs glasses."

Ms. Sexton lets out a huffy sigh, oblivious to the way this comes across as a setback, like she'd solved the case and any new evidence should be inadmissible. Then she surprises me as I witness genuine concern blossoming around her eyes.

"His grades are starting to slide. Only today I seated him at the front, not as a punishment, but hoping it might help, and maybe it does, but he still seems preoccupied. And it's not that he acts unhappy. I've even caught him smiling to himself several times. Whatever it is, Jasper seems to think something inside his head is far more important than what we're currently learning."

I maintain unblinking eye contact and will my facial muscles still, but my mind can't help but wonder whether this recent decline in Jasper's performance in class has any correlation with his ongoing, unhealthy obsession over all things dog, doubtless heightened by the arrival of our latest acquisition, Whistler. Add "disruptive at school" to my long list of reasons for vetoing a canine roommate.

"We wondered," says Ms. Sexton, gesturing to the other members of her hit squad, as though hoping to share the blame, "if something had changed at home?"

I don't flinch, even though I notice the nonchalance and the royal "we." Of course she's prying, but I can tell it's borne of a desire to help Jasper, rather than a quest for titillation or gossip. Briefly, I consider the beautiful, healthy, and vibrant young woman seated opposite. Ms. Sexton's left hand bears no rings, her whole life ahead of her, much as mine had been at that age, not a care in the world—ambitious, immortal, coated in pure Teflon because not a single woe or trouble would stick. "No," I say, "no change. But I'll talk to Jasper and definitely discuss this with his doctors. It may just be a dosage problem with his Adderall."

"Right," says Ms. Sexton, "right, right, right," she adds, confirming she's no longer listening, easing back in her chair, as though a cue for Coach Taft.

"Well," says Taft, "can't speak to the deafness, but," he smacks a clenched fist into his open palm, "big game this weekend."

For any other parent, this preamble might have led me to acknowledge the coach, to praise his leadership, guiding the sixth-grade boys' soccer team to a winning season. But, again, when you're Jasper's mother, his intro spells danger.

"Yep," says Taft, "we win, we go to states."

"Jasper is very excited to be a part of this team. It means a great deal to him."

I could have kept quiet, but it was worth it, fueling his discomfort, watching him squirm in his seat, crisp Adam's apple swallowing hard.

"Yes, Dr. Blunt, I appreciate that. However, at this phase of the season, state rules limit the squad of eligible players to fifteen, and there are some parents who have expressed concern that a valuable place in the squad is being . . ." the coach begins verbally sprinting, as though the faster he can get his point across the better his chance of scoring a win.

So what if I nudge him toward the finish line. "What? Squandered?"

I appear to have made his eyes jerk around like a compass in search of magnetic north.

"Taken, by a player who . . . has certain limitations."

If Taft had gone first, I might have leaped to my feet like a Momma grizzly, demanding names, ready to embark on a verbal killing spree. But now the element of surprise has passed. This kind of passive-aggressive attack is nothing new and nothing I can't handle. In my situation, when you lash out in public, people think you've lost it, finally cracked. If you keep your cool, you've got a shot at something far more valuable—respect.

"I could remind you, Coach Taft, that this is sixth-grade soccer, that this is not the World Cup, but my son would argue against that point, because he takes this extracurricular activity extremely seriously. I could mention that Jasper is legally disabled and wonder how the local newspaper might feel about what sounds like discrimination, especially at this stage in the season. But, instead, I'd like you to ask his teammates what they think. Ask them what Jasper brings to their squad."

This may be a risky play, but I've watched the other players, even the really competitive ones, and I can see they have a measure of respect for Jasper's knowledge and understanding of the game, even if they keep their distance. For all the countless hours my son has spent watching soccer on TV, he comes up with priceless ideas and tactics regarding set pieces, corner kicks, free kicks, and offensive formations (his language, not mine). He helps out during training and, from time to time, he's even got a walk-on part—literally—in those last few minutes of the game; coming on as a substitute, reveling in the applause, oblivious to the fact that his team was so far ahead they couldn't possibly lose. But now Taft is making out that Jasper is dead wood, their ball and chain, a charity case, that they no longer need their "mascot."

"Dr. Blunt?"

It's Ms. Sexton speaking.

"Sorry," I say.

"Coach Taft would like to get back to you *after* Sunday's game."

"Sure," I say, rising from my chair, wishing I'd worn heels so I could stretch even taller, wielding height like a weapon, forcing them to stare upward, at my stern countenance and frosty blue eyes. I wonder if they see through my Nordic ice queen performance. I wonder if they suspect that it is far from impregnable.

Following an uncomfortable round of weak handshakes and fake smiles, I realize I've left Jasper's medication refills in the truck. With a promise to be right back, it's a relief to crash through the school's front doors and be assaulted by brilliant sunshine, clicking the key fob as I book it across the freshly mowed lawn to where I parked.

The meds are in my pocketbook—pancreatic enzymes that Jasper must take with every meal or snack in order to digest his food; a new puffer to be huffed deep into his lungs, dilating the congested airways but making his hands shake and his heart race as a side effect; and then there is the Adderall. I check the instructions label on the bottle.

"Half a tablet three times a day."

At the time, I seriously questioned the diagnosis, and I've been vindicated, weaning him down to the single dose Mrs. Fisher delivered at noon. Today had been the first time in two years anyone has even mentioned his possible ADD. I would never deprive my son of a vital medication—maybe it's time to increase his dose? But do I really want to? More importantly, can I afford to?

Nothing to think about. I click open the bottle of Adderall and spill two thirds of the contents into the empty Advil container in my pocketbook. I'm about to snap the lid shut when a "little blue helper" cries out to me and I slip the tiny pill between my lips.

"Thought I'd save you the trip," calls a stealthy Mrs. Fisher, already only a few yards behind me.

You'd think the shock would help me swallow it dry but the damned tablet is superglued to the roof of my mouth. I fumble for the medications, turn, and hand them over. It's a struggle to make my lips and tongue say "thank you" without a lisp.

As I drive away, Mrs. Fisher disappears in my rearview mirror. If she'd caught me, surely she would have said something?

At least I fear she would.

15

Jasper

Nurses are always asking me, "How're you feeling? How's your pain?" They bring out a smiley-frowny face chart with a scale from one to ten, one being "no biggie," ten being "hit me with some morphine," their pointy fingers drifting past Cheshire cat, through flatline, all the way to exploding eyeballs and upside-down *U*. If a nurse asked me right now, with Burt, Martha, and Mom arguing, I'd be scoring a solid seven.

They're in Mom's office and I've got my back to the wall, next to the open door where no one can see me. It's hard to hear, but what I can pick up is scaring me.

"X-rays don't lie," says Martha. "That dog's cough is a major problem."

Mom mumbles a reply and Martha responds with, "I'm just being practical. Someone's got to be."

Martha has issues with the loudness button on her volume control and when she gets angry her voice cuts like glass. Burt tends to over-chew his words, all low and hissy, and Mom is farthest away and might as well be speaking Swedish.

From what I can tell they're arguing about space, or the lack of it. See, the shelter has this big room, with a massive skylight so it's bright and there are these nice runs with fake plastic couches and cozy beds and this is where the people can come to check out which dogs they want to adopt. Burt calls it "The Showroom" (he used to work at a Honda dealership) and says our isolation ward is like a parking lot out back where new shipments get checked out and spruced up before they get to the public.

Trouble is the showroom only has fourteen runs. No matter whether you're a Great Dane or a Chihuahua, each dog gets its own run, and they're always full, and more dogs arrive pretty much every day. Mom goes all Dr. Blunt on me when I complain, saying it's the fairest way, but it never seems fair to me. Fourteen runs means fourteen days to find a forever home, or, after two weeks, if no one cares enough, it's time for the kind of forever that makes for a really bad goodbye.

"Waste of time," followed by a "then we'll have to bump Pudge." These words batter my eardrums, courtesy of Martha. Make that an eight on the smiley-frowny scale.

Pudge is a little black dumpling of a pug with an eye problem called glaucoma so he's blind in one eye. Tomorrow is Saturday but, more importantly for Pudge, it's day fourteen. Two more big dogs (a German shepherd and a Lab cross) came in this morning, and math may be my least favorite subject, but even I know something's got to give. Bump is not a nice four-letter word. Bump is an unkind way of saying "put to sleep."

Burt comes back at her, growling like a grumpy lion. I still can't hear what he's saying and I'm not trying to be mean, but I think Martha made a mistake with the note she taped to the bars of Pudge's run. Usually she writes helpful things like "loves kids" or "not good with cats," but sometimes she adds stuff from their behavioral evaluation and Pudge got a "hates vacuum cleaners." Since Whistler arrived, I've tried tuning into other dogs, and it's nowhere near as easy, but when I was with Pudge my stomach twisted into knots when someone outside was mowing the grass. Pudge might not *like* vacuum cleaners, but I think he *hates* lawn mowers. Now he's about to become a day-fourteen dog, because who wants a pet in a home you can't clean?

"All I know is we've got two dogs, and only one run. You're the boss. It's *your* choice."

The word *choice* gets lodged in my head. Does this mean Mom has to choose between Pudge and another dog? Wait a minute. Does this mean Mom has to choose between Pudge and Whistler?

Burt comes storming out of the office, right past me without noticing.

I'm not so lucky with Martha.

"Your mom's asking for you," she says. "She's got some bad news."

16

Kate

My LITTLE GHOST of a son appears from nowhere, hands by his side, shoulders hunched forward, the trademark posture of a kid forced to spend more time coughing than growing.

The look in his eyes has me on my feet. "What's the matter?"

"Nothing," he says.

I've seen Jasper wear this desperate, fearful expression many times, often when he's waiting for the results of a pulmonary function test that will dictate whether he gets to go home or spend another three weeks imprisoned in a hospital bed.

"Martha said you wanted to see me." Pleading oozes from his killer blues like melting ice. What did she tell him on her way out? Martha's tough on all the volunteers from high school, but when it comes to my son, I sense there's something more going on. Whether it's nepotism, me bending the rules because he's underage, or a perception that she hates caving to the boss and her glorified after-school program, it's hard to tell.

"I spoke to Ms. Sexton," I say, coming around my desk to perch on a clutter-free corner. "You want to tell me what's going on in class?"

As soon as I hit him with another day-fourteen dog dilemma he'll shut down. Best to lead with something less painful.

Jasper offers a cough shrug combo but keeps quiet.

"She seems to think you might be going deaf. Are you?"

All I get is an indifferent head shake. It's obvious he's bracing for the main event. I make a mental note to get his hearing tested at our next doctor visit. Deafness may not be part of CF, but permanent inner ear damage is a well-known side effect of one of his vital medications. If they tell me Jasper has to trade deafness for staying alive, I'll check into the nearest mental institution and throw away the key.

A sigh gets away from me. I don't want to come across as exasperated, but Jasper and I have done this dozens of times. You'd think he'd have learned by now. Or maybe, you'd think I would.

"Two new dogs turned up this morning, which means Whistler can't stay in isolation. We're out of runs. Tomorrow is day fourteen for Pudge the pug, so, as usual, I've got a difficult decision to make."

Jasper unlocks his stare, distracted by something through the window over my shoulder. I follow his line of sight. It's Burt traipsing across the lawn, holding on to a leash.

"The thing is, several volunteers have expressed concern about Whistler. And it's got nothing to do with his appearance." I pause. "The fact is you're the only thing on two legs or four that he seems interested in. I know he hasn't been properly evaluated and I know dogs can act weird when they're forced into a shelter, but you've got to admit he's not your average mutt. Not to mention his . . . health issues."

Jasper tries his best to tame the tremble starting to contort his lower lip.

"For that reason, I've decided to give Pudge the weekend. See if he can find a home."

The first fat tear clings for dear life to a lower lid, loses its grip, and spills down his cheek. My boy wears his empathy like a badge of honor and sometimes my job makes me feel as though I'm ripping it from his boney barrel chest. The irrepressible, hacking cough, stoked by emotions, bursts in my ears.

But Jasper breathes as before. It comes again, thick, struggling to clear, and I realize it's not in front of me. It's behind.

I turn to see Burt once more, right outside my open window. He's staring in with absolutely no expression on his face. I don't need to see who is on the other end of his leash.

"Everything okay?" I call.

The coughing stops but Burt never takes his eyes off me. "Yes," he says. "How about you?"

Both the question and his timing trip me up. Most people never ask, because I don't give them cause to ask. It's easier this way. It only brings people down. It only pushes them away. But every now and then there's that temptation to shed my shroud of bulletproof glass.

So why don't I? Simple: one little crack, and it might just shatter.

I don't answer, turning back to my son, catching the way the tears have begun to dry on his pale cheeks. Of course I want to cave, to soothe his pain. If I gave in every time, animal control would arrest me as a canine hoarder. And where would the "just one more" end? Regardless of size, shape, or texture, Jasper will never stop trying to save every day-fourteen dog.

"Stop. Please," I plead, hugging him to me, spurring his sobs. When was the last time he cried this hard? Like so many boys his age, Jasper thinks tears show weakness, their absence in times of pain proof that he is big and tough and growing up. But when it comes to this mangy mutt, he's undone, all stoicism abandoned, this child who endures so much. How has this creature become so important so quickly? It's unexpected, jarring, and I can't help but feel afraid.

Out the window Burt and Whistler have moved on. Why would Burt have wandered toward my office? He never does. No one ever does. Random exploration, bizarre trail of scent, or did the ugly dog from Oklahoma yank him in our direction on purpose? Now I sound more like my son.

"Listen to me. I have a suggestion. And that's not the same as a solution."

I know I will regret this, but not nearly as much as the grim alternative.

"What if Whistler comes home with us for the weekend, so I can evaluate him myself?"

No immediate response. Maybe he really is going deaf. Then his head angles up and I feel the tight squeeze of his arms around my hips, surprise and hope catching in his breaths, stammering the tears.

Peeling back his grip, I grab a small brass key hidden under a glazed pink conch shell on my desk and unlock the bottom right drawer.

Jasper paws at his wet eyes. "What's in there?" he asks, like he's wondered for some time.

I pull out three bright red canine vests—small, medium, and large. Each vest is boldly labeled in big white font: SERVICE DOG—DO NOT PET. Like most people in my profession, I'm not happy about the concept of impersonating an intensively trained dog with valuable work to do. However, when needs must, and you have the day-fourteen dog conversation as often as I do, I figured it couldn't hurt to be prepared.

I toss him the large vest.

"Hey, you're not the only one who shops online. This is just in case. And don't put it on him yet. Whatever happens, we can't afford to lose the apartment. We'll do a thorough behavioral evaluation and he's right back here on Monday morning, to be adopted, or the other, you understand?"

Jasper can't even nod but he's smart enough not to ask how long I've been holding on to the vests.

"Go wash your face, get the dog, and meet me by the truck while I explain to Martha."

17

Jasper

THERE USED TO be a show on TV called *The Pet Psychic* only Mom called it *The Pet "Psycho."* This old, blond woman went into people's homes and told them exactly what was wrong with their pet. She'd stick her ear in front of their snout, narrow her eyes, and then say things like, "Yes, I agree, it's no fun being left alone for eight hours a day," as if only she could hear the animal talk inside her head. I thought she was making it up, but every now and then she'd say something amazing, like when a Maine coon told her he had a tummy ache and the next thing you know there's a vet finding a hairball in the cat's stomach. I hope the Pet Psycho started out slow like me, because even with Whistler sitting right next to me on the back seat, I still can't tell what he's thinking.

Mom catches my eye in the rearview mirror.

"You're sure you understand?"

I nod for the both of us. Best behavior seemed like the least I could do, even if Whistler acts like he's never been in a vehicle, let alone seen a seagull or a beach or a rotary. It's as if he's trying to remember which way we're going, like Officer Dapolite said when he came into class and told us about having a code word so you don't go off with strangers, and if you ever do get locked in the trunk of a car, to use your senses so you know where you are, like listening for the sound of a passing train or the rattle of crossing a wooden bridge.

"Because I don't want this to be a big deal come Monday morning."

I lay my hand on his back. If I'm tuning in right now I'm sensing happy, but not crazy happy, like he's got something else, something more important, on his mind.

"It won't," I say. "Promise."

The big blue eye in the mirror does not look convinced. Mom can be scary good at spotting a lie, even though I'm not lying. Having Whistler over is actually going to be a *huge* deal way before Monday morning.

I've been working on a new plan for how to convince Mom that we should keep Whistler. Pointing out that the only person not afraid to adopt him has a cough that sounds exactly the same won't work. It's not enough. I have to go big, bigger, to the biggest thing she focuses on. Me. Keeping me healthy. Beating CF. Mom will do anything and everything to make me well, and that's what got me thinking. What if I could show her that Whistler is good for me and good for my disease?

Proving to Mom that I can actually feel what is going on inside this dog would be really good, but I don't know how. And it's not like Whistler can tell her. Maybe Ms. Sexton is right about me going deaf. Maybe that explains why I'm connecting with Whistler. If I'm losing one sense, maybe another sense is getting stronger, letting me understand Whistler.

The road twists away from the choppy ocean and Mom steers our 4Runner inland. Mom had this truck from before I was born. She says it's a "he," "Norman," and even though it's covered in rust and kind of screeches if you go too fast on the highway, she claims it is still one of the only men in her life she's ever trusted.

We leave the neat green walls of privet that protect the waterfront properties from nosy tourists and pass a gas station, an art gallery, a coffee shop, and a restaurant with a big inflatable orange lobster strapped to its roof. Whistler takes note of every landmark like they're crumbs on a forest trail, like he's prepared to find his way back to the shelter if necessary.

Mom indicates that she's turning left at the next set of lights, taking us off course. "I've got to pick up some meds from the pharmacy and a few other things. Won't take a minute."

While we're caught up in traffic, waiting to make the turn, Whistler eyes a shaggy brown and white terrier on the sidewalk. The dog's tied to a metal rack outside a store that rents bikes, and as soon as he spots Whistler, he lunges, front legs coming off the ground, his bark totally out of proportion to his size, all big and snappy and ferocious.

Whistler moves closer to the glass, acting more curious than surprised, and even though his black hackles quiver, he doesn't come close to barking back. Maybe he can't be bothered. Or maybe he just can't bark after all.

Mom pulls into the pharmacy parking lot and struggles to find a space. According to Mom, summer needs to be over on Cape Cod.

"Why aren't they shutting down their second homes and pulling their boats out of the water?"

I guess it will be Thanksgiving before Mom stops complaining about the traffic, her "crazy long commute," and threatening to buy an "I'm not on your vacation" bumper sticker.

"Finally," she says, zipping into a spot in front of a bench outside the store entrance.

There's a man seated on the bench. His hair is kind of ratty and it's hard to know where it ends and his beard begins. He's dressed in a winter overcoat that seems wrong for the hot weather and he's holding a white cup.

Mom switches off the truck and twists around in her seat. "I'll be quick."

"Do they sell dog bowls?" I ask.

Mom makes a grab for her pocketbook. "There's a leash, collar, his jacket, and dog food in the wayback. That's all he needs, and he can make do with one of our bowls."

Guess I won't ask about a dog bed and some chew toys.

"Sit still and if anything happens, honk."

"What's going to happen?" I ask.

"Nothing," she says, eyeing the man on the bench, "but I'm going to lock you in."

Mom has this thing about strangers, especially if they're panhandling. She says the Cape is full of trust fund babies who drank away their inheritance and are now broke and homeless.

One time, after a guy asked her for change, she said she wanted to move up to Maine because "the cold weather keeps out the riffraff."

"But Mom, what if there's a solar flare while you're inside the store and me and Whistler fry and you end up arrested for reckless endangerment of a minor and a dog?"

Mom drops her chin, rolls up her eyes, and says, "Crack the window," as she hops out, pressing the fob in her hand, checking the driver's side door is locked, even though we heard the beep.

Like two cops on a stakeout, Whistler and I watch Mom until she disappears through the automatic doors.

"Now what?" I ask.

And when I turn to my partner on the back seat next to me, he's staring directly at the bearded man on the bench, scratching at the door handle with his paw.

I guess I have my answer. Maybe I'm not so different from the Pet Psycho after all.

18

Kate

ON OUR DETOUR to the pharmacy, my eyes keep straying from the road ahead, drawn to the bottle of little blue pills pretending to be Advil. It nestles inside my open pocketbook on the passenger seat, right next to an unopened packet of tissues, and its presence feels all wrong, a rotten tooth my tongue can't help but worry. I flash from the road to the rearview mirror, to the image of my beaming son next to the worst-looking, least-adoptable dog at the shelter. Jasper radiates purity, innocence, and this compounds not only my guilt, but my weakness. At this precise moment the Adderall is more than just a drug. It's a paint bomb in a bag full of cash, meant to catch me, taint me, and mark me as a criminal.

When you've rehearsed a rational argument you're prepared to defend, in public if necessary, is it too late? Are you, by definition, already an addict? Or can you justify a deluded logic—

convinced it is as plausible as it is reassuring—that this is little more than a harmless vice?

I mean, it's not as if I'm brain doping. The dose is tiny, nothing for an adult, and normally I take it twice, three times a week tops, and never on weekends. I'm not a student cramming for a test. I'm not a lawyer with a court date or a journalist on deadline. I don't need to be or pretend to be a supermom. But I do need to be a full-time mother of a sick child that requires me to be totally on top of his disease, while working a full-time job. There is no other parent. The burden is mine alone. I don't need help to make it *bearable*. I need help to make it *possible*.

Taking the dog home with us felt more like Sophie's choice than Solomon's wisdom. Of course I'm not blind to Jasper's weird and premature kinship with the creature in the back seat, the one acting more like a sugar-high kid on his first trip to Disneyland than a dog. Everything we pass is eye candy, that scarred zebra snout weaving back and forth, not wanting to miss a detail. But he's not pacing, panting, barking, or drooling, like a typical carsick dog. I wonder why he runs away from every good home that takes him in. Is Whistler the one still looking for that special someone?

Finally a space opens up in the pharmacy lot. It seems like way too many washashores have ignored Labor Day and the unofficial end of summer: how nice for them. But as soon as I pull in, I see the man on the bench clutching a polystyrene cup.

We get a few drifters and homeless, like all tourist destinations, but something about this guy feels off. It's more than the oily jeans, sandy sneakers, and the way he's wrapped like a loaded burrito in a heavy woolen coat. The beard looks thick enough to nest a piping plover and then I spot it. He's wearing a wristwatch. Strange for someone begging for change? Or maybe he's just drinking a coffee? Harmless hobo or level-three sex offender? Maybe I should park somewhere else.

"You two stay put," I say to Jasper, grabbing my bag, deciding to lock them in, wishing the bum would turn my way as the key fob beeps so he might catch my maternal glare. He never flinches, arm extended, cup in hand. I'd best be quick.

Bad elevator music, bright lights, narrow aisles, and a sea of humanity assault me en route to the pharmacy proper in the back. Grabbing a basket will only slow me down, though it may prove useful as a battering ram. I weave and bob, squeeze and apologize my way to the flustered folks in white coats dispensing their chemical hope.

"Hi, Kate," says Sanjay, looking up from his pill counter. It's never a good sign when you're on first-name terms with your drug supplier. He points a finger in the direction of the counter set aside for "consultations with a pharmacist" and goes to grab my stash.

"Here you go," he says, handing over a brown paper parcel of medications that looks more like a family order of takeout. "You're going to have to speak to your doctor about getting another override. They want Jasper to switch from Advair to Symbicort. Apparently it's cheaper."

He raises an open palm before I can gripe.

"I know. It's not right. And now they're refusing to fill a script for more than two weeks at a time."

"So I guess we'll be seeing even more of each other," I say, matter-of-factly. Sanjay is a sweet, kind father of four nearing retirement. Even if he was Matthew McConaughey I wouldn't be flirting.

"I gave you as much gentacin as I have and more should be coming in on Monday. The Pulmozyme is wrapped separate and on ice, so don't dally on your way home."

He winks and I hand over my credit card. Who can afford to drink themselves into numb oblivion with the cost of co-pays?

Painfully slow and deliberate people obstruct every aisle necessitating a circuitous route to the exit. And then a shortcut opens up, an empty avenue lined by cosmetics and hair products. It's the mirrors, or to be more accurate, my reflection in them, that slows me to a standstill.

I'm wearing a gray fleece jacket over green surgical scrubs, blue crocs on my feet. The scrubs are my work uniform. They're practical and I can always pick up a clean pair. But it's not my clothes I notice. It's my hair. I wear it short, more pixie than soccer mom, and one of my few vanities had been a trip to the hair salon the first Tuesday of every month. These days, with the spiraling cost and number of Jasper's drugs, best to touch up the roots myself. I look around, poised to inspect my scalp in a mirror.

There's a man in the opposite aisle. He's checking me out. About my age, a smidge taller, with thick tousled black hair, most women would label him as cute. I cold-stare back and he smiles the smile of a man who thinks he can pick up women wherever he goes.

I ignore him, check the gray feathering in my part, and grab a box of dye. Mothers of children with chronic disease age faster than a two-term president. Who has the time or energy to work on attractive? Besides, he was standing in front of a shelf full of hemorrhoid creams.

I pay for my box of pricey peroxide but never make it to the truck, rooted by one of a million parental nightmares—my vehicle is empty.

The man on the bench is gone.

Where's Jasper?

A woman pushing a stroller across the lot turns in my direction but keeps going. A car horn blares off to my right. A dirty tan Winnebago with tinted-glass windows sits waiting for a break in the traffic so he can pull out into the road. Incipient panic kicks in, tempting me to hit 911 on speed dial, but then I hear it, the cough, unrivaled and unmistakable, and I spin, seeing the bearded man in the overcoat with his back to me, standing on a patch of grass on the far side of the lot.

As I close the distance, the bearded man turns and takes a step back, exposing a figure crouching down next to a big dog.

"Mom," says Jasper, jumping to his feet. "This is Neil."

I ignore the bearded man. I ignore the dog. "What did I say about staying in the truck?"

Jasper knows he's in trouble, not arguing, keeping his head down as he takes Whistler by the leash and begins their slow death march back to the 4Runner.

"Here," I say, rummaging through my purse, shoving a dollar bill in the hobo's hand, before catching up with my son.

"Whistler wanted to say hello to Neil. *He* wanted to make him feel better."

And while I reel and bite my tongue, there's a shout from over my shoulder.

It's Neil. "Thank you," he calls to us. "Thank you," his voice tentative and scratchy, making me wonder if his gratitude is aimed at me or my son or the dog, and for what.

Back in the truck, belted up, key in the ignition, I watch the boy skulking in his seat appearing appropriately chastened. So why do I feel guilty, as if I'm the one in the wrong, as if I should have indulged their innocent little meet and greet?

"Look, I get it, you were just being friendly, but believe me, no mother wants to walk out of a store and find their kid missing. Okay?"

Jasper nods, but refuses to meet my eyes. This is totally out of character. The dog by his side may look more like a dejected dairy cow, but he's the catalyst for this sudden and fearless change in behavior. I'm sure of it.

I start the engine and glance in the rearview mirror. Is it possible to love a child too much? Or has his disease intensified our attachment, amplifying normal maternal instincts to paranoia? Perhaps I should press Jasper for an explanation. Then again, can I handle a canine clairvoyance fairy tale? Best not to look under a rock if you're afraid of what you'll find. Best to drive home, blame love, and say no more.

19

Jasper

Because I'm not famous or special or know many people, I don't have a Twitter account, but if I did, I guarantee my tweets would be trending at #bestsaturdayever.

It starts with a sleepover. I know, right? Me at a sleepover. Mom has finally calmed down—even if she won't let go of the word *kidnapped*—and is making me set up Whistler's bed. I toss one of my old duvets on the floor in the kitchen. I have to promise not to kidnap him in the night. Rookie mistake. She never says a word about me visiting him. So I set my alarm clock for midnight, and stuff it under my pillow, but when I hear it and wake up, Whistler is already on my bed—brilliant. He lies on his side, legs stretched out, eyes closed, paws twitching, whimpering like he's having a bad dream. I concentrate really hard and try to connect, but I'm tired and need to pee and when I come back from the bathroom he isn't doing it anymore. We snuggle for a while and he does his weird slow lick thing (it's like an awkward handshake) on the end of my nose and then he goes all floppy and grunty when I rub at the base of his gnarly right ear.

By morning he's gone. I check all over my comforter for long black hairs but there aren't any, just a warm, neat dent right next to where I slept. Maybe he doesn't shed? Or maybe it's because more of his body is covered in scars than fur.

Mom's made me a massive breakfast.

"Your pretend service dog decided to perform his early morning ablutions in a hazardous spot." She slides a plate to me loaded with scrambled eggs, bacon, and a bagel lathered in enough cream cheese to spackle half of my bathroom ceiling. She always expects me to eat way too much food.

"What?" I croak.

"Whistler took a massive dump in Mr. Crabtree's roses."

Instantly I come awake. Mr. Crabtree lives in a house across the street and he manages the apartments. Here are the top five reasons why I don't like Mr. Crabtree.

1. He hates dogs.

2. Actually, he hates all animals but especially rabbits and deer and moles and all life-forms that might in any way ruin his backyard.

3. I am on this list as a life-form known for accidentally kicking a soccer ball into his precious hydrangeas.

4. He refused to donate to my CF fundraiser.

5. He has really bad breath.

"Did he catch you?" I ask.

Mom looks at me like I'm an idiot. "You think either of us would be alive if he did? Here, take your enzymes."

She offers me a massive glass of milk and drops a handful of brown capsules into my palm. If I don't take them, I don't absorb my food, I won't grow, I won't be able to fight my disease, I'll need a feeding tube, I'll waste away . . . I've heard it all before. Easier just to take the pills and try to eat enough to stop her from saying, "Is that all?" Weird, but for the first time in forever, I actually feel like eating a big breakfast.

Whistler sits at my feet, watching everything, his head angled so far up the whites of his eyes make little waxing crescent moons (see, Ms. Sexton, I pay attention). I can tell—and it's more than just the drool—that he's hungry as well. Unless . . . of course . . . I'm not the one craving breakfast—he is. I'm tuning into him.

"Mom, did you feed Whistler?"

"Not yet," she says, disappearing from the kitchen and coming back with a fake plastic hand on the end of a long wooden stick. "Thought you'd want to watch this."

I put down my fork. "Now?"

I've seen this trick before. It's for Whistler's first behavioral test—guarding.

Mom opens a can of dog food, plops it into a bowl, and invites Whistler to have his breakfast. Whistler checks in with me before taking his first bite and I silently warn him to be on his best behavior. Halfway through eating, Mom takes out her creepy little plastic hand and starts prodding and poking and trying to steal the bowl back from him.

I have a coughing fit ready to go, but I don't need it. Not a grumble or growl, not a bark or a bite.

"Pretty good, right?" I say to Mom.

But she is all business, making the hand disappear, trading up for a squeaky green frog. "Here, you two go play with this."

No fair, moving straight from food to toys, but I do as I'm told, teaching Whistler to play catch, fetch, tug-of-war, and peekaboo, and he goes crazy, eyes wild, scampering and scrambling like he's never had a stuffed toy in his life.

"Good," says Mom. "Leave him for a while."

With the limp green amphibian hanging from his mouth, Whistler trots off, lying down in a corner, the frog pinned between his crossed front paws as he starts to suck on its head.

After five minutes the plastic hand returns, a nasty crab puppet sidling across the hardwood floor, petting Mr. Froggy before dragging him away in its stiff and spooky grip.

There's no denying the sadness in Whistler's eyes as he stares at Mom. But the way he makes me feel inside is much worse. I've never stolen a thing, not counting the book about dog breeds that I keep meaning to return to the school library. And anyway, borrowing's different. But if I did steal something special, something important, and got caught, I imagine it would feel how

Whistler made me feel when Mom took his frog. More than sorry. Guilty. What must have happened in Whistler's past to make him feel guilty for playing with a stuffed toy?

Mom refuses to praise him, just nodding.

"Take your orals, finish your treatment, get dressed, and we'll do barriers next."

Barriers are part of protective aggression, where you try to see if a dog is going to freak out when there's a stranger outside a window, or through a glass door, or when the doorbell rings; and whether they're okay with women but lose it around men, or men in baseball hats, or men in baseball hats and sunglasses. I'm not worried about this one. No matter what Mom does to surprise him or bait him, I know there's one thing Whistler will never do, and that's bark. Mom even pries open his jaws and inspects the back of his throat.

"Vocal chords look fine," she says. "He's got no excuse."

"No," I say, patting his head, "he's got excellent manners."

Mom fake smiles, the one she uses when people ask how I'm doing, so I know she's not convinced. "I need to run some errands. Grab his special vest and let's see how he does in the real world."

Wow. Back at the shelter new arrivals get tested over a couple of days, not a couple of hours, but sometimes Mom gets like this when she drinks too much coffee. Whistler stands, fretting and uncomfortable while I dress him up. Cinching down the Velcro straps on his vest I began to feel itchy, like that time Auntie Gwen bought me a mohair sweater for my birthday and Mom made me try it on and wouldn't let me take it off. I reckon the material must prickle his scars.

We drive into town, park, and Mom, Whistler, and I start going into stores. Mom holds his leash and Whistler keeps dragging his feet and bumping into people—he won't take his eyes off me—but he doesn't make any big mistakes, even when a kid paws at his face and squeals in his ears. Seriously? His jacket may be fake but how come no one reads the "Please don't pet me while I'm working" warning?

Mom says we need to find a birthday present for Grandpa, so we go to this sporting goods store, searching for a golfing gift (currently Grandpa's obsessed with golf), and suddenly I feel this panic attack coming on, like when I have that dream where I turn up for school and everyone's laughing at me 'cause I'm butt naked. We're right next to the camping section so I'm thinking it's because I still haven't sent that tent back to Amazon, but then I notice Whistler. Eyes shut tight, lying flat on the floor with his legs out straight and rigid, it's like he's refusing to walk past a row of shiny metal golf clubs.

"How about some golf balls?" I say, yanking Mom by her elbow down a different aisle, hoping she doesn't notice, hoping Whistler tags along and fortunately he does.

By the time we check out, the woman behind the counter says, "He's calm, isn't he?" Mom agrees and Whistler turns my way. I let him know it's okay and he's doing great, but then the woman laughs and says, "But he sure is one ugly mutt for a service dog."

She thinks this is funny. I think she is stew-pid (in England they say "stew-pid" not stupid). When we leave I silently tell Whistler that he can pee all over the entrance to her store. Unfortunately his bladder must be empty.

We pick up some groceries and some wrapping paper and then Mom says it's my turn.

"For what?"

Mom hands over his leash. "Let's walk down Main Street. Go ahead. I'll be watching."

I grab it and wait for a signal from Whistler. I tune into scared and excited, but then he tilts his head to one side and it looks like a "What are you waiting for?," so off we go.

The next ten minutes are brilliant. Whistler is brilliant. He is Gorilla Glued to me, keeping the beat of my footsteps. Nothing can faze him. Three cyclists scream past in a blur of sweaty spandex; not a twitch. He drags me across the street to avoid a man smoking a cigarette—protecting my lungs, and his. A throbbing Harley backfires at an intersection; he never flinches. People stare, swerve, shout, and laugh, and we keep going like the world can try and stick out a foot but we are too fast, too cool, too catlike, to trip up. It's like Whistler actually knows what he's doing, like he's a real service dog. Then it hits me. Maybe there's a better way to convince Mom that we need to keep him.

I never see her tailing us—Mom would have made a great spy—but suddenly she appears from nowhere.

"Want to get something to eat?"

I don't but say, "Sure," because wanting to eat makes Mom happy.

It's still hot, T-shirt weather, and we find this deli with outdoor tables and little wooden picnic benches and sit outside. I stay in the shade because I burn easily thanks to one of my antibiotics. Mom orders salad and I get a cheeseburger. The best perk about having CF, she says, is that you can eat anything you want and never get fat. She knows I'd much rather not have CF and just get fat.

While we eat, Mom checks out the people gawking at Whistler as he lies at my feet. I'm happy and he's happy, especially when I sneak him bits of my burger under the table. Then I notice two girls finishing up, grabbing their trash, and heading our way. It's Lexi Perez and Olivia Cox, only the two most popular girls in our grade.

"Hi, Jasper," they say.

I just smile because the only words popping up in my brain are, *How do they know my name?*

"Is he yours?" asks Lexi, and I don't know what to say so I check in with Mom, who chews over the question (literally), making me squirm, before raising her eyebrows like she's just as interested to hear my reply.

"He's in training," I say, staring back at Mom when I add, "guess we'll have to see."

"Can we pet him?" asks Olivia.

"Sure," I say. "His name's Whistler."

Both girls are wearing tons of makeup and these really tight tops and really short denim shorts, so I'm shocked when they kneel down in the grass to pet him and don't say a word about his scars or ear or anything.

Then Olivia's phone pings, she checks the text and announces, "We gotta go."

They get up, and as they leave, Lexi says, "You should bring him to school on Monday," but they're gone before I can reply.

Across the table, Mom's still chewing, but she's got a pleased sparkle in her eyes.

"They seem nice," she says, pissing me off because I know, I just know, she's dying to add something annoying like, "Is one of those girls your girlfriend?"

Best to put my head down, eat, and hope the chewing hides my smile because the dog who stole most of my burger made the two most popular girls in school want to say hello to me. Somehow Whistler gave me a little bit of his cool.

Fortunately, Mom's phone rings. It's work.

"Guess what, Pudge the pug just got adopted," she says after hanging up. "Some old guy from the trailer park. Doesn't have a vacuum cleaner."

How the man keeps his home clean doesn't bother me. I worry he might have a lawn mower.

"Anyway, that means there's a run free for Whistler."

Amazing. Not one word about how great Whistler has been, or how well he's done on all his tests. No mention about how he is a natural as a real service dog or how he would be perfect as *my* service dog.

"But what about the new arrivals? What if Martha wants to give the run to one of them instead? You've seen how good he is as a service dog." I lean in closer and lower my voice because the woman at the next table is trying to listen in. "What if we got him properly trained so that I can keep him?"

Mom has a wad of oily lettuce halfway to her lips. She stalls and fixes on me, and for a few seconds I think she might be about to crack, but then she recovers, producing the stare kids fear, the one where she's trying to work out what you're really thinking.

"Look, we don't have to take him back today," she says, landing the fork in her mouth before jabbing it at me, chewing between words. "'Cause I need you to continue your evaluation of this dog. Something makes him keep running away from every good home that adopts him. Perhaps something frightens him. Or drives him crazy. If we know what it is, we'll know what he needs to avoid next time around."

I feel Whistler slow-lick my ankle, above my sock, and suddenly it hits me, the way Mom's got it totally the wrong way around. Sure, Whistler's been bouncing from one place to the next, but his problem is not about what's been *present*, but about what's been *missing*. I'd bet a new pair of lungs on the fact that Whistler found me because I'm the first person who can actually "hear" him. It makes total sense. He didn't keep running from something bad. He kept running until he found someone who gets him, someone he can "speak" through. What's been missing in Whistler's life is me.

"Besides, Zack Cruz's mom called me. She asked if you wanted to join them down at Crystal Lake after two."

Zack is on my soccer team. He's one of our captains. He never asks me to hang out with him. Almost no one ever asks if I'm free.

"How come?"

"No idea. Maybe he wants to tap into your vast soccer knowledge before the big game on Sunday."

Possible, I think, *but not likely.*

"What about the sun?"

"It's called long sleeves, a baseball cap, and SPF 50."

"And what about Whistler?"

"Mrs. Cruz says he can come, so long as he doesn't bark, and I told her he passed that test with flying colors."

"And what are you going to do?" Like I said, going off with friends is rare, but Mom always hangs around, in case something happens.

Her neck recoils and she stares at me with an attitude like, *I have a life as well, you know.* She isn't fooling me.

"I've got to make something for Grandpa's birthday party at five. You can't stay too long. And it's a minute down the road. You've got your phone? It's charged, right?"

"Yeah, but don't forget I'll have Whistler."

Mom didn't add him to the list of reasons why I'd be fine. It makes me wonder if she hopes he might run away again. She already has a bag ready with my puffer and enzymes (in case they offer me a snack) and four juice boxes and a bag of Cheetos (in case they don't).

It's called Crystal Lake but actually it's a kettle pond, which has something to do with glaciers, and contains fresh water not seawater. There are lots of them all over the Cape, but this one lies at the bottom of a deep basin surrounded by trees. You can park high up in the woods and, because it's October and enough of the leaves have fallen, you can see the entire lake way down below. After Labor Day, no one seems to care if you bring along a dog, and besides, today there are only two other cars in the lot.

Mom recognizes the Cruzes' Suburban.

"Take your sneakers off on the beach," says Mom. She's referring to my brand-new Nikes.

"But what if someone steals them? And how am I supposed to kick a ball barefoot?"

No quick comeback, which means the Nikes can stay on.

Next she attacks me with sunblock, on my face and neck and legs below my shorts. Then she surprises me by removing Whistler's jacket—because this isn't really work—leaving it on the back seat and carefully applying lotion to his scars.

"What?" she asks because I can't help staring. "You think dogs don't get sunburn?"

Knowing Mom cares enough feels good, and then she walks us down the long wooden staircase that zigs and zags its way through the trees and down to this big empty beach in front of the pond.

We say hello to Zack's mom and dad. Mrs. Cruz has set up a beach chair under a green umbrella and Mr. Cruz looks like he is about to do something fun with a paddleboard. Mom waves goodbye and Whistler and I head down the beach to where Zack kicks a soccer ball.

"Hey," I say.

"Just so you know," says Zack, "this wasn't my idea. Guess your mom called my mom and my mom feels sorry for you."

I don't know what to say. I wasn't invited. Why would Mom set me up?

Zack keeps the ball up in the air with tiny precise little kicks. He's good. I count twenty-four.

"Dude, what's with the ugly dog?"

Whistler checks in with me, like he wants me to say, "What's with his ugly face?" Zack has pimples on his forehead and every now and then his voice cracks.

"This is Whistler. He's from my mom's shelter."

"How come you've got him?"

"Training to be *my* service dog."

I don't know why I say it out loud, but the ball hits the sand. Zack drifts closer but keeps his distance.

"Does he do tricks?" he asks.

"Don't know."

Zack seems to think about this, boots the ball down the beach, and screams, "Get it!"

Whistler watches it sail away, but his body remains still, seated with his bum caked in sand, tail twitching ever so slightly like it's taking a lot of his concentration not to bolt.

There are so many ways this next bit could go wrong: Whistler ignores the ball and disappears into the woods; Whistler attacks the ball and kills it; Whistler ignores me completely. But I step in front of him and, making sure Zack can see, flick the index finger of my right hand in the direction of the ball, slow and casual.

Whistler explodes in a sandy spray, back legs pumping, gaining speed before launching himself at the ball and, with phenomenal snout skills, dribbling the ball across the rutted beach, nudging it up to Zack's feet before backing away.

The captain seems to think about a "wow" but goes with "Cool" and asks, "You think he can play in goal?"

I don't see why not, so we set up a goal on the edge of the beach in the shade using some big sticks to make the posts and I tell Whistler what to do. I'm not saying we have an actual conversation in which I explain to a dog how he might become a goalkeeper. I'm not saying Whistler can channel his inner Tim Howard (the American guy who made the most saves of any goalkeeper in a World Cup—sixteen) and start flying through the air. I'm saying I just kind of imagine it, I hope for it, and with Zack watching, I really want it. The next thing I know, Whistler comes at us, closes down the angles, gets his body, a leg, even a paw, in the way like he wants to stop you from scoring a goal.

I'm not actually doing much, except being amazed by my "ugly" dog. Zack does most of the running. Every now and then he'll ask me what I think about some set piece he's been thinking about and I show him this trick I saw Beckham do one time from a free kick. I think we're having fun. I'm on my own, without Mom, and my cough is okay. I'm with my dog, and I'm pretty sure my dog is the one making this possible.

Then the Kerry twins show up.

Martin and Trevor are central defenders on our team and they totally ignore me. Their dad, Mr. Kerry, shouts louder than anyone else on the sideline and he curses every time I come on as a substitute. Even when we are winning by miles. Which is the only time I ever come on.

Zack looks shocked to see them running down the beach and then embarrassed, bolting in their direction, taking the ball, not saying another word to either me or Whistler. The three of them start kicking the ball around. Mrs. Cruz sits under her umbrella, slumped low in her chair like she is asleep. Mr. Cruz is way out on the water, splashing away.

"You okay?" I ask Whistler as we stand together at the water's edge.

In the Pet Psycho world I might nod and say, "Good, me too." But in the real world the only thing that happens is I feel good inside. I'm used to playing on my own—I get plenty of practice—but hanging with Whistler, the two of us trying not to laugh as a duck face-plants a water landing, this feels better than good. This feels calm. Happy. Brilliant.

The water is totally clear, the bottom sandy, tiny waves lapping at our feet. I pick up a flat pebble and try skimming it across the surface. Pathetic. Good thing no one's watching. Suddenly, Whistler turns around and trots back toward the shade, returning with one of the goal posts, a pretty large stick wedged across his mouth.

He drops it at my feet.

"You want to play fetch?"

No reply. No surprise.

I pick up the stick and toss it out across the water as hard as I can. I check down the beach to see if anyone is watching. Zack and the twins are focused on heading practice. Mrs. Cruz might actually be dead. Mr. Cruz is a stick figure on the horizon, about to be "lost at pond."

I stand in front of Whistler and do the exact same flicking finger gesture as before, bracing for the splash.

Nothing.

I use my whole hand, jerking my head toward the water, telling him, "Get it, go get it."

Still nothing.

The stick bobs up and down, out where the sand falls away and the water switches from yellow-green to total black.

What am I doing wrong? Does he prefer to chase balls? Is he afraid of the water? Maybe he's never learned to swim?

I look at him, his eyes jerking between me and the stick, me and the stick. That's when I get it. And I can even tell he knows I get it.

I fake a lunge toward the pond and he shudders forward, four paws in the water. I do it again and he smiles, twitches, and coils up, ready to go.

I don't know why I do it. Maybe because I'm hot. Maybe because I'm not thinking straight. Or maybe because Whistler makes something inside me say, "Why not?" Right there and then I know Whistler doesn't want to play fetch. He doesn't want me to stay put and watch him swim. He wants to race. He wants to race me for a stick floating in the water.

I skip the "Ready, set," and hit "Go," clothes, sneakers, and baseball cap still in place, the water surprisingly soupy in the shallows, switching to icy cold as soon as the bottom slopes away and I reach the creepy black.

Whistler enters the pond like a pro, displacing water cannonball style, taking an early lead, porpoising the first few yards until the depth forces him into a doggy paddle.

Because Mom insisted I swim every week at our local Y to

improve my lung function (fortunately, trumpet lessons were abandoned due to complaints from our neighbors) I'm a pretty good swimmer. With clothes on my strokes are kind of slow and splashy but I still get there first (or maybe he lets me), grabbing the stick, shouting and coughing and gurgling that I'm the winner just as the two of us simultaneously realize we are freezing and wet and, at least for me, a little scared of being bitten by a snapping turtle.

Why is it that clouds always pull in front of the sun when you need it most? Not that I care. Whistler and I crawl onto the beach, catching our breath, coughing our brains out, stinky water spraying off his shaking body, pouring out from my baggy sleeves, dribbling from the bottom of my shorts, and I can't stop laughing. I can't stop feeling good. And that's when I realize no one else on the beach has noticed. No one has been looking. Which makes me wish I had a Twitter account so I can share my news about what we've done on this, the best Saturday ever. And that's when Whistler suddenly plops down in the sand, looks right past me, and starts to tremble.

I don't need to turn around. It's written on his face.

"She's behind me. Isn't she?"

20

Kate

I BLAME MYSELF, and Jasper, but mostly I blame the dog.

Yes, I know I've lost it, and yes, it's totally unreasonable, but when you watch your child half-drowning, half-choking to death, don't try and palm me off with a glib "boys will be boys." And so what if I'm ranting? Given my circumstances, no one in their right mind would be in their right mind.

This is precisely why I refuse Jasper's pleas and harden my heart to his tears. My son is the perfect mark, a total sucker for any dog. His response to Whistler was always a given, committed to an instant kinship. It's Whistler's response to him that came as a surprise. More than being a quick study, the coyote ugly mutt with ulterior motives visibly checks in and responds to Jasper in a way that's in a different league to the other hopeless canine causes that came before. I'm detached enough to wonder if he's simply a clever dog going through the motions. Unlike a ditzy golden happy to go home with any stranger, Whistler's play is more subtle than friendly, less crude than flirty.

Believe me, I know this mind-set is not normal. Seen from a different perspective, I'd grab a brush and be the first to paint me as selfish, mean, or even jealous. After all, how can a veterinarian deny her dog-loving son a shot at this type of companionship? An unpleasant, unappealing streak of pettiness and vanity makes perfect sense. Until you dare to stop and drop into my version of a life and acknowledge how the smallest variable can threaten to bring you down.

I admit it: I'm afraid of change. Living with this disease has rendered me fluent in fear. Change apartments—how hard can it be? Take your dog to work—what's the problem? You're a vet; you've even got the health care issue covered. But let's say I find a new home that's perfect for Jasper and money pours into the shelter so I don't need to look for a new job, I've still got to worry. And it's more than who's going to clean up an accident because our doctor's appointment ran late or where on earth the dog will stay when we're trapped in the hospital for three weeks at a time. It's the guarantee that a dog will influence my focus on Jasper, distracting me in small, innocent ways, forcing decisions, unnecessary considerations, and, worst of all, extra responsibility. This sounds trivial because it is trivial, but for a single mom with a sick child, the prospect of caring for something, anything more, feels like a burden, a final straw, guaranteed to make our already precarious existence bow, falter, and crack.

And then there's the other reason; a truth that lies within a trait fundamental to each and every one of us—the desire to be perceived as normal.

Like I said to Coach Taft, kids with cystic fibrosis can be considered legally disabled, but it's a disability that prefers to hide. Unlike a disease that robs you of your hair, deforms your body, twists your mind, or confines you to a wheelchair, CF—for the most part—has its fun on the inside. Everyone sees a kid who looks normal, with a cough that could be nothing more than a niggling cold. So when you slap a disabled sticker on my truck, certain small-minded people take notice, suspicious that I'm trying to park for free. Slap a disabled sticker on my son and those same people think something contagious or tragic must lurk beneath his normal exterior. The curiosity is bad enough. The pity is unbearable. Without a sticker, no one notices. Today, Whistler, a ramshackle, well-behaved mongrel in a fake vest, became that sticker.

Trying as best we can to be "normal" keeps Jasper and me in the real world. After all, what kind of future could I offer my son if I spend my time saying goodbye? Health constraints constantly challenge Jasper's version, but I've got no excuse. People expect normal. People relate to normal. People can handle normal. Mention a child with a terminal illness and even though they say, "I'm sorry," all I hear is, "Sorry for your loss." Talk about the battle to keep that child alive and their world becomes trivial, inconsequential by comparison. This response is perfectly reasonable. It's not a fault. Hey, until Jasper's diagnosis, that was me. Then it got complicated. When burdened with an unadulterated truth, you risk becoming a pariah, at first by your presence, and then simply by your existence. Why invite the downer to the party? You're the reminder of why I shouldn't bitch, gossip, boast, or complain about life and, when you think about it, for so many of us, where does that leave us?

Normal may be an act, it may be thankless and draining, but it is the only performance that gives you a chance. Of course I want Jasper to be as normal as he can be. Let others add "even though" or "in spite of" to his short list of ordinary achievements. But in my version of normal, his health has always come first. At least it did until I caved to an unlikely adversary.

In town and at lunch, I looked on as strangers noticed the word *service* on Whistler's vest. I could tell a few suspected a fake, a few appreciated a tight relationship between dog and boy, but the majority were unified by what they wondered most—what invisible disease requires canine assistance?

That was why I let Jasper and Whistler go to the pond. It was a reflex, a need to fight back with proof that my son could be normal, go play like a regular kid. I broke down and called Mrs. Cruz, heard what she was up to, and suggested Jasper would love to tag along. What was she going to say? And it wasn't that I trusted Mrs. Cruz. I don't. I was always going to stick around. What mattered was Jasper believed he was alone. Jasper imagined his mother trusted him, and if that made him feel a little bit closer to normal, so be it.

From the lofty Crystal Lake parking lot, no more than a quarter of the way down the steps, there's a side trail that leads to a beautiful spot, a bench donated by the Cape Cod Audubon Society, offering a vista of the pond below. More importantly, it provides an unencumbered view of the entire beach. There's only one way down and one way out. After yesterday's scare with that bearded hobo, I'm not taking any chances.

"Have fun," I said, pretending to be busy, pretending to be happy, leaving my only child with a woman focused on getting a tan, the next chapter of her paperback, and not being a primary caretaker for a precious few hours.

And instead of saying, "Will do," or "Sure, Mom," Jasper came back with, "Thank you," as though the most important thing to him was to have my permission, my blessing, killing me with how he still puts his desire to please me first.

So I withdrew to my lofty vantage point, like the creepy overprotective parent loitering in the playground bushes on the first day of school. And, for a while, I was glad I did, standing alone, my face caressed by a willing sun, afforded this rare, candid view of Jasper at play, smiles and laughter honest and spontaneous, trees and distance helping me out, silencing his cough, making him appear, well, normal. Moments like this are jolts of purpose, the missing Post-it note that reminds you where you left your smile. They are the glimmers of possibility, and if you find just the right angle, and let them catch in the light, for a split second, they might even lessen the burden of caring for a sick child. Despite the hurdles, I will always help him over, lower the bar, chainsaw my way through, because these are the times when I realize I am nothing without my son in the race.

Zack Cruz doesn't hang out with Jasper. They'll interact at soccer practice, but Zack is smart, athletic, and popular. So I'm shocked to witness Zack's enthusiasm to engage Jasper and shed his cool until I recognize the new variable in their equation—Whistler.

To be fair to the dog, he definitely changed the dynamics. Whether Whistler is the icebreaker or my son's confidence builder, it's hard to tell. What's undeniable, however, is Jasper's grin, his belly laughs, and the dog's gift with a soccer ball. That this four-legged soccer savant can play makes no sense. His scars suggest a history of trauma, if not abuse. Where did he learn the ball control of a Brazilian soccer star?

Just as I'm second-guessing my choice of antibiotic for Whistler's cough, the Kerry boys show up, their boorish father noticing me from the wooden staircase, coming over for a chat about tomorrow's game, me struggling to look past him, seeing my son instantly abandoned and pretending not to notice.

And that's when I hear the splash and see two dots bobbing about on the shiny black surface below. I silence him midsentence and begin to run.

By the time I get down to the beach, they are back ashore; bedraggled, shipwrecked, doubled over, coughing up lungs the pair of them.

"What the hell?"

From the other end of the beach, Mrs. Cruz emerges from under her umbrella, hand raised against the sun, squinting my way, too far away to shout. Mr. Cruz might need the coast guard.

Jasper endeavors to find his voice.

"I wanted to swim," he says. Bad enough, but then he adds, "We both did."

Head bowed, he can't meet my eyes, like he might find a

decent excuse buried somewhere in the sand. And that's when I notice the dark water oozing between the lace holes of his brand-new sneakers, one neat white Nike swish streaked with a nasty brown stain.

"Who goes for a swim in October on Cape Cod, fully clothed?"

Perhaps he wants me to find the answer in his stare, fixating on that trademark swish, as though marketing had indoctrinated both of them and they had heard the call.

Just do it.

21

Jasper

WE'RE ON OUR way to Grandma's house and Mom's knuckles make me worried—too pale, too shiny. She breaks a seven-minute silence with "Unbelievable," angry mirror eyes burrowing into me.

I hang my head in shame. Whistler looks like he's seen a squirrel. I give him a nudge.

"Whistler stays in the truck and don't you dare 'but Mom' me. Not after today's stunt. I would have left him behind, but God knows what he'd do to the apartment and you know how Grandma is about dogs. We'll crack a window and I brought a blanket. You can visit and take him to the bathroom, but make sure you pick up after him."

I do the bobblehead nod, the rapid overexaggerated version that begs forgiveness. But Whistler coughs and then so do I.

Mom shakes her head, reaches into her purse for a bottle of Advil.

"Headache?" I ask.

"What? Oh, yeah. Must have been from watching you two choke on ten gallons of pond swill. And before I forget, Grandma says keep away from the tree house."

I groan. Mom's old tree house is the only fun thing to do at Grandma's.

"The tide's been astronomically high these past few nights. Apparently that part of the backyard is like a swamp."

"Okay," I say as we pull into the horseshoe driveway, hearing Mom using a swear word under her breath. Maybe it's 'cause we're always the last to arrive.

"How come Auntie Gwen has left her Mercedes running?" I ask, noticing a thin trail of smoke trickling from the exhaust of her big white SUV.

"Not a clue," says Mom, snuggling up behind Uncle Bob's shiny new BMW.

Mom makes me sit still for one last inspection under the dome light, her saliva fingers fussing over my part. She sighs, throws up her hands, and sets up a blanket nest in the wayback.

"Take a nap," I tell Whistler. He looks confused, so I send him a silent "Trust me, you're better off staying in the car," and he leaps over the back seat, circles once, and flops down.

I carry the birthday present—we chose a golf glove and a golf cap. Mom carries a tray of stuffed mushrooms. Yuck.

The front door swings open before I have a chance to knock, Grandma standing there, arms folded across her chest.

"Are there no working clocks in your house?"

I do a quick mental count but before I can answer, "Yes, seven," she continues.

"I told you we're having beef tenderloin. It's your father's favorite, and you know how he hates it overdone."

Grandma kind of scares me. She wears bright red lipstick like a hungry vampire, never smiles, and bathes in so much old lady perfume that even I can smell it. Her feet, if she has any, are always hidden under long skirts and dresses, but I think she levitates, never making a sound, able to appear from nowhere. Fortunately, my cheeks remain smudge free because she only ever pats me on the head and tells me to run along. Mom swears it's nothing personal, saying Grandma never gave her hugs or kisses back when she was a kid. In fact she still doesn't.

"Sorry," says Mom, but she looks about as sorry as Grandma looks surprised. "Jasper's cough needed an extra—"

"I'm sure it did," says Grandma, already gliding away, mumbling.

The house is huge and dark and frilly with lots of rooms and space to spread out, but everyone always squeezes into the kitchen, bumping into each other, scrambling for drinks like they just crossed the Sahara, hunting for food with their dirty fingers, pretend laughing and speaking too loud. As usual, Mom makes me say hello to the grown-ups first.

Grandpa waves (might be "hello," might be "go away") without turning our way, slumped inside his La-Z-Boy, hypnotized by the TV.

Uncle Bob and Auntie Beth synchronize raising their chins but keep their distance, as if my CF is contagious.

Though Mom says nothing, guiding me in silence, it's obvious she's hoping for more of a reaction. Fortunately, Auntie

Gwen delivers, earning a smile for being the only person to hug me so tight I can't breathe; or rather I can breathe even less. Her rapid-fire kisses smack in my ear. Mom says that sometimes Auntie Gwen drinks too much, which makes her giggly and a little emotional. That must be why I catch her wiping away a tear.

"Auntie Gwen, you forgot to switch off your Mercedes."

Auntie Gwen takes a gulp from her goblet of red wine, screws up her face like I must be mistaken, and wobbles off in search of a refill. Weird.

Dinner means sitting at a separate table with my cousins. Auntie Gwen and Uncle "Away on Business" Scott (he never shows up to these parties) have three kids—Jessica, six; Tim (not Timmy), eight; and Todd (his mom pronounces it "Tawd"), ten. I like Jess and Tim but Todd is a total plonker.

Uncle Bob, Mom's oldest brother, and Auntie Beth (his second wife) have two kids in college. No one's seen either one of them in years.

Before sitting down to eat, Mom slips me a palm full of enzyme capsules together with a glass of milk.

"What you doing?" asks Todd, loud enough to make people turn and stare just as I'm cramming them into my mouth.

Mom stiffens and mouths, "Ignore him."

I swallow hard, lean into Todd, and whisper, "Cyanide capsules. Want one?"

He thinks about it, like I might be offering him some new kind of candy, before taking a seat in front of a volcano of food. Mom says, "Cousin Todd likes his vittles."

We eat while the grown-ups blab and then we sing "Happy Birthday" and Grandpa blows out his candles but goes back to watching golf without even trying a slice of his cake. All I can think about is Whistler. What if he needs to pee or if he's afraid of the dark? What if he's chewing his way through Mom's seat belts because he's bored?

Mom says some CF kids are like cows, preferring to graze on food throughout the day rather than eating meals at set times. Useful excuse. Even though my cousins are still strapping on a feedbag, I sneak over to Mom, tell her I'm full, and ask if I can "check on our truck."

She smiles, but it's one of those smiles like she's given up and doesn't want to argue. Everyone else is talking about taking trips and flying to places and she's just moving her food around on her plate in a way that would get me into big trouble. I give her a quick hug because she looks like she needs one, and run outside.

It's totally dark, but warm enough that I don't need a coat. Whistler stands on the driver's seat, as if he's been waiting for my return.

"Hey, take it easy," I say, trying to lasso that rooting zebra snout in my leash, his tail hammering the dashboard.

I catch the sweeping arcs of light before I hear their screams. The cousins are loose and headed my way. They each carry a flashlight.

"Jeez, what's with the wolf rat?" Todd says.

Jess and Tim hang back, cackling, placing the beam under

their chins to make spooky faces. Todd's the one being rude, closing in, his beam determined to blind poor Whistler.

"He's mine. His name's Whistler."

"Where'd he get those sick scars?" he asks, pointing at his muzzle.

I'm pretty sure Mom and Burt know the truth behind the zebra stripes, but it's got to be bad because they pretend they don't.

I'm about to go with a no-clue shoulder shrug, but then I think about how Mom's always telling me to stand up for myself, to give as good as I get, so I reply, "He's a military attack dog, just back from Afghanistan. One word and he'll have your throat for dinner."

"Yeah, right," says Todd. "Looks like a mangy mongrel. How old is it?"

His question annoys me mainly because I don't know the answer.

"Ten," I reply, pretending that I do.

"Well," he says, "maybe it's best you get an older dog and not a puppy. Know what I'm sayin'?"

Yeah, I get it, Tawd, but it's not like I've never heard it before. A couple of mean kids at school sometimes say stuff like, "Quit spreading your virus, cough boy" or "Why go to class if you're never going to finish high school?" or "Why don't you get a transplant already?" Mom says they're ignorant, destined to bag my groceries, but I've been online, I've read the blogs of kids a little older than me, the ones waiting for new lungs. To be honest, the worst part about Todd is he says stuff without acting mean, like he's telling the truth, so how could he get into trouble?

I look over at Whistler and think, *How come dogs never bad-mouth?* I've watched them for hours at the shelter and they never care if you smell funny, are having a bad hair day, or seem to be missing a leg. Dogs don't gossip. Dogs don't backstab. Dogs don't do mean.

Todd's comment might bother me, but not half as much as it seems to bother Whistler. Whistler stands his ground and I can sense a wave of disgust rippling through his scarred shoulders.

"How come your mom's Mercedes is still running?" I say, as another exhaust cloud drifts our way.

"Who cares? She says it's something with the engine. Shut up and take this."

Todd tosses me a flashlight. It's a lot smaller than his.

"We're playing flashlight tag and you're it. The lamppost is base and you're only tagged if the beam gets you right in the eyes. Not legs or body, eye contact only. Count to a hundred, no peeking."

"Only if Whistler can be on my team."

"Whatever," says Todd, switching off his beam and charging off into the darkness.

At sixty-six, I realize that Jess and Tim are hiding around the back of their mom's SUV. I can hear them whispering. Grandma lets us play this game because she can't wait to get us out of the house, and Todd loves it because he always wins and he loves to scare the crap out of me. The dog sniffing at my pocket in search of a treat tells me this time will be different.

"Ready or not, here I come."

Ignoring the Mercedes (too easy), I head out across the lawn, Whistler clinging so tight we might as well be in a three-legged race. Normally I'm jumpy, anticipating an explosive "boo" in my ear. Tonight I haven't even turned on my flashlight. No need. I'm fired up—not alone and not afraid.

"Let's do this," I tell him, knowing Whistler is in control, pressing his body into my left side or my right, herding me in the direction he wants us to go.

My grandparents' backyard is really big, with all kinds of trees and fancy flowerbeds, a massive deck, a hammock, neat rows of white Adirondack chairs and a view across the marshlands to the ocean. Most of the trees are kind of skinny—less than ideal for hiding if you're Todd—so, with Mom's old tree house out of bounds, that leaves the shed, the garage, the picket fence, and the hot tub.

I look back at the lamppost. Jess and Tim stand in the glow, trying to catch moths and calling me names, because they made it safely back to base. I don't think they can see me, but if they could, I bet they'd see a strange single silhouette—part boy, part dog.

Downstairs light can't reach this far from the house and the only sound comes from the crashing waves and the branches overhead, scratching against one another in the wind. Whistler hesitates, like he's thinking, and suddenly my arm shoots out of its socket and I'm dragged past a mountain of black mulch, heading for a woodpile covered by a huge nylon tarp.

For a split second I turn on the beam. Whistler looks nothing like a pointer but his body is rigid, good left eye trained on the distorted lump in the middle. *Brilliant.*

Like a magician unveiling his trick, I rip back the edge of the tarp, and thrust my torch beam directly into the blinking, stunned eyes of cousin Tawd.

"Get out of my face. Using a dog is against the rules."

"What about using a mangy mongrel?"

"Cheat," snaps Todd, marching back to the lamppost. "See if I care. You'll never find anywhere to hide from me."

Without saying another word, Todd presses his head into the crease of his raised elbow resting on the lamppost, pretends to close his eyes and begins counting. The other cousins scatter and Whistler drags me into the darkness, like he's a speedboat and I'm on water skis. We end up behind the garden shed just as I hear a cry of, "Coming, ready or not."

That's when a cough begins to build in my lungs. It starts as a little tickle, a scratchy itch deep down in the lining of my airway, begging for a soothing hack. I can feel it building, expanding, about to get away from me, when, without warning, Whistler slips his leash and disappears into the night.

I clasp a palm to my mouth, the cough escaping like muffled gunfire. Todd must have heard.

Suddenly, I'm alone in the darkness and the old jitters rush back. Gritting my teeth, I call for Whistler. Nothing. What if he's run away again?

"Come out, come out, wherever you are."

I hear a twig crack, yards away, see the beam slicing through the glass window on the other side of the shed. I should let myself get caught and fetch Mom to help me look for Whistler.

And then there's the sound of my cough, booming and familiar, but it's not coming from me. The beam stops, drops, and sweeps back across the lawn. The cough comes again and the flashlight starts to drift away.

Peeking around the shed, I make out Todd's circle of light, off in the distance, growing brighter as it crawls up the trunk of the thickest, strongest tree in the backyard—the one with the tree house.

What happens next happens fast, starting with the scream. To be fair to my cousin, it's a really good one, totally out of a horror movie, a shock in the silent night, but it's spoiled by a wimpy cry of "Help." Only when I hear the squelching, the sound of muddy swamp trying to swallow him whole, do I realize what's happened. It's followed by a run of curse words that would get most kids my age in serious trouble.

"Todd, Jess, Tim, come on we're leaving." It's Auntie Gwen, standing alone, making her way to her truck.

My youngest cousins pop up directly in front of her, conveniently using the same hiding place again.

"Todd, come on, hurry up," Gwen says, climbing into the driver's seat.

Should I go and help Todd? Should I fetch his mom? While

I'm trying to decide, I switch on my flashlight and suddenly Whistler is once more by my side.

"Where did you get to?"

No time for an answer because the creature from the brown lagoon emerges from the shadows and begins sloshing my way.

"This is your fault," says Todd. "The tree house was off limits. I'm telling Grandma."

Todd is smothered in a slimy goo like barbecue sauce. It's plastered to his jeans, caked across his butt, and he's hobbling, having lost a sneaker and a sock. And that's when it hits me. Todd wanted *me* to go hide because he wanted this to happen to me. He was banking on no one telling me about the swill pond pooling around the tree house.

"You're so dead," he snaps, and then laughs. "Maybe even deader."

I can't let this one get past me.

"Well you . . . you, you smell like hot garbage." Even though I can't smell a thing and I feel guilty for being mean.

"Come on, come on," says Auntie Gwen, powering down her window without looking. "Quit your whining, Todd, whatever it is we can sort it out at home."

So cousin Todd opens the back door to his mom's shiny white Mercedes SUV, smearing the door handle, admiring the clean leather seats before jumping in, his look saying, "Hey, you asked for this."

I stand under the light as Auntie Gwen pulls away—hoping she notices that my clothes are completely swamp-free—but instead of waving goodbye, she blows me a kiss and breaks into a hysterical laugh. Then she slams on the brakes, and screams into the back seat, "Tawd, what the hell happened? Did you crap your pants?"

I look over at Whistler. Whistler looks up at me and it's obvious he's smiling, his droopy eye like a slow wink, like he wants me to know, "I've got your back."

I shouldn't encourage bad behavior. Still, I can't help but give him a little pat on his head. Just a little one.

22

Kate

THE LIST OF essential items loops like endless ticker tape around the inside of my skull. In addition to all the standard stuff, I dare not forget the portable nebulizer with car charger (in case its battery runs flat), an EpiPen (in case Jasper's allergic to something other than bees or penicillin or sesame seeds), and, lest the other mothers stone me with their eyes, two dozen washed and quartered oranges for halftime.

The trouble is I'm distracted. No, I'm fascinated. Standing at the kitchen window, overlooking our postage stamp of a backyard, I can't get over the pregame warm-up unfolding before my eyes.

Once again, Jasper and Whistler play with a soccer ball. Strange, but no longer such a big deal, until you pay attention to the specifics of their game. Jasper talks, not that I can hear what he says, but his mouth opens to speak in bursts, with breaks of silence, as though he's pausing in a conversation. There are nods, head shaking, laughter, and smiles like something the dog has said or done is either funny or poignant. I know, how can a dog be poignant? And there's the way in which they use the ball, as though this might be an actual training session.

If I ignore the use of four paws and the excessive oral ball control, the dog appears to be showing Jasper how to be fearless, to charge in without a care, 100 percent committed to winning every tackle. Between the posts of the little hockey net Jasper uses for practice, Whistler flies, flips, and pirouettes, determined to leap and parry and stop Jasper from scoring a goal. Forget an untrained eye, anyone can see this dog is on fire. Yet, for all the drool, a ravenous grin is permanently plastered to his lips. Even his wonky, weeping right eye laser locks onto every pass and flight of the black-and-white sphere.

This is not a nothing moment for me. It is not just play. My son is having a blast, and if I didn't know better, if I wasn't watching this unfold like a silent movie, and if it wasn't a dog standing opposite him, I'd swear their interaction looked more like a lesson, a teacher and a student. Don't make me say who's who.

Yet I can't help but worry. That a boy believes he can communicate with a dog may be just a game, innocent make-believe, but what if others see a lonely boy acting delusional, a sick kid who's disabled and weird. It's another step away from "normal" and one more check in the "do not get a dog" column. The way Jasper acts around this dog would make them mock his brain as well. Kids can be cruel. I might as well send him to school wearing a bow tie.

Fifteen minutes later, as we trek toward the soccer field behind Jasper's school, I notice how the usual suspects have begun to congregate on the touchline. Like most parents, a huge chunk of my social life lies at the mercy of our children. Every weekend we gather, united as spectators, the helicopter parents frightened to miss the milestones. Over time, factions have evolved.

There are The Obsessed, epitomized by the oafish Mr. Kerry, father of the twin boys, Martin and Trevor. Come rain or shine, Mr. Kerry records every second of every game with his video camera, supposedly so he can sit down after the match, critiquing each play in a postmortem from which the twins must learn and do better.

Neatly situated along the sideline in their high-tech beach chairs—the ones with the double cup holders and the integrated roof—sit The Gossips, a quartet of wannabe yummy mummies convinced that, with enough makeup, any woman can banish the prospect of winter ugly blues. They cackle, lean in close to share snarky tidbits, and they always act annoyed when one of their kids scores, like it's the kids fault they weren't watching.

Then there's The Blasé. Mrs. Owen is a perfect example. Her son, David, plays in goal. She's juggling five kids and, by her own admission, she's usually clueless as to where they all are at any moment in time. More often than not she drops David off and, hours later, loops back to retrieve the kid kicking the curb in the parking lot.

As for me, I shoot for The Revered. The other parents are polite and friendly, but it's obvious how carefully they tread.

Hardly surprising, when you think about it. Unlike school or college or work, we don't gravitate based on mutual tastes, or a growing kinship. We are unceremoniously tossed into a melting pot, forced to bind together for the sake of our children. There is no choice. Sometimes we hit it off, more often we make do, but in the long run, chances are these are not friendships that will last.

Jasper bounces ahead to join his teammates leaving Whistler with me. I'm fairly confident I could have left the dog at home, but being in a noisy crowd is actually a good opportunity to test him. This time around the fake service dog vest stays in the car. I'm getting more than enough attention from certain parents anticipating my showdown with Coach Taft if we go to states and he decides to drop my son from the team.

"Okay if I leave these here?"

Taft glances my way as I plop down a large Tupperware container full of cut oranges on his collapsible table near the halfway line.

"Many thanks," he says, eyeing Whistler. "That dog's not going to bark, is it?"

I smile, say, "No chance," and drift away, having spotted Mrs. Cruz, head down, pretending that she hasn't seen me. She should be embarrassed. My son could have drowned on her watch.

Whistler and I find a spot farther down the touchline and, probably for the first time since bringing this mutt home, I'm grateful to have his company. He creates a degree of separation from the masses, a barrier they are unsure they want to, or should, broach. Hopefully I haven't mistaken the label of revered for the stigma of alienated. Over the years I'm pretty sure I've earned a semblance of respect. Whether it's being a single mom, maintaining a career, or what I have to handle with Jasper, I'll take it. After last night, anything is better than the insipid chiding from those you cannot choose—your family.

When Mom went off on me for showing up late it was all I could do to pinch my lips into a thin, white, "do not cross" line. I know I'm overly sensitive about Jasper, and maybe she wasn't being unreasonable, but there's this disparaging streak to her attitude and, for whatever reason, I'm noticing it more and more, every time we're together. Oh, she may smile, never raise her voice, and happily bounce from one predictable nicety to the next, but in the gaps between the words, in the looks I'm not supposed to catch, I keep coming back to the moment I decided to keep my boy, and a fear that my mother harbors a grudge.

"Who cares if Dad's precious tenderloin turns into beef jerky?" I wanted to scream. "Let's you and I hash this out, once and for all."

But it's not how we do it in this family. Blunt by name, not by nature.

"No use crying over spilled milk," she said. But deep down, where insecurity fuels insinuation, I heard, "Keeping Jasper was a mistake." Naturally, she'll deny it, insist I'm wrong, confused, being ridiculous. She'll recall her well-intentioned warnings of life as a single mom, and of course they came true, but sometimes—and I wish I didn't see it this way—I'm convinced of a simmering smugness, like she loves to rub a little salt into my wounds, Jasper's CF the whipped cream on a told-you-so sundae. In my darkest moments, part of me even wonders if she thinks his disease is my punishment.

That's why I say nothing. When it comes to the difficult topics regarding Jasper, we've evolved from words. For me, what's the point, I'm serving my sentence. For her, it's an argument she won long ago; to say more is wasted energy. Perhaps, by remaining silent, she thinks she can help me get over the shame.

My father pretty much checked out the moment I graduated high school, claiming his parental responsibility over, replaced by a vague, tepid indifference—"So long as you're happy"—that feels more like rejection. He's mastered the art of veiling his apathy and self-imposed exile from family life as comic regret, citing the way things turned out, in my case, "not becoming a *real* doctor."

There's my brother, always odd and self-absorbed, and his annoying wife, always happy to point out, "Still haven't met anyone?" Our (her) running joke only highlights the problem: that without a partner I lack credibility, I lack proof that at least one other adult believes in what I'm doing. Which makes me an outlier, if not an outcast.

Then there's my little sister, Gwen. Poor Gwen. Affectionate and concerned but in constant need of propping up, as if her own grief over Jasper requires greater support than mine. I love her to pieces, but she can be such a pill. Sloshing wineglass in hand, unsteady in her latest Jimmy Choo's—she's always been more girly than me—she had pulled me aside and said, "About Thanksgiving. I know it's my turn, but can you host again this year? You're so much better at it than me. Oh, and we're still on for Monday, yeah?" Into my confusion she added, "Taking the kids. I'll pick them up by nine, nine-thirty at the latest."

And then she took my silent incredulity as an affirmative, tottering off before I could muster a "Why?" and "What about your husband?" It seems I may be the only unmarried mother in our family, but I don't appear to be the only single parent.

Whistler sits beside me, tight and square, and I pat his misshapen head in approval. He ducks away and I can tell he's distracted, perhaps puzzled when Jasper takes his usual chair at the scorekeeper's table, ready to document the plays rather than joining his team on the field.

Our team, the Tide, wears sea-foam green. Today's opposition, the Sharks, play in white and slate-gray stripes. As the whistle blows I overhear one father informing his indifferent wife that the Tide can tie and still qualify for the playoffs. Only a loss stands in their way.

From the moment the whistle blows, Mr. Kerry, video camera panning and zooming, bellows to his boys, shouting orders, not encouragement, criticizing the referee for every controversial call that goes against the home team. It's as if he thinks a Division 1 college scout might be in attendance. He paces the sidelines like a barking dog trapped inside his pound, trying to outdo his opposite number (there's always one) from the Sharks.

Whistler appears to follow the ebb and flow of the game as the ball flies around the field, but he's restless. He stands, he sits, he tries to peer between and around legs as though looking for Jasper. I don't think his dilemma lies with the crowd. It's the separation, and every so often I catch Jasper leaning back in his chair, checking in. These two have something between them, and once again the mother in me anticipates a problem.

Not that Whistler is a bad dog. If anything, right now, he lends me a certain amount of credibility, the well-behaved street dog, this scarred canine warrior, proof in the power of nature over nurture. Given his skills with a soccer ball and his instant bond with Jasper, he's clearly used to being around kids. Of course I appreciate the way he enticed those girls from Jasper's school to say hello, the way he wowed Zack Cruz—absurd how this mutt can seduce strangers, and inspire such confidence in my boy. I mean he probably could become a proficient service dog, if we ignore the freak out in the store (how could I not notice) when he spotted the golf clubs. How many times was he on the wrong end of a seven iron? And that manic detour—spotting the brawny redhead smoking a cigarette, bolting for the other side of the street like his life depended on it, like he was running from the devil—did the man remind him of his captor, or was it the glow of burning ash, his weapon of choice? God knows what this poor creature must have endured in his former life?

But that's not it. For all the tests and behavioral evaluations, for all the mysteries of his provenance, one thing is undeniable: Whistler is a runaway, a deserter, a repeat offender, and therefore, when it comes to my son, a potential heartbreaker. And let's not forget the dog's penchant for risky behavior. Jasper would never swim in an icy pond. And those traces of muddy paw prints across my back seat tell me he was up to no good in my parent's backyard. Clearly he's incredibly influential.

No, Whistler may not be a bad dog, but he is a bad-boy dog, a troublemaker. When your child hangs out with the wrong kind of kid, you know it, and you do something about it. What halfway decent mom wouldn't interfere? Bottom line: Whistler will make a great pet. Just not a great pet for my son.

A collective gasp brings me back, panic washing through the crowd as the Sharks attack. Led by a squirrelly redhead named Daz (short for Darren, not Dazzle, according to a proud but loud-mouthed parent from the opposition), they have scored a goal.

It remains one to nothing at halftime.

I take Whistler for a potty break and, walking back, can't help but notice the way Jasper chats with each player on his team. It's become his thing, what he does. By watching lots of British soccer on TV, he knows so much about the game that he's able to offer sage advice in a way that Coach Taft, who'd rather be playing basketball, never could.

"They're good," says Jasper, finally coming over to see Whistler, grappling with the smiling dog writhing on his back, in need of a belly rub. "We've just got to get a goal and park the bus."

"Park the what?"

"Park the bus. Drop everyone back into defense and run out the clock. I got to go, Mom, they're heading back."

"You think you'll get to play?"

Head-shaking as he jogs off, Jasper unloads a cough into his sea-foam sleeve. The noise has heft, it's more junky and definitely getting worse. I glare at the dog by my side—the architect of the risky misadventures that compounded his lung disease.

Twenty minutes into the second half and even the Gossips are engrossed in the game, none of them offering to get another round of venti soy lattes. For the first time ever, Mr. Kerry has quit filming and looks like he might succumb to a coronary.

And then, like a jolt from a defibrillator, Zack Cruz, the boy who abandoned my son on the beach, steps up to a free kick, and with a dipping, curling, practiced shot, scores the goal that pulls the Tide level.

Cheers of relief and hearty fist pumps off the pitch synchronize with high fives and hugs on it. Funny; as the two sides return to their starting positions, Zack accepts the praise of his teammates, but his thumbs-up is aimed not at Coach Taft but at my son. Jasper makes me melt, flashing his biggest grin, returning the sign, screaming for everyone to "Park the bus, park the bus," while only Coach Taft looks clueless.

Unfortunately, in the process of "parking," there's a fender bender of disastrous proportions. To be honest I was distracted by Jasper battling a coughing fit to see exactly what happened. One moment our goalkeeper, David Owen (he of the absentee mother), is diving for the ball, the next Coach Taft is charging onto the field, medical bag in tow.

One of The Gossips eases out of her chair and scans the crowd, merely to confirm to her besties that, "Surprise, surprise," Mrs. Owen is nowhere to be found.

Normally they pull out an ice pack and minutes later the kid's back on the field. This time a crying boy hobbles off, wincing in agony, and I can't tell who's more distraught, the goalie or the coach.

"Put in my boy Martin," says Mr. Kerry, muscling his way over, his tone both grave and panicky. "There's no one else."

"I can do it."

I can't actually see into the swarm around the coach, but I recognize the little voice. What does Jasper think he's doing?

"We need Martin in D. He's the only one who can handle that redhead kid, Daz. And I play in goal all the time during practice."

"That's only because . . ."

Kerry catches himself, thinking better of saying it out loud while casting about among other concerned faces for backup.

"Martin," he shouts, waving at his son, the one pointing a finger at himself. "Yes, get here now."

And then, to my surprise, Mrs. Cruz, who has been hiding behind sunglasses, sheds her disguise, reveals her raccoon tan, and says, "Coach. Let Jasper do it. He's right."

Slowly, Taft's head pivots my way. Maybe he thinks of me as an overbearing parent, but in that moment I actually shrink a little. Instead of daring him to say no, the biggest part of me says no for him.

Good old Coach Taft. Always lets you down. Without saying another word, he reaches into an oversize sports bag, pulls out a green shirt and a pair of goalkeeper gloves, and hands them over to Jasper.

I'm speechless as my son takes the field. Mr. Kerry, however, is not, leaning into Taft's ear, threatening bodily harm if this play goes awry. There's no excuse, but while I'm caught up and caught off guard by an epidemic of trepidation and doom, Whistler snaps his leash from out of my hand and he's gone, bolting down the sideline, making a neat, ninety-degree turn at the corner flag before coming to a stop, perfectly centered behind the open goal, just as Jasper takes up his position.

Jasper coughs into his upper arm and locks eyes with the dog. When he turns back to face the play, I can't tell whether I imagined what I saw. All around me facial expressions exude various stages of panic, but I can't be the only person who noticed how my son gave the dog a stern confident nod.

Corner kick, the ball sweeps in, high in front of Jasper's goal, disappearing into a quaking wall of bodies and for one long second, united by a collective breath hold, we wait to see the inevitable bulge in the white netting as the Sharks score a second goal. But as the players back off, one by one, a little boy in a green shirt emerges, pulling himself from the dirt, the ball clasped to his baby-bird chest, patting down the air with his oven-mitt hand, the gesture delivering a clear message: "Stay calm. I've got this."

Eight minutes to go and as I'm trying to rationalize how ten other boys should be able to shield my son from inevitable trauma, that rabid red squirrel, Daz, lets loose with a booming right footer from just outside the box. All eyes are on Jasper. All eyes except mine. It's not that I can't bear to watch, it's just that I'm watching the dog because even before Daz's cleats strike the ball, Whistler leans right. I see it clear as day, a distinct flinch, like the dog standing behind the net knows exactly which way the ball is going to go, a split second before the ball has been kicked. And that's when my eyes catch up, Jasper launching himself at full stretch, out to the side. It happens so fast, and I can't believe I'm saying this but I'd love to see Mr. Kerry's video, because I swear Jasper takes off at the very moment the ball is kicked, guessing right, the only way he could possibly get his fingertips on the ball and push it around the post. There is a roar. There is a groan. But mostly there is applause, applause for my son's save. Even Mr. Kerry has fallen silent.

Four minutes to go and the ball has bounced back into their half, Jasper coughing hard, no attempt to conceal it, like he's dying to clear his lungs. The green shirt fits him like an army surplus tent, the oversize gloves ridiculous, pseudo–Mickey Mouse, exaggerating every movement into busy jazz hands. He needs his puffer. What will happen if I march over there right now and give it to him?

Into the final minute, and the seconds refuse to die. With the Tide pushed forward, trying to keep the play away from Jasper, a looping ball flies over the heads of the Kerry brothers, our last line of defense, and, from nowhere, into the empty space darts Daz.

It's one on one, and, thanks to Jasper forcing me to watch the World Cup on TV, I've seen it before. Does the goalkeeper go out, narrow the angles, and hope the striker will panic and fluff the shot? Or does he stay put, protect the goal, and hope his defenders can get back in time?

Whistler appears to make the call, claws scrambling on the spot, neck lunging forward, and Jasper responds, up and running, that's right, running, and it's as if, once more, I'm standing at our kitchen window, watching him practice in the backyard, only Jasper has become the dog, resolute and fearless, and the ball is his, will be his, was never going to be anything but his. This wunderkind Daz is a determined little bugger, convinced he can get there first and I watch, helpless, as my son, without a care, takes off, glides, and lands on top of the ball, like he's ready to make the ultimate sacrifice, pouncing on a grenade, taking a barrage of brutal kicks into the curl of his tiny body.

Jasper hangs on.

The whistle blows.

And suddenly my son vanishes, lost in a sea of hugging, high-fiving, back-slapping players, desperate to congratulate the teammate who saved their season.

Relieved parents invade the field, but I stay put. To my right, Mrs. Cruz flashes me an olive-branch smile, and I even manage to smile back. Mr. Kerry dares to squeeze my shoulder as he jogs past to join his boys, offering me a relieved "Never saw that coming." Alone, I find myself focusing on the dog with the scars, the chewed ear, and the droopy eye. Whistler hasn't moved. He sits quietly behind the net, content. This canine nomad had his chance to run away. But he didn't. He chose to stay. He chose to stay with my son.

Finally, the crowds part enough for me to see him, my little green giant, still clinging to the ball, struggling not to cough, stealing breaths, but most of all smiling. And in this moment, enough to notice, the weight, that eternal cinder block that lies across my chest, eases up, just a little, for just a second, affording me one, lighter breath, as Jasper basks in an echoing mantra of "Good game, good game, good game."

23

Jasper

Mom has finally calmed down because on the drive home she flinched every time my cough got out of control, and totally lost it when I changed out of my muddy kit, slapping a hand across her mouth like she had to hold back a scream.

"God, look at those bruises."

I run to the bathroom, twisting around to see in the mirror. "Yes! Battle scars."

My skin is kind of pale, okay, mashed potato white, but there are these great big black and blues on my back and shoulders and hips, like ink, like tats, like war wounds. To me they are the price of victory, even if the game ended in a draw.

"Not cool. If your school nurse sees them, she'll report me for child abuse. Here, take a Motrin, then I want you in that shower. And make sure there's plenty of steam. It'll loosen the junk in your chest."

The steamy shower doesn't help my cough one bit, and secretly I feel sore all over, but so what, I'm going to spend the day chillin' with an actual proper dog, inside my home.

I do my homework (maths—Mom hates it when I add an *s* like in England), I do lots of extra nebs to stop her nagging (closing the bedroom door so Whistler can suck down some of the stray mist into his lungs), and then we sit on the couch to watch a soccer game I've recorded, even though Whistler prefers to close his eyes with his head on my lap.

From time to time Mom checks in—offering drinks, snacks, "You sure you two are okay?"—but around four, she takes a phone call in the kitchen. My Grandma.

"No, Mom," I hear her say, "it's not like that. I can't simply . . . switch off." Her voice often gets loud when she's talking to Grandma. "I know you do, and I appreciate the offers of help, but babysitting Jasper is not like babysitting one of Gwen's kids."

Mom's pacing back and forth. Never a good sign.

"Because," she says, "because . . . no one in this family seems to understand how hard it is for me to relax. I try not to let it bug me, so why should it bug my brother if I'm not bursting with excitement over his next ski trip to Breckenridge or his next cruise to Bermuda."

And then, actually shouting. "Look, Mom, if you've got something to say, then just say it."

Whistler and I pretend to be really into the game and when Mom hangs up she pretends to be happy and says, "Okay if I take a bath?" She's already holding a big glass of white wine and a bottle of some foamy bubble stuff, so I'm not sure why she asked.

As soon as we're alone I turn to Whistler and say, "She worries me."

Whistler sits up, a string of drool connecting my lap to his chin.

"The way she gets mad and sad. And I know it's my fault. Like when she's talking on the phone and says, 'I can't, I've got Jasper,' or 'No, Jasper's sick . . . again.' We never talk about it, but it makes me scared. Not for me. For her."

No response except droopy chocolate eyes.

"Don't you ever get scared?" I ask, and Whistler tilts his head off to the side. Maybe he wants me to know that at least he's listening, even if he doesn't have any advice, and the look on his face makes me realize that sometimes, getting a reply doesn't really matter, because it feels pretty good just being able to share, to let it out, knowing my secret's safe.

Even though Whistler's coughing has been almost as bad as mine, Mom still wants him back at the shelter tomorrow. If I keep bugging her about us keeping him, I know she'll shut me down. If I sulk, she'll call me out. If I ramp up to full-blown crying, she'll get mad because tears make my cough ten times worse.

"How are we going to make her want to keep you? Are you even listening anymore?"

He's snoring and I'm trying not to be sad but I can't help it. Maybe it's contagious. Maybe that's why he's not that interested in "talking." Then another explanation pops up in my brain.

This weekend was the best because of Whistler. What if he's depressed because he thinks he did everything right, everything he could to be my dog. What if he can't understand where he went wrong?

Ten minutes later Whistler flips from deep, twitchy-paw sleep to totally awake at least two Mississippis before I hear the knock at the door. I shush him, index finger bouncing off my lip, realize of course he's not going to bark, switch to a flat palm stay command, and creep into the kitchen.

Mom's bathroom is down at the far end of the apartment and I can hear water running. There's the knock again. I should call her. I should ignore it. I should not open the door.

I open the door.

It's Mr. Crabtree—or as Mom likes to call him, the Apartment Nazi. He leans in close, too close, bad breath close, bursting spit bubble in the corner of his mouth close, and says, "There's been a complaint about a dog."

If Mr. Crabtree were a dog, he'd definitely be a bulldog, kind of chunky and snuffly with way too much floppy skin around his neck and cheeks. I think it stops him from being able to smile properly.

"Your Mom there?"

"I'm afraid she's busy, Mr. Crabtree. Can I give her a message?"

Mr. Crabtree sniffs, his piggy-nostrils flare, and all these curly gray nasal hairs get sucked up his nose, like a hiding sea anemone (I like nature TV shows). Did I mention how he's seriously old and crusty?

"Huh," he grunts, "I believe this belongs to her."

Like a police officer flashing me his badge, Mr. Crabtree shoves a lumpy plastic bag in my direction.

"Dog turd. Found it among my rosebushes this morning. Hope you've not got a dog in there?"

Remember how I said lying makes me panic, which kind of gives me away. I've learned it is easier not to answer directly. "Dogs are not allowed, Mr. Crabtree."

"That's right, young man. No loud music after ten at night. No outdoor fires. No parking other than designated spaces. And no dogs."

"Service dogs are okay though, right?"

"You telling me that's a service dog?"

He points and, from nowhere, Whistler is by my side, grinning, rear end turned to wobbly Jell-O like Mr. Crabtree is a friend and not a foe. I guess I need to work on our stay command. I guess I need to work on judging character. Or . . . wait a minute . . . what if I'm wrong about Mr. Crabtree and Whistler is right?

"If I said yes, could he stay?"

Mr. Crabtree shakes his head. Good job he doesn't actually drool. "I'd need to see papers, legitimate papers, not something fake you can buy online."

"But if I got proof, he'd be all set, right?"

Mr. Crabtree sighs. "Look, I don't make the rules, but if I catch you with a dog again, let alone a dog crapping on my yard, I'll have to report you. Your mom signed a contract. There's a waiting list to get into these apartments. We don't do second chances. Know why? We don't need to. Trust me, you don't want to have to look for somewhere new to live."

Again he holds out the plastic bag like he wants me to take it, but Whistler catches his eye and Mr. Crabtree hesitates, seems to change his mind. After a second of grunting and grumbling, he turns and hobbles off, swaying side to side like an emperor penguin, keeping time with the wag of Whistler's tail.

24

Kate

IN THE FIRST meaningful stretch of silence between thunderous coughs, my phone bursts into life and Gwen's name appears on the screen.

"You still up?" she asks.

"Jasper can't get to sleep."

"Fever?"

"Coughing. It's school break the week after next. It may be time to schedule another round of IV antibiotics in the hospital."

"Oh, Kate, I'm sorry. But then he'll be better, right?"

I catch the optimism in her voice, a plucky, rising intonation that believes in happier days ahead. Try as I might, undone by hours of relentless coughing, all I hear is the naivete of someone who means well, who truly cares, but doesn't really get it. At best, a few miserable weeks in the hospital might earn Jasper a temporary reprieve. Right about now I'd kill for a cure instead of a Band-Aid.

"Sure, I just hate having to put him through it again and again."

The line goes silent, followed by a stifled snivel.

"I don't know how you do it," says Gwen, unable to control the quaver in her voice. "I could never be strong enough."

How many times have I heard some version of this line and wanted to say, "Like I have a choice." A while back one of the other soccer moms took me aside to whisper, "When I think my life sucks I think about you, and realize how lucky I am. You're such an inspiration." It was all I could do not to scream in her face, "Thanks but I don't want to be an inspiration. I want to be normal. I want to get through a day without needing to cry."

"Of course you could," I say. "Don't get upset, Gwen, he's going to be fine."

I hear the rustle of a tissue, the blow of a nose, the restoration of composure.

"Anyway, why're you calling so late?"

"Because I want you to meet this old college buddy of Scott's."

"Oh, no, Gwen, please, a blind date with one of your husband's frat bros is the last thing I need right now."

"His name's Holden Patterson," says Gwen, ignoring my plea, "he's a doctor, the MD kind, single, fed up with the online dating scene, and, wait for it, inherited a boatload of family money and property. Waterfront. Incredible private beach. Worth millions."

"Holden Patterson?"

"He's interested in getting a new dog so I told him to visit your shelter. Thought you might show him . . . what's on offer."

She giggles at her attempt to make this sound salacious. Is she drunk? "Oh, and did I mention he's adorable?"

"No, but then I bet you failed to mention that I'm about to turn forty, still rent an apartment, have at least another ten years to pay off my college debt, and raise a sick kid with a terminal illness."

"I'm just looking out for my big sister. And it's not even a date. It's you offering professional advice to a guy who's thinking about getting a dog. Zero pressure. You hit it off, you two go out for a coffee. You don't, maybe one more shelter dog gets adopted."

For a sleepy, irrational second, I succumb to the logic of her suggestion, seduced by the dream of having someone in my life prepared to take *us* on, prepared to share *our* burden. Then again, what sane man would want my kind of baggage?

Gwen rambles in my ear, persevering with her pitch, and I try to remember what it's like to be courted, to be wooed—that shows how long it's been—going on a date, being on the nice end of a compliment, daring to flirt, standing in front of my wardrobe (let alone my underwear drawer) and deliberating over what to wear. But, as ever, reality slaps me awake—my role as lifelong caretaker, and the grief, the omnipresent anticipatory grief. Jasper knows how much I wish I was the one living with CF, not him, and I wonder if this eternal ache is my penance, the price I must pay for giving him my half of his crappy DNA. Then again, I wish it were just an ache, just pain, because, if I'm being honest, sometimes it's jealousy, jealousy of people leading normal lives, my imagination craving the day-to-day stress of a humdrum life without fighting this constant, losing battle.

I drift back enough to catch, "You deserve a life as well you know."

I hear a slurp, a swallow, and then, "I mean I just want my sister to have what I have."

Um. Three bratty kids. An absent husband.

"And what's that?" I ask.

"Security, of course."

I so want to say, "Financial, not emotional, right?," but opt for, "Security sounds great, but there's got to be more to a relationship."

"I'm sayin' it helps. Less for one person to worry about."

"You mean someone else to share my burden?"

"Don't be like that. People find each other all the time. God, you remember Sarah Gold from high school. You should see the stud she bagged and she turned into such a sea hag. At least you're still an attractive woman."

I laugh. "Thanks," I say, and mean it. "I haven't been on the receiving end of a compliment like that in forever."

"What? You're joking, right? By the time I turned twenty-one you always got more attention than me."

Gwen is petite and beautiful, but growing up, if we ever went out together, men backed off, intimidated, reading moody or aloof, convinced she'd be out of their league. I may not have had her looks, but back then I could flaunt an edginess, emit a magnetism that turned heads and drew men closer. These days I can barely remember the woman that used to be me.

"Holden Patterson. Okay. If he swings by, I promise I'll help him find a dog."

"That's all I ask, but I swear this one's a keeper. I'll text you his address and phone number, in case you feel like Googling him. Got to go, Todd's screaming for a glass of water."

She hangs up. What's wrong with me? Gwen will never be the sister who leaves a cooler full of prepared meals on our doorstep the day we get out of the hospital. She'll never show up uninvited to babysit Jasper so I can take a spontaneous night off. This setup, blind date, call it what you will, this is her way of showing how much she cares. Yet here I am, wound tight and getting tighter, thumb hovering over the redial button, ready to renege on the deal.

Forget a fear of dating. This problem runs deeper, broader, and is more of an aversion than a dread. I'm talking about an ingrained unwillingness to accept help or support in whatever form they take.

"Charity is a fancy word for debt," lectured my father during our formative years, insisting we "work harder, sort it out on our own, and sleep well knowing there's nothing to pay back, no need to get even." What kid wouldn't grow up believing indebtedness was a sign of weakness?

A minute later, the phone pings with the arrival of a text regarding Dr. Holden Patterson, MD. It's tempting to press delete but I hold back. I hate feeling like a disappointment, like I've let everyone down, because people like Gwen expect me to be in control and sometimes I want to be precisely how I feel—insecure and defeated and vulnerable and scared.

That's when a cough explodes from just outside my bedroom door, and I'm up, grabbing a bathrobe and slippers, slinking across hardwood to check on Jasper. Propped up high on pillows my son appears to be fast asleep. Ditto the dog curled like a giant comma on his blanket in the kitchen. How strange. Was one of them listening in on my conversation?

25

Jasper

DURING SCHOOL LUNCH break I came up with two new plans for how to solve the Whistler problem, now that he's back at the shelter.

Plan A is all about ways in which I get to keep Whistler for myself.

1. Continue to work on Mom by convincing her that Whistler is good for my "mental health" and my lung function (because of soccer).

2. Convince Mr. Crabtree not to tell on us keeping Whistler so that we don't have to change apartments.

3. Surf the Internet for really good fake service dog certificates.

4. Surf the Internet for other nearby apartments that we can afford to rent, that take pets, which means take Whistler.

Plan B is only if Plan A fails.

1. If I can't have Whistler, I have to at least keep him alive and that means getting him adopted by someone nice in less than fourteen days.

2. Ideally this nice person should live nearby and let me visit.

3. Better still, this nice person might want to marry my mom and invite me and Mom to live with him and Whistler in his huge mansion on the ocean with an outdoor shower and a Jacuzzi and a trail down to his very own private beach.

This last part of Plan B might sound strange and I didn't mean to listen in on Mom's conversation last night or check her phone this morning or go on Google, but I guess a man called Holden Patterson might be dropping by the shelter later this week in search of a new dog. If I can make sure he chooses Whistler, maybe Mom can do the rest.

When I arrive at the shelter after school, I dump my stuff and find Whistler with Burt in the room used for dog training. It's really big and empty and echoes like a basketball court, and they're joined by Tru, a shelty (day ten); Mojo, a pointer mix (day eleven); and Reggie, one of our shelter cats.

"Someone knew you were nearby," says Burt, letting go of a new purple collar around Whistler's neck as my scar-faced ugly mutt shows he's missed me as much as I've missed him. "Thought this little get-together might be useful."

This is why Burt is my best friend and the best dog person I know. He's always looking for new ways to get good dogs adopted, especially if they're close to being day-fourteen dogs.

"All three of them have been fine around Reggie," says Burt.

Reggie is a fat tabby who used to live on a horse farm. He's here as bait and he knows it. Reggie is not the least bit scared of dogs. Burt says he's like a retired Italian mobster. "You don't mess with him, he won't mess with you. But you cross him and he'll make sure you regret it."

This is a good result. Now Burt can tell people who have cats that Whistler and Tru and Mojo will fit right in.

I like cats. I like Reggie. But every time I see if I can connect with him, I get nothing—and I mean nothing; total blank, not a hint, twitch, or buzz. I can't tell whether I need to practice more or if cats jam the signal on purpose because I'm pretty sure Reggie knows what I'm up to. Maybe cats prefer not to be understood. Maybe that's how they stay cool and mysterious.

Mojo is missing a back leg because Mom hacked it off. He had a tumor (English version "chew-more") in his knee, but he's doing great now; and it wasn't such a bad cancer, so he should live for years and years, but Mom says some people get weird about adopting a tripod even though, according to her, "Dogs are born with three legs and a spare."

Burt thinks the main reason why no one's adopted Mojo is because he's totally hyper. When Mojo first arrived at the shelter—before Whistler, so before I started to figure out my new talent for dog communication—I was standing near him and all of a sudden my heart started pounding. I never told Burt because I'd just come from soccer practice and the Kerry twins had forced me to chug a can of Red Bull, but, looking back, I think Mojo wanted me to know he needs to be adopted by someone who hates sitting still and loves to pass out from exhaustion at the end of every day.

Right now Mojo tosses a tennis ball into the air, sometimes catching it, sometimes dropping it, and I tell Whistler to "go play," but he ignores me and begins closing in on Tru. The shelty is off in a corner, trembling, head down, and instead of bouncing over, Whistler's careful, taking one step at a time, nice and slow, not wanting to scare her, closing in until, eventually, their sides gently touch.

"Tru's a nervous wreck," says Burt.

I nod. Tru's like Reggie; she won't let me in. A few days ago there was this English bull terrier in the run next to Tru—like Bullseye, the mascot for Target. Anyway, seeing this terrier made me remember "The Incident," as Mom calls it, when Auntie Gwen kind of left me behind in the toy section at Target. Maybe it was a coincidence. Or maybe Tru made it pop inside my head, wanting me to understand how she feels.

"What if she has no confidence? What if she thinks her mom and dad will be back to pick her up any minute?"

Burt does this cartoonish scrunchy face. "Mom died, Dad had to go into a care facility, and the daughter never liked the dog in the first place. I'm afraid Tru needs to come out of her shell and fast."

Neither of us speak, watching Whistler, certain that all he wants to do is make a sad dog feel better.

"Looks like she'd do well in a multidog household," says Burt. "Somewhere she might make a new friend."

I keep quiet, mainly because I'm sad, sad because Whistler is the best, kindest dog ever, and he needs to be with me.

"How's his cough?" I ask.

"A bit better," says Burt, watching me, like he's trying to decide, before adding, "Your mom change her mind?"

Wow. How did Burt know what I was really thinking about? I shake my head. "Even if she did," I say, "Mr. Crabtree, the guy who runs our apartment complex, hates dogs."

"Hate's a strong word."

"Maybe, but he doesn't seem to like them much. Then again, he doesn't seem to like anyone or anything."

"Did Whistler do something to upset him?"

"Only if you count taking a massive dump in his rosebushes."

Burt adjusts the baseball cap on his head, taking it off, sweeping back his nine strands of hair, and putting it back on again.

"What's he like, this Mr. Crabtree?"

I shrug. "Obsessed with his yard is all I know. Always mowing and pruning and spraying and planting stuff."

"Is he? Well, if you want to change his mind about Whistler, you might want to find out what he doesn't like about dogs."

"He won't tell me."

"How do you know unless you ask?" Burt lets loose a smile, the big one, used most often when he remembers where he put something.

Martha's blue troll hair pokes around the door. "Hey. I've got dogs that won't walk themselves you know."

"Coming," I say. "You seen Mom . . . Dr. Blunt around?"

Her face pinches like she just got a flu shot in her arm. "She's busy showing a potential donor around. Just walk the dogs you've been assigned. Please."

And without saying another word she's gone.

"You'd best get on," says Burt.

"Ah, we're fine," I say. "Martha's all mouth and no trousers."

New seismic wrinkles crack across his face.

"It's not rude. It's British. Like she's all talk, her bark is worse than her bite. Sorry. I can't practice my British slang around Mom."

Burt takes his time, comes back with "Why?" and I'm not sure whether he's referring to Martha or life at home or becoming an Anglophile. I go with Anglophile.

"Because I'm half English. The male half."

"Your father?"

"Yeah, but Mom and my Auntie Gwen don't call him that. Sperm donor might be the nicest thing they call him. I've never met him."

Burt grunts, cracks his knuckles real slow. Definitely thinking.

"But you want to?"

I shake my head.

"It's more complicated than that. I'm just trying to keep my options open . . . in case I need to swear my allegiance to the Queen. Mom says it's good to have a backup plan, so this is mine, if English doctors have to look after me, when I'm older."

Burt nods but his eyes can't fool me. I've totally lost him.

"Hey, choose a stuffed toy for Whistler on the way out," he says, obviously trying to get back into his comfort zone. "He'll like having something from you while he's staying here."

There's a big cardboard box next to the door full of donated toys, safe toys like kongs and thick, braided tug-of-war ropes. They are supposed to give the dogs a distraction, something to do while they sit and wait and hope. I dig and rummage around but wish I had brought Henry, my stuffed dog from home, because Henry would smell of me the most. I settle on a green frog, like the one from Mom's behavioral test, because Whistler seemed to like it so much.

"This one," I say. "Where's Whistler going to live?"

"I'll put him in the run next to Tru."

I look over at my strange four-legged friend as he's giving the shelty a trademark slow lick to her left ear.

"Burt, why don't you take Whistler? That way I'd still get to see him."

Burt snorts a piggy laugh.

"If I added a sixth dog, my wife would go from just hating me to killing me."

This sounds like a good reason to never get married, but I just smile and say, "Catch you later, Burt."

Crossing the lobby, ready to change into my volunteer shirt, the front desk phone rings. Normally I'm not allowed to answer calls—according to Martha I sound like a baby with a bad smoking habit—but after about ten rings even I can hear her screaming, "Can someone please pick that up?"

Everyone must be outside doing afternoon walks because I go slow enough that any grown-up who's free could beat me to it, but no one does.

"Hello."

There's a pause.

"Sorry, maybe I dialed the wrong number," says a man with a bendy American accent like a cowboy. "I'm tryin' to reach the animal shelter."

"This is the shelter."

Another pause. Maybe he prefers shouting across a prairie to using a phone.

"My name's Clayton Silver and I'm calling from Texas. I believe you might have found a dog of ours, went missing several years back."

My mouth stops working like I can't remember how to talk. Geography is one of my favorite subjects and Texas is scary close to Oklahoma.

"You still there?"

I croak something close to a "yes."

"See, we got a call from a dog rescue group, Panhandle somethin' or other. Woman said your shelter found a dog kind of fitting the right description."

This can't be. What kind of dog owner finally decides to hunt for a dog that went missing years ago? Not a good one.

"What does this dog look like?" I ask, not caring if I sound suspicious.

"Well, it's a he, big, black, and a total mutt."

Real dog owners never say "it."

"We have lots of those," I say.

"He went missing in a twister. A bad one. Sounded like this particular dog got cut up pretty bad. Lucky to be alive."

I think of Whistler's scars, his droopy eye, his gnarly ear and his missing toes. Could these have been caused by a tornado? Why did I pick up the phone?

"Perhaps I could speak to Doctor . . ."

I hear paper rustling.

"Dr. Blunt. Is he available?"

"I'm afraid *she's* busy," I blurt out, thinking I need to hang up before he either says something I don't want to hear or, worst of all, he forces me to lie.

"Then can you take down this number?"

"Hold on."

I grab a pen and paper and tell him to go ahead.

"Have her call me, yeah?"

Instead of saying "yes," I mumble, "Uh-huh," and hang up before he can add "soon."

I take the piece of paper, fold it in half, and go hide it in the front pouch of my school backpack. Hopefully I'll remember to give it to Mom when we get home.

Hopefully.

26

Kate

I TURN OFF my royal wave and let the fake smile slide from my face the moment their fancy Audi spins out of the driveway.

"Those prospects gonna cough up?"

Ah, Martha, my prickly guardian of the downtrodden and the abandoned. And she wonders why I don't let her give potential donors a tour of our facility.

"Doubt it," I say. "They promised to swing by with a check at next week's fundraiser, but I'm not holding my breath."

Martha clacks her barbell tongue piercing back and forth against her xylophone-like incisors, making a hollow, tinkling sound of disapproval.

"Hmm, the KGB won't be happy. Sounded as if she was counting on them."

Martha's right, but what can I do.

"I'm starting to think we should cut back on paid staff," I say, but before I can reassure her that she's not about to be fired, a glossy red convertible pulls into the driveway, sweeps past, and for a second I think, *Oh, no. Holden Patterson. The guy Gwen wants me to meet.* But then a man in his early twenties, sporting a slick tailored suit, pops out and, right away, I know it's not him (in case I forgot, Gwen texted me a photo this morning). The thing is, instead of relief, I register a shocking and unfamiliar twinge of disappointment. Somewhere, buried deep, I guess I'm more interested than I thought.

"Leave this to me," says Martha, heading him off before he can reach the front door.

I watch from a distance as she ignores his handshake. I hope to God he's a rep, or a salesman, and not a potential donor because she plants her feet, folds her arms across her chest, and shuts him down with a stare caught between contempt and disgust. He reaches into his briefcase for a pamphlet or a brochure, but she's having none of it. I think of Jasper, the way he's always opening our front door to sketchy ex-cons pitching asphalt driveways or solar panels, and practically inviting them to dinner. Where did Martha learn the art of hair-trigger hostility? She's my right-hand woman yet I know so little about her. Is that because she never shares or I never ask? I know she cares deeply about the mission of the shelter, and she can scare the crap out of the high school volunteers. But, by relying on the usual excuses, I've never reached out. I may bitch about some of the soccer moms, but in this regard, aren't I no better than them?

Martha takes his business card and waits until he's back in his car before heading my way.

"Real estate developer. No interest in the shelter. Just the land. You think KGB's thinking of selling and forgot to let us know?"

"I hope not. I thought maybe you knew him."

"I know the type."

This is probably my cue to find out more, but I do the next best thing.

"Thanks for getting rid of him. We live to fight another day. I was about to say we should try recruiting more volunteers. I refuse to reduce the number of dogs we put up for adoption."

"Which," says Martha, "brings us to this new dog of yours."

She's been standing next to me, but only now do I stare into those creepy purple contacts. "We're calling him Whistler," I say, "and I know you have reservations about him based on his age, appearance, attitude, and health, but I swear he'll make a great pet for the right person."

Instead of a sassy rebuttal, I'm treated to a weighty pause and "are you done?" eyebrows.

"First, his ex-owner dropped by while you were at lunch with Mr. and Mrs. Moneybags. And before you go off on me, of course I tried to get him to take the dog back."

"What? Who?"

I curse the timing, instantly (if irrationally) convinced that my diplomatic skills might have ensured Whistler found a home.

"A kid. Young-looking, but old enough to drive. Address in Eastham. Said he was going to surrender him anyway. Claims the dog never listened, constantly ran away. Lots of talk about a new job with plenty of travel. Couldn't sign the paperwork fast enough."

For the briefest of moments I think about this wasted opportunity, how Martha blew our best chance to discover information about Whistler's past, valuable information that may impact his future. But then she adds, "Believe me, the dog's better off without him," and, treated to her scariest scornful face, I'm reminded that we're still on the same side. Martha may take her love for animals over people—especially children—to extremes, but on this occasion she's absolutely right. The coldness of Whistler's abandonment hits home, the ability to trade a signature for the convenience of simply walking away, and I realize this stranger never had anything to contribute. The dog deserves the last word. Not him.

"Second of all," says Martha, "now that he's *our* problem, how do we handle the scars on his muzzle? People deserve to know that he's had a history of abuse. Not to mention the lung issues. That cough."

My mind flashes on Whistler's chest X-rays, their striking similarity to Jasper's lungs, and I will my face to convey just how risky this conversation has become.

"Every dog deserves a chance," she says, "I totally get it, and I hope you know I do get it, but there are worthwhile causes and there are lost causes. With KGB breathing down our necks and hands tied by time and money then surely we've got to play the odds and stop betting on losers."

Martha's got a point, trying to be practical, and fair, but she's oversimplified our situation, seeing the world as clear-cut, black and white, with no in-betweens. She's overlooked the most vexing variable in this particular equation—my son.

"Like I said, this dog will make a great pet. I don't care how many cons you've got on that list, Whistler gets the same chance as all the others."

Only now do I register how tightly I've been clenching my jaw muscles.

Martha avoids eye contact, slow nods, and makes to walk away. But when I think she's finally taken the hint, she spins around and asks, "Why don't you just take him?"

Maybe it's me, but the question feels like more of a dare than a helpful suggestion. And my lack of a response appears to be the answer she expects, the proof that she is right, that poor Whistler is a predictable lost cause, destined for a date with a lethal injection.

27

Jasper

THE PLAN SOUNDED simple when Burt went over it, but that was with Whistler by my side and things feel different when he's around. Now I'm alone, finger about to press Mr. Crabtree's doorbell, holding on to a dozen flyers for our next shelter fundraiser—my excuse for dropping by.

Of course I'm not completely alone. Mom is the silhouette standing in the window, across the street, watching my every move. She thinks I'm wasting my time with the flyers. She doesn't know why I'm really here.

"What?" growls Mr. Crabtree, popping up from behind a hedge like a Jack-in-the-Box. I notice he's gripping a pair of scissors in his fat sausage fingers.

"Hi, Mr. Crabtree, sorry to bug you, but I wondered if I might be able to—"

"You got rid of that dog, right?"

That wasn't supposed to be the next line.

"No? Then you must be here to show me some official service dog paperwork?"

Remember I said that Mr. Crabtree reminds me of a bulldog. Well, I like bulldogs. I like the way they puff up with confidence, that "ugly" is your problem not theirs. But sometimes, when you meet them and they get all snorty and strut about, it's hard to tell the difference between upset and pleased to see you.

"I wanted to . . . I hope it's okay to . . . to put up a few flyers around the neighborhood."

I hand one over; it features a picture of a smiling goofy dog covered in soapy bubbles—it's a dog wash fundraiser. For a second, I think he's going to scrunch it into a ball, but then he says, "Sure."

And without waiting for a reply, he wobbles off, headed for a row of stick trees where his neat green lawn meets untidy woodland.

"So you don't hate dogs?" I shout.

That stops him in his tracks. Turning around takes a little longer.

"Why'd you say that?" His cheeks seem to droop lower than normal, making him look sadder, if that's possible.

I think about saying, "Because you're the one who wants to rat on Whistler," but keep quiet, even as he closes in, his stinky breath about to make me gag.

"I've had dogs my whole life." Mr. Crabtree says this as though it proves he's a dog person, but then I remember the way Whistler came to the door to greet him when Mom was in the bath. Did canine instincts pick up on someone we can trust?

"Why not now?" I ask.

He taps the handles of his scissors in his crusty palms. They are filthy, covered in soil. "How old do you think I am?"

I let my shoulders shrug my answer.

"Seventy-six. Said goodbye to my last dog three years back when I had to take this job."

"Don't you like dogs anymore?"

"Like? I love them too much."

Now I'm really confused.

"Son, at my age, a new dog would outlive me. Wouldn't be fair on the animal."

This makes no sense. Loving a dog is not like picking up a remote and turning a TV on or off. You're either into dogs or you're not. The most useful thing Martha ever told me was, "Dogs are like herpes. Once you get them, you're infected for life."

"But a dog can stop you feeling lonely," I say.

He makes a noise caught somewhere between a burp and a grunt. "I've got a wife for company."

Hum. "What about making you laugh?"

A great big frown line zips across his forehead like he's thinking about his wife again and this time she's not the answer to my question.

"A dog can make you safe. Scare away burglars."

"Son, I'll go with a nine-millimeter bullet over sharp teeth any day."

I let out a sigh, but a mucus plug somewhere deep in my lungs trips it up and I break into a cough.

"You okay? Need a glass of water?"

I raise a "just a moment" finger. Being around Whistler has made me realize there are so many good reasons why people need dogs.

"Yeah . . . well . . . what about exercise? Having a dog makes you go for walks, get out and about, meet people, and make new friends."

Head shaking sets his cheeks to vibrate. "Have you seen my yard? I get all the exercise I need and then some. Look, living here, not being able to have a dog, keeps me on track. It also makes sure . . ."

Mr. Crabtree's lower lip does this pouty thing like he doesn't know whether to go on or not.

"Makes sure of what, Mr. Crabtree?"

His droopy eyes take forever to decide but then he finally says, "Makes sure I don't get my heart broken. Again."

Wow, this is a big share, but it makes total sense. Mom is always trying to keep me from the day-fourteen dogs. If I lose Whistler, I can tell something inside me will break.

"But Mr. Crabtree, isn't getting a dog worth the risk?"

I consider saying something about "falling in love" but Burt said this chat should be "man-to-man" so I wait, and for a second I think he's going to smile but maybe there's too much weight in those bulldog cheeks for his mouth muscles to overpower.

"Hey, make yourself useful," he says, pulling a spool of fishing line from his pocket and handing me one end of the clear nylon. "Run this down to that tree over there."

I do as I'm told, hoping my slog constitutes a run in Mr. Crabtree's book.

"That's right," he shouts, "keep it shoulder height, loop it around the trunk and carry on to the next."

"What's it for?" I ask.

"Trying to stop the deer from ruining my clematis."

"Fishing line?"

"They don't see it. Spooks them. They run away. At least that's the plan. Friend from the garden club's idea. I've tried motion-activated sprinklers and floodlights. Coyote urine worked for a while."

I know my hearing is off so maybe I heard wrong. "Did you just say coyote urine?"

"Yep. But it's hard to come by."

Naturally I think about Whistler, about all those different breeds in his mix, and suddenly I get this brilliant idea. There *has* to be a coyote in there somewhere.

"Hey, Mr. Crabtree, what if I told you I have the perfect solution, totally free, and guaranteed to keep deer out of your yard forever?"

28

Kate

JASPER SITS AT the kitchen counter, paralyzed by the homework assignment, blank sheets of lined paper still bracing for the first scratch and smudge of his crude penmanship.

I blame his teacher, Ms. Sexton. What was she thinking?

"There must be somewhere you've always wanted to go, other than Orlando, Florida?"

Jasper sighs, slumps, lets an elbow slide across the granite before setting his chin on his forearm.

"What about famous people you'd like to meet?" I ask.

"What sort of people?" His words come out garbled because he refuses to employ his lower jaw.

"Sit up, Jasper. Why not a famous soccer player or a pop star?"

He frowns at the phrase "pop star" as though I might have said gramophone instead of iPod.

"Or the president, or an astronaut, or an actor? Or maybe it's doing something crazy, like, oh I don't know, climbing Everest?"

"You really think a kid with CF can climb Everest?"

"Sure," I say, without giving him the satisfaction of the slightest hint of hesitation. "Why not? Same goes for diving the Great Barrier Reef or running the Boston Marathon. It's a bucket list she's after, right, so dream big."

On the outside I'm the Mom with gentle back pats of encouragement, smiling as I slide over a glass of cold milk and a plate stacked with Oreos. On the inside I'm upset by the insensitivity of his teacher.

Back in first grade we had the humiliation of the family tree. Sure, I get it, discover and discuss where we all come from, our diversity, our roots, but what about the single parent kids, the adopted, the divorced. Poor Jasper's tree was so lopsided it would have toppled over. He looked like the product of an immaculate conception. Now it's the things to do before you die. I'd love to take her aside and share my version of Jasper's bucket list—living long enough to graduate high school, to drive a car, to legally get a drink in a bar, to kiss a girl, let alone get married. And what kind of a girl would be brave enough to marry him? What woman in her right mind would want to share the responsibility of his care?

"Mom. You're not listening."

"I'm sorry, what did you say?"

"I said I think my list should be a teacup and not a bucket."

"What are you talking about?"

He nibbles on a cookie, sparkly blue eyes unfocused, drifting across the counter. "It's harder for kids with CF to make a list long enough to fill a bucket because CF kids don't live long enough. Maybe a teacup list makes more sense."

I stare back at him, ignoring the ice-cold steel sliding through my heart, determined not to succumb, trying to gauge his motivation. He's been acting out of sorts ever since he came back from visiting the crabby Mr. Crabtree.

"Is this about Whistler again?"

He takes a swallow of milk, swipes away the white mustache with the back of his hand, and leans forward, suddenly animated. "How about buying a fake service dog certificate online?"

That goddamn dog again. I knew it.

"That's a horrible thing to suggest. Service dogs are intended for people who desperately need their help to live some kind of a life. Fake certificates are for selfish people who think the rules don't apply, that their dog is so precious that he or she deserves the seat next to them on a plane, or to lie under their table at a favorite restaurant. Service dogs are not *special* pets and trust me, anyone can spot the difference."

I've made him squirm. Good.

"Is it expensive to train a service dog?"

Unbelievable. He puts the question out there, faking general interest, and all the while we both know who he's hoping to sign up for lessons.

"Okay, let's put this to bed. Service dog training facilities are few and far between. I've been told it costs about twenty-five thousand dollars to graduate a dog, and only a select few make the cut. More importantly, to answer your real question, they don't train any old pet. They use puppies or carefully selected and receptive shelter dogs."

"But Whistler is very recep—"

He jumps as my palms slap the counter.

"No. Stop. I . . . we . . . can't handle a dog. You're all banged up after soccer, your cough is out of control, dogs are not allowed . . . shall I keep going?"

Keeping his eyes cast down, he mumbles, "We could move?"

I stifle a scream, snatching up paper and pen, sliding in next to him.

"Here, this is how much I make a month."

Numbers fly across the paper.

"This is roughly what I pay for food, gas, utilities, and your medications."

This last number catches him by surprise.

"After paying my monthly college debt, this is what we have left for living and rent. Do the math, and you tell me if we can afford to move."

I notice how his nostrils flare with every breath even though he just did his treatment. He's having a harder time breathing than he's letting on.

Without a word Jasper reaches for his open laptop, scrolls through online history, and up pops a listing for an apartment.

"This place costs the same, and it takes dogs." He pivots the screen my way, clicking and pecking at keys, showing me badly framed photos of a dark, dingy, outdated two-bedroom condo, and all I see are plush, mite-laden carpets, mold-spewing ventilation, and the look on his face, big, hopeful eyes praying for a reversal of fortune. How can I tell him no, crush his dream? And then I spot it, in the details, the devil come to save me.

"Let's say we do it. And let's say I'm okay with an extra ten-mile commute to work each way. How would you feel about having to change your school, mid-term? More importantly, how about having to quit your soccer team?"

And like that, I snuff out the flicker of possibility dancing in his eyes and slowly he reaches forward and closes the laptop shut.

I must not cave. I mean, look at me. Just talking about getting a dog puts me on edge because I have no reserve, no wiggle room. Financially and emotionally we just about get by, but I'm the juggler with four balls in the air. No way can I handle a fifth. And besides, Whistler is less of a ball and more of a chain saw. But then I look at my boy—sick and getting sicker. Why does the logic of doing the right thing for his health and for my sanity feel so wrong?

"We'll never have a dog, will we?"

I hug him to me, but he's limp, unresponsive, heightening my awareness that this is my problem, that I'm the one in need of reassurance and forgiveness.

"You think I'm that mean? Look, over the next few weeks I'll start checking out other places to live that take pets, only maybe we should think about something smaller than Whistler."

Jasper stretches out his chin to look up. I don't think he believes me. I'm not sure I believe myself.

He untangles himself, settles over a fresh piece of paper, and scratches out his first sentence, "1. Have a dog of my own."

Pen hovering over wish number two he asks, "Can I work in the showroom for the rest of this week?"

He looks as if someone stamped dark inky circles around his eyes. It's the coughing, keeping him awake at night.

"I'm not sure Martha will be too happy about—"

"Please. It's important. If I can't have him, I have to make sure Whistler goes to the right home."

I hear a plea borne of panic, and for a split second the outrage of all that is wrong in this so-called life washes over me, that a kid who suffers so much cannot simply have the mutt of his dreams. It's not too much to ask; yet it could be everything.

"Of course," I say. "I'll speak to her first thing. We'll make sure Whistler is all set."

29

Jasper

MARTHA TOTALLY HATES my guts.

"Stop bugging people," she hisses in my ear, making her black zombie lips smile at a young couple who stood in front of Mojo, the three-legged pointer mix.

She's not interested in my reply, pacing the showroom like the principal when we have tests at school, constantly popping up from nowhere, hoping to catch someone cheating.

Martha wouldn't understand my plan so I'm not sharing. I've been at it all week after school, ever since Mom (and Mr. Crabtree) made it clear I can't have Whistler. The clock is ticking. He's already got less than sixteen thousand minutes left—yeah, I'm counting. What do I care if people think I'm acting like a creepy salesman? It's better than the alternative. Besides, there's a big difference between bugging and trying to make sure Whistler ends up with Mr. Right and not Mr. Wrong.

Between the hours of two and six all sorts of people crowd around the runs in search of a dog and I'm supposed to answer questions only if I'm asked. Trouble is no one trusts the skinny kid with the bad cough who looks like he stole an oversized volunteer T-shirt. Fortunately, Burt's advice, which he learned from working at the Honda dealership, has been very helpful.

"Do you like soccer?" I say to this big guy wearing a Patriots shirt as he passes Whistler's run. The man glares at me as though I might have asked if he likes baking or painting his nails.

I go back to the tall, thin woman and the tall, thin man standing in front of Mojo. They look like they might do lots of exercise. I try to will Mojo to be cool and stop spinning in circles. It doesn't work. I get dizzy just watching him.

"Excuse me," I say, to the stick man, making sure Martha's not watching, "if you had the choice between a granola bar or a Snickers bar, which would you pick?"

He smiles the smile of someone who feels sorry for me. Trust me, I've seen it before.

"No, then how about which bumper sticker fits you best—'26.2' or 'Keep calm and watch TV.'"

The stick woman pulls the man away, looking like she's going to report me.

"Mom, Mom, can we get that one?"

It's a little girl sucking on a green Popsicle—food isn't allowed in the showroom but if it shuts her up I'll let it fly. She's jumping up and down like she needs to go potty in front of Tru, the shelty, hiding in the shadows at the back of her run.

"Oh, that's so pathetic," says the big woman answering to "Mom." "Poor thing looks scared to death. Look, Kaitlin, she wants you to have her frog."

Martha rounds the corner, just as I'm about to open my mouth because it's Whistler's frog, and it's not for your daughter, it's for Tru because the best dog in the world wants to make a sad dog feel better.

"Do you have questions about any of the dogs on display?"

Maybe Martha can't help it, but her best smile is about as warm as the Joker from Batman.

"Yeah," says Kaitlin, "why is that dog so ugly?"

For a second I think Martha might say something nasty about Whistler, but instead she snaps back with, "Those are scars. It's not his fault. Poor dog's obviously been through a lot," and "You know you're not supposed to eat in here, right?"

Sweet. Kaitlin's mom gets all in Martha's face like she might deck her, but then she grabs her daughter by the hand and snatches her away, Kaitlin staring back over her shoulder, more upset at dropping her half-eaten Popsicle than not leaving with a pet.

"Could you get that?" asks Martha, continuing her patrol.

"Sure," I say, loving how she stuck up for Whistler.

I grab paper towels and begin to wipe up the mess, just as I hear the word *Patterson* loud and clear over the background chatter and barks. Standing by the entrance there's a man in a black leather jacket introducing himself to Martha and all of a sudden she switches up from confused to acting super friendly and pretending to be nice. Then I think, *Oh my God, it's him, it*

*must be Holden Patterson, Dr. Holden Patterson, here to look for a
dog and a date with my mom.*

Trying not to stare is tricky, but eventually Martha does this
big dramatic swoosh gesture toward the runs, like a magician's
assistant, and Dr. Patterson is alone, strolling my way, stopping
at each dog, taking his time, like he's studying paintings in a
museum. I pounce the moment he gets to Whistler.

"Hi," I say, slipping in next to him.

"Hi," says Dr. Patterson. We look at each other and then we
look at Whistler. Whistler's tongue is sticking out, like it does,
because of his lack of front teeth to hold it in.

"Know anything about this dog?" Dr. Patterson's voice is
deep, but smooth. Every hair on his head is a different shade of
gray. Even his eyes are a pale gray. "Sure," I say. "As you can see
he's unusual, with bits and pieces of lots of different breeds and
even though he's been through some tough times, he's not mean
or aggressive."

The man studies me before squatting down, beckoning Whistler to come closer. "What's he like with other dogs?"

I sneak a mini, unseen "come" with my fingers and Whistler
trots over, but he stands in front of me and not the Doc.

"He's great. Very sociable. Loves to play games, especially if
you like soccer."

"I love soccer. Play in a league with a bunch of guys from
work every Sunday."

I keep my *brilliant* to myself.

"Those scars are big. And his ear's a mess. You sure he's not
been a fighting dog?"

"Definitely," I say, looking around, making it look like I'm sharing a big secret. "Between you and me, I think he's the best dog here. Knows all his commands. And totally loyal."

This is what Burt calls "closing the deal."

Suddenly Whistler coughs and not just a tickle or a polite ahem, it's a boomer, loud enough to bring a moment of silence to the entire room.

"Wow," says Dr. Patterson. "That sounds bad."

I want to say, "Then listen to this," but I should keep my CF on the down low, at least until he and Mom have been on a first date.

"He's on antibiotics for a little chest infection. But he's getting much better."

On cue Whistler lets loose a cough even bigger than the first, impersonating a jackhammer, getting his whole body behind it, making me open the run and step inside, running my hand over his chest, asking Whistler if he's okay and that's when it hits me, a buzz inside my belly, making me jump, like he's giving me a shock or some sort of a warning.

"He's a funny-looking fella," says the Doc, coming around to stand beside me, reaching out to touch the big scar, causing Whistler to startle, step away, and put me between this stranger and his stripy snout. "And he's old, right?"

"He's mature," I say, "but Dr. Blunt says 'eleven is the new seven' for dogs."

See the way I did that, getting Mom in the conversation, baiting the trap. But I get nothing, just fingers working gray stubble and the nose wrinkle of a man trying to make a tough decision.

"You know I thought about that three-legged dog, the pointer thing. But he's exhausting just to look at. Whereas this dog . . . what's his name again?"

"Whistler."

"Yeah, Whistler. He's cool. He's unique."

Another buzz flares inside me and it doesn't feel good.

"No, this Whistler has got something that makes you stop and stare. Makes you feel sorry. It's like he's asking for pity. And he's old. That cough is bad. Poor guy can't have much left in the tank. Much safer than getting stuck with a puppy."

Doc Patterson seems to be talking to himself and I want to interrupt because that bit about pity is not true, but he keeps going.

"Get a shelter dog and women know you care. Get an abused shelter dog and . . . well . . . now they know you're someone special."

He turns to me and says, "I think you are absolutely right. Whistler is perfect."

My lower jaw is stuck in dentist open-wide mode. What just happened?

"There you are," says Martha, standing at the bars, "I just called Uncle Pete, let him know I'd help you find him a great dog."

"I'm confused."

That was meant to stay inside me but it slipped out.

"We're cousins," says Doc Patterson, but he says this in a kind of whisper, a "please don't tell anyone" kind of way. "Second cousins. Haven't seen each other for years, but still, Martha calls my dad her uncle Pete."

I may not be good at math, but I can do family trees. That makes Dr. Patterson Uncle Peter's son.

"You thinking about this dog?" asks Martha.

Wait a minute. Peter's son. *Peter's son.* Not Patterson. Peter's son. Stew-pid Jasper, stew-pid.

"Yeah, I think he'd be perfect. And let's face it, I'll be the one taking it for walks."

Did they cover me with a cloak of invisibility? It's like I don't exist. And that's when I see it, the "pop" in Martha's eyes, like a slot machine coming up lucky sevens. She's always acted as if Whistler was a lost cause, a waste of money and a waste of space. Suddenly, from nowhere, her creepy second cousin shows up and here's her chance to unload our unadoptable dog.

"Then maybe you and I should do some paperwork and make my uncle Pete a happy camper."

This man is *not* the Dr. Patterson from Auntie Gwen's text. This man is *not* Dr. Patterson, future husband of my mom and future stepfather to me. This man is Peter's son. A total plonker. He's only interested in borrowing a dog to help him get noticed by women. What happens after that? Ignored, bored, left alone, and desperate to pee? Patterson and Peter's son don't even sound that alike. My hearing is in serious trouble. But more importantly, thanks to me, so is Whistler.

30

Kate

As I PLACE the last suture, there's an insistent rap on the large glass window, making me glance up and over the rim of my surgical mask, past the neat spay incision, beyond the drapes and monitors, everything routine and orderly until the moment I see his face. Neck extended, mouth open, wide-eyed, Jasper hungers for air as his heaving body slumps against the operating room door.

Tearing at my paper gown, bouffant cap, and mask, leaving them where they fall, I come around the OR table, dropping to my knees beside him.

"What the hell happened?"

He places one flat palm on his chest, holding me back with the other.

"I couldn't . . . find you . . . need your . . . help with . . . Whistler."

His words syncopate breaths. Not good. Worse still, his lips are more mulberry than their usual lilac.

"Take a seat. When was your last puffer?"

I reach for a nearby chair, scraping it our way, but he's shaking his head and jerking me up and onto my feet.

"No time . . . come on."

Jasper drags me down the corridor that leads to our lobby. It's packed, hopping, like a mall on Black Friday, people milling around, taking happy dogs for walks, the prospect of finally posting bail written in lolling pink tongues and pricked ears.

"Hold on. You need to tell me what's happened."

He drops my hand, squeezes into a gap in the crowd, and stands on tiptoe, scanning for something or someone. By the time he pushes his way back, the expression on his face has amped up from concern to full-blown panic.

"It's my fault. I thought he was nice. But Whistler knew. He tried to warn me. And now it's too late."

"What's too late?"

"Man in a leather jacket. Adopting Whistler. He's bad."

"Bad? Bad how?"

I take in my son and wonder how much of the fear dancing in his eyes is due to difficulty breathing or to the possibility of failing that inescapable mutt. Just when I thought we were done, their flaky telepathy gimmick is back with a bang. What is the cold-hearted cynic in me supposed to do? Go along with another bout of ridiculous dog-speak, pretend it's just a phase, as innocent as a child who plays with an invisible friend, as ridiculous as a great-aunt burdened with premonitions? Or do I accept what is undeniable?

"He just is," snaps Jasper, as though we don't have time for this.

Slowly I drop my chin and my eyes roll up, letting him know that if I'm going to help he needs to make time.

"He doesn't want Whistler like I want Whistler. He wants to use him to get attention. Especially from women. Mom I swear I'm not making it up."

No matter how he reached this assumption, scrawled across every inch of Jasper's troubled face is an absolute conviction that something must be done, a wrong in need of righting, and that I, his mother, am the only person who can make this happen.

"Go to my office and if it's been more than two hours since your last puffer, take another hit."

"But Mo—"

"Go. I'll deal with this."

And I watch and wait as the fight goes out of him before searching for "bad guy in leather jacket."

Fortunately Martha's blowtorch blue hair illuminates the way and there he is.

"Hey," she cries, waving me over. They're seated at a desk doing paperwork and she's beaming. Jasper was right. Something must be seriously wrong.

"Kate, this is Ron, he's a relative of mine . . ."

"Distant," interjects Ron, as though this clarification is vital, getting to his feet, offering me a hairy knuckled hand. I take in the premature gray of his hair and beard, but most of all the way his shark eyes scan me up and down, like my body is a bar code and it takes forever before he hears a beep and lets go. Definitely earns a check in the "creepy" box.

"He's after a new dog for his dad and wants to adopt Whistler," says Martha. "Isn't that great?"

I'd like to think Martha means well, but she can barely contain her excitement at the prospect of dispatching our lost cause. Meanwhile Ron seems to have noticed the indentation on my forehead from my surgical bouffant cap. I think I'll tell him it's a frontal lobotomy scar.

"Right," I say, shooting for casual and upbeat, "and it looks like you're nearly done with the paperwork. How was Whistler on your walk?"

Martha mimes a karate chop to her own throat, Ron not catching her "what the hell's wrong with you" glare.

"It's fine," says Ron, "no need to go for a walk. Some kid raved about him. Said he was the best dog up for adoption. Said he's well trained and likes to socialize, so he's got pretty much everything I'm looking for."

My eyes dart from smug Ron to vindicated Martha. I can't say for sure whether Jasper's hunch is right or if my son is being a brat, unable to lose this dog to someone he deems unworthy. Profiling a stranger in sixty seconds is wrong, horribly judgmental, but not even bothering to take your new dog for a walk feels rash, bordering on dishonest. Maybe Whistler *should* be included in this decision.

"And you're fine with his cough, giving him antibiotics."

Ron's nod is halfhearted at best, like how hard can it be, sickness is something you can always cure with a pill. Shutting this down might be harder than I thought. Maybe I should play for time.

"That's great," I say, leaning in close enough to smell leather, "but if you're going to buy a truck, surely you're gonna want to take it for a test drive."

I smile the smile of a woman trying to flirt, hoping I haven't misread a weakness for female attention. Unfortunately I'm out of practice, my lips more twitchy and nervous than come-hither, and Ron seems puzzled. Maybe I should have suggested he test drive a convertible rather than a truck, but then he says, "Okay then. Want to join us?"

Martha appears to have heard enough, muscling in like this deal is going south and she's about to lose her commission.

"I'm not so sure that's a good idea," she says, wrinkling her nose, acting coy. "A pair of cockers got dropped off while you were doing spays. They're going to need an evaluation."

Is this Martha's way of saying, "I know, cousin Ron's a dick, but with the arrival of yet two more dogs, he's still a whole lot better than the day-fourteen alternative"?

"Not to worry," I say, raising my chin, like I get the message, appreciate the heads-up, but I'm all over this. "Ron, you from around here? Yeah. You know Jackknife, down the road?"

Jackknife beach is a narrow strip of muddy brown sand on the bay, running alongside the golf course, unpopular enough with the tourists to be open to dogs year round. To be fair, during the summer, it offers scenic views of the moored boats and small islands that guard the cut into the ocean and at low tide there's a lovely walk for a mile or so up to the yacht club.

I barely wait for his fog of confusion to clear.

"Great. I'll get Whistler. This time of day there'll be plenty of other dogs down there."

I leave out "and lots of women" and disappear before Martha can object. Not that there's a method to my madness. I still don't know how to stop this adoption. Technically I have the power of veto, but on what grounds? Impersonating a douchebag? And what if this is Whistler's ride on the last-chance express? Ron may be a skin-crawling letch, but even so, with every passing day, the dog's running out of options.

Whistler stands at the front of his run acting like he can't believe what's taken so long. My reward for slipping on his leash is a single, measley, left-right sweep of his tail.

"Forgotten me already or too cool to say hello?"

Scarface looks up, cants his head to the left. There's no one else around, no one even remotely interested in adopting our desperado in the corner.

"Just so we're clear," I say. "This was Jasper's idea."

If he reacts to my son's name I never notice.

What follows has nothing to do with me buying into the madness of direct communication with a dog. I just know that when I get debriefed on this mission, and trust me I will, I need to be able to tell my son I swallowed my pride, spoke slowly, and enunciated every word. That's why I squat down, eye to eye, taking in all the dings and flaws and disfiguring asymmetry, reaching out to the dog inside as I say, "If you have a problem with this guy, you have to let us know."

"WHAT IF HE'S not there?" says Jasper swinging back and forth like a trapeze artist, strapped into the back seat as Norman-the-

4Runner destroys what little is left of his suspension negotiating the Jackknife parking lot potholes.

"He'll be there," I say, sliding into an empty parking space. Judging by the number of other vehicles, our timing is perfect. The tide is low and the beach, off in the distance, is peppered with moving archipelagoes of dog people and off-leash dogs.

"Grab the binoculars out of the back."

When my mother first heard how Jasper suffers limitations on his ability to exercise, she bought him a pair of binoculars, insisting he get into more sedentary pursuits such as bird-watching. Thanks, Mom.

I take in Jasper as he hands the binoculars over—still terrified, and where the rim of his soccer shirt dips low enough to expose his collarbones, dark hollows suck deep with every breath. He never coughed on the ride over. Are his little lungs so infected and plugged up with junk that he can't get it out?

"Find him?"

I survey the waterfront, ignoring the dunes in the foreground and the diminishing October flotilla of sail and powerboats in the back, hunting for a man in a leather jacket and a dog with leather for skin. "Not yet," I say, determined not to panic. There have to be at least fifteen humans and twice that many dogs. Whistler is unique, but he's no Waldo. My eyes pick their way through kids in clunky life vests, lost in rigging and sails, preparing to launch a pair of Sunfish for what might be the last time this year, and loose dogs playing chase around empty kayaks, rowboats, and Hobie Cats, beached above the high-tide line.

"Got him," I say at last, unwilling to take my eyes off my target.

"Can I see?"

I make a mental note of Whistler's coordinates—off leash, sticking to Ron's side, headed toward a group of what appears to be three women with two goldens, a Lab, and three Jack Russells among them.

A lack of height to see over the intervening marshland, lots of squinting (definitely time to see an optometrist), and the struggle of shaky hands (one hit too many on the puffer) and Jasper passes them back, close to tears.

"Just tell me what's going on?"

"Sure," I say, "but what's the plan?"

He looks broken, bordering on hopeless.

"We can't just assume that Whistler will run off. I mean, maybe this guy's okay. Better than . . . you know."

"Stop, Mom. Please, just find him. Whistler will think of something. He will."

I make a show of sweeping back and forth, tweaking the focus.

"He's a bad man. He only wants Whistler as a babe magnet."

My eyeballs suction out of the rubber eyecups, taking in my son's head shake. Babe magnet?

"What a plonker," I say, hoping to raise a smile. No such luck.

"Mom, I know you don't believe me, but we really can communicate without words."

Tempted as I am to jump all over this statement, I have to remind myself that I'm only standing here because my son got a hunch from a dog.

"But maybe I'm too far away to reach him."

I finally lock onto Whistler again. Damn, he's on his best behavior, just like over the weekend, receiving the sniff of approval from the Jacks, playing politely with the goldens and the Lab, all as Ron appears to be holding court, the three woman engaged as he no doubt spins a yarn about his "new" dog's troubled past. Did one of them just adjust a loose ringlet of hair behind her ear?

Suddenly Jasper coughs and everything changes. It's a big one, bone-jarring and explosive at close range, practically ricocheting around the boats in the bay and, thanks to my binoculars, I'm able to see how the ears of every dog flinch and rotate in our direction, honing in on the source. After a second or two, sensitive ears relax, at ease, back to what they were doing. All except for one imperfect pair.

"You okay?"

"Think so," says Jasper. "What's happening?"

I don't know where to begin. Ron may have turned up with a creature capable of luring the opposite sex, but everything changed the moment Whistler heard Jasper's cough. More than hearing, the dog flinched then froze, his maimed face twisting into an expression I've made a thousand times—recognition.

And like that, gone is the carefree canine, the social butterfly, instantly mutating into social misfit bent on crazy time, inciting an impromptu tangle of gold and black and gray fur as the four dogs tangle and twirl like a loaded washing machine on spin cycle, making the colors blur. Then, as if flung from a kid's merry-go-round, Wildman Whistler races off at a tangent, carousing his way from a toy poodle butt sniff to stealing something edible, maybe a sandwich, from a couple trying to enjoy a picnic, to disappearing between the hulls of two sailboats.

Before I can give Jasper an update, the entire beach hears the banshee wail, its ferocity helping me track a gray-haired woman waving her arms and running like she's trying to take off. She lets loose a tirade of expletives before getting to the nitty-gritty, shouting down the beach, "Whose dog just took a dump in my boat?"

I feel Jasper tugging at the bottom of my scrub shirt, desperate for news. The skeptic in me can't argue the fact that Whistler changed the moment he recognized a cough that telegraphed one simple message: "I'm here." But why misbehave, and to what end? How would a dog think acting up wins him a ticket back to the shelter?

I pan back to Ron, catching the way he's trying to laugh it off with his attentive harem, trying to turn his back on Whistler, imagining how he'd love to tell the gray-haired lady, "That dog doesn't belong to me." But Whistler, like a heat-seeking missile, is locked onto his target, his new owner, and just to make sure those around appreciate how much this new master means, that ugly beautiful mutt lunges for Ron's thigh, locking on, dry humping his leg like he's discovered the long lost love of his life.

"Mom? You're killing me."

The phrase hits me like a slap and I jerk back from the binoculars, taking in the boy ready to hang on my every word. Jasper is in trouble, and it's far more than his yearning for Whistler. It's everything in our lives that I can't change. Everything that makes their ridiculous union, their eccentric bond, flawed, pain-ful, and, ultimately, impossible.

"Whistler's going nowhere," I say, knowing exactly what I have to do next, thinking a consolation prize might somehow soften the blow. "Let's go get him. And maybe he should stay with us tonight."

31

Jasper

Usually I sleep through coughing fits at night but this one is a big alarm clock in my chest and the snooze button doesn't work. I sit up in bed, wishing I could wring out my lungs like a wet face cloth, and start over. Mom rushes to my bedroom just as I'm getting a grip.

"Okay?"

I nod and grunt from the pain.

"Intercostal?"

Mom wants to know if I've pulled a muscle between my ribs, from coughing so hard.

"Not sure," I mumble, rubbing my left side. "Too tired."

When Mom said we could take Whistler home with us I went mental with excitement—until she explained why. Reason #1: She didn't want to deal with Martha back at the shelter. Reason #2: She wanted to make me feel better about her bad news.

"Sorry sweetheart, you need to get up." I feel her lips on my cheek, the back of her hand on my forehead. "No school today. Dr. Dan's managed to squeeze us in at ten, but we've got to drop Whistler off at work on the way. Here, let me help you into your vest."

Whistler appears at my doorway. Another sleepover was fun and better than nothing, but it's still a reminder of what I'm missing.

As soon as I've finished my treatment, I'm picking at a bowl of Cap'n Crunch when Mom gets a phone call and for a second I worry that it might be that guy with the accent wanting to speak to her, Cowboy Clay from Texas. What if I'm in big trouble for not passing on his number?

"What?" says Mom. "Calm down. How d'you know it was stolen?"

She mouths, "Auntie Gwen." Phew.

"Since when have you been going to church on a Monday morning?"

Mom listens, pulls the phone away from her ear, and listens again.

"Did you call the police? Now? But I'm leaving for the hospital. Jasper had a horrible night of coughing."

It's a while before Auntie Gwen lets her get another word in.

Mom sighs. I can tell she's given up.

She finishes with a quick "Yes, yes, yes," followed by another long, drawn out "Yeees," and hangs up, grabbing the kitchen counter so tight she might break granite.

"This family," she says, dialing another number on her phone.

"Hi, Burt, it's Dr. Blunt. You at work?"

She waits her turn.

"No, that's great. But can I ask a favor? My sister's car has been stolen and she needs a ride home. I know. The thing is, she's stranded in the opposite direction, I've got Whistler, and I have to pick her up before Jasper's doctor appointment at ten. Any chance you could meet us and take the dog? Otherwise I'm never going to make it."

There's a pause, a smile, and she finishes with, "Burt, you're a lifesaver. St. Marks, on Ocean Drive. See you there in fifteen."

Mom lied. It takes us twenty-two minutes. Unlike every other car ride we've been on, Whistler won't take his eyes off me. It's like he knows something is up. Or maybe, like me, he's tuned into the just-in-case bag in the wayback. It's a large canvas bag containing slippers, pajamas, my laptop, and Henry, the stuffed dog, the one I should have given Whistler, the one from when I was little. Not that I need it or anything. Mom must be donating it to poor kids with no toys. Anyhow, she packs everything "just in case" I get admitted to the hospital. If she's packed the bag, it's never good.

St. Marks is a little white church overlooking a bay. It's so close to the water there's a sign for a boat ramp down the street. And there's Burt, waiting for us. What's he doing talking to a police officer?

Mom pulls over and stops behind a police cruiser. There's another policeman standing with Auntie Gwen. She's crying. A lot.

"Take Whistler over to Burt, and I'll go and see what's wrong with my sister."

Mom gets out and there's more wailing and hugs and lots of swears and all I can think is, wow, Auntie Gwen must have really loved her truck. But then, on the way down to the boat ramp, I see something big and white, floating in the water.

"Hey, Burt."

"Hi, Jasper, this is Officer Sweeney. He found the stolen car." Burt jabs a thumb toward the white object and now that I'm closer I can make out the back end of Auntie Gwen's Mercedes. I'm about to ask why anyone would steal a car and then dump it in the ocean, but maybe I already know the answer.

"Whoever stole it probably realized it was broken."

"What?" says Burt.

"Auntie Gwen had to leave it running all the time. Something up with the engine."

Officer Sweeney laughs but not a real laugh, more of a sarcastic one, the ones adults use when they're trying to make you feel small and dumb. "The car wasn't stolen," he says. "It rolled down the hill and straight into the water. Probably thought it was in park, but she left it in neutral."

Burt's eyes narrow and he kind of leans back like he doesn't believe the policeman.

"The driver has a previous DUI and the vehicle ignition was fitted with a Breathalyzer two weeks ago. Only starts when you're sober. Happens all the time."

What does DUI stand for—difficulty understanding Italian? Time for a Google search as soon as we get home.

Sweeney twists closer to Burt, but I can still hear, "They wake up in the morning, turn over the car, and, so long as they leave it idling, they can drink and drive all day long. Even after attending an AA meeting. Ah, finally." Officer Sweeney steps into the road, waving and shouting orders over the piercing beeps of a tow truck as it backs up.

"How's he doing?" asks Burt, nodding toward Whistler. "Your mom finally changed her mind?"

"No," I say, "but I can tell she really likes him, even if she won't admit it."

I go to place my hand on Whistler's head, but he dips in under my palm and takes a seat at my side, like it was his idea.

"Burt, can you make me a promise?"

"Depends."

"If I'm gone for a while, if this doctor's appointment means I'm stuck in the hospital, you'll make sure Whistler doesn't get . . . you know."

Whistler's body remains perfectly still but his eyes flick to find mine.

"I mean, you'll make sure he goes to a really good home, right, maybe close enough so I can visit?"

Burt raises his chin like he's thinking about this and I notice silver stubble sparkling along the folds of his neck like he forgot to shave this morning. "It's a deal," he says. "What should I tell people about him?"

"Tell them he's curious. Fast learner. Funny."

Perhaps I should write this down. Then I notice Whistler is still staring my way, tilting his head to the side like, "That's all you've got?" It makes me think about a website I visit, a forum, where kids with CF talk about their disease and some of them wonder what people will say about them after they're gone.

"And really smart. Good swimmer. Amazing with a soccer ball."

Burt grins his little yellow-toothed grin. "What about his looks? It's going to put some people off."

I think about it because Whistler's still waiting, curious to hear my answer.

"His looks will only put the wrong people off. Even if he's a two on the outside, doesn't mean he's not a ten on the inside."

I liked that. So did Whistler. So did Burt.

"In all the years I've known you," says Burt, "never seen you bond with a dog like I have with this one."

It's true, only it's much more than Burt's idea of bonding. I mean, okay, a special bond has to go both ways, and yeah, I've had some trouble getting Whistler to answer *my* questions, but I can tell he wants me to understand him. And maybe that's because what Whistler has to say is incredibly important, and I'm the only person who can help him say it, so he's desperate for me to translate. I wonder if Burt should mention our bond to Mom but then I notice Auntie Gwen being helped into one of the police cruisers.

"That's nice of them," I say. "Giving her a ride. I wonder if they'll put the lights on."

I'm thinking cool, but Burt doesn't seem impressed.

"Come on," shouts Mom, heading for Norman-the-4Runner. "Thanks, Burt, I don't know what we'd do without you."

I drop down to give Whistler a wide, gentle hug—Burt says dogs don't like tight hugs. Even though we're kind of pressing our hearts together Whistler isn't in the hug. He's not hugging back.

"He doesn't want to say goodbye," I tell Burt.

"Maybe he thinks if *he* doesn't, *you* can't."

I get to my feet.

"I wouldn't worry," says Burt. "Chances are he'll still be around, long after your doctor's appointment."

"I'm not worried about people wanting to adopt him. It's whether he wants to adopt them. He's the one doing the choosing. Aren't you?"

I reach out for one last touch. "See you in a bit."

But Whistler doesn't look so sure.

Maybe he's still thinking about my just-in-case bag.

32

Kate

GOOD THING I packed that bag.

Every doctor's visit begins with weight (bottom tenth percentile), height (bottom tenth percentile), and vitals. Jasper loves the pulse oximeter, the little clip with the glowing red E.T. light that attaches to his index finger, flashing a measure of the oxygen-carrying capacity of his blood. He's learned how a good coughing fit can fool the machine, artificially helping him into the high nineties. He flashes me his blond brows when he cracks 97 percent, like he's cured. His temperature begs to differ: 101.2°F—low-grade fever.

Dr. Dan Whitehead is the product of a new generation of pediatric pulmonologists. Early thirties, beginning to bald, with enough heft to his belly to make you question his eating habits, Dr. Dan has the smarts, but he makes the parent feel like an interloper, a guest who joined the party without an invite. All conversation is directed to Jasper. If I interject, ask a question, or raise a concern, I'm little more than a pesky inner voice. Rarely does he address me eye to eye. They say it's part of helping their young patients take responsibility and learn to advocate for themselves. Sometimes I want to point out that Jasper has a hard time remembering what he had for dinner, let alone whether he has an allergy to fluoroquinolones or cephalosporins.

Before Dr. Dan arrives I must endure the worst part of any pulmonary consult—the pulmonary function test or PFT. For Jasper, it is painless; for me, it is torture. With nose clips pinching his nostrils and a nebulizer-like contraption in his mouth, he's hooked up to a fancy laptop while he imagines he's blowing out a hundred candles on a birthday cake, and failure to blow out every candle will result in the room catching fire. Taking the deepest breath his little lungs can muster, he blows out as hard, as fast, and for as long as he can. He coughs, wheezes, struggles, and flushes with the effort. And every single time, no matter how hard I try not to, I take the exact same breath and blow with him, and the fact that he has to stop so soon scares me to death.

The technician asks me if I want a printout. Of course I don't. That it's bad is enough. Who needs to know how bad?

"Yes, please," I say, tossing in a polite smile, and a minute later he's back, handing me the sheet like I'm the judge and this is the jury's guilty verdict. The cold objectivity of numbers and trends cannot lie. All parameters are down. Way down. Jasper is in trouble.

"Bad?" Jasper asks, cheeks as red as they will ever get from working his lungs so hard.

The truth is mine alone and as much as I want to cry or scream, for his sake, this charade must continue.

"Okay. Not great. Let's see what Dr. Dan thinks."

Jasper scrunches into the thin layer of white, crepe-like paper coating the examination bed. So many germs. He's sitting up, legs dangling. *Please*, I think, *don't touch a thing*. I reach for my bottle of Purell (I wear it like most women wear perfume).

"You really think Whistler will get adopted?"

Good. Keep his mind off what's to come. "Hopefully. Especially if his cough continues to improve."

Jasper waits a beat.

"Do you think he's ugly?" My boy looks worried.

"Duh, yeah," I say, "but that's part of his charm. Think about it, people only stare at both ends of the spectrum, beautiful or ugly. And for a dog, ugly gets far more attention."

That did the trick, and then there's the familiar rap on the door, Dr. Dan's signature *dat-da-da-dat-dat*.

"Jasper, my man," says Dr. Dan, the fist bump so wrong for a guy wearing a Smurfs tie.

Dr. Dan settles in his swivel chair, boots up his computer, and studies his copy of the PFT results. It's like I don't exist.

"How's school?"

"Okay. Our soccer team made the playoffs."

"He played in goal for the last ten minutes," I interject, "throwing himself around like crazy. His bruises seem excessive, though he always runs low on his platelet count. You think he might have a clotting problem?"

Dr. Dan jerks his head ever so slightly to one side, raises his chin, and frowns, as though he's killing it at stand-up comedy and I might be the heckler spoiling his routine.

"You feel like you've got a fever?"

"No."

"And how about the cough?"

"About the same, a bit worse. My side kind of hurts."

Dr. Dan untangles the stethoscope from around his neck, asks for deep, slow breaths, and takes a listen.

Jasper's face reflects total concentration, like he's performing at a school piano recital.

"A few crackles, especially lower left." The doctor taps around dull ribs with his fingers. "It hurts when you breathe?"

"When I cough."

"And can you lift up your shirt? Whose colors are these?"

"Barcelona."

Those goalkeeping bruises on his shoulder and sides have ripened to yellow.

"I also wanted to have his hearing checked, if possible. His teacher thinks he might be going deaf."

Dr. Dan eyes Jasper, but nods for my benefit in the affirmative.

"Even if I am going a little deaf," says Jasper, "it's okay by me."

I snap, registering the breaking point, and the words get away from me, swift and hot. "Jasper, why would you say such a thing?" I can play their little game only so long and only so much.

"Because it's true. You said one of my meds can make me go

deaf and another of my pills can make my fingers numb and tingly. It's like I've started to lose sound and touch and—"

"Jasper, that's enough, we'll talk about this later."

But cool Dr. Dan can't resist, reading Jasper's sincerity, the misplaced enthusiasm, certain he can score points. "Tell me," he says, settling back in his seat.

Jasper hacks up a cough and I swoop in with a sterile container, a little plastic spittoon, so they can grow and label the invisible killers destroying his lungs. I had hoped it might be a distraction. No such luck.

"I think it's a bit like blind people," says Jasper, nostrils flaring, breaths punctuating words and phrases. "You know, you lose one sensation, and another gets stronger to fill the gap. That's what's happening with me and Whistler."

There's no point in trying to get Dr. Dan back on track. So I go with a stare laden with fury, stopping just shy of drawing a finger across my throat.

"And Whistler is—"

"A dog at the shelter, really smart, smart enough to let me know what he's feeling. It's true, Mom. Ms. Sexton at school talked about this thing in science where every time you lose something you have to gain something else and it's the law."

"Newton," says Dr. Dan.

"Yeah, him," says Jasper. "Mom doesn't believe me, but sometimes, not all the time, but sometimes, what I feel inside me is really what he is feeling. How else did I know his name? And . . . and . . . why do you think I was able to do such a good job in goal?"

"Hence the bruises?"

Jasper nods, tries to appease me with a "sorry but I couldn't help myself" shrug.

Dr. Dan does this sour thing with his lips, twisting them off to one side.

"Interesting" is the best he can manage. And then, "So, based on the PFT, the low-grade fever, the chest pain, and the crackles, I don't think we've got much choice. You need to be admitted. Sooner the better."

Jasper cringes but the protest is feeble. Maybe he just wants to feel better. I knew this was coming, and still, when reality gets packaged and delivered by a doctor, it's always a sucker punch to the gut.

"School's out next week. That might work out fine."

Dr. Dan mouths "Excuse me" to Jasper, pivots in his chair, turns to me, and says, "Your son can't afford to wait, Mrs. Blunt. This is serious. We need to get started right away."

THE LONGER JASPER lives, the more complicated his treatment becomes. Dependence on heavy-duty antibiotics means Jasper needs a PICC (peripherally inserted central catheter), essentially a long white strand of linguine slid into a vein, ready to deliver a payload of bacteria-killing medicine, in spitting distance of his heart. Sounds reasonable, until you consider that Jasper is practically a junkie, his veins overused, narrowed, and tortuous, heightening his anticipation and dread when a stranger starts digging for a vessel, forced to Roto-Rooter through scar tissue, desperate to get it to thread.

"Such a cute kid," says the nurse wearing scrubs covered in gooey, doe-eyed puppies. I know she means well, but I ignore the compliment, kiss my son's salty forehead, and watch as his wheelchair whisks him away, to a place where he will be sedated to endure pain, where he will cry for his mother, and all I can do is fret as another small part of me dies.

Sitting in the waiting room, I bask in the flickering glare of closed-captioned cartoons from an overhead TV as squealing kids squirm on floors or maul sensible toys or suck on their fingers, oblivious to pervasive superbugs. Distractions are everywhere, but I am with Jasper, imagining every step in the process, his little chest hooked up to monitors, swallowed whole by sterile surgical drapes, the glint of a scalpel blade catching his eye, or maybe a needle, or a steel guide wire. I know he feels alone. And what if he's not adequately sedated, flinching at the snap of a latex surgical glove drawn over a scrubbed hand? What if he sees blood, his blood?

"Cute kid." That's what the nurse said.

Cute.

I flash back to the day that changed my life, Jasper a sickly two-year-old, the doctors sitting me down, the diagnosis incontrovertible. By the time they reached the phrase "incurable" I was numb.

But what stayed with me were the words of the nurse's assistant who helped us to the car. She was so kind, situating Jasper in his seat, quick with the tissues for my tears. And then she told me how children with CF struggle to say the name of their disease, so they go with the next best thing, something adorable, accessible, something that made sense. "'Sixty-five Roses' instead of cystic fibrosis. Isn't that cute?" said the assistant, and even now I can see her face. Here was the moment my life changed forever, the moment a new version of me was born, blind to the sincerity in her eyes, convinced that she just didn't get it. *Cute*—like a dimple or a lisp. *Cute*—like learning to play peekaboo or say "Mama." How cute can it be if your kid never grows old enough to properly say the name of the disease that kills him?

I check my watch—seven minutes gone. At times like this I pay the price for relishing every second with my son.

I call work, tell Martha what's going on, and encourage her to email or text me with any problems.

"We're fine," she says, and I can't tell whether she's really saying "we've got your back," or making my absence sound like no big deal. "KGB called. I said I couldn't find you, but she says you'd best get back to her today. Still can't believe that stunt you pulled with Whistler."

Part of me wants to say, "Me either." The same part prepared to accept the blame if Whistler ends up put to sleep. But then, into my silence, Martha sighs a bitter, "God, I hope he realizes—"

Then I lose her, deafened for several seconds by an overhead page, only catching a tiny part of her sentence, one specific word hanging awkwardly between us—*lucky*.

Lucky. Such an incongruous word as I sit, helpless and alone while my son undergoes medical torture. Where's the luck in all of this? In my current state of anguish, I heard an adjective, when it could easily have been a name, Whistler's former name, some new problem with our unadoptable stray. But if this is true, why did the word jump out and practically bite me?

"Oh, and I spoke to some guy from Texas. Thought it was another of those real estate developers trying to buy up the shelter. Said it's important. Said you never called him back. I told him you were in the hospital so he gave me his number again."

"Email it," I say, ready to call her out, to rewind and have her clarify that bizarre "lucky" comment, but she begs off, needing to go, before I can ask.

How long can I keep this job given Jasper's illness? With Katrina Goddard-Brown hovering over every metric and balance sheet this perfect gig might be coming to an end. There are plenty of other vets out there, equally driven to home adoptable pets, and they've never used a sick day in their lives. And what if the shelter closes? Who else is going to hire me, a single mom who may need to drop everything to take care of her son? Sure, add a dog to the mix, what could possibly go wrong?

Nothing has changed—eleven minutes gone. I should call Gwen, because it feels like I'm the one who's been asleep at the wheel, not her. I thought we were close, maybe not enough to know where the bodies were buried, but enough to confide, to unload. Apparently not. Her second DUI in less than a year—where was I?

Sure, at family gatherings, Gwen pounds the chardonnay pretty hard, but then who can blame her? And yes, I've noticed the word-bending slurs, the heavy-handed glug of wine, and the chink of glass on glass, punctuating her late-night phone calls, but in my head it was always an innocent stress reliever, something to take the edge off. When did it become an addiction? Gwen might come across as a spoiled, stay-at-home mom, but her ditzy and disorganized parenting style seems to work. She's always been the opposite of me. At least that's what I thought, until now. Then again, is alcohol her crutch, in the same way that a little blue pill is mine?

Everybody knows her husband, Scott, uses his notoriety as a high-powered attorney like a perk when he wants something bad enough, and like a sick note to get out of something unsavory. Obviously his clout kept her first violation out of the local papers. Given the embarrassing circumstances of what happened to her Mercedes, good luck with the second.

For me, it's the not sharing that hurts. Then again, like I said, when your child has a chronic disease, people hesitate, deliberate, and shut down, unable to stick to the usual format. Maybe my sister can see through my veneer. Here I am projecting unwavering optimism, trying to make things easier, to let the world in, and it turns out Gwen's not buying it, trapped in her own version of a life more endured than enjoyed.

Scrolling through my contacts, I find a quiet (the quietest) corner of the room and dial Gwen's number.

The phone keeps ringing, she doesn't pick up, and I think, *What if she's still in custody, locked up?* But then I hear a voice.

"Hey," I say.

"Hey," she replies, just as tentative.

We both hesitate to go first.

"You home?" I ask.

"Yeah. Scott pulled some strings."

I force myself not to say, "Bet he did," and go with, "That's good."

She parries with a petulant huff, then silence.

"Gwen, you know you can talk to me?"

"Talk about what?"

"Come on."

"Look . . . I had a few drinks last night, got up early. Guess it was still in my system."

"But you were at an AA meeting."

"Only because I got to keep my driver's license. It's not like I'm not in control. It's not like I can't quit."

"Please, Gwen. What's going on? Let me try to help you out."

"Right, like you're such an open book."

Blunt by name, not by nature. Must be something about the way we were brought up. I head for safer territory.

"What d'you tell Mom?"

"Nothing," she snaps back.

"Really."

"I told her the truth. I told her the truck got totaled. Then she offered to pick up the kids."

"That's nice of her," I say, but my mind's already jumping ahead, looking at the bigger picture. "But what about tomorrow, and the day after that?"

"I dunno. The kids are going to have to start taking the bus to school I guess."

I give her another silence, hoping she'll jump in and open up. Still nothing.

"Everyone's going to notice you not driving, especially Mom."

"Scott says it'll only be a year, tops. Maybe I'll tell her I've got something wrong with my eyes, that my doctor says not to drive for a while. She'll never know."

I'm getting nowhere, but can't resist one last push.

"How's Scott in all this?"

"He's fine. We're fine. Why wouldn't we be?"

The connection crackles like the tension between us.

"Anyway, aren't you supposed to be at the hospital with Jasper?"

"Yeah, that's where I am right now."

"Oh, Kate, don't worry about me. I'll work this out. You need to focus on the little man. Tell him I love him."

"I will and he knows you do."

"It's going to be fine. My trainer says I need to get off my ass and ride my bike more. And then there's always Uber. Worst case, Scott can hire me a chauffeur. Someone cute and buff and at my beck and call."

I huff a laugh.

"Okay, but I'm here for you. When you're ready."

"Right back atcha," she says, and we hang up.

The reality of her situation washes over me. Not in a vile, bitchy, schadenfreude kind of way. Her situation reminds me that none of us is immune. We all battle our way through life. At least Gwen does try to be supportive, unlike so many of the other moms who limit their involvement to a magnanimous "You're so strong" while singing my praises. In my darkest hours I wonder if they play up my superhuman powers so they won't have to comfort me. It's the perfect out. An excuse to be absent.

I could work on email. I could read a magazine. But I'd rather stew, churn, ache, and repeat. The pain has set in. Not that it ever goes away. It just changes shape and texture—sharp, dull, deep, superficial, piercing, shooting—no anesthetic can touch it. There's no choice. Best learn to live with it, get by, and function in its presence. This is the difference. This is what stops me from being normal. Most people live with pain in their peripheral vision, something glimpsed from time to time. For me, it's tattooed on the inside of my eyelids.

Time passes. Forty-seven minutes.

The bargaining begins. At fifty minutes I will ask the officious power hungry B word behind the reception desk—with the fancy fingernails, likely surfing the net for shoes, or clothes, or boyfriends—whether she can find out if there's a problem with my son.

At forty-nine, the puppy-scrubs nurse appears.

"The PICC's in. He did fine. Took a few tries is all."

I stop listening at "fine." He's still alive. I still have a son.

Then the wheelchair appears; Jasper slumped in the seat, Stephen Hawking Junior, lids leaden and fluttering, fighting the sedatives. "Sorry, Mom," he croaks.

I buckle at the knees, kiss his ashen face. "Why sorry?" I plead.

"Because . . ." His words slur, my little sleepy drunk. "Because my veins were crappy."

We head straight to the intensive care unit because, to top it all, Jasper is deathly allergic to many of the antibiotics essential to keeping him alive. Thank God there's a solution. Get a peanut allergy, you avoid peanuts. Get an allergy to a vital antibiotic, go straight to the intensive care unit to get desensitized. That's why we're shrouded by machines that blink and chime and beep, hoping to fool Jasper's body into tolerance, and not anaphylactic shock.

This is where Adderall comes in handy. Sure, I trust the nurse, but two sets of eyes are better than one and medical mistakes happen. And besides, by keeping my dose low and infrequent, I tell myself I could quit anytime. But isn't that the addict's mantra? Did Gwen profess the same belief about alcohol? It helps knowing how cold-turkey Adderall withdrawal promises unhappiness, anxiety, and insomnia. How would I notice? It's a trifecta I've already got covered. So, I pop a pill, sit, observe, and wait for success or an emergency EpiPen dose.

Darkness settles on the room, Jasper still sleeping after his ordeal, disproportionately cheery nurse heads appearing at the door, wondering if they can get me something. I politely decline. Sitting here with my son is what I need, comforted by the rhythm of his heart, the tone of the pulse oximeter, the subtle movement of his chest. I see the marks at the crease of his right elbow, the needle sticks of multiple attempts to hit a vein. Jasper coughs and it shakes him half-awake.

"Hey, you."

"Hi, Mom."

I jump out of my chair, stroke back a sweaty fop of hair from his forehead, and offer his chalk-dry lips a tiny red straw attached to a juice box. He drinks, lids closing, a baby on the breast, and it kills me, the way I can never kiss this better.

He falls back into his pillow as he says, "You won't forget about me, will you?"

"Why would I forget about you?"

"When I'm dead," he slurs. "Because . . . because . . . it might be easier to carry on . . . if I never happened in the first place."

I gasp, take his body in my arms, and hug him, fiercely tight, dangerously tight, praying it's the drugs talking, that they've messed with his head, rendering him delirious and not uninhibited. It takes the limpness of sleep before I let go, tuck him in, return to my chair, and allow the tears to flow.

I was twenty-seven years old when a urine-soaked plus sign broke the news of my pregnancy. Keeping this child made no sense. I was broke and unemployed, my ex wanted nothing to do with "it," or me, and my family—okay, I'm singling out my mother here—could only offer irritating platitudes like "I'm sure you'll do what's best." In the end there was nothing to decide. Forget my stubborn streak insisting this accident didn't have to be a mistake. Forget morality or religion or a naive conviction that I could be at least as good a parent as my own parents. When I looked down at that little blue plus sign, something flipped inside me, something visceral, and in that instant, I swear I could feel the thrill of his tiny heart beating somewhere inside me.

Jasper, there has never been a time when I have not wanted you in my life, but once again, witnessing what you endure and suffer, is best for me, fair to you? What if I hadn't got pregnant, would I still be with Simon? How long before I figured out he was a total dick? And what if I'd had a child without CF, would my relationship with my parents be any different?

I succumb to a new round of tears, biting down on my knuckles, trying to be quiet, certain of just one thing. The mistakes of the past, and all the imperfections of the present, have nothing to do with my perfect child.

Instead, they say all that needs to be said about me.

33

Jasper

AFTER THREE DAYS and three nights I get to move to my regular ward where they give me the best room ever, with a couch and living room, a sweet sixty-inch flat-screen TV, a huge bathroom, and this crazy view of the heliport.

So far I'm not itching, the first sign of an allergic reaction, which makes Mom very happy. She's been by my side the whole time—sleeping on the ledge next to the window—except when she goes off to get me juice boxes or snacks. I'm not allowed to leave my room—risk of infecting other sick patients—so it's a bit like prison, except I've got nurses instead of guards and they're really nice. Ms. Sexton at school says being punctual is a good thing, so she'd appreciate the way my nurses show up within seconds of me needing my next antibiotic, even if it means waking me up in the middle of the night.

Most of the time I watch movies or hop on Fortnite to see if any of my friends are online. It's sick to outbuild someone or to carry a squad. It makes me feel like any other player. All my Fortnite friends think I'm a ninja with perfect lungs and an endless supply of skins.

Mom lets me buy stuff online, like a Tim Howard goalie shirt or V-Bucks. Mom says Auntie Gwen would love to visit but the Mercedes is totaled so she's stuck, and Uncle Bob and Auntie Beth live far away so they sent me flowers instead.

Mom can get a little loopy during my hospital stays and by loopy I mean she might say or do magical things. One time I really thought I had a shot at Disneyland, until she came to her senses. This means I should be solving the Whistler problem, but I don't want to feel like I'm cheating because Whistler would definitely tune into Mom's regret if she decided to cop out of the deal.

One of the worst things in the hospital is the way doctors constantly show up at bad times, like when I'm about to eat dinner. Some resident from Child Psychology appears at my door, promising he'll only need "five minutes, tops." Mom's obsessed with me gaining weight and she knows how I hate cold pizza. So why would she jump up, say, "Sure, I'll give you two some privacy," and leave the room?

He's new to me, with a diamond stud in his ear, a tattoo peaking beyond the shirt cuff on his wrist. Instead of just taking a seat, he grabs a chair, spins it around, straddles it back to front, and leans in.

"It's okay to be angry," he says. "If I were where you are, I know I would be."

I'm pouting because I want to eat, but I reply, "A dog wouldn't be angry."

"Why's that?" he says, all interested, as I try not to stare at a juicy slice of pepperoni.

"Dogs growl, and show their teeth, and of course they bite, but it's a reaction. It's instinct. Fight or flight. Being angry is different. You have to *think* about bad stuff to get angry."

He rocks back. "You never think about the bad stuff in your life?"

"I try not to. Unless I can make it better."

His frown looks more worried than that he doesn't believe me.

"Your mom's a vet, right?"

Has he memorized my file?

"That's why you're into dogs?"

"I want to be a vet when I grow up."

"Very cool. What do your friends think?"

"I haven't told anyone. Except Mom."

"Really? No BFF? Someone who can keep a secret? Wait, you're going to tell me no one keeps a secret better than a dog. Am I right?"

I smile.

"But if you needed to speak to someone other than your mother, to . . . say . . . a guy, about, guy stuff . . . then who would it be? Your grandfather? A teacher at school?"

Guy stuff? What's he talking about? Girls? Puberty? Sex? Is this doctor suggesting I talk about sex to Grandpa or Coach Taft?

"And what about your biological father? Do you ever think about him?"

Whoa. Where did this come from?

"Ever try to Google him? Stalk him on Facebook? It would be perfectly normal at your age. Starting to question where he is and why he's not around. You've had time to think." And then, "Time to get angry."

He flashes me a little touché eyebrow, and that's when it hits me. Did Mom feed him these questions? Does she think I want to find my father? Is that why she left us alone?

"I'd talk to my best friend, Burt. He's my bro. If I need him, Burt's got my back."

Before it can feel weird, weirder—calling a seventy-seven-year-old man my "bro"—nurse Debbie comes to my rescue.

"Jasper, why aren't you eating? You took your enzymes?"

"Yes."

"Well they can't help you digest that pizza unless it gets into your stomach. Isn't that right, doctor?"

The resident from Child Psychology takes the hint, dismounts his chair, and hands me a business card.

"Have your mom call, set up an appointment." And then, tapping the long list of contacts on the card, says, "Friend me on Facebook."

I nod but keep quiet. Maybe I should tell him that *not* being on Facebook is one of the ways to make bad stuff feel better.

JUST BEFORE LUNCH on day four, I recognize the *dat-da-da-dat-dat* on the door.

"Hey, Buddy," says Dr. Dan. "If your mom's cool with doing your treatments at home, maybe we should get you out of here. Sound good?"

Why is he asking me and not Mom?

"And you were right. Your hearing test results show some loss with the higher frequencies. No biggie, at least not for right now, but we switched one of your meds." About to leave he catches himself. "If you really are trading one sense for another, might as well teach your mom to speak dog while you recover, right?" He gives me a wink and he's gone.

"I wish you'd let it go," says Mom, picking up today's menu to see what I've circled so she can phone in my order.

"Let what go?"

"You know very well. This . . . talking to dogs obsession. It's not normal. People will think you're weird."

"It's not talking. It's not about words."

"Then what?"

"It's like . . . thoughts and sensations inside me are talking for them."

"Jasper, come on, you're being ridiculous. It needs to end, now. Do you know what you want for lunch?"

My upper teeth bite into my lower lip, trying to stop the tremble but it's too late. I never cried while they stabbed me with their shiny needles, but I'm crying now, words getting stuck down my throat.

"Hey, hey, hey, it's okay," says Mom, squeezing onto the edge of my bed, her hand reaching to pat my shoulder.

I swat it away before it lands.

"I'm serious, Mom. What if understanding dogs is the only thing I'm any good at?"

"What do you mean? You're good at lots of things."

"No, you don't get it." Air keeps snagging as I breathe in, like a bad case of hiccups. "There's got to be something more. There's got to be a payback. There's got to be a reason . . . for me having CF . . . for having to live with all of this."

34

Kate

"THANKS FOR GETTING us such a nice room," I whisper to the nurse.

"No problem," she says, eyes focused on a fluid bag hooked up to a pump. "It's for . . . " she checks to make sure Jasper is not listening before adding, "end of life. Sorry, nothing else available."

Forget being offended by her insenstivity, we'll take it, and to be fair, the hospital staff has been great, Jasper favoring those who have dogs, quick to mention what his mom—the woman with the scary smile, working on her laptop, pretending not to listen—does for a living, inevitably describing his budding gift as an animal swami. When his favorite, Debbie—Rufus, Irish setter, does agility on weekends—rises to the bait and hopes Jasper might be able to teach me a thing or two about conversing with dogs, I nearly lose it.

"Aren't these lovely," says Debbie, bringing in a huge bouquet from my brother in lieu of a visit, the generic, cold "Get Well Soon" remotely typed.

I come back with a perfunctory "Beautiful," thinking, *What bedridden eleven-year-old boy wants flowers*, until Jasper looks up from his laptop and proves me wrong with an enthusiastic smile. Who knew? And just like that, I'm actually grateful someone in my family made an effort.

"You know how your father despises hospitals," said Mom, when we last spoke. "They make him feel like he's walking on thin ice over his own grave." This almost believable rationale rendered me speechless, less out of acceptance and more out of sadness, sadness for Jasper, that he might think his suffering doesn't affect them, that they really don't care. Presumably, by misinterpreting my silent desire to cry as anger, she added, "Look, Kate, when everything settles down, we'll go out for a coffee, just you and me. It's time for us to clear the air."

Clear the air.

She hung up while I was still in a state of shock.

And as for Gwen, she's promised to visit but the cab ride alone would cost a fortune, and who's going to look after the kids?

Our own families always come first. It's the way it's always been. And I realize it's the same for me.

Just then I hear footsteps turn into the room and nod at the resident standing in the doorway. Normally, when Child Psychology contacts me, I inwardly groan, knowing it'll be an awkward waste of time, Jasper projecting a vague robotic positivity, keeping his responses superficial and generic. This time, however, the resident called my cell, in advance, requesting a private, introductory, one-on-one session.

"CF can be particularly tough on adolescent boys. Peer pressure. Negative body image. Slow to pubertal changes. And I noticed in his file that you are a single parent. I wonder, does he ask about his father?"

I might have been offended—the way a doctor I've never met makes "single" sound like a defect—but he got me thinking and I ended up sharing my concerns about the English slang, the obsession with soccer, the furtive Internet surfing. Is this Jasper's way of trying to discover the truth about Simon Swift? I know it's wrong, me pussyfooting around his father, but it's a painful reminder of my own bad choices. How do I balance my greatest joy, Jasper, with the termination of a relationship that I will forever regret?

So, when the resident shows up, I leave them to it—fifteen minutes instead of the allotted five—only to return and find Jasper alone, gnawing on pizza crust.

"How'd it go?"

Chewing, lots of chewing, followed by a slow, slow, swallow. Is this his build up to venting, to asking difficult questions?

"Fine," he says, totally indifferent, handing over the doctor's business card.

Maybe now's the time to push, to build on what they discussed, and call Jasper out. But all I can imagine are the questions he will ask of me, the perfectly reasonable, predictable whys certain to pick and poke at the scab that never truly heals.

So I pocket the business card. As soon as we're out of the hospital, I'll set up an appointment.

Or not.

ON THE FOURTH day, Dr. Dan pays a visit, happy to (a) kick us out of the hospital and (b) playfully suggest Jasper tutor me in the art of canine communication. I don't know what disturbs me more, Dr. Dan thinking he's being funny or the look of validation written across my son's face.

"Come on, listen to what you're saying. It's not right. Do you know what you want for lunch?"

And there I am, scanning the menu, trying to choose between a strawberry or vanilla high-calorie shake, between mac 'n' cheese or a hot dog, and my son comes apart, his face twisted by a sadness, a fear, or a pain.

He doesn't have to gesture to the walls of his cell or the tentacles of tubes and wires tethering his ravaged body. I get it. It is just him and me, fighting with everything we've got to defy Darwin's law of survival, refusing to surrender, and yet how easily we can be unmasked and undone. Years ago I gave up bartering with God. Today my son prays his suffering, his misery, his endless fear, scores enough points with a higher power to earn him an impossible gift.

"What if, thanks to Whistler, I'm meant to find out what can't be said in words?"

His crazy talk is like a bucket of ice water down the back of my neck. I take his raw, wet cheeks in my palms and hope my forced smile stops me from saying something I'll later regret.

Isn't it always the way, life's turning points catching you off guard and unprepared? Perhaps the upside of being broadsided is more receptive, more indelible. Perhaps the best part about the biggest moments is the way they can be so small.

Having forgotten to order a drink with Jasper's lunch—hey, I was a little distracted by his breakdown—I head to the small galley kitchen on our floor, eager to filch a free six-pack of cranberry mini–juice boxes from the communal fridge. There, in front of the microwave window, transfixed by a plate of spinning food, stands another mother, sans makeup, sporting a familiar uniform—sweatshirt, pajamas bottoms, fuzzy slippers—with greasy UPS brown hair clumped in an unruly bun by a giant turquoise clip. We size each other up, and in milliseconds it is obvious we're thinking the same thing, no need to speak, just smile with the recognition of another survivor. Scary, the way she might be a version of me in ten years time. At least I hope it takes ten years.

"The person who invents a place to get a massage and a hair cut in a hospital is going to make a fortune," I say.

The woman laughs. "I was thinking more about a bar."

"Definitely," I say, rummaging around at the back of the fridge, discovering nothing but orange juice and ginger ale.

"What're you in for?"

Her question takes me by surprise, but when I close the fridge door, primed to unleash a blunt "None of your business," she's looking right through me and there it is, written in the subtle folds and creases of acquiescence around her eyes. I've seen it often, especially in the mirror. It's the secret that requires no handshake, and it's no badge of honor. It's the look of PTSD, only, for us, the *P* has a different meaning, not *post* or in the past or behind you, but *permanent*. CF is the natural disaster from which you will never recover. Like me, this woman exudes the weariness of a soldier back from battle, a soldier who knows the war is far from over.

I think about a smile, tossing out "Little lung infection," and being on my way. But a children's hospital can make any parent unmoored. Perhaps it's the presence of professional caregivers giving you a false sense of security. When you don't have to be on all the time, the mind can drift, allowing your mood, ever so briefly, to lift, secure in the knowledge that, for right now, you're not completely alone.

"CF," I say.

She lets me see the faintest of smiles.

"Thought so."

Guessing at CF isn't really a stretch, since as one nurse pointed out, about 75 percent of the patients in this ward share the disease. Ironic, the way kids not meant to be in contact with one another get lumped together.

"Me too," she adds, but without enthusiasm. "Amy. Twenty-two."

"Jasper. Eleven."

This isn't me—open, even chatty—but my latest episode with Jasper has me off balance. I don't do support groups or shrinks. Yes, I tried, but my coping strategy is personal. This is my grief, and no one else can tell me how to live it. All I know is there is something between us, something more than the disease and the fact that neither of us wears a wedding band. I can tell this woman gets *me* because she gets *it*.

"He doing okay?"

I nod, grateful for the age and sex difference between our kids, hoping she doesn't want to compare severity.

"Never thought all this," she gestures to our surroundings, "would be the biggest part of raising a kid."

Fearful of where she might be going with this, I inject a little rigor into my hunt for juice alternatives. Still, I notice how she looks away, hesitates, ignores the food-ready beep of the microwave, and comes back to me. Now I've done it—opening the door to a complete stranger.

"Do you ever wonder about the way everything became *before* and *after*?"

She reads my confusion.

"Before and after the diagnosis. Before and after CF."

I say nothing even though I want to say, "Only all the time." I search her face for obstinate, crazy, or irate, but the only expression I recognize is our burden.

"I do. I think about that moment, that turning point, a little too often, you know." She forces a laugh, bitter and clipped. "People ask me, and I tell them it's like being out on the town, dining at your favorite restaurant, with the people you love the most, friends and family, and you're having a blast, easy and relaxed, with that certain vibe you get, you know, magical, the one when everything is clicking. And then, quite unexpectedly, the maître d' whispers in your ear, escorts you to the door, and tosses you out onto the street, and, as best as you can tell, nobody notices, and you're hammering on the glass, looking in, and everyone is still smiling, tossing back their heads, laughing and enjoying a life you thought you had, a life that ended in an instant, without an explanation, and not one of them can understand you anymore."

Astonished and breathless, my brain says, *How can you know me so well,* while my mouth can only muster a deep, unsettled "Wow."

She clasps a hand to my upper arm. "Enjoy this time with your son, this now . . . oh God, please, no, I didn't mean . . ."

Of course I'm going to take that the wrong way. What other way is there? Who needs a lecture on Jasper's inevitable decline from a woman with a ketchup stain on her chest and flecks of toothpaste caking the corners of her mouth? But she won't release her grip.

"I mean this age, while they're still young. I used to think I was in control of Amy's illness. Every med, every neb, religious, no exception; sleepovers, summer camps, vacations, forget it, if they might interfere with her health. Even refused to let her go to college. Made her commute from home. Babied her, I admit it, made every decision for her and in *my* best interest. Believed that as long as she followed my rules, stayed within my grasp, this disease couldn't win."

Her intensity is palpable and I dare not speak.

"But, here we are again," she says, the spell of her upbeat tone belied by the anguish in her smile. "Thought I knew what it took to keep the kid alive."

"Easier said than done," I say, finally, my eyes sliding left to where she's still gripping my arm.

She lets go and turns back to the microwave. "This disease sucks, whichever way you cut it," she says, pulling out a steaming Tupperware bowl, but still staring hard at me. "When I look back, I know my biggest regret will be the way I pushed my version of Amy's life, and wishing I'd let her live more of her own."

I don't smile, I don't nod, I just have to wait, to settle and let the room stop spinning.

"Just keep swimming," she calls, as I make to leave.

Such a strange thing to say, but it makes me smile. I glance back over my shoulder, letting her know I get it. When your ship is sinking and there's nothing out there but open water, you can never quit. It's what you do.

Less than halfway back to his room the full impact of what she suggested hits me and I falter, fumbling for the wall, turning and letting my back slide down, knees buckling into a crouch. I'm aware of the hospital smell, the way it should be the smell of hope, and not despair. I never asked her name, or what she saw in me that made her share. But it was what she said, her warning, her regret for taking over every facet of her daughter's life. It felt like I was being handed a pair of glasses—prescription, not rose-colored—invited to take a fresh look, and though they can never make the world that different, or get rid of the blur, or alter my focus, maybe, in small and meaningful ways, they can cut down on some of the glare.

When it comes to Jasper, I know I'm super-obsessive and hypervigilant, but if I take a step back, lighten up, or even dare to put myself first, how can I not feel like I'm neglecting him or, worse still, trying to live without him? The punishment of this disease is a guarantee of plenty of time for that later. Her cautionary tale insists that I cannot outrun our reality, and though I appreciate the wisdom of her hindsight, what's our alternative? What's the plan? How do I safely let Jasper live to the max? We need a future that scares me less, not more.

Outside Jasper's room I interrupt a pair of nurses putting on disposable gloves, gowns, and masks. One of them turns to me and says, "Hey, Mom. We're just going to change the dressing on his IV."

It's too good a chance to miss and the timing is perfect—ten to fifteen minutes to clear my head. There's only one place to go. I head for the elevators, down to the first floor and the hospital gardens.

Some people call it "novocaine for the soul"—this escape, this green sanctuary, this chance to bask in the relief of open space and natural light. Whenever Jasper goes into the operating room, an improbable half-acre at the heart of this medical chaos is where I often come to panic and pace and feel less trapped, less afraid, and closer to something approaching comfort.

Outside it's cloudy and drizzly and the garden is empty aside from a nurse pushing a boy in a stroller, a raw tattoo of surgical staples snaking across the child's shaved scalp. He's hooked up to an oxygen tank and a fluid pump, and I smile as I pass them, and will my mind not to get sucked into another tragic story as

I head for a particular bench hidden behind a row of thick aza-
lea bushes, where I can sit, and breathe, and try to pull myself
together.

Unfocused as I round the corner, I'm shocked to barrel into
a shadowy figure, a man, shorter than me, almost knocking him
over, and in the gap between surprise and apology my mind picks
out two things about him: his age—at least sixty; his cheeks—
smarting, streaked by tears.

"I'm so sorry," I blurt, but the man's already on the move,
waving away my apology, head down, shuffling off without a
word. When he passes the nurse and the kid he says something
but keeps going, scurrying back into that cold world of fluores-
cence with its chemical bouquet.

"Is he okay?" I call, walking over to the nurse, noticing the
stethoscope around her neck labeled "Cassie."

"Sure," says Cassie, visibly puzzled by my concern.

"He seemed upset."

She shrugs, encourages the boy to throw a broken cracker at
a fat squirrel.

I could walk away, I should walk away, but I ask, "Wasn't he
kind of . . . old . . . compared to most of the parents in here?"

"Maybe he's a grandparent. Or maybe he *was* a parent."

Now she's done it. *Was* a parent. All I hear is the way the
past tense sounds like failure, like it didn't count, like he had a
chance and screwed it up.

"What do you mean?" I ask.

"They come here," she says. "All the time." She glances down, as if making sure that the boy is distracted. "They come back . . . to remember."

I don't want her to go on, but I can't move.

"For some sick kids, this"—she gestures around us—"may be all they get. It's a slice of what passes for normal, for fun, even. That's why they come back, the parents of the dead. A chance to relive a few precious memories."

In a blink, the old man's face comes into a kind of focus— the way he used his hand as a shield, attempting to hide his grief—as if embarrassed that this ordinary and inconsequential place is all he has, clinging to a sliver of joy left by a child lost too soon.

Cassie bites her lower lip and her eyes smile like they are sorry for telling it like it is and I stand there—dewy grass below, gray sky above—having taken in her every word, letting them hit me like bullets, like friendly fire, and all that emotional Kevlar I've tried to put between me and the pain of Jasper's disease disappears, the target inside my chest torn wide open.

And like that I'm gone, sprinting out of the garden, down the corridor, hammering the up button on the elevator, praying no one else gets on, finding my floor, and only catching myself when another nurse chases after me, fearing a code blue, before bursting into Jasper's room without knocking.

His eyes are wide and gray. "You think if we use his special vest, that Burt could sneak Whistler in for a visit? Hey, you forgot my drink."

I conjure up a mental image of the mutt, my son's Comforter in Chief, this relentless yearning for his company, and I almost laugh, the way I strive to be in control, calling the shots, providing safe passage when the reality of this hospital room proves that for all my bravado, *we* remain enslaved by a disease. If we can't stop CF, if despite our best efforts this disease is going to win, at least we can dictate how the game is played.

"Let's do one better," I say, still panting. "How about we adopt Whistler ourselves?"

35

Jasper

DEBBIE, MY NURSE, comes racing into the room.

"You okay? Your heart monitor went crazy."

I'm still not able to speak.

"It's fine," says Mom, turning her face away from me because she knows I know she's wiping away a tear. "He just got a little excited."

Best I can do is nod and grin.

Brilliant.

36

Kate

I WILL MY mind to wallow and bask in it, to permanently ink the image of my son flashing the biggest smile of his life. I'm not thinking straight and it feels amazing and totally worth it and a big fat tear gets away from me and I can't help but laugh because inside my head I'm screaming at the top of my lungs, *In your face, CF.*

I hate the word *epiphany*. Being the victim of a Road to Damascus experience suggests everything that went before was wrong, fatally flawed, and misguided. Sure, I'm vulnerable, the way this place gets to me, but the truth is something has been stirring for a while. Does it coincide with the arrival of this dog? I'm reluctant to give him that much credit, but maybe. He turns up and now a part of me feels like I'm the one wandering through life, that I'm the real stray. No question, Whistler has disturbed the sediment of our lives. The bigger question is, why risk his influence on my son?

I rarely tell people what I do for a living. It's a green light to be tyrannized about the merits of vaccines, raw diets, and how best to treat niggling skin disorders. Yet occasionally friends with pets will ask end-of-life questions—how far should I go, what would you do if this were your dog? I give them variations on the same answer every time—your choice should allow you to look back, beyond the end, and see the vast real estate of happier times. Perhaps this policy shift with regard to Whistler means I'm finally listening to myself. Maybe this stranger in the kitchen—can't believe I never got her name—unnerved me. Or maybe Cassie, that nurse in the garden, scared me into making a commitment. Whatever the reason, the universe appears determined to put this dog and this boy together. Who am I to interfere?

"I'll call work, right now." I pick up my phone and the disproportionate thrill revamping Jasper's face nails down the lid of my coffin a little tighter. "Hi, it's Dr. Blunt, who's this?"

"Stacy," says a meek voice.

"Oh, hi, Stacy," I say, having no idea who this can be, probably some high school volunteer. "Is Burt around?" Easier to deal with Burt than Martha. "I need to talk to him about Whistler."

"Who?"

"Big black dog, lots of scars."

Jasper hangs on my every word, done with the distraction of Nickelodeon.

"I know the one. Hang on."

Minutes pass, and then too many minutes, and what starts out as frustration quickly escalates into uncomfortable apprehension.

"Something's not right," says Stacy, sounding as though she might be about to burst into tears. "Burt's been walking the dogs and . . . like . . . I think he might have messed up."

"I'm not with you."

"Um . . . I found Tyson in Whistler's run and Tyson's run is empty. No ID card on the bars. No bedding. No water bowl. Nothing."

"But Tyson's a day-fourteen—"

My vocal chords clamp shut as my mind sees the catastrophe unfold. Senile old man accidentally puts the wrong dog in the wrong run, someone forgets to check the name tag, no one asks, everyone assumes, and, like that, one animal gets a reprieve while another gets an early death penalty without a fair trial.

"Oh, God, tell me there's not been a terrible mistake."

The line goes silent, and I wonder if Stacy doesn't know or is too afraid to answer, until finally, she mumbles, "You still need me to find Burt?"

37

Jasper

I'M DYING HERE. Mom won't tell me what's wrong. She flops into her chair and buries her head in her hands, emitting the growl she only makes when she's crazy angry.

"What?" I scream.

She angles her head up. That slight tick in the corner of her left eye has been magnified into a psychotic wink. Is she proper crying?

"Jasper," she says, and I hear my name get all wobbly in her throat. "I've got some bad news. Some really bad news."

Slowly she sits up, taking forever, killing me, nothing but the words *terrible* and *mistake* ping-ponging inside my head, and I think, if this *is* about Whistler, I'd know it, I'd feel it, I'd be on my knees, I'd be begging for oxygen, and I'm not, I feel the same, so he has to be okay.

Finally she takes a deep breath, about to confess, when her

phone rings and Mom's on it, once more leaving me hanging. "Martha, what the hell's going on with Whistler?"

Mom listens, her face scrunched tight, looking like she might crush the phone in her trembling hand. Her eyeballs are darting left and right and she's still not saying a word until finally she lets loose with, "Oh, thank God. No, I'm glad," and then, after a while, "Yes, I'm sure you are."

Mom hangs up and begins pacing in front of the window.

"Someone else has adopted him?"

She stops and slowly lets her head rock way back, like she's only just noticed the Big Dipper constellation sticker on the ceiling above her, even though it's daytime.

"How did you know?"

Incredible. She actually looks surprised. What part of special communication is she not getting?

"I'm so sorry, Jasper. I've been such an idiot. But I swear, nothing's changed. I still want you to have a dog. Not just soon, now, when we get out of here. We'll move. Do whatever it takes. Only, thanks to my stupidity, it can't be Whistler."

Compared to a tragic day-fourteen mistake this is not good news, but not as bad as it might have been. She rushes over and plops down on the side of my bed, practically catapulting me into the air, grabbing for my hands like she wants to dance while I want to cry. Instead of thinking dog, any dog, I'm thinking Whistler, so of course I'm sad. It's like someone said you just won the lottery and it turns out the jackpot is five bucks and not a million dollars.

"Who adopted him?"

"Don't know. But you can ask Burt yourself. He wants to drop by after dinner, see how you're doing, if that's okay?"

I nod and Mom squeezes my hand.

After a minute she says, "If I were to believe in this dog-speak thing, and I'm not saying I do, but if I did, and if I want to learn, and if you promise this conversation goes no further than this room, then what would you teach me?"

One Christmas, Auntie Gwen gave me a magic kit—a wand, special cards, a couple of pieces of rope, no rabbit—and in the instruction book it said the most important part of doing magic was something called *misdirection*. Mom does it all the time, especially when bad stuff happens. She's doing it now because she feels guilty about Whistler.

"It's hard to put into words."

"Try." Mom inches closer, squeezing tighter, and inside her eyes there's a sadness that promises, "This is not a bribe." Even if she's not really that interested, I can tell she is really sorry for messing up.

So I think about Whistler and say the first thing that pops into my mind.

"Dogs aren't afraid to die. That's why they're so excited to live."

And she lets go of my hand, like I gave her an electric shock.

38

Kate

FOR STARTERS, I should have kept my mouth shut. I don't ad lib. I don't go off script. I maintain direction, have a plan, know where I am headed, and to know is everything. If I'd called work first, discovered he'd been adopted, Jasper would be none the wiser, his heart aching but not broken. Not broken by me. But now, thanks to my lapse, my moment of spontaneity, I gave him hope, I let him dare to dream, only to snatch it away.

For seconds, when my boy wonder bounces back, he has me rattled. When your time is running out, you should be able to say whatever you like and get away with it. But what normal eleven-year-old boy preaches a canine philosophy on life?

Like it or not, life is a chronic disease. Though it promises beauty, horrors, and everything in between, for some of us, life has a sick concept of time. We've all used or heard the phrase "Life's too short." Usually it's a verbal carrot or a stick, meant to provoke a new outlook, to get off your ass and actually live.

Filtered through my ears, it is the constant reminder that Jasper will never be with me for long enough. And then, in my professional capacity, it is the inescapable truth about sharing our lives with animals.

As humans, we are not meant to outlive our children. It goes against the natural order of things. Yet my days are full of people who love pets no less than if they shared their DNA. Our dangerous liaisons with animals almost always guarantees that we will lose this "child" in our lifetime, destined to face a future that feels vast and dark and unimaginably lonely.

Why would any kid foster a "dogs are excited to live" delusion? And I find it hard to believe the events of that wild weekend with Whistler was all the proof Jasper needed. I think back to the boy waylaid by a lonely hobo in a parking lot, that senseless swim in an icy pond, exacting revenge on a demon cousin (yes, Gwen told me what happened), and learning to play like a World Cup goalie. Whistler was outrageous and willful and my son loved every minute of it. The experience may have left him more obsessive, effusive, perhaps even more articulate about dogs, but has Jasper really changed? No. He's still the same dog nut. The about-face on getting a dog belongs to me. Whistler is *my* catalyst and, like it or not, that makes me *his* changeling.

I fuss with the sheets and blankets around Jasper's feet. It's the "dogs aren't afraid to die" line that disturbs me most, the niggling fear that he was about to add, "And neither am I." I have never let Jasper anywhere near an animal that has to be put to sleep. So how could he possibly know? When forced to carry out the worst part of my job, can I make this leap of faith, whispering affection, staring into sad wet eyes, praying my interpretation of acceptance and relaxation is more than trust, more than forgiveness, and a certainty of something better to come? Maybe, but for right now, the best I can do is agree, telling Jasper, "All dogs go to heaven, and when you get there, which will not be for a very long time, you, my love, are in for a whole lot of licking."

39

Jasper

"I NEED TO pee."

Mom helps me out of bed, still attached to my IV pump.

"You had two phone calls while you were asleep," mutters a voice against the locked bathroom door.

Out of her sight for twenty seconds and still, this is her way of making sure I'm okay.

"One was Ms. Sexton. She's emailed you some schoolwork. Stuff you missed. She says not to worry if you don't feel up to it through next week's vacation."

There's a pause.

"Jasper?"

"Still here, Mom."

She waits a beat before saying, "The other was Coach Taft. Guess what? He asked if there was any way you would be better in time to be their goalkeeper for the playoffs."

"What did you tell him?"

"I told him Manchester United has offered you a three-year contract so you won't be able to make it."

"Mom," I shout, washing my hands.

"I told him it'll be at least another week, maybe more. But isn't that great?"

I catch my reflection in the mirror, and my eyes remind me that I was only able to play in goal with Whistler there to coach me.

It's no surprise that Burt is my first and only visitor, even though I'm supposed to be going home tomorrow. He shuffles in, looking kind of worried, like he might be visiting the wrong kid in the wrong room.

"Burt," shouts Mom, springing out of her chair to give him a big bear hug (bigger than Grandma or Grandpa usually get). "This means the world to him. And me."

He hugs her back, says, "Me too," and for a second, they just stare at each other and I worry 'cause Mom looks like she's about to cry.

"Burt, what you got there?" I ask, before this gets even more awkward.

That breaks the spell and he hands me a gift—no wrapping paper, just the Amazon box it was shipped in, which reminds me, I've still got to send back that two-man tent hiding in the back of my closet.

"What is it?" asks Mom.

"Cool," I say, reading the title of a book. *"Dogs That Know When Their Owners Are Coming Home and Other Unexplained Powers of Animals."*

Mom doesn't even try to hide her eye roll.

"Thought you might like it."

"What do you say?" prompts Mom.

"Thanks, Burt." I flick open the back of the book jacket.

"Rupert Sheldrake. Look, Mom, he's from England."

Mom smiles and adds a cheery "Of course he is," barely moving her lips.

Burt hovers by the side of the tower of monitors, awkward and not sure where to stand until Mom helps him out.

"Here, Burt, have a seat. I'm going to grab something for dinner from the cafeteria. Can I get you anything?"

Burt shakes his head. Mom makes me promise I'll text her if I have any problems over the next twelve minutes. *You're driving me mental, Mom.*

"Who adopted Whistler?" I ask as soon as we're alone.

Burt's coffee-brown eyes light up like he knew that would be the first question I asked.

"Older couple. Early sixties."

Wow, really old.

"Both retired. Live two miles from the shelter. Big backyard. I've seen it. Grandkids come by most weekends. Boys. Love to play soccer."

I should be happy, but I can't find the happy switch in my brain, let alone flip it on.

"What about Whistler's cough?" I ask. "His medications?"

"They seemed fine with it. And no one's heard him cough for days."

"Did you tell them about him not barking?"

"I did. But they said they didn't need a guard dog; in fact, some of their neighbors complained about their last dog so being quiet was a big plus."

"But you liked these people? They were nice?"

Burt thought about this.

"Jasper, I know how much this dog means to you. They're good people."

"But what about Whistler? Did he like them?"

This made Burt rock back in his chair, lace his fingers, and cup his belly.

"Whistler acted fine, but . . . put it this way, he didn't act like he does around you."

I try not to smile, but not too hard. I could tell Burt about old Mom being beamed up by aliens and the new version they sent back changing her mind about a dog. But why bother? It won't get Whistler and me together, and if other people find out, it will only make Mom feel worse.

"What about Mojo and Tru?"

Sometimes it's better not to ask, but now that I'm in the market for a dog, I can't help it.

"Both found new homes. But don't worry, there are fourteen more for you to worry about when you get back."

"You're sure about this?" says the woman from home health with the scratchy man-voice—Mom says people who work in hospitals really shouldn't smoke cigarettes. "Three different intravenous antibiotics running for six hours out of every day will be really tough."

Mom swats the air, puffs out a "No biggie" tut, and says, "I'm not worried. I don't have a problem staying awake."

And so, after nearly a week, I get to break out of prison, Norman-the-4Runner our getaway vehicle.

"I still feel bad about Whistler," says Mom, ending the silence of our ride. "But I'm glad he found a good home. And there'll be other dogs, right?"

Mom's reflection looks more focused on watching my response than the highway. Then it hits me. With Whistler out of the picture, is she thinking about blowing me off again? I mean it's not like I have a specific dog in mind anymore. Am I back to square one? Me getting a dog might take weeks, months, never.

"Hope so," I say, making an effort to be quiet and pretending to be really sad.

Worried mirror eyes try to read me while she thinks what to say next.

"I've already put in a call to a realtor who swears she can find us a new home."

I manage a pretend shrug and stare out the window. The trick is not to give in and see if she's still looking.

Another long delay—which is good—and then she says, "I'm serious, Jasper. It's time to change both our lives, starting with a dog."

"Sure," I say, hoping Mom thinks I'm playing it cool, when

really I'm falling asleep, blanking out the rest of the journey until she pulls into the carport and cuts the engine.

"We're home. Leave all your stuff in the truck. Let's get you set up."

I'm tired and cranky and my legs are mushy from spending a week in bed, so Mom comes around to give me a hand. If this is how it feels to be a little old man, I'm not missing much.

It's dark, mainly because the streetlight outside our apartment is still broken. Mom's complained to Mr. Crabtree about replacing it, but he's probably too busy trying to fix his deer problem.

Shuffling along, I'm about to ask, "What time's my next treatment?" when Mom scares the crap out of me, pinching her stubby talons into my shoulder, forcing me to a dead stop, doing a bad job of whispering, "Did you hear that?"

"What?"

She's acting jumpy. Maybe she has a hard time sleeping at night because she watches too many scary movies.

"That," she says, like I must be deaf—which is almost true—because I've no clue what's freaking her out until a motion detector outside a nearby apartment suddenly flicks on.

I'm tired but awake enough to work out that neither of us could have triggered the outdoor light, and there's this spooky pause, long enough for us to look at each other before one of our rhododendron bushes explodes and I go blind, smacked backward into Mom's arms. Okay, slight exaggeration. I can still see, only my world has gone black, squashed by a suffocating layer of warm black fur.

Mom has time for "What the—?" but I cut her off.

"*Whistler.*"

The ugly mutt is in my face, on my face, licking my face, dancing and turning tight figure eights, tail in helicopter mode, and man, I am so hyped!

Even Mom is on her knees in the wet grass, loving him up.

"I told Burt," I say, "it's not about who chooses Whistler, it's about who Whistler decides to choose."

Mom shakes her head and drops an s-bomb, but it's the good kind, the one that's a rude version of "Wow, this is incredible." With her hands on Whistler's shoulders, taking him in at arm's length, she says, "Why did you run away? And how did you get here? What's wrong with you?"

She ruffles his head, rough and tough like he loves it, and he dips into it like he knows this attention is because he's done good.

"You are a freak dog," says Mom, "stubborn, dangerously willful, and not exactly handsome. Don't ask me how I'm going to make this happen—the embarrassing phone calls, the begging, hoping they understand, changing all the paperwork—but I'd have to be an idiot not to realize that you two are meant to be together."

"We can keep him?"

Mom looks at me as if I might need to stay back a year at school. "Like we have a choice," she says, before cracking up.

The grown-up tears of joy concept never made sense to me—pain, yeah, sadness, sure, but not joy. I was wrong. For the first time ever I am so happy I realize my eyes are getting watery so I bury my face in Whistler's neck, just in case things get embarrassing.

We head inside and Mom says, "You should get him something to eat and drink while I unload the car."

I bet he is hungry and thirsty and tired, but when I try to tune in, I can't tell which bit is me, and which bit is him. Why didn't I know Whistler was waiting for me? This was a big moment for both of us, so how come I never had a clue?

Then it hits me. What if he didn't let me in because he wanted it to be a surprise? What if I'm not the one in control? What if he's the one choosing whether he communicates with me and not the other way around? That makes total sense. That's why cats say no. That's why it's not all the time and not all dogs.

"You okay with pizza?" says Mom, carrying in a huge pile of junk mail and a few bills. Obviously she forgot to cancel the mail before we left for the hospital.

"Sounds great," I say. Whistler's zebra snout attacks my bowl full of kibble—in max vacuum cleaner mode—before it hits the floor.

Mom pauses on the way to the freezer, distracted by the number four on the answering machine. Almost no one calls our home number. She hits the play button as she pulls on the freezer door.

Message one is Grandma. "Would it help if I drop by with dinner tomorrow night, and if so, what would you like, and what time is best because I've got to—" Mom shocks me by pressing the delete button.

"I'm sorry, Jasper, I know Grandma means well, but sometimes there's no point in offering if all the burden is on me."

Message two is Auntie Gwen. "Tried your cell but you never

picked up. Hope Jasper's feeling better. Tell him he needs to be well for Thanksgiving. Love you both. Bye."

Guess we're hosting Thanksgiving again.

Message three is a robot reminding us I have medicine ready for pickup at the pharmacy. Boring.

Message four is not boring. Message four is scary.

"Hi, Dr. Blunt. Sorry to hear you were in the hospital. Hope you feel better. One of your colleagues passed on this number since it is a matter of some urgency and I have been unable to reach you. My name is Clayton Silver and I am eager to talk to you about a dog in your shelter's care, a real special dog, a dog that belongs to us and goes by the name of Whistler."

40

Kate

THE FIRST TIME I listen to the answering machine I'm barely paying attention, thinking, *Nice, Mom, whatever happened to you and me "clearing the air"*; and *Unbelievable Gwen*, squeezing in that passive-aggressive Thanksgiving reminder; and damn, totally spaced it, that guy Martha mentioned while Jasper was getting his PICC. Second time around I ignore the family drama and lock onto the stranger's details—his knowledge of the name Jasper chose for the dog and, far more disturbing, the phrase "belongs to us."

As I write down Clayton Silver's number I say, "Isn't that nice of Martha, giving out our home phone number . . ."

I turn and the two of them stare back at me, the hint of pink that had finally begun to color Jasper's cheeks gone, washed bone white, goofy black dog enhancing the contrast.

I'd be lying if I said it never crossed my mind, the notion that, once again, here was fate offering me a bona fide excuse to be rid of this dog. It's right there, flickering into life, independent, beyond my control, and, before this last visit to the hospital, no question, I'd have let it catch fire. I'd be sensitive to Jasper's frustration, but I'd stress this Mr. Silver's persistence, how his claim on Whistler sounds perfectly valid. And on the inside, I'd be quietly basking in the relief of not having to hunt for a new apartment, once more neatly sidestepping the responsibility of a four-legged variable in our lives. But now, I recognize the notion for what it is—an easy way out, inertia—and that's why I snuff it out.

For all my resistance, and skepticism, there's no denying one indisputable fact: Whistler, a dog who's drifted from one good home to the next, has gone out of his way to be with my son. Amazing how he got here in one piece. Amazing that *here* was where he needed to be. There's clearly something—I'm still not ready for "magical"—going on between them and I refuse to wrap my head around the notion that Jasper might be telling the truth about his so-called gift; but here's the thing: this improbable, impossible dog has given me a second chance. I don't think I'll ever forget Jasper's joy. Only now I bear witness to something far worse—the horror of watching that joy ripped from his face.

"Hey," I say, rushing to him, to them, "it's okay. Martha probably mentioned Whistler by name. My fault. The guy called days ago. And don't forget his microchip had Whistler registered to someone in Wellfleet. Technically he used to be Lucky, so this is almost certainly a case of mistaken identity."

"But the number Mr. Silver wants you to call, that's in Texas, and Texas is near Oklahoma, and we know Whistler was shipped from Oklahoma."

This slip-up, the fact that Jasper knows that three-digit area code equates with somewhere in Texas, is hard to ignore, but now is not the time.

"Don't worry," I say, guiding him to the couch, coaxing the Sasquatch to tag along, earning looks of confusion.

"What? Just make sure there's more scar than fur on my cushions. I'm going to start up another antibiotic. Then I'll bring you a slice. Sit tight, okay?"

I get a cautious nod and slowly the two relax, lock onto one another, and I raid a fridge laden with more medications than food.

The invention of the Eclipse is one of the main reasons why I said yes to leaving the hospital. It's basically a pressurized ball—smaller than a tennis, bigger than a golf—containing antibiotic that delivers the correct dose at the correct rate without the need for a cumbersome electric pump. Simply attach it to Jasper's PICC line in his arm, and, over the next hour or so, in it runs. He can be on the move, or fast asleep. All I have to do is make sure he gets it at exactly the right time.

Hooked up, chewing on Hawaiian pizza, he's not fooling me with the TV volume turned down low enough to try and listen in as I make my call. I would never wish hearing impairment on anyone, but right now, it might be for the best.

I introduce myself and in return receive an exaggerated "Finally," followed by a "My apologies, ma'am. We've been waiting a long time for this call."

"My son has been sick. Still is." Normally I wouldn't play the CF card from the get-go, but he asked for it.

"Sorry to hear that. Hate to pester you except this is most important."

He takes my silence as an invitation to go on.

"Perhaps I can explain our situation," says Clayton Silver. "We're in the service dog business, a nonprofit we call Paws Unlimited. Select, raise, train, and place special dogs for special folks in Southeast New Mexico, Northwest Texas, parts of Oklahoma, southern Kansas, and southern Colorado."

Is Clayton Silver a dog trainer?

"Six years back we spotted a dog in a local animal shelter, total mutt, really unique, but there was something about him. Didn't know what at first, but that's usually how it goes, take a chance, see what happens. Turned out this dog possessed a rare gift. Don't see it so often."

Part of me fears he's about to tell me the dog can "speak."

"Seizure alert. Alert, not response. Quite different. The ability to sense a seizure coming on in an epileptic long before it happens. Now the dog's partner can get help, find a safe place, take a preventative medication. It's a total game changer."

I glance back at the dog watching me, not even pretending, and I wonder if he recognized Clayton Silver's voice on the answering machine.

"Long story short, we placed him with a gentleman in Beaver Creek . . . Beaver Creek, Oklahoma."

Beaver Creek. The name sounds familiar and Silver obviously

thinks I should know it. School shooting? Thwarted terrorist plot? Last stand for a religious sect?

"The guy was dealing with up to three seizures a day before he got Whistler."

Up to this point I'm being polite, going through the motions, but hearing the dog referred to by name, so matter of fact, makes my stomach clench.

"Then the EF4 hit."

Got it. Beaver Creek. Destroyed by a massive tornado—notable for many fatalities.

"Whistler's partner didn't survive."

Silver inserts a pause for dramatic effect.

"The dog, nowhere to be found."

"Hold on. Service dogs get microchipped."

"Yes, ma'am."

"But the only microchip on the dog *we* call Whistler had him registered with a former owner on Cape Cod."

"Oh, I'm not surprised," says Silver. "Not after seeing the photographs you emailed."

Shock takes shape on my tongue, questions beginning to form, until it hits me—Martha.

"We tried everything to find that dog. Missing posters in every police station, alerts at every animal shelter in six counties. Whistler had a Facebook page, a YouTube video, all the local papers, radio, and TV stations shoutin' 'Anybody seen this dog?' But no one came forward. Not even after offering the reward."

He pauses, but if he's waiting for me to ask, "How much?"

my mind is too busy elsewhere. Yes, I spy on Jasper's browsing history and yes, sites listing lost, missing, and abandoned dogs frequently pop up. But what are the chances that my son literally recognized Whistler, a high-profile mystery dog? Is that how he decided on the dog's name?

"The big scar on his side, stretching over his shoulder blade," says Silver, "that's where his chip would have been."

How could the dog sprawled across my couch have survived a twister? Are his wounds consistent with trauma from flying shrapnel? Maybe, but not all of them.

"The scars across his snout. You're aware that he was probably—"

"Yes," says Silver. "Someone kept him against his will, someone who made sure he couldn't bark, couldn't alert a neighbor. Probably why no one could find him. The shelter from where he was shipped is over ninety miles away from Beaver Creek. And four years had passed. Without a chip, can't blame anyone for not making the connection."

I'm pacing the kitchen, nervous habit.

"But you seem to have made one."

Even to my ear that sounded hostile. He waits a beat before saying, "Cindy, from the Panhandle rescue, nice lady, gave me a call, totally out of the blue." Little laugh. "Like one of those TV murder mysteries, the break in a very cold case. She mentioned a dog her group had shipped out of Oklahoma, years back, a dog who'd been through the wars, a dog that kept running away from every good home that took him on. She said you were afraid this dog would be impossible to adopt. It got me to thinking—what sort of dog can't settle in a good home? And all I could think of was a dog that's looking for something and what if that something is a way back to Oklahoma? As soon as I saw the pictures, I knew it was him."

Time to wander into the privacy of my bedroom, closing the door behind me.

"Mr. Silver, even if this is the dog you think it is, you're too late. He's been adopted. He's happy, well taken care of, and I can guarantee he won't be running away ever again."

Silence and then the faintest hiss, almost a whisper. Is someone else with Silver, listening in?

"But, Dr. Blunt, I understood you—"

"Circumstances have changed. My son and I are going to keep him."

Another pause, long enough to suggest consultation rather than deliberation.

"Ma'am, I'm not sure you're grasping what I'm saying. This is a highly trained service dog. He belongs to us. Strictly speaking he is not available for adoption."

"Wait, you want to put him into service again? This . . . this dog is getting on in years and . . . and he's got a lung condition . . . a severe lung condition. I'd be happy to show you the radiographic proof. Really, after what he's been through, doesn't he deserve a decent retirement?"

"Dr. Blunt, this—"

"And my son's legally disabled. He's been asking for a service dog. And . . . and . . . now he's losing his hearing, so this works out perfectly. I mean . . . it's like they can't get enough of each other. You don't know me, Mr. Silver, but I do this for a living, and I swear I've never seen a stronger bond than I have with these two." The words scurry away from me, fast, without thinking, and it hits me—I've picked a side, Jasper's side, Whistler's side, and it feels good.

He hesitates before asking, "Does your son suffer from a seizure disorder?"

I'm tempted to lie but my indecision is all he needs.

"Dr. Blunt, this dog has a unique gift. What if your child had epilepsy? Wouldn't you want a dog, any dog, who could warn you, prevent a loved one from suffering the trauma of even one more seizure?" Clayton Silver sounds a little wooden, a little rehearsed, like he's reading from a script. "This dog is too valuable to be a pet."

Valuable? Is this about money?

"Mr. Silver, I'm going to need to see some kind of proof of ownership."

I hear a chuckle. "Dr. Blunt, here's what I'm going to do. This is a crazy week for us, busiest of the year, graduating our annual class of service dogs. Fortunately, our advisory board is around and meets again tomorrow. I'm happy to plead your case, but I wouldn't hold out too much hope."

"And what if I refuse to give him up?"

I mean what is he going to do, fly out a group of Navy SEALs to abduct Whistler in the middle of the night?

"Please, doctor, no one wants this to turn into an ugly custody battle. Imagine if the media got ahold of this story, printing a headline—'Selfish animal doctor denies sick child a service dog.'" He sucks down a sharp intake of breath like he's already got the media on standby.

"Unpleasant. Unnecessary. Far better to go with—'Hero animal doctor returns service dog missing for four years.' Much brighter ring to it, don't you think?"

I don't answer, but I don't have to.

"Like I said, I'll speak to the board and get back to you, but please, don't paint me as the bad guy. Whistler has the ability to transform a sick child's life. In good conscience, how can you stand in his way?"

He hangs up and I think, what am I going to tell my son, and, more importantly, why doesn't Whistler get to choose?

41

Jasper

ONCE, WHEN AUNTIE Gwen was babysitting, she forgot to give me my enzymes with dinner and my intestines began to ball up like the worst knot of Christmas lights you can imagine. The exact same thing happened when Mom pressed play on our answering machine, because as soon as we heard Mr. Silver's twangy cowboy voice, I felt the way Whistler jumped out of his scars. My mouth went sloppy—the English call it gobsmacked—and while I twitched and panicked, I couldn't tell if Whistler's surprise was the good kind or the bad.

"No one's taking him away just yet," says Mom, getting scary intense, making me lock onto her eyes when all I really want to do is cry.

Part of me thinks I might be about to die, like she's hiding something really bad about my disease. Why else would she act so opposite about keeping Whistler?

"And it turns out he's a highly trained service dog."

Despite the badness this was brilliant news.

"Then Mr. Crabtree will have to let him stay?"

"Definitely," she says, but she doesn't seem excited like me. "Look, Jasper, I'm going to find out everything I can about this Mr. Silver and Paws Unlimited. I'm not giving Whistler up without a fight."

So we start with their website.

"No shortage of ways to help you donate money," says Mom, clicking on a picture of a kid my age hugging a yellow Lab. I don't read as fast and she clicks on something else before I can finish but I still have time to focus on their happy faces and see the words "—changed my life forever."

"Guess this service dog graduation is a big deal."

Some famous congressman guy (I'd never heard of him) is giving a speech (yawn), there's a demo of service dog skills (cool), and tons of awards and certificates being handed out.

Stalking Clayton Silver is more tricky. There is no picture and he doesn't have a title like treasurer or secretary, but his bio says something about "integral to the success of our Capital Campaign" and "a true ambassador for Paws Unlimited."

Then Martha calls and Mom smiles and says, "This should be fun," putting her on speakerphone.

"I knew it. And the people who adopted him were perfect. Did a rabid beaver impersonation on their antique wooden chairs, and went psycho mole in their backyard. I listened to you, he had his chance, but when animal control tracks him down—"

"They won't," says Mom, eyeing me, "because he's here in my kitchen. Don't ask me how. He found us." And then, shocker of all shockers, she says, "You were right, Martha. I should have listened to you. I should have adopted him sooner."

Whoa. That shut her up. Then Martha comes back with, "Guess that microchip wasn't lying."

Mom and I keep quiet, but we turn to each other and our faces say, "What's she talking about?"

"His name," says Martha, "Lucky."

"His name's Whistler," says Mom, loud and snippy and kind of over the top.

Then she switches off the speaker, puts the phone up to her ear, and says, "Martha, back when I was in the hospital, d'you remember you called me and said something about Lucky the dog, or maybe someone being lucky . . ." Pause. "Okay, maybe he is, but . . . it was the way you said it. Your tone." Longer pause. "'Cause it sounded, well, kind of mean, kind of accusa-tory." Pause. "Nearly a week ago, when we first got admitted." Pause. "Really? Nothing?" Longest pause ever. "No, that's fine, I just . . . yes . . . sure . . . yeah . . . I'll be in touch."

Who's lucky? Can't be me.

Mom blows out a breath, lips fluttering, and says, "I don't know about that girl. She finally opens the door a hair, a crack, makes to let me in, but the moment I step forward—*bam*—she slams it shut in my face."

Unlike Mom, and without using words that make no sense, Whistler and I exchange our own exact same look that says, "What is she talking about?"

But Mom never shares, and even though Whistler's sort of been my dog for . . . twenty-five hours and . . . thirty-seven minutes, deep down, something still doesn't feel like I'm his or he's mine. The fact that we're keeping him locked up in the apartment like a fugitive isn't helping. And right now, I'm on lookout, standing on a chair, balanced in front of our kitchen window, ready to warn Mom by knocking on the glass if Mr. Crabtree appears while she's sneaking Whistler across his yard for a pee. Still, I told Mom she might as well help with his deer problem and it's a good excuse if they get caught.

Now the flashlight beam hasn't moved for thirty seconds—probably number two and hopefully not near the rosebushes—when the phone rings, my new height (standing on the chair) giving me a bead on the caller ID, and there it is, the same number with the Texas area code—Cowboy Clay is back.

Mom is a tiny twinkle in the distance, too far away for me to shout. Let it go to voice mail? No way. I've had too many hospital visits where grown-ups try to sugarcoat the truth. Stew-pid phrase. Who makes a coat out of sugar?

"Hello."

"Ah, Jasper, nice to speak to you . . . again." He's using my name like we're best buds. "Your mom there?"

"Not right now."

"That's okay. Better to speak to you, anyway. I mean, you're the one who wants the dog, right?"

"Right."

"Here's the thing. I'm sure your mom told you that Whistler has a special gift."

"I already knew."

"You did?"

"Yes." I know Mom wants me to keep it a secret but I add, "He can tell me what he's feeling. If he wants."

"Hum. That's . . . great, but I was thinking about his ability to anticipate a seizure, before it occurs."

"I get it. He reads me all the time, only I don't seizure."

"Exactly. And that's my point. You have cystic fibrosis."

I can't tell if he's asking a question or stating a fact. Did Mom say something or has he been checking me out?

"Yes."

"Truly sorry," he says, and there's something about the way he says it. Maybe it's the "truly" but when some people find out and say sorry, it's like I told them I got a paper cut or need a filling for a tooth. Cowboy Clay's "sorry" sounds like he really means it.

"Tough disease to live with, but, from what I've read, your brain is perfectly fine. See, we need Whistler back in our program because there are so many kids, kids your age, whose brains are not perfectly fine."

I think about Andy Peach in the year below me at school, peeing his pants when he had a seizure in class, some of the mean kids making fun of him.

"What this dog can do is nothing short of amazing. It's a gift and incredibly rare. Some facilities train service dogs, place them with an epileptic, and hope the dog will bond and learn to predict a seizure. It might take months. It might never happen. Whistler is the real deal. He's already proven he can do it."

I wonder how rare it really is? I bet most dogs are screaming, "You might not want to drive that car right now," but we're not smart enough to feel them.

"Think of it this way," says Cowboy Clay, "if I told you I had a dog who could stop your coughing, you'd want him, right?"

This is probably a trap but of course I say, "Yes."

"Well, Whistler is that dog for children who have epilepsy." Seconds pass before he says, "You ever donate toys or games to poor kids in your community, at the holidays? Drop a few quarters in the Salvation Army box? Sure you do. So you know how it feels better to give than to receive."

Now he's lost me. It's one thing to give away some toy you'd kind of like to play with yourself. It's totally different to give away something you physically love.

"Look, there's a girl here, about your age, her name is Emily, Emily Smart. She has epilepsy and she's been at the top of our waiting list for a seizure alert dog for way too long. We'd love to offer her Whistler."

I think about the phrase from their website—changed my life forever—and part of me wants to say, "What about my life?"

"But you live in Texas."

"I do, but our facility is based across the border in New Mexico."

"Are you going to send someone to take Whistler away?"

"Sure, if that's easiest. I can organize to pick him up, drive to Boston, fly him out to Oklahoma City, and we'll take it from there. But . . ."

He leaves me hanging and I'm thinking, what kind of a dog lover would he be making Whistler fly cargo? He must have read the stats on air travel for pets. What if Whistler overheats or freezes or gets lost?

". . . if I did, you wouldn't be eligible for the reward."

Wait a minute. Mom never mentioned a—

"Didn't your Mom mention it? Set up by one of our donors shortly after the tornado. Big deal with the media, made them realize the importance of service dogs. Still stands, but the language of the reward is clear—*Safe return*."

"How much?"

"Twenty-five thousand dollars. Think about it. Not only do you get to do something selfless and special for a little girl in need, you also have enough money to get a service dog of your own, a dog perfect for your specific needs."

But Whistler is that dog, I want to reply until I remember something Mom says every time we're in the hospital. "Look around, Jasper. You're not alone. There are plenty of kids far worse off than you."

I can see the kid on the Paws Unlimited website hugging his yellow Lab. If someone really needs Whistler more than me, then I think they should have him.

"I know it's short notice, but we'd like him back in time for our graduation this weekend."

"But that's only five days from now." I keep the "and what about my IV antibiotics" to myself.

"Yes, but I'd love for you to be the one to present Whistler to Emily. I want you to see her face, her smile, her tears, as you give her the gift of a dog who can make her feel normal."

Wow, he's better than one of those ads for starving children in Africa. I guess I could get my own service dog, but I'd be just as happy with a dog from the shelter. Then we could use the money to find a new place to live and help pay off Mom's college debt.

"Jasper, can you help me convince your mom?"

I don't know what to say. Staring at the floor in silence is my normal reply to difficult questions.

"Why don't you and your mom bring him out here? Think of it as an adventure, a fun way of spending your last few days together, a chance to say a long and meaningful goodbye."

It turns out (though I would never tell Mom), I'm already pretty good at saying goodbye. There's this online forum for kids with CF where we whine about our treatments, our coughs, and our crappy lung function tests, but sometimes it gets competitive, like with my friend Josh, from Cleveland, who's my age, saying, "My five weeks in ICU beats your sinus surgery with complications any day." And every so often, someone who's really sick, like Morgan—thirteen, from Hawaii, season one veteran in Fortnite—will play the ultimate trump card: lung transplant. No one can top this. Getting on the list for a lung transplant is bad, sands-running-out-oxygen-tank-on-empty bad. Somewhere in cyberspace, on the other end of a keyboard, we're left to wonder: Does this kid get a future? And if her posts go quiet, did the new lungs work, did she finally get to breathe, able to forget about her fellow sufferers, or, despite her last chance, did she run out of time?

Whistler deserves the best send-off ever. No question. But how can he teach me everything I need to know about dogs in five days? I want to cry. I don't want to be brave.

"Jasper, can I count on you to make this happen? Jasper?"

Part II

How many things would you attempt if you knew you could not fail.

—Robert Frost

42

Jasper

"My name is Jasper Blunt."

The bald guy in the blue TSA uniform smirks and flutters my birth certificate in the air. "Not you. The dog."

Whistler sits by my side, the noseband of his Gentle Leader denting the zebra stripes, fake jacket snug and masking the biggest scar.

"Whistler."

"Service or therapy?"

"Service," I say.

Bald guy, too lazy to get off his stool, leans out to the side of his podium, looks Whistler up and down, and comes back to Mom with an expression that wrinkles his forehead.

My hands are shaking. This is the scary bit. Cowboy Clay emailed us a letter to show security, explaining our trip, but Mom says, "It won't hold up in court"—whatever that means. I read online that sometimes, totally random, TSA will ask to see a service dog license. If they do, we're busted.

Bald guy thinks about it, pen hovering over our boarding cards before laying down some chicken scratch and gesturing for the three of us to move on.

Don't smile, don't celebrate, stay cool. There's still more work to be done. Next up, the metal detector.

Whistler takes my sit command, waits for me to pass under the tall, silent rectangle and then, responding to a finger flick, trots through. We've practiced going through open doorways, but what if something metallic in his vest sets it off, he's stripped naked and I have to explain away the big, big scar.

No alarm bells. Still, the boys and girls in blue stare, dying to know—what's the disability? But here's the best part: They're not allowed to ask, except questions like "What does my dog do for me?" Switching on lights, opening doors, and fetching toilet paper might not cut it. Warns me my blood sugar is running low feels too specific. So, if asked, I'm going to go with "He keeps me calm," together with a raised eyebrow, just to freak them out a little, like they might want to order up an air marshal.

43

Kate

"GATE A19 IS this way," says Jasper, loud and fake, glaring at my guilty smile, desperate for me to stop looking like the shoplifter who didn't get caught. He and his wreck of a crooked dog head toward a mechanical walkway and I think, *I'm sure there was a time when this idea made sense.* But as the three of us weave and bob through a rowdy crush on our way to the gate, the glitches in my plan leave me feeling too indulgent, too spontaneous, and worst of all, too exposed.

Here's my original train of thought. Jasper is doing well and out of school for the next week. Home or not, I can handle his grueling regime of IV antibiotics, thanks to my illicit stash of little blue helpers. Another unscheduled absence from work is awkward but in my email to KGB, I stressed how I was using vacation time to "unburden the shelter of an unadoptable dog." She's yet to reply.

Jasper's conviction that a little girl named Emily needs

Whistler more than he does is impossibly endearing and impossible to contradict. Even though I thought Paws Unlimited was acting more like a covert government agency, tracking down a valuable asset gone rogue, it's obvious they want Whistler back for the right reasons. If Mr. Crabtree busts us for keeping a dog in the apartment, we'll be sleeping in our truck. So why not get on with it? Of course I'd prefer a fast goodbye. But part of me believes this trip is a small concession to a boy prepared to give up the canine love of his life.

When I lay it out like this, and squint hard, I can make out a semblance of logic. The shelter will be okay—though I'm not exactly sure where I'll find the money for quarterly taxes and next month's payroll—thanks to Doc Wickham, seventy-two years old, still twice as fast as me at canine castration, and happy to cover as needed. But I can't escape the intangible influence of a sick child enlightened by a magical dog. I can still hear Jasper's drowsy bedridden mutterings, the prattle of an older (maybe wiser) CF mom, and it's more than being haunted, I don't want their message to fall on deaf ears. My son is living with his disease. Thanks to me, maybe he's not been living enough. By agreeing to this odyssey, no one can say I didn't listen.

To be clear, I don't like to fly.

"We could make this a road trip," I offered. "Take Norman."

"Mom, Norman can barely make it over the Sagamore Bridge, let alone the nineteen hundred and eighty-four miles to New Mexico."

This led to a nonnegotiable stipulation. Direct flight (therefore not Oklahoma City), no planes small enough to double as a crop duster, and flight times that work with the antibiotic schedule. To get to Lincoln Peak, New Mexico, we're flying to Dallas and renting a car. From there it should be a seven-hour drive, give or take. Quicker to go through Denver, but the flight gets in late, and I've read about those crosswinds whipping off the Rockies.

Aside from a mother trying to console a crying baby and a pair of lip-locked teenagers, the stares begin again as soon as we find a seat at the gate. Never thought I'd wish for one of those portable green oxygen tanks, give my boy some overtly disabled credibility. I can tell what they're thinking, there's nothing physical, so it must be mental. Autistic, bipolar, schizophrenic? Will he freak out midflight and charge the cockpit? What if he uses his dog as a weapon?

Whistler is fueling more skepticism than curiosity. Not that I can fault his behavior. His performance has been impeccable. It's his breed, or rather lack of it, attracting the wrong kind of attention. The public is used to service dogs plucked from the Labrador rainbow of yellow, chocolate, or black. Whistler's genetic goulash looks wrong. And the vest can only hide so much. Shouldn't a service dog be normal, not disabled? What if the mute dog finds his voice on take off? If he misbehaves, will the pilot be forced to make an emergency landing, so he can kick us off the flight?

I listen for the overhead page, ready to pounce—"Any passengers with small children and those in need of extra time"—maybe we should have driven after all.

44

Jasper

"Wasn't he brilliant?" I say as soon as Mom, Whistler, and I head for Dallas/Fort Worth International Airport baggage claim.

"'Course I knew he wouldn't bark but not even a whine at take off or landing or when we hit that turbulence. He must need a bathroom break. You know some airports have pet toilets with fake grass, even lampposts and fire hydrants so that dogs will want to—"

"Jasper, dial it back, will you? Have you been mixing Red Bull with your antibiotics?"

Whistler checks over his shoulder blade, eyes me, but keeps the beat. I can tell he likes leading the way. Maybe Mom's right, maybe I am getting a little overexcited.

Whistler easily finds our luggage on the carousel (I placed a couple of Milk-Bones in the front pockets of mine and Mom's suitcases) and we follow arrows to the car rental desk.

"You have a reservation?" asks a guy without looking up from his monitor.

His white shirt is creasy, his black tie narrow, the knot too loose below an open top button—Grandma would be all over him. His name tag says "Dwayne."

Mom slides over the paperwork I printed out and that's when Dwayne notices Whistler.

"Sorry, but no pets allowed in rental vehicles."

"He's my service dog."

Dwayne does this goofy snort and pushes the paperwork back in Mom's direction.

Mom leans across the counter and growls, "Look, Mr. Dwayne, maybe you'd prefer I speak to your manager about your violation of my son's civil liberties according to the Americans with Disabilities Act."

Mom can be really scary when she wants to be. Safe to say Dwayne got us into our car real fast. And best of all, he never tried to sell us on an upgrade.

45

Kate

WHAT HAVE I done? Jasper was the one who researched and booked our flights, but I own the stark and glaring mistake that is our choice of rental car.

"Dwayne promised it's got AC," says Jasper, peering into the tiny, brilliant white, two-door Fiat 500.

"Yeah," I say. "I'm sure it's also got seats and a steering wheel, but that's about it."

If I said this trip had nothing to do with the reward money, I'd be lying. Unlike the professional cyclist who never doped or the surgeon who never has complications, I acknowledge the $25,000 elephant in the room. Yes, it's crass and it should be irrelevant, but come on, I'm not stupid. If Jasper is getting a dog, which I swear he is, we're not moving to his version of a dog-friendly apartment. Staying in the same school district will require a bigger first and last and bigger monthly payments. Even if my accountant buys this as a business trip, I'm still the one with significant out-of-pocket expenses. Anything I can do to minimize our costs and maximize this unexpected nest egg, I'm doing for my son, and that includes my choice of rental car.

Silent but brimming with jubilation, Jasper slips in next to me, up front—no booster seat (I didn't want to push our luck with Dwayne)—while Whistler sprawls across the rear passenger seats and still manages to look squashed.

"Okay, everything's in the trunk. You're belted up. How's your Eclipse?"

"My Eclipse is smashing," says Jasper. "About ten more minutes and I'm done. Want me to navigate?"

I ignore "smashing," distracted by the fact that this particular model lacks a GPS navigation system. Like I said, we're on a budget, and besides, isn't that what smart phones are for?

"Sure," I say, firing up this tin can on a roller skate, negotiating our way out of the airport, heading northwest on highway 287.

Having spent most of my life in New England, where so many highway vistas are limited by dense forest, I'm struck by how far I can see; because everything is so flat, spirit-level flat, endless-horizon flat. It's like this place has extra sky.

"How come no one lives here?" says Jasper. "Too many gaps between the trees."

"I kind of like seeing this much open space."

Jasper thinks about this, doesn't look convinced, and concludes, "Too empty."

Behind us, Whistler fidgets, unable to settle.

"Can you make that dog calm down?"

Jasper twists around, tries to pet pacing fur, but the dog is especially restless.

"He's telling me he definitely knows where he's going?"

For that my son earns a sideways glare.

"Jasper, we talked about this. We're going to make the best of this trip and I'll try my best to make it fun, but you promised to lighten up on the dog-speak and the English speak, remember?"

I earn a "Sorry, Mom," and ignore the twitching blackness filling my rearview mirror.

By hitting the road a little after four in the afternoon, I had hoped to knock off the bulk of the drive today, stay over at a motel, and get to the Paws Unlimited facility late tomorrow morning. Thirty minutes in and my copilot and his copilot have other ideas.

"Mom, I'm hungry."

Undone by the change in time zones and my pathological inability to deny Jasper any interest in calories—hunger means he's feeling good—a lengthy and tedious detour is rewarded with the culinary delights of the golden arches. No sooner are we back on the road when Mr. Whistler—he of the defiant "I don't need to pee or poop" stare when he had his chance—decides to fill the gap between the front seats, attempting klutzy three-sixties, briefly blinding me with his tail like I'd best pull over or else.

Finally, ablutions performed and everyone, including the beast, excessively fed and watered—this part of the world is making my brain think in cowgirl—we scrunch up in our faux Italian wheels, pretend to be comfortable, and thread our way down a needle-straight highway that rapidly saps at my brain. How much fun can this road trip possibly be? Silver confided that they plan to surprise Jasper, make a big deal about him returning Whistler at their graduation ceremony, and I hope he enjoys it. But what if it feels like a straight trade—dog for money?

Way off in the distance, I notice a tiny vertical smudge, and, as we get closer, it mutates into a stick figure, standing by the side of the road.

"Slow down," shouts Jasper, the dog lunging forward, practically on his lap, straining at the glass, trying to get a better look at a rare life-form.

The figure comes into focus—tall and rangy, arm outstretched, thumb extended, the back of a dark hoody, the words *Go Buffs* trapped in the beam of our headlights.

"We should stop," says Jasper. "I've never met a hitchhiker."

I take my foot off the gas and slow enough for the man to glance our way—dark eyes, pale face, drawstring pulled tight to his head. His body comes around, walking backward, hopeful that his luck has changed.

Then I gun the accelerator, past him so fast he's a blur, pulling back his arm just in time, Whistler out of the passenger seat and pressed into the rear window, transfixed by the image of a man shrinking into the distance.

"Mom. Not cool. What if no one picks him up?"

I don't know where to begin. These two clearly have a thing for hobos and drifters, but what about rapists and serial killers?

"Not sure if you've noticed, but it's a little cramped in here. And how do you know he didn't just escape from a maximum security prison?"

Jasper checks in with the yeti once more filling the gap between us.

"Don't answer that. Look, it's a nice gesture and I agree, there aren't many other cars around, but I've got to think about our safety. Could you take a look in my purse and pass me the Advil?"

Jasper comes back with a childproof container of my inappropriately labeled pills. I've read articles about moms getting hooked and having problems with self-confidence because they think their achievements stem from the Adderall. Not me. When you're a parent living with CF, you live with three constants—fear, guilt, and doubt. You give in to any of them and you're doomed. No drug, especially this drug, is going to take any credit away from me. And besides, the same article said most moms need Klonopin to get to sleep. I'm pretty sure the occasional swig from a bottle of NyQuil doesn't count.

I down a pill and take a slurp from a water bottle as Jasper slumps into the door. This is when I justify my vice. What better way to concentrate on driving and stay awake for his round of nighttime antibiotics?

"Thanks, Mom." He smiles, but his fluttering lids tell me he's ready for a nap. It's been a long day.

"For what?"

"For making this happen."

"Who wouldn't want to drive a lonely highway across Texas in the pitch black with a dog cutting the worst farts ever?"

"Did I mention how much I love you, Mother?"

"No, I don't think you did."

About to reach over and pat his hand, I catch myself, thinking he's already asleep, but then he mumbles, "Why did I never have a brother or sister?"

What? Forget about Adderall, I'm wide awake, wondering where on earth that came from. Since when did Jasper want a sibling? But before I can ask, he's snoring, the mutt imploring me to keep my eyes on the road. I do as I'm told, hands at ten and two, hearing Whistler flop down, sigh, and join Jasper in dreamland.

I should be grateful I don't have to answer, but now I'm alone with my thoughts, left to wonder if this is really about him or me. Is his passion for a dog borne of loneliness—his lack of friends except for Burt—or is he beginning to see our future in a new light? Up until the Dr. Holden Patterson incident—Jasper confessed that he had mistaken what he called a "promising suitor" for Martha's scuzzy second cousin—my son has wavered between revulsion and apathy whenever Gwen mentions my lack of male companionship. What's changed? His need for a father figure? His belief that I'd be happier with a boyfriend, partner, or husband? Secretly I'd love a special someone to sweep me off my feet, but let's get real, my prospects are limited. Since Jasper I've become less of a woman and more of a mom, and that's my choice because, for all those moments when I rail against my lot, when I scream and curse and lose it over the hand that I've been dealt, no matter how crushed and defeated I feel, I never do blame. Our situation is nobody's fault. If my son notices what I may or may not have sacrificed, he's realizing it on his own.

The night before we flew out to Texas, I weakened and found myself stalking the mysterious Holden Patterson online. From his hospital website photo—Gwen was right, not bad-looking at

all—I perceived a genuine kindness in his eyes, a softness, something compassionate, something you can't fake for the camera.
Without thinking, I scoured his bio, willing him to be a pediatric
pulmonologist. But would it help, for me not to have to explain
our situation, or hinder, for him to know more than enough to
run screaming? "Please don't be a plastic surgeon," I said out
loud, and my prayers were answered. Sort of. "Specializing in
geriatric medicine." Guaranteed he never sees a patient with CF.

Drafting an email to a complete stranger felt kind of futile,
but harmless, an opportunity to thwart Gwen's meddling. I kept
it brief, innocent, mentioned my sister, my brother-in-law, and
made a standing offer to help him find the right dog through our
shelter. I read and re-read the paragraph, hunting for innuendo,
flirtation, anything unprofessional or open to interpretation.
And there was something cathartic in the process, a thrill in
writing to a man I don't know, a man who may be right for me,
for us, but in the end I couldn't bring myself to press send. It's
still sitting there in the drafts folder, biding its time, destined
for a date with the delete button, just like my romantic future.

To be honest, the thought of having more children always
came down to one thing: risk. If things had worked out with the
infamous Simon Swift, the chance of CF in Jasper's sibling was
one in four. Out in the wider world of dating, if you are white,
the chance of hooking up with a CF carrier is one in twenty-
three. Maybe Jasper feels differently, but the risk that stops me
cold has nothing to do with long odds. It's the risk that my son
might feel replaced, and, worse still, an imperfect millstone
around my neck. It's a risk I'm not prepared to take.

Time and miles slip behind us but Jasper's question lingers, worming around in my mind, when we're dazzled in the high beams of an oncoming eighteen-wheeler. It screams past, the Doppler shift rattling our flimsy Fiat, and Jasper wakes up.

"Where are we?"

"Ask the guy in charge of navigation."

He reaches into the foot space where the phone has slipped off his seat. "It's dead," he says.

"What do you mean?"

"I've got full power, but no signal."

There's nothing to see outside the window except black, impossible to tell whether the occasional twinkle is a star or a residence, heavenly or earthbound.

"Maybe it's a bad patch. Try again in a bit."

And then the first burst of color pops into my visual field—bright red, shaped like a wrench, and coinciding with a seismic shudder from somewhere beneath my feet.

"Sorry," I say, chastened, way too late for the runaway swear. The engine recovers but the warning light stays on.

In the glow of the dashboard Jasper looks over but doesn't speak. Life with Norman-the-4Runner has us acclimatized to roadside disasters.

"If I could get a signal, I could tell you how far to the next town or rest stop or gas station."

A minute passes. The steering wheel dithers in my grip.

"If I could get a signal, I could tell you how far a Fiat 500 can safely travel when the red wrench lights up."

I'm guessing that means he still can't get a signal.

"Did we pass a station when I was asleep?"

I think back, look over at Whistler. He stares back. If this is me understanding "dog," then he's as clueless as I am.

"God, Jasper, I don't know." I play around with the controls until I can get my high beams to work. "Keep an eye out for anything that might be a gas station or a town. Or alive."

Crushing the rising anger between my clenched molars doesn't help. This is everything I feared. This is precisely what happens when you're a weak, overindulgent parent. Our situation would be annoying for a parent of a regular kid, but it's potentially disastrous for the parent of a kid with Jasper's medical needs. Time to jettison regret and go straight to self-loathing.

"There," shouts Jasper, pointing, and I see it, a white fuel pump logo, an arrow right and below it, "One mile."

Whistler heaves a sigh—relief, boredom, disappointment, don't ask me.

I pray to the Fiat gods for the little engine to hang in there, willing it to survive, grateful for every yard of asphalt gained and suddenly we see it, another fuel pump sign together with an arrow at what appears to be an unmarked exit. I try not to focus on the fact that the sign does not conform to the usual State Highway Department standards and looks as though it has been painted by hand.

Swerving right, the beams lock onto a narrow two-lane highway, an empty billboard, barbed-wire fencing, and rocky scrub peppered by the occasional scraggly bush. Coasting softens the metallic grinding sound of the engine, lessens the rattle of the chassis, and on little more than momentum, we glide at least another mile.

Then the road does the unthinkable.

It comes to an end.

There's only one sign to help us out—a standard red stop sign. No arrows left. No arrows right. I'm beginning to wonder if this is some kind of prank or something more sinister? Are we about to be carjacked, or worse?

The engine bucks but doesn't stall. I stifle a scream.

"Left or right," I say, way too loud, too jumpy and impatient. I'm thinking about how much power is left in the portable nebulizer. How long before the travel cooler is no longer cool and Jasper's meds, his vital antibiotics, start to crystallize and turn useless?

I half expect my son to shout the answer, any answer, like a blind coin toss. Instead, he powers down his window, considers me, and then, I kid you not, he confers with the dog. By this I mean they stare at each other for a full five seconds before he comes back with a confident "Right, definitely right."

Right it is.

And three miles later, in the middle of nowhere, the engine succumbs to a violent and sudden death.

46

Jasper

BACK AT THE stop sign, just before the Fiat died, I rolled down
the window, checked in with Whistler, and he totally agreed.

Definitely turn right.

That's because of the list I made of all the things I need to get
done on this trip, knowing some of them will be harder than others.

1. Learn everything I can about dogs and what they're
   thinking before I have to say goodbye to Whistler.

2. Make sure Whistler doesn't think he's being abandoned.
   This is tricky. He's going to know where he's going,
   and if I were him I'd probably feel like a bit of a reject,
   kind of like Wayne Rooney signing with the MLS.

3. Try to be happy. Also tricky because there's this rock,
   heavy and sad, that I can feel inside me and it won't

go away and every now and then I remember that it's there. I worry that Whistler knows where it's buried and he's going to try and dig it up.

4. Get Mom to believe me and teach her how to do what we do. She needs to know that I'm not making this up, that "speaking dog" might prove useful on her résumé if she needs to look for a new job.

5. There's another, more important reason why I want Mom to believe me, but if I tell her she'll feel really sad so I'm keeping it to myself.

6. Have fun. Make this trip an adventure. Whatever it takes to remember my last few days with the best dog in the world.

Idea number six is the easiest of the bunch. I mean, I'm glad we're doing this and I like spending time with Mom, but this is still a seven-hour road trip and after a while we're going to run out of stuff to say. Why not shake it up, give a hitchhiker a ride? Better than staring out the window, right? And he didn't look like a murderer to me. Sometimes, when I eat over at Auntie Gwen's, her cooking tastes kind of bland and I don't want to be rude so I ask for ketchup or A.1. Sauce to spice it up. I figured that's what I'd have to do on this trip.

Seems like the Fiat wants to help me out as well.

47

Kate

THE CHIRP OF crickets fills the silence, the blackness absolute.

"Phone still dead?"

Jasper checks. "We can use it as a flashlight."

I think about Morse code, but based on the absence of any surrounding light, there's no one out there to receive our SOS signal.

I slap the steering wheel. Actually I pummel it with both hands, growling before scrambling out of our toy car, slamming its door shut, screaming until every last pocket of air has left my lungs.

"Goddamn it," I bark into the abyss. "Why is this happening? What did I do wrong? What did *he* do wrong? Why can nothing ever go right?"

Coming around the front of the car, I hang my head and lean into the bubble hood. The headlights are still on high beam, but are barely denting the black.

I chose to do this, I elected to do something spontaneous for my son, and this is how I get paid back—trapped in the middle of nowhere in the smallest, stupidest vehicle on the planet, breathing in an ugly dog's colonic by-products, and . . . and . . . no, Kate, not now, not when I need to be . . . The tears are away from me, the sobs visceral, raw failure and frustration bursting from my core, leaking from my eyes, shaking loose from my shoulders and chest.

"It's okay, Mom."

Jasper sidles up to one side, his wool-less mammoth gets the other.

"Someone will drive by. It won't be long. This road has to be headed somewhere."

It takes another thirty seconds before I can put an arm around my boy. Time to snap out of it.

"Definitely."

For a while we sit, staring forward, letting our eyes adjust, and slowly, despite the darkness, a sensation of space, of vastness opens up around us.

"It feels good to be outside at night," I say.

The night air is comfortable and still, a perfect mild humidity. No bugs. No need for a jacket. There's no moon, no stars, but there's this awareness of being on the edge of something. I pick up a stone and toss it out. It ricochets off rock, skitters, and stops. I guess we're not about to drop off a cliff.

"Okay, let's reassess our situation. We have a perfectly functional, if cramped, shelter. I can still do your treatments even if your chest PT will be suboptimal. We have plenty of water and Gatorade. The car battery works, so if we need to, I can still charge your nebulizer."

I keep the problem of refrigeration to myself.

"What time is it?"

Jasper consults the phone.

"Nine seventeen."

His ten o'clock antibiotic has to be precisely on time. It's about four miles back to the highway. We'll definitely find a passing car but that's a long way for Jasper to walk and there's no way I'm leaving him here. Three miles back to the stop sign but how much farther to this mysterious gas station? I lash out at a rock but it doesn't budge, the inanimate object making me stub my toe.

"Come on." Once more I'm shouting at the heavens. "Somebody. Anybody. Don't make us sleep in a sardine can."

We sit there, for ten minutes. Nothing.

"Promise you won't be mad," says Jasper.

Every mother knows no good can possibly come from hearing that line.

He wanders off to the trunk of the car, pulls out his suitcase, and returns carrying a chunky black nylon bag in his arms.

Jasper speaks before I can ask.

"Remember when I said my suitcase was already full."

"Yes," I say, discovering a sarcastic tone, "thanks to your meds, I barely had room for underwear, let alone actual clothes."

He shakes the bag and it clanks.

"What is it?"

"Only the lightest, most compact, most portable two-man tent in the world."

"Jasper," I screech, loud enough for the sound to linger like a pseudo echo, a reverberation to give emphasis. "I thought you sent it back?"

"I meant to, but . . . well . . . this is supposed to be an adventure, right? And I thought camping would be more fun than a hotel. Aren't you glad I didn't send it back?"

"No."

"But this way I can do my chest PT lying down, and we don't have to wait in the car."

Sneaky little . . . he's got all the answers.

"How and where are you going to set it up?"

"Right here on the gravel, next to the car where it's flat. It's quick and easy. I watched the how-to video on YouTube seven times."

My son spends way too much time surfing the Internet. What else is he watching?

And so, cell phone flashlight in hand, I shine my beam in the right places as he erects the tent like a camping pro. Five minutes and it's up.

Whistler insists on being first to pad across the threshold, while Jasper grabs a sweatshirt and my one and only sweater to use as a pillow. I bring in the nebulizer and the rest of his nighttime medications and get started on pummeling his lungs.

"We're finally camping, Mom." The words get chopped up into stutters by the chest PT. "Isn't this great?"

He reaches out to touch Whistler's paws, closes his eyes, and grins.

"As soon as a car drives by we're done. I hope you can break down this tent as fast as you can put it up."

Jasper nods but once again he's getting tired.

"And what if we're attacked by a bear, or a mountain lion?"

"Mom. We've got Whistler. He'll scare them off."

"Right, with that big booming bark of his."

Whistler squirms and cozies into the far end of the tent. The definition of *two-man* is clearly less than one adult female, one boy, and one moose of a freak dog.

At ten o'clock on the dot, I hook up the IV antibiotic and wait as it infuses his blood over the next ninety minutes. Jasper is asleep. Whistler is asleep. All medications and treatments have been delivered appropriately and on time (including those for the dog). Despite our circumstances, despite my fear and frustration, normal services have been resumed.

One o'clock comes and goes and I'm still awake. I can't stop listening, waiting for the faintest murmur of an engine, ready to hurl myself in front of a passing vehicle like I'm committing insurance fraud. At this rate, come first light, we'll have no choice but to walk back the way we came to get help.

Wait a minute. According to my son, he could just ask Whistler to do his best Lassie impersonation and rustle up a rescue party.

I'm still pondering this possibility when a tangerine glimmer of light hits my eyelids and I realize they've fallen shut. I've been asleep. The sun must be coming up. I shuffle over to the sealed flaps and, careful not to wake my fellow campers, tease open the zipper.

Before me, cast in the palest flicker of a golden glow, lies a valley, a canyon cut into rock. The air is fresh and fragrant, the view top heavy, big sky above a sliver of rugged earth, the effect humbling and breathtaking. Despite the ache in my shoulder from sleeping on a crag, despite the twitch in my brain from the caffeine-deprived headache beginning to brew, it's hard not to be awed by this location.

I turn to look at Jasper. His head rests on Whistler's big scar, but more importantly, for the first time in such a long time, he's sleeping on his back. Usually his diseased lungs fight this configuration. Not tonight. It reminds me of when he was a baby, of innocence, profound security, and the certainty that I will take care of him forever.

For a second Whistler raises one eyelid, his good left eye. It's as if the dog is appraising my appraisal of the situation and having read my approval, he's confident he can go back to sleep. It makes me wonder. Did the two of them plan this? Did I play into another one of their crazy schemes?

I glance outside once more and realize I'm experiencing an unusual sensation—contentment. Maybe the wrong turn was the right turn after all.

Then I hear the noise.

48

Jasper

WICKED COOL.

It's big, really big and it doesn't purr, it roars, deafening and scary. Mom's jumping up and down in the middle of the road, screaming and waving her hands, but as the motorbike crests a rise and comes into sight she instantly stops.

The biker slows and crunches to a halt, plants his black leather boots, and cuts the engine. Whistler sits at my side, tail sweeping the gravel back and forth into neat little ridges. He's as excited as I am. I glance at Mom. Her left eye twitch is back.

"Morning," he says. "Car trouble?" His voice is deep and gritty. The bike is like a black stallion—scary, wild, and massive. I guess it has to be to carry its owner. He's wearing a sleeveless leather vest, dirty jeans, sunglasses, and he's got this crazy gray beard that reaches to his belly and tattoos that cover his arms. Then I notice the best part. There's a holster on his hip. He's carrying a gun.

"Yes," says Mom, sounding as though she's not sure. "But the tow truck is on its way."

The man checks out Mom and then breaks into a smile. He's got teeth.

"Right," he says before turning to me, saying, "cool place for camping. This your dog?"

"Not really," I say, "we're taking him to New Mexico. We're from Cape Cod."

Mom glares at me. Sometimes I think she needs to lighten up and be more friendly to people.

"What's his name?" asks the biker.

"Whistler."

I notice the way the two halves of his beard pull apart like curtains when he smiles.

"Whistler? As in James Abbott McNeill Whistler, the artist? What was it he said . . . yeah . . . 'art for art's sake'; that's his famous line."

Whistler the dog shuffles forward, sniffing the bottom of the man's jeans.

"Interesting," says Mom, way too chirpy, circling around to get close beside me. "But let's not bother the . . . the nice man. I'm sure the tow truck will be here any minute."

"I thought the cell phone still couldn't get a—"

"That's enough, Jasper. Thanks for stopping, but we've got this."

Mom wraps her arm around my shoulder and fake smiles, but I can't help sideways stare at her hand because it's trembling.

The biker eases back into his leather seat and nods so slow

that I can tell he knows Mom's lying. He leans out to Whistler, waving him to come closer with great big oven-mitt hands, as Mom flinches, talons digging into my skin. What does she think he's going to do? Kick him? Pick him up by the scruff and shoot him? Whistler doesn't hesitate. Why would he? He's straight into a slow-lick greeting (definite approval).

"Ray's Garage is back the way you came, about two hundred yards past the stop sign. Can't miss it."

He winks and fires up the kick starter.

"By the way," he shouts, throttle wrist ready to twist. "Your dog. Totally badass."

And with that he's gone, ripping off into the distance, too fast, too far, to see my grin or hear my "Thank you."

We watch him go and Mom only speaks when the roar of the engine disappears from my ears.

"Jesus Christ, Jasper, a Hells Angel shows up and he's . . . he's . . . packing heat, and all you want to do is . . . is tell him where we live so he can send over his East Coast brethren when we get back home."

Using the phrase "packing heat" is a little embarrassing and definitely shows Mom's age, but I let it go.

"Whistler liked him, and he doesn't like everyone. And the biker man knew about art so he can't be a total redneck, right?"

Mom looks troubled by this fact, like she'd noticed and it didn't make sense to her either.

"Look, I've played along with your camping trip, but now I want you to pack everything into the car. We'll lock up and walk back to the Interstate. Yes, it's a long way but God knows when someone else will drive by who doesn't look like Grizzly Adams."

Mom's gone before I can ask, pulling stuff out of the tent.

"Bet you can't fit it back inside that little bag this time," she says, making her eyes into slits, trying not to smile, her version of sorry for snapping.

I check in with Whistler but he's staring down the road. "Wow, Mom, you were telling the truth."

Her brows go all magnetic and snap together to make a "What?" face.

"There really is a truck on the way."

49

Kate

Perhaps I was a little judgmental. But come on, the man had a gun, out in the open, like a shoot 'em up cowboy. Anything could have happened, and none of it good. Still, the arrival of a truck—albeit more pickup than tow—and the announcement from the driver, "Hear y'all could use a ride," is all the boy wonder needs. Biker guy went to get help, proof my "judging a book by its cover" philosophy is in need of some serious re-thinking.

I try to keep this in mind as a woman drops down from the cab. She's taller than me, significantly older, and could definitely handle the adjective "strapping." Her long, pure-gray hair is wild, like it's been blow-dried in a squall, and she wears what appears to be a neck-to-ankle sackcloth dress.

"Laureen. Pleased to meet you."

Crushing handshakes and a skull thumping pat on Whistler's head.

"Sorry, tow truck's in the shop, but I've got a phone you can use at home. The car's a rental, yeah?"

I manage to nod at our Samaritan.

"Toss your stuff in the flatbed and let's go bitch them out for renting you a lemon."

Ordinarily it takes bribes or threats to motivate my son to tidy up. Suddenly, under Laureen's spell, he's tireless and enthusiastic as we break camp and switch out our luggage. I leave a note under the windshield wiper to explain where we've gone. Not that I expect anyone to find it.

"Okay if the dog sits in back?" asks Laureen.

Whistler doesn't wait for my reply, up and over the side like an agility dog over an A-frame. This woman is rounding us up like we're lost sheep.

"Guess that's a yes," she adds, sliding in behind the steering wheel.

The cab has one long seat and Jasper sits in the middle, happy to handle the small talk—husband, Ray, died years ago (the cancer), as did Ray Junior (second tour in Iraq), she runs the business alone, and yes, of course, has a black Lab and two Siamese cats—and though I couldn't be more proud of the way my boy is polite, attentive, and strives for eye contact, I'm still hung up on his response to our visit by the biker. He saw what I saw, and yet he saw everything I *chose* to ignore. Jasper recognized good, and not in a gullible, impressionable, childish way. Somehow, for Jasper—and, let's not forget, this dog—it was instinctive.

Ray's gas station is a crumbling forsaken garage along the frontage road to the Interstate, and as we get near, the heady aroma of gasoline drifts through Laureen's open driver-side window. Surely a dog with a superior sense of smell could have caught the whiff of fuel in the air from the nearby stop sign?

I tell myself, *Don't go there*, not wanting to suggest that the decision to turn right and not left was premeditated, making me the victim of a camping conspiracy.

Rolling tires trigger the sound of a distant bell. There's a solitary pump for regular gasoline and a pump for diesel, an empty wooden rocking chair parked between the two and a sign touting "full service only." The forecourt is more dust than asphalt, but there's a shop adjacent to a mechanic's bay, and over to one side of the wooden building, we pull up to a double-wide trailer.

"Make your call," says Laureen, helping Jasper down from the truck. "And while we're waiting, you two can grab a shower and I'll get us some breakfast."

"Oh, that's very kind of you, but—"

"Excellent," says Jasper. "I'm starving. Is this Homer?" Ignoring me completely, Jasper gets caught up by the long-lost-brother treatment from an old, wooden, calorically loved Lab, a dog who probably wishes his knees and elbows worked half as well as his tail. Whistler has to wait his turn, their exchange more restrained and focused on the subtle aromas of each other's nether regions.

Laureen leads the way up a short flight of stairs and across a wooden deck to the trailer's unlocked front door. "Phone's by the TV. Shower's down from the kitchen on the left. Plenty of towels and hot water. Don't be shy."

She raids the refrigerator for a box of eggs and a packet of bacon. It's like she's been expecting us, like people break down in these parts all the time. Maybe she's glad of the company. Or maybe she's just a good person and I need to get comfortable letting good people do what they do best.

I check in with Jasper. "You okay?"

Big happy eyes and a big exaggerated nod. It doesn't take much to please this kid.

"Then I'm gonna call the rental company. You grab your bag of toiletries from the suitcase and I'll be by in a minute to wrap your PICC."

Ziploc bags and surgical tape were invented for showering with a sterile catheter dangling from your arm.

With a replacement vehicle on the way and Jasper clean, damp, and rosy, hooked up to his first IV hit of the day, I take my turn in a stranger's bathroom and try not to notice how easily I've taken off my clothes and washed up behind a transparent plastic curtain decorated with rows of yellow ducks. Truth be told, after the flight, the drive, and the impromptu camping trip, this could be the Four Seasons.

Refreshed by the shower and a change of clothes, I allow my nose to lead the way, seduced by the smell of a hot breakfast, past the framed folded American flag and the photo of a young, handsome man in military uniform, and into the kitchen.

"Out here."

It's Laureen, calling from the deck, and before I can join her she's jabbing a finger toward the pumps, at Jasper, antibiotic ball in one hand, squeegee in the other, straining upward and across to swipe away some frothy bubbles from a car's windshield. The pump handle protrudes from the open gas tank and, close by, gently swaying in a rocking chair, sits Whistler, head held high, overseeing everything. Jasper catches me watching, smiles, but doesn't wave, like he needs to be serious, like he's got an important job to do.

I feel Laureen's eyes on me, taking me in, before she reaches out a hand and pats my arm. I glance over, fearing a "There, there," but instead her subtle smile telegraphs, "He's okay," and, more importantly, "No need to explain."

"Mom, Mom," shouts Jasper, running from the pumps to the deck, waving a five-dollar bill over his head. "The nice man gave me a tip."

I can't speak. I should insist, "That belongs to Laureen," but my son is running, running, and he's not breathless or coughing.

"Good job, kid," says Laureen. "But let's get your mom something to eat."

Jasper and Whistler ignore me, slide into Laureen's slipstream, plop back down in the kitchen, and pick up where they left off with breakfast—one chowing down, the other drooling saliva.

I'm left stranded on the empty deck with the lasting image of my beaming son, the way he takes so much pleasure from the little things, the forgettable, nothing moments of a normal life, as if pumping gas was on that dreadful bucket list project from school and now he's checked it off.

"You eating or not?" cries Laureen.

I apologize, slink into the kitchen, and pull up a chair beside Jasper as Laureen slides a plate loaded with bacon, scrambled eggs, and pancakes my way.

The bell rings—another customer rolling up to the pumps.

"Thought this might happen," says Laureen. "My version of rush hour." And without another word she abandons us for a large SUV.

Jasper swallows down a mouthful of food—he's eating like he's going to the chair—checks that we're alone, and says, "She's real nice, isn't she?"

Real nice. Since when did my son turn northwest Texan? He's such a mimic. I guess I should be grateful that he didn't go all English on me and say she was "smashing."

In my hesitation he adds, "You need to check on Homer."

"Why? What's wrong with him?"

"When you were in the shower I was petting him and he and I had, you know, our thing . . . our . . . 'silent correspondence.'" Out come the air quotes. "I know, I'm supposed to be dialing it back, but I've kept it to myself, and it wasn't my fault, it just happened, and I'm sorry, but I'm worried and because you're a vet and because Laureen has been so nice, I thought, well, maybe you should check him out. Give her a free consult."

I glance out the window; that SUV must have a thirty-gallon tank—Laureen will be a while. Back to Jasper, catching the unmistakable, hopeful glint in those baby blues. My son is right, she's been an angel, and it's the least I can do—but if I examine her dog, unsolicited by his owner, in the absence of overt discomfort or disease, prompted only by the instincts of an eleven-year-old boy, aren't I buying into his fantasy? Aren't I condoning a delusion that upgrades my son from disabled to disturbed?

I pick up a rasher of bacon, crunch down on one end, and

point the other at Jasper. "Okay. I'll do it. But only if you do a better job of telling me what it is you *think* is going on between you and dogs. Promise me there's no actual talking."

He winces. "That'd be lame, Mom."

"So?"

He puts down his knife and fork, sits up, his body practically crackling with animation like he wants to get this right.

"I just try to be open, talk normal, like I would any animal, but not baby talk and not a pretend conversation. Most of the time I don't get anything, but that's because I'm not the one making it happen. It's like I place lots of calls and they don't pick up, only every so often they do."

Laughing, dropping a sarcastic comment might be easier, healthier, but there's something about his demeanor—innocence, maybe honesty. I just hope he doesn't utter the word *telepathy*.

"It's hard to explain, but sometimes they make me feel something, anything, could be happy, sad, angry, curious, hungry, scared, or whatever."

"But Jasper, how do you know it's not what *you're* feeling, what *you're* imagining?"

"I don't," he says. "But then there are lots of things that are impossible to explain."

"Like?"

"Like . . . like . . . why cats purr? And what makes salmon migrate, and Arctic terns, and monarch butterflies? And that sensation you get, deep down in your belly—"

"A gut feeling."

"Yeah, when something is definitely wrong or definitely right, and you just know. You trust it. None of us have a proper explanation, but we all get it."

Whistler checks in with Jasper and the two of them stare back, all full of themselves, like they just blew my argument out of the water.

"And Homer made you feel something?"

"Yeah, I felt full, like I'd eaten too much, like I was stuffed, but this was *before* I ate any breakfast."

The forecourt bell rings again.

The specifics of this description have me worried. Jasper's intestines are in a constant battle with the buckets of medications they absorb. I hope there's not a problem.

"You took your enzymes? You need me to feel your tummy?"

"No. I need you to feel Homer's tummy."

Homer hasn't moved, flopped over on the tired pink carpet in front of the blank TV screen, two circles of lilac fur bookending a couch, the cats, a copy of *Reader's Digest* and *TV Guide* between them. Strange for a Lab, missing out on the possibility of a dropped table scrap, the enthusiasm of his initial greeting forgotten, as if he used up his supply of energy for the entire day.

I get up from the table, tail thumps telling me Homer approves of my attention, a language that makes sense, and I feel his body relax into an expectation of a welcome belly rub. But as I get down on my knees, hands transitioning from petting to palpation, Homer flinches, especially as my probing fingers bump up around the perimeter of the softball-size mass protruding from his spleen.

"Well?"

I'm down on the floor, Jasper and Whistler overhead, expect-ant relatives bracing for bad news.

How is this possible? Lucky guess? Did Laureen confide? I doubt it.

"Homer has something in his belly, a mass, probably coming off his spleen."

No fist pump, no hubris, just a reassuring pat to Whistler and a worried expression I've seen more times than I can count. "That's bad, right?"

I get to my feet, strain to look out to the pumps where Laureen leans into a passenger-side window.

"It can be," I say, "more often than not."

"What should we do?"

I take a deep breath and take in the reality of the threadbare couch; the chipped, scratched, outdated furniture; the stains on the old carpet; the cheap chintziness of the owl figurines on the windowsill. This kind and generous widow, having lost a husband and a son, is getting by—but only just. How can she afford expensive diagnostics and surgery and whatever else Homer needs? What kind of a person would I be for saying, "Thanks for everything and by the way your dog's got cancer"?

"I don't know."

"Well, I do," says Jasper. "We tell Laureen. If something bad is going to happen to me, you'd want to know. Right?"

I flash to the other CF mom in the hospital kitchen, and the old man in the hospital garden—my ghosts of Christmas future—and will my face to conquer the brooding fear of what lies ahead. But then again, after the incident with the biker, perhaps I should ignore my instincts, and trust Jasper's. For all I know, Laureen might be a millionaire.

Having finished breakfast and Jasper's chest PT (Laureen insisted we use her bedroom), she and I sit out on the deck with coffee, waiting for a new Fiat 500 to arrive as Jasper flits between trucks and cars, basking in the financial rewards of his new vocation as a "fossil fuel replenishment specialist." He and Whistler, though content to linger around the pumps, keep checking my way with looks that say, "Did you tell her yet, did you tell her?"

Laureen and I say little. It's just after eight, the sound of Interstate traffic picking up in the distance, and already the October sky is a dazzling blue. There's nothing particular to look at but an easy quiet flourishes between us as we stare out, like old friends watching a child at play on a beach. Here I can forget about my lack of sleep, about the ache in my neck and shoulder muscles. Here it is possible to ignore the silent indignation when I told Dr. Dan of my plan, ignore the fear that this was a waste of time and money, the fear that I might be causing my son serious and potentially irreparable harm to his health.

Then, quite unexpectedly, she says, "He's going to be fine."

And instead of my knee-jerk response of "No, he's not," or "How can you know?" I'm suffused with this certainty, this truth beyond hope that somehow she is right and I just need to see what she sees and make it happen.

"When I lost my son, folks reminded me that the Lord only hands it out to those who can handle it."

I flinch. I can't help it, the desire to lash out instinctive and visceral.

"What a load of crap," she adds. "Bunch of idiots. Reckon we all suffer, one way or another. Might be sudden, might take years, might be a baby, might be a granddaddy, but that's life, and there ain't nothing none of us can do about it. No point in askin' 'bout that son of yours 'cause I can see what's in front of my eyes. Looks like he's got it all figured out."

She's staring directly at him and I want to say thank you, but it feels so trite and inadequate.

"And that dog of his, he may be butt-ugly, but boy, they're something, those two."

It doesn't feel like the perfect segue, but in part it's driven by a fear that she's going to let slip how Homer is her saving grace, the last vestige of a tangible connection to her late son or husband. "Laureen, you're too polite to ask, but I'm a veterinarian, and ordinarily I don't go around examining other people's dogs . . . but Homer has a health problem, and it seems only right to let you know."

"If it's that lump on his hip it's just fat. My vet checked it out. Been there forever."

"No, this is inside his belly, probably on his spleen. I hate to be the bearer of bad news, but Homer's going to need blood work, probably an abdominal ultrasound, chest X-rays, and then there's—"

"I'm on it," Laureen says, getting to her feet, checking her watch. "I'll call Doc Nelson the moment he opens at nine. Get him right in. Whatever it takes for my boy."

What was I worried about? Just because a client pulls up in a brand-new Mercedes doesn't mean they'll pay for a shot and a worming tablet. Once again my son was right. Homer was going to get the best care possible.

I stand and Laureen insists on giving me a hug.

"And there was you thinking I was the one doing the rescuing. Try telling me we didn't cross paths for a reason."

I don't have an answer, but fortunately I don't need one. A tow truck from the rental company rolls onto the forecourt, and—shock of all shocks—it looks like Dwayne has decided to give us an upgrade.

50

Jasper

MY BUM'S GONE to sleep from all this driving and even though our brand-new shiny black Chevy Tahoe is sick, it's so big that Mom won't let me sit up front. On the plus side, Whistler is spread across my lap, head inches from mine, making sure I see a canine version of the world from between his ears.

I'm wearing my Lionel Messi Argentina soccer shirt, white and sky-blue stripes, the one Auntie Gwen gave me for my last birthday. It was nice of her, finding out that Messi is the best soccer player in the world, but England and Argentina had this war over some island, like, decades ago, and they still have beef, so wearing the shirt always makes me feel like a bit of a traitor.

"Okay back there?" asks Mom, waiting for my nod in the rearview mirror. "Just a couple more hours."

My hand rests on the big Antarctica scar, slow calm heartbeat just under my fingers, like a countdown to goodbye. It gives me a bad feeling.

"Mom, do you think Whistler's ever had his DNA tested?"

"Doubt it," she says, and then, giving me the suspicious mirror eyes asks, "Why?"

"Well, if I was Emily, the girl with the seizures, I'd want to know what kind of service dog I was getting. You think Mr. Silver showed her the photos Martha sent?"

Mom squirms in her seat, which doesn't make much sense because they're really comfortable. Then she says, "People see what they want to see, one breed in his ears, another in his legs, his tail, whatever, but you know what, I love the fact that Whistler's a mutt, a mix, a mongrel. Whichever label you choose, you still have to call him a very special service dog. He's living proof of the potential in an underdog. I may not see Chihuahua, or pit bull, or dalmatian, at least not on the surface, but so what, it's in there deep down. Know why?"

"Why?"

"Because I think Whistler is every dog."

I like this answer, and that makes Mom smile. I don't tell her, but I notice when she's happy, like when she and Laureen had big goodbye hugs.

Mom says she'd give me her lungs any time, which is meant to show how much she loves me, but sometimes—especially at night—I hear her on the phone with Auntie Gwen, and it's obvious that I'm the reason she's sad. People talk about one dog year being the same as seven people years because time passes too fast for dogs. My disease makes Mom sad because it makes time pass too fast for me. That's why kids with CF have a shorter life than normal, sometimes as short as a dog's life, and anyone who knows dogs knows how hard that can be on those who love us.

"Mom, now do you believe me?"

I get the narrow mirror eyes instead of a "Believe what?"

"About Homer, about the thing I have."

"I believe that dogs are definitely more receptive to you than me. But . . ."

"But?"

"Well . . . diagnosing a splenic tumor with, what . . . a hunch? It's hard for me. You're on so many medications I'm more worried that 'feeling full' means you're constipated. And guessing that something had to be seriously wrong with the dog wasn't rocket science. A Labrador with no interest in freshly cooked bacon? Hard to believe he's still alive, let alone sick."

Mom reaches for her bottle of water and takes a really long swig. Fortunately, she notices my best angry pout.

"*Believe* is a strong word, Jasper, and when you get older and study science subjects like biology and chemistry, you'll see that it takes more than one example to prove a point. I do know you have a certain way with dogs and they have a certain way with you. Especially the ugly one trying to crush you right now."

That's it. That's all I get. But then:

"Sometimes the things we choose to believe in should stay private and personal, you know, like God, or heaven, or ghosts, or . . . I don't know, aliens."

She makes it sound like she's really saying, "Keep it to yourself," and, worse still, "Don't embarrass me." I didn't want to have to do this, but Mom's leaving me no choice. It's time to spill, share the *big* reason, the one that will make her upset.

"Mom, remember that time in the hospital, the one when I kind of lost it, 'cause I really wanted there to be something good to make up for all the bad things that happen with CF?"

"How could I forget? You almost never cry."

"Yeah, well, sometimes when you and Auntie Gwen talk on the phone, I accidentally hear you getting upset, and you cry after hanging up. Lots. And it scares me, you blaming yourself for what's happened to me, because it's not like you meant to give me CF, which means it's not like it's your fault. That's why I want you to believe in what happens with me and dogs because if you do, you'll stop feeling sad."

Her mirror eyes are locked on mine. If she makes us crash then I take it back, 'cause me dying will definitely be her fault.

"You know I can't smell properly and my hearing's not right and I probably need glasses and the ends of my fingers keep getting numb and tingly, and I know it's nothing compared to my lungs, but instead of five senses I'm down to, like, two and three-quarters, and it totally sucks, but . . . it's like a trade, for something totally awesome, a hundred times better, and when the magic happens, it makes everything *we* go through a little less bad. So, if you want to blame yourself for giving me CF, then go ahead, but guess what, that means you also gave me this thing, this gift, and that's why I want you to believe, because if you do, you'll never ever have to feel guilty again."

Whistler nudges me, checks in with a "Now you've gone and

done it" stare, while Mom slides out of the rearview reflection, deflating like a punctured bouncy castle. I can't get a read on her reaction, but there's definitely some sniffling going on.

Eventually she comes back with, "You said 'we,' what *we* go through."

"So?"

Her ninja grip on the steering wheel eases up but her voice sounds sad and small. "I love you to pieces, Jasper. I love that it's you *and* me, in this together. But . . ."

She'd best not make me sound like a total momma's boy.

"You're almost a teenager. It's normal to want to distance yourself from me. I, we, can never give up, but one way or another, CF will hold you back, and when it does you're going to lash out. You'll blame me. Getting angry with your parents is what teenagers do. It's what I did with my mom and now look at us."

I play dumb. Better to zip it than say, "I don't want us to end up like you and Grandma."

"So, two things: first—stop listening in on me and Auntie Gwen. Everyone's allowed a bad day now and then; second— guilt is just another way for me to worry about you. It's my problem, not yours."

"Okay," I say, "but I won't be a teenager for . . . like . . . twenty-two months, so in the meantime, what have you got to lose?"

No answer.

"Look," I say, "Ms. Sexton is always going on about telling the truth, 'cause when you lie, you make a choice, you actually have to go out of your way to make stuff up. Like when you *knew* you were lying about Santa. Not that I'm complaining."

No response. She's still slumped in her seat.

"Me understanding dogs is totally different because even if I don't know how it happens or what it is, one thing is for certain, and I need you to look at me now, Mom."

Finally she sits up, puffy eyes filling the mirror, definitely crying.

"Good."

I reach my arm around Whistler's head, and press it next to mine, the two of us staring back, deadly serious, passport photo serious (not that I've got one).

"Give me your best polygraph stare. The scary one. Yeah, that one. Now, read our faces. Nothing to see, right? 'Cause no matter what, *we* are not lying."

Two empty seconds pass and then Mom cracks up, laughter turning on her tears, and in the hunt for a tissue she avoids giving me an answer.

THERE'S STILL NOTHING to look at out the window. Way back there was this billboard that said, "Don't Mess with Texas. We enjoy gunfights. If you kill someone, we will kill you back."

"You want me to find something on the radio?"

I shake my head. Time to get Mom out of her comfort zone— say nothing, stare at nothing, stay cool. Oh, and don't look into her mirror eyes.

"You going to miss him?"

See, there it is, she cracked. Now I have to take my time. Like Grandpa used to say back when he was obsessed with fishing and not golf, "Don't reel in too soon."

Sad slow nod with no eye contact.

Then she goes and tricks me by saying, "Me too," and the surprise makes me look in the mirror. She's back to smiling, and I hope it's because she means it.

"What if we could keep him for longer?" I ask.

Mirror glance. "Life is full of what-ifs. What if you'd never met him? Would that have been better or worse?"

"Worse," I shout, earning a slow lick on the cheek like I need to calm down.

"Then that's good. Even if Whistler wasn't around for long enough, it was better than nothing."

I scratch his muzzle scars and we press heads.

"Mom, do you think humans should learn to live more like dogs?"

She laughs. "Where's this coming from?"

I don't know what to say. I definitely don't know how to explain it. Ever since Whistler turned up, certain things have started clicking inside my head, falling into place, making total sense, feeling obvious, like when Ms. Sexton showed me how to do fractions in math, and when I got it I couldn't understand what took so long. Only Whistler teaches a much better subject.

"You mean sniff each other's butts, pee on lampposts, attack mailmen?"

"I'm being serious, Mom."

She straightens and pulls her shoulders back. I can't see her face so she might be pretending.

"Think about any dog from the shelter," I say, "any dog that gets adopted. Think about the way they live their life."

"What about it?"

"See, I reckon dogs don't just show up. I reckon they live, like dogs *really* live, doing everything to the max." I need examples. "Remember the other day, when we went to the beach to rescue Whistler?"

Back of the head nod.

"As soon as all the dogs got off leash they went crazy, running around like their butts were on fire. They don't stretch or warm up or pace themselves or worry who sees their white legs. They just do it, all or nothing, because they want to have fun. They're all about fun. I mean, when was the last time you saw a dog do grumpy or whiny or embarrassed? If we ate the exact same meal, day in, day out, we'd go nuts, we'd go on a hunger strike. Not dogs. They jump up and down, tail set to crazy time, snarfing down their kibble like it's prime rib. And, and, and even when they sleep, they give it everything, out for the count, able to flop down anywhere. I mean, when was the last time you saw a dog chugging on a bottle of NyQuil?"

Forget the mirror, this earns me a quick, direct, over the shoulder glare.

"Two hands on the wheel, eyes on the road," I shout. I've heard my cousin Tawd use this line when Auntie Gwen tries to text and drive.

Mom laughs and I try to get a read on Whistler, hoping for

sad about saying goodbye but prepared for nervous or excited about a new home. Instead I get nothing except pins and needles in one of my legs.

"You still want to be a veterinarian, right?"

"Hopefully."

"Well, there's a big problem with your idea of being able to directly communicate with an animal."

"There is?"

"Of course. I mean, there'd be no need for X-rays or blood work or lots of other tests if an animal could just tell us where it hurts. We'd go out of business."

I think about this.

"Human doctors can talk to their patients and they don't go out of business."

That makes Mom go quiet.

I ask, "Do you think Whistler is too old to work?"

"I don't know. But I do know he has a unique gift and if he can still use it, he probably should."

I wait a few seconds. Ms. Sexton does the same thing in class after screaming someone's name. She calls it "dramatic effect."

"Mom, do you think dogs go to heaven?"

"Of course," she says, without a pause, without even thinking. Sometimes I just don't get grown-ups. "Do you?" she asks.

"I hope so," I say, "but I also think dogs don't take any chances."

Curious mirror eyes.

"I know I haven't been around dogs for as long as you, but everything I see tells me they live their lives like this is heaven, as good as it gets, like if we only get one go around, they're not going to miss a thing."

Eyes disappear and she slowly shakes her head. "Why don't you make yourself useful." She tosses her cell phone onto the back seat. "I need to pee. If this is working, find out how far to the next rest stop."

I get bars and while I'm scrolling on Google Maps Whistler pushes his way up front by placing both front paws on the center console.

"Service station in about twenty—"

And suddenly Mom's braking, hard and fast, and we're veering over and something whips past the glass on my right.

"I hope I don't regret this," says Mom, powering down the passenger-side window, twisting around in her seat to look directly at me.

I have no idea what she's talking about, but then I notice Whistler, checking over my shoulder, tail drumming the leather. That's when I recognize the hitchhiker, the one we passed way back, with the "Go Buffs" on the back of his sweatshirt. Mom's stopped for him, only, as he loosens the drawstrings on his hoodie, turns out it's a she and not a he.

"Where you headed?" asks Mom.

The girl dips down and leans in. I'm not good at guessing ages, but she's got bad skin and no wrinkles so she might be in high school. Maybe she's on vacation like me.

"Boulder, Colorado. But anywhere near Denver's fine."

"We're not going that far," says Mom. "But I can drop you off at the next rest stop, if that helps?"

The girl doesn't answer, just opens the door and gets in. Whistler wants to say hello, sniffing and rooting, making it hard for her to put on her seat belt. She makes no effort to pet him.

"Sorry," says Mom. "Whistler, get in the back. I'm Kate, and this is my son, Jasper."

I smile but she doesn't look my way.

"How far to the next stop?" she asks.

"According to Google Maps, twenty miles," I say.

She doesn't reply, just finds the controls to ease back her seat and closes her eyes like she's going to take a nap.

Mom sneaks a side-glance meant for me in the mirror. I shrug my shoulders. Whistler chooses to sit rather than lay, like he doesn't want to miss a thing. I can't tell whether he approves of this girl or just the idea that we picked up a person in need.

Mom pulls back onto the highway and I begin to wonder if this girl's silence is a bit like my Jedi mind game with Mom.

"We saw you yesterday," I say, "trying to hitch a ride."

I get a grunt and a sleepy "What?"

"I recognized your sweatshirt."

She snaps open her eyes. "But you never thought to stop." She's speaking to me while staring straight at Mom.

"Didn't realize you were . . . female," says Mom.

"Right, that makes sense," says the girl, shaking her head before flopping back into her seat.

"So what are Buffs?" I ask. "Your sweatshirt? 'Go Buffs.'"

"What? Oh, University of Colorado, some mascot . . . thing."

"You a college student?" asks Mom, sounding way too hopeful.

The girl digs her elbow into the armrest and cups her left cheek in her hand, mumbling a "No."

"Then what takes you to Boulder?"

The girl sniffs, sits up, and comes this close to rolling her eyes like she wants Mom to back off and let her go to sleep.

I'm with Mom on this one. If you're getting a free ride, the least you can do is be polite, and better still, entertain us.

"Look, my name is Cotton, I'm eighteen, and I'm visiting a friend in Colorado. I don't have money for a Greyhound so I figured why not hitch. Cool?"

Mom nods but not in a "that makes perfect sense" kind of way. More like a "you picked the wrong person to mess with" nod.

"Must be a bit scary—on your own?"

I can see through to the passenger side foot space and notice the way Cotton nudges her backpack with the toe of her sneakers. I hope Mom doesn't ask if she's "packing heat." Then again, what if she is?

"I'm a big girl. I can look after myself."

Judging by her grubby sweatshirt, smudgy eye makeup, and greasy hair, I'm not so sure.

Cotton leans forward, pulls her backpack onto her lap, reaches a hand inside, and begins rooting around. Forget about oncoming traffic, Mom can't take her eyes off the girl and what she's searching for, like she's convinced she's about to be staring down the wrong end of a Glock 9.

"Borrow your charger?" says Cotton, whipping out her iPhone

and hooking up to the dangling adaptor in the console without waiting for a reply.

Mom lets out a breath, pretending to be cool as we veer back into our lane. She's tapping the steering wheel with her right hand. It's the driving equivalent of the left-eye twitch.

"Someone you need to call?" asks Mom. "Let them know you're okay?"

"I'm not a runaway," snaps Cotton.

"Never said you were," says Mom, her comeback just as snappy.

"Sorry," says Cotton, "what was your name again?"

"Kate."

"And I'm Jasper and this is Whistler."

"You're only a runaway if you're underage. I'm old enough to choose, and I choose not to live anywhere near my mom's boyfriend."

Then Mom asks, "Would it be helpful to talk to the police?"

Whoa. What's going on? Suddenly this conversation has turned totally serious. Did I miss a clue? Is Cotton's mom's boyfriend a murderer or something?

"Look, forget I said anything. It's fine. I got a job lined up, waitressing. My friend says I can sleep on her couch. It's all good."

Mom's mirror eyes check in and it's obvious she's not happy. This makes me feel bad because I'm the one who made Mom feel guilty for not picking up a hitchhiker and now she's stressing her out.

Whistler hasn't budged even though Cotton refuses to offer him a single scratch, pat, or rub. It's like he's invisible to her but—here's the weird part—he's not upset. Why would he be pleased that Mom was stopping to give her a ride? She doesn't seem very nice or grateful, but if he's cool with her, I'm guessing she's okay.

"My dog likes you," I say. "Actually he's not my dog. We're returning him to a place that trains service dogs in Lincoln Peak, New Mexico."

"Service dogs?" Cotton leans right, squints, but barely looks at Whistler.

"There's a graduation ceremony and we're getting a reward."

That makes her sit up.

"What sort of a reward?"

"My son exaggerates. It's just a certificate, a formal thank-you. Jasper, are you sure there was a rest stop in twenty miles?"

"Yes I am, and it's not just a certificate. I'm getting a big fat check because he's a very special dog. We've come all the way from Cape Cod, Massachusetts. That's how much they want him back."

Cotton slips off her sneakers and folds one foot under her other thigh in order to twist around and talk to Whistler and me. I hope she's interested for the right reasons. I try not to notice how her socks are dirty and they don't match.

"What can he do?" asks Cotton, reaching out to touch his zebra stripes.

"Mainly he tells people if they're about to have a seizure, but he can do lots of things if you ask him in the right way."

"You mean tricks, or stuff like sniffing for bombs or drugs?"

Mom's eyes definitely flick down to the backpack in the foot space. "Finally," says Mom, her voice bigger than necessary, "I thought we'd never get here."

Up in the distance a big sign towers over the highway—Toot'n Totum. They're weird out here.

Cotton begins to pull on her sneakers as Mom pulls the Tahoe off the road and rolls into a parking space.

"Nice meeting you," says Mom, forcing Cotton into a weird in-car handshake.

We get out, I clip the leash on Whistler's collar, and the four of us start following a trail of people headed for a big convenience store.

"Maybe they have some paper or cardboard," says Mom, "so you could make a sign, let people know where you want to go."

Cotton's "Really?" expression is ten times better than mine.

"Mom, I need to pee as well."

We're nearly at the entrance. Why is Cotton still hanging out with us? I tug on Mom's sleeve because I only want her to hear, "real bad."

For some time Mom and me and public toilets have had a problem. When you're really little it's bad enough, and I know, bad people hang out in toilets, ready to kidnap kids, but anything is better than the shame of following your mom into the ladies room at my age.

"Let me watch the dog," says Cotton. "You guys go. We'll wait right here."

Mom goes to say something but stops herself. Maybe she spotted the NO DOGS ALLOWED sign on the door. Maybe she's mad because I left Whistler's fake service dog jacket back in the Tahoe.

"Okay, Cotton," says Mom, leaning in real close, unleashing the total eye contact, "I'm going to trust you on this one. Please, don't let us down."

Mom takes Whistler's leash out of my hand and places it in hers.

"Let's go," I hiss, trying not to focus on a nearby water fountain or the poster of a waterfall, grabbing Mom's sleeve and shoving her through the front door.

There's a big red digital clock over the gas pumps, flicking between the time and the temperature. It takes us exactly six minutes, but when we get back, Whistler and Cotton are not where we left them.

I look around, thinking they've wandered off—Whistler hunting for a pee spot of his own—until the high-pitched screech of tires makes me stare at the gas pumps. And that's when I hear a woman starting to scream.

51

Kate

OF COURSE SHE'S gone. And taken Whistler with her.

We're on the sidewalk where we left them, and I'm spinning three-sixties, desperate for a glimpse of grubby sweatshirt or black fur, and I don't know what's worse, the anger at my naivete, or the fear of losing Whistler.

I'm sure Jasper's innocence—mentioning the reward—planted the seed, but it was me who handed the leash to a complete stranger (I don't even know her last name) like I was giving away twenty-five grand in cash, no questions asked, with a five-minute head start in case I change my mind.

Humiliation leaks from every pore. I am such an idiot, letting myself get infected by Laureen's warmth and generosity, my maternal resolve undone when Jasper pointed out my guilt issues over CF. I just wanted to do the right thing, help someone in need, pay it forward—the most stupid, and irritating, concept ever. Now I feel duped and ashamed, like the brunt of a joke, the victim of a scam.

Trucks and cars pull up and pull off, a bass pulses from a nearby convertible, there's the stench of unleaded gas heavy in the air, and all around, regular people go about their business. I order myself to get a grip. Chances are she's still here, somewhere. But what if I'm wrong and she's gone, taken Whistler with her? She might just want a dog for company or security. But maybe she's desperate, Whistler nothing more than a commodity to barter for food, money, or drugs?

Clench-jawed, ready to pull out my hair, a screech of rubber on asphalt slices right through the background noise, and I pivot toward the gas pumps, the woman's scream, long and feral, like an exclamation point, confirming the coordinates. But it's the sound sandwiched in between that lingers inside my head, the thud not just dull and sickening, but final.

"Come on," I shout, snatching at Jasper's hand. "Now," I order, shattering his confusion, dragging him with me, people staring, like I might be the one doing the abducting. My glare and raised palm dares ongoing traffic to defy me as we run toward the rows of self-service pumps, bursting onto a scene, the angles of the cars all wrong, sexy lines and contours, scratched, crumpled, and deformed. But the small crowd that has gathered ignores the wreckage and the drivers screaming at one another, because their silent semicircle is aghast, staring down at the creature on the ground.

No one is making a move because Whistler is dead.

52

Jasper

Obviously he's not dead. He's just pretending.

Whistler lies on the ground, rigid, his one good eye closed, "I can't see you so you can't see me," just like that time at the sporting goods store when he freaked out in the golf section.

Mom drops my hand and orders people out of the way saying, "I'm a doctor. He's ours."

Two reasons why this is cool. One reason why this is not so cool.

First: I bet Mom's been dying for a chance to say, "I'm a doctor" in a pet emergency situation. Second: Now that she's said, "He's ours," in public, I know she definitely loves him. Third: A couple of people are looking at her like, "What kind of an animal doctor let's their dog get hit by a car?"

Mom's down in the dirt, running her hands over his fur and scars, checking for cuts and bleeding, laying her head gently against his chest, listening to breaths, apologizing nonstop by whispering "sorry," over and over.

I'm not tuning into any pain in my head or belly or bones but I can feel a very specific type of scared, exactly like when I'm hiding from Cousin Todd in Grandma's backyard and I know he's about to find me. Who was Whistler hiding from?

"He never got hit."

I turn around and there's this skinny kid pumping gas, hair twisted up in a man bun.

"Guy in the Honda swerved, missed the dog, but took out the front end of that Porsche."

He jerks his chin toward the smashed cars, but my eyes follow the tire marks curling back to where Whistler went down.

"Is the dog okay?"

It's Mr. Honda, shouting to Mom as he jogs over.

"Think so," says Mom.

Mrs. Porsche obviously doesn't like pets because she's more interested in screaming into her cell phone while fingering the dents on her car.

"Where is she?" asks Mr. Honda. "The girl?"

"Gone," says Mr. Man Bun, topping off his tank. "Bummed a ride from some dude in a pickup. Big guy, redhead, smoking a butt. Jerk. Who smokes at a gas station? The dog took one look at him and freaked out, like he knew him, like he thought about booking it, but decided to play dead, like the guy was a bear or something."

Mr. Honda looks totally gobsmacked. And so does Mom. Weird.

"I wouldn't worry," says Mr. Man Bun, waiting for his receipt, "I see two, three cameras. The cashier will have it all on film. Never got the license, but it was definitely a Colorado plate."

I forget to ask the only questions that matter: Did Cotton let go of the leash, or did Whistler pull away? I forget because I'm distracted.

Whistler is sitting up, slow-licking Mom's face.

53

Kate

WHISTLER MADE ME do it.

Yes, I pulled over to pick up a hitchhiker for Jasper—a chance to right a wrong, to save face—but (and it kills me to admit this) Whistler instigated the whole thing.

Wedging his way into the gap up front, the mutt got me noticing his scars, the little ones, imagining the worst—the burning tip of a cigarette, a gouge from a swinging seven iron. Yet Martha's Lucky stared ahead, undaunted and no less noble, like he was on watch, a resolute sentry, searching the horizon for danger. And long before I actually saw the hitchhiker, his snout began rooting under my elbow, digging into my armpit, making me curse and swerve. I hit the brakes by default, to swat him away, and there she was, the coincidence too much, as if here was the dog offering me a second chance. It felt impulsive, reckless, and potentially dangerous, but after the biker incident I had to prove myself capable of catching Whistler's goodwill virus.

Discovering he was a she was a win, but any relief was short lived. Her name, Cotton, smacked of hippy-dippy roots, and I'm sorry, but any kid who pushes their age from the get-go is lying. Probably fifteen, at most, skipping school or already a dropout. Not that I doubted her motivation. All I could think was, where did she sleep last night? Who did she have to sleep with? Worst-case scenarios filled my head as I pondered what Cotton must have endured at home. Physical abuse? Psychological abuse? Sexual abuse? I couldn't go there, but it did make me think about my relationships with my mother, my sister, my son. Sometimes it's a little too easy to forget there are far worse things out there in the world, far greater evils, and for a while, I buzzed with the certainty that, for all my discomfort, my original intention had been good.

The backpack she carried; now there was a problem. It seemed too small, just the essentials, but what were they? A handgun? A spray can of mace? Plastic syringe, hypodermic needle, and a bent spoon?

Only now, back on the highway, Jasper practically wearing Whistler like a fully deployed airbag, can I try to find the positives from our encounter with Cotton.

I'm guessing she would have asked around for a ride, wondering if a dog helped or hindered her quest, hopeful when she spotted a Colorado license plate at the gas pumps. And maybe it was a "leaving right now, you're either coming or you're not" ride. No time to find us. No way to leave a note. Then Whistler saw the driver, a brawny redhead smoking a cigarette, and he panicked, his captor come back, and suddenly he was bracing for the swing of a golf club or the jab of red-hot ash. Maybe this redhead was a good guy, a dog lover, but, having gotten this far, Whistler wasn't taking any chances, determined to escape, instigating the crash until, knowing he was caught, cowering, wishing he were dead, waiting for the pain to begin.

I hope Cotton never intended to take Whistler with her. I hope the redheaded driver never said, "No dogs," and in that instant she chose to drop the leash. And, just before Cotton nods off in another passenger seat, I hope she realizes I was a stranger who made a choice, recognized need, and, inspired by that hairy lug in the back, tried to help out.

Currently, our hairy lug in question stands on the back seat, scanning left and right, looking like he's searching for another adventure. And it strikes me that, while I'm still stewing and fuming—second-guessing Cotton's motives—the dog has already moved on. Of course Whistler gets the luxury of distilling his life down to simple actions and emotions: engage in the now, hunt down the joy, and on to the next. But clearly it's working. He's permanently smiling, like he's on to something, like what's the point of doubt and self-recrimination? As though, when you're living what matters most, by definition, every intention has to be good.

54

Jasper

I THOUGHT I was pretty good at the silent treatment, but Mom is a million times better than me, and right now she's hunched over the steering wheel and definitely speeding.

"Mom, you think Cotton's okay?"

Mom pushes back in her seat, slowly raises her chin, and then twists her neck, hard left, hard right, getting a crack in both directions. "Right now, Jasper, I'm just glad she's with someone else."

Mom doesn't do well when things don't go the way she planned. Auntie Gwen says that's why she tries *not* to get outside her "comfort zone." But if you never take chances, if you never try, you never fail, but you miss all the shots you don't take.

"Well, I think that when you and I went to the loo, Cotton probably—"

"Jasper," Mom snaps, giving me scary angry eyes in the mirror, "what was our deal?"

I glance over at Whistler and he glances back. We both agree. Say nothing.

"You promised me you'd go easy on the dog whispering and the excessive use of English lingo. Remember?"

Nod. Eyes down. I elbow Whistler to follow suit but he's distracted by a tumbling tumbleweed.

"I think I've been incredibly tolerant. I've kept quiet, I've even been indulgent. But there's been no let up on the dog-speak, and for weeks now, you've done the Anglophile thing to death. Enough with the soccer, the 'brilliant' this, the 'knack-ered' that, and no more whinge, arse, smashing, or *loo*. I've tried not to talk about your biological father because I don't like to, and it doesn't feel right, but with this endless love for England you're not leaving me much choice. Simon Swift has never been a part of our lives and likely never will. I don't want to be mean, but as far as I'm concerned, he doesn't exist, a man who will be remembered for being forgotten. It sounds harsh but sadly, it's the truth, and maybe the sooner you learn to accept this fact, the better."

My mouth flaps open. I try to absorb what Mom's saying. This might be a good time to throw out a junky cough, but I can't brew one up—stew-pid antibiotics. "I don't care if I don't have a dad because I've only ever needed a mom."

Nothing but the sound of rolling tires on blacktop.

"Then why the love of all things English?"

I think about ways to explain, better ways than when I tried to tell Burt.

"I just thought an English passport might be useful."

The Tahoe slows. "What are you talking about?"

"Remember when your work was changing to a new medical insurance plan and you said I'd best get a decent job by the time I'm twenty-six because by then I'm not allowed on your plan anymore?"

Her mirror eyes say "Not really."

"You've told me I'm half American and half English. That means I should be able to get an English passport, but there's probably some kind of a test, so I need to study and I need to be ready."

"But why do you need an English passport?"

"So I can get in. Because England has free health care. If I can't get a job by the time I'm twenty-six, maybe you'll let some British doctors look after my lungs."

Seconds pass, the center console clock clicks through another minute and Mom still says nothing, until she finally lets go of the wheel with one hand and scratches an itch in both her eyes. "God, Jasper, if your disease doesn't kill me, the way you think will."

I'm not sure what she means, but ask, "So, is plonker okay again?"

55

Kate

DESPITE A FAR-OFF mountain range—stark, craggy, and frosted by cream-cheese clouds—to spice up the mind-numbing monotony of our drive, my thoughts linger on the creepy dog staring my way, the one who somehow knows I'm thinking about him, the same one who—yes, I'm finally prepared to admit it—I am afraid to lose. Back at the gas station, flailing in that rush of panic, the reward money never once crossed my mind, because I wilted to a previously unthinkable knee-jerk response—my son needs this dog; this dog needs my son.

Though I haven't discussed it with Jasper—I'm done getting up his hopes—if circumstances present themselves, I intend to plead a case to keep Whistler, one last time. Yes, there's guilt and a need for redemption, but right now, the crux of my argument—cystic fibrosis—is in serious trouble because the deflating antibiotic ball on the seat next to him is the only visible reminder that Jasper has an incurable illness. Being small for his age and painfully cute won't be enough to win the sympathy vote we so desperately need. And a besotted mother exulting Jasper's many virtues feels crass. No, the powers that be need to experience what I've experienced, to witness the magic of what can happen when this boy and this dog connect.

Jasper killed me with his British passport logic. What American kid his age even knows about the National Health Service? There I was focused on a subversive plot, desperation to make a pilgrimage. For weeks I fluctuated between possible motives; natural curiosity, attention-seeking, or, worst of all, wanting a different parent, choosing "the hated one" over the woman prepared to sacrifice everything. And it turns out this bizarre obsession with everything English was for me, for us. The logic may have been off, but the intent was heartachingly perfect. Right about now I'm good with every "brilliant" or "stew-pid" that comes out of his rosebud lips.

Maybe this is the Jasper the Paws Unlimited advisory board needs to see: the optimist, glass half-full, brainwashed by a dog to think, "I can die, but I'd rather die living." I know, silencing the cough and sleeping on his back have left me impressionable—dare I say whimsical—convinced that this round of treatments will be different, that it will stick, giving us six months, maybe a year, before we have to do it again. And I never learn, because every time feels like a chance for a fresh start, a do-over, the excitement of New Year's Eve with resolutions to be made. Thing is, New Year's resolutions never last. So why bother?

I'll tell you why. Because, thanks to Jasper and the scar dog,

I can finally see what they've seen all along. If Jasper's decline is inevitable, then what is not, and what will set our lives apart, is deciding to make the most of every moment he is well.

In the rearview mirror, the two of them stare out the window, distracted, as we crawl down Main Street, Lincoln Peak. Jasper has muted his nonstop commentary, but there's nothing awkward about their silence, no fear of running out of conversation, of offending, of hurting, or saying the wrong thing. How easy, I think, the relationship between a boy and a dog, the kind of love affair most of us would kill for.

I set my mind adrift, wondering about work and how I can appease KGB, get her off my back and keep the place afloat. What if I put more effort into fundraising? What if I won over some big corporate sponsors, eager to underwrite a capital campaign aimed at finally becoming an open shelter? And it wouldn't hurt to be more tolerant, more engaging, of Martha. I think about Gwen, and dwell on the fact that she's been afraid to ask for help. I think about my mom and dad, and wonder, have they backed off or have I shut them out?

Plaques inform me we're snailing our way through the historic district—a fabricated avenue of strategically planted saplings line the sidewalks, rows of old brick and stucco buildings, nothing over three stories tall, words popping from bustling storefronts— cowboy, new age, locally sourced, artisanal.

"Do you think our hotel room will have the soccer channel?"

"Definitely," I reply, stopping at a red light, flashing to memories of his last soccer game, his aerial exploits in goal and how, aside from Whistler, I stood alone to watch. What if I've been going about this back to front? What if pretending all is well with the world is freaking people out?

I'm critical of those who live a so-called Facebook life, skewing the truth, letting the online world see only what they want you to see. But now that I'm being honest (or pre-menopausal, or giddy from sleep deprivation), aren't I the same way? I cannot let you in. You cannot handle my reality. That's why I never post. I click "like" to be polite. I'd rather click "jealous," "you're killing me," "I never thought I could hate you more," or "no one gets to live like this." We all edit and filter, but at least you have decent material to select from, a scrapbook full of smiles, holding a glass of wine, standing in front of somewhere nice. My scrapbook has far too many empty pages. Perhaps it's time to fill them up. Perhaps it's time to unleash a new version of me—flawed, vulnerable, and, if I dare to go there, real.

I've been my own worst enemy for far too long. Sure, I can claim I was brainwashed by my father's pigheaded aversion to any form of debt, but his sins are not mine. I own this flaw. My need to be in control of Jasper's disease, to prove I can do it, to be independent, has made me defiant, convinced that accepting help shows weakness. And at the same time, bitterness festers inside me, convinced that no one really wants to help us anyway. Time to welcome the casseroles, the offers to visit in the hospital, the invites for a drink, a coffee, instead of shutting them down. Time to ditch "I'm busy," "We're eating out," or "That's kind, but Jasper's allergic." If people are cautious around me, so what? Isn't it reasonable *not* to know what to do, *not* to know how to help, to fear saying the wrong thing? Silence is not the evil twin of indifference. Sometimes silence is as innocent as not knowing how to make you feel better.

WE PASS OUR hotel—too early to check in—a Holiday Inn Express on the far side of town (my son wanted to tell people at the graduation ceremony that that was where he stayed last night; it's also the cheapest place around), and after another five miles, Jasper announces, "We're here," first to spot the paw print inside a handprint inside a heart, the logo of Paws Unlimited.

The place is sprawling, an adobe-style compound, with signposts to guide the confused, speed bumps to slow the impatient, green spaces with poop bag dispensers for the unprepared, and plenty of parking. I follow the directions to reception.

"You think he needs his fake vest?" asks Jasper.

I go with pained expression, coming around the Tahoe to flush Jasper's line with heparin and seal it shut.

"Let's do this," he says, maybe to me, maybe to Whistler, and I fall into place, as we walk three abreast, gunslinger style, across the lot to the sliding glass doors of the main entrance.

Familiarity fills my nostrils, the smell of wet dog, dry kibble, and pet-friendly floor cleaner. I'd say it was like I never left the shelter, except for one major difference: the silence—no barking.

"You okay?" I ask, squeezing Jasper's shoulder, his head set to automatic nod, his mind elsewhere. No need to guess where as a jumpy Whistler twitches by Jasper's side.

"Hello," I say to the woman behind the desk. "Kate and Jasper Blunt, here with Whistler. We have an appointment."

The woman raises her chin and smiles. Her mouth is huge

and she's all teeth, dazzling, Hollywood white, lip-stretching, impossible to restrain teeth. She really should be a receptionist at a dentist's office. She consults with a computer monitor, taps a key, and offers an enthusiastic "Yes. Welcome. Have a seat and Terri will be right with you."

Jasper mouths, "Terri?"

I shrug.

We sit opposite a wall covered top to bottom with photographs of dogs and their human partners—men and women in uniform, in wheelchairs, children caught mid-laugh and always a dog in the picture, the catalyst, the crutch, the saving grace.

"Look, Mom."

Jasper points to a large gold plaque, but I'm too distracted by the front page of a discarded newspaper on a nearby chair. It's a copy of this morning's *Lincoln Peak Tribune*, and, above the fold, there's the headline "Missing Miracle Dog Offers Hope to Albuquerque Girl with Epilepsy." The reality of why we're here and how much it means to a total stranger hits me like a fist to the solar plexus.

"Mom, come see."

I remember to breathe, make sure Jasper's not looking, and flip the paper over to hide the caption.

"'Retired names—our tribute to their faithful service,'" he says, reading from the plaque. Dog names are listed in alphabetical order, from top to bottom, and next to the dog's name is a date, and next to that, the sponsor for the name. Jasper's finger has gone straight to the only "W."

"If they still want to use him as a service dog," asks Jasper, "then why has Whistler's name been retired?"

I don't have a clue. Besides, I'm distracted, curious as to who is (or was) Whistler's sponsor, a D. H. McClennon?

It's Whistler who saves me, spotting a woman headed our way. At first I notice his awareness, instantly alert, the private realizing there's an officer on deck. But as the woman gets closer, slowing to a stagger, theatrically clutching her chest, our yeti morphs into a bronco, dancing on his back legs, pawing the air with his front.

Without a word, without even a glance in our direction, the woman drops to her knees and the two of them come together, no hesitation, no holding back—Whistler working his butt like a Hawaiian hula dancer, generous with enough slow licks to take care of her tears.

"I'm . . . I'm . . . speechless," she says, half-crying, half-laughing, getting to her feet. "Blown away. Lost for words. Terri. Sorry, I'm Terri, Whistler's old trainer. Former trainer. Not that old."

I'm guessing she's a little older than me, outdoorsy skin aging ahead of schedule, flecks of untouched gray in straight, shoulder-length, auburn hair. Her plain gold-rimmed glasses say "service-able" not "chic," just like her uniform—blue jeans, sneakers, and a Paws Unlimited sweatshirt.

"I hope it's okay," she says, looking at Jasper, turning serious, "but I really need to give you the biggest thank-you hug ever."

Jasper nods his approval, beaming despite being crushed in Terri's arms, and he's so small and fragile, yet visibly thrilled that he's the one who made this possible, this moment of joy for a total stranger, that suddenly, swept up in the pure simplicity of this reunion, I'm in danger of bursting into tears myself.

Whistler provides some welcome comic relief, his determined zebra-snout investigating Terri's only concession to flair, a Barbie-pink nylon pouch hanging off her hip—I'm thinking doggy treats.

"Sorry about that," she says, slipping him a bribe before coming over to me, clasping her hands around mine. "This means so much, knowing that Whistler is alive and well and able to share his special brand of magic with the world."

For the first time—and it's shocking that it's taken until now—I actually register Terri's words, seeing what she sees, realizing how this funny-looking dog, this forgettable mutt, possesses a gift that can change lives. Her sincerity is palpable and penetrating, and any concerns, any fears I harbor that we are doing the wrong thing in giving him back vanish as I take in her gratitude.

"You're welcome," says Jasper, as though traveling two thousand miles to give away his perfect canine companion is no big deal.

"How long has he been with you?" asks Terri.

It's seems like forever ago since animal control swung by our shelter with a mangy mutt *not* answering to the name Lucky.

"A few weeks," I say, hoping she appreciates how Jasper and Whistler have had more than enough time to forge an undeniable bond. Right about now I wish I could say unbreakable.

"Is this where Whistler learned to be a service dog?" asks Jasper.

"Some here, some across the lot. We've got an early-learning center where the eight-to-sixteen-week-old pups start out before going to prison."

"Wait, prison? Real prison?"

"That's where our dogs get the bulk of their training."

Jasper's face tells me Terri just blew his mind. She's talking about one of the buildings being a house where dogs train with their new partners, see if things work out, learn how to turn on a light switch, to open a refrigerator, to run a bath, but I can tell Jasper's mind has stalled at "aren't prisons for bad people?" like he can't see the value in learning the art of street fighting or how to fashion a shiv from a plastic spoon.

"Here he is," says Terri, as a big beaming man lumbers in our direction.

Mr. Clayton Silver exudes the soft, burly warmth of a man whose body size makes him perfect for the part of Santa at Christmas fundraisers. He may have traded a full white beard for a bristly walrus mustache but his glistening eyes declare an unbridled delight to see us.

"Kate. Jasper. Whistler. This is fantastic. Can't thank you enough. The rest of the board are dying to thank you as well. Terri, why don't you head upstairs to the training room, see what Whistler remembers, what he's forgotten, then you and I can get together again after lunch, discuss your findings. Two-thirty?"

Terri agrees and out comes her Gentle Leader. I watch the wriggle and jiggle of Whistler's unhelpful snout as she tries to put it on, as if the dog regards the nose loop as less of a teaching tool and more of an unnecessary restraint.

The insistent tug on my sleeve begs for attention, but when I glance down, Jasper makes my heart stop. Jasper is afraid and fearful, the severity of his expression something I've witnessed only one other time, the first time he coughed up blood; and even then, it wasn't the crimson blob in the white tissue that made him panic, it was registering the alarm written on *my* face, the alarm I—his careless mother—had failed to hide.

"Mom," he whispers. "Is this it? Is this where I have to say goodbye?"

Clayton Silver overhears, frowns his concern, and interjects, "Of course not. There'll be plenty of time for that."

Silver checks in with me, his expression bordering on furtive, and I wonder if he's been thinking this over, if the entire board has been wondering how best to handle this "indelicate" separation. Are they anticipating a scene? I'm sure our eagerness to keep Whistler has been discussed. Maybe they've hired security.

Jasper opens his arms, Whistler curls into place, and the two press heads together. Something gets whispered in a ratty, cauliflower ear, something vital, like my son doesn't believe Silver, or isn't taking any chances, and then Jasper pulls away, shuffling awkwardly, shyly, just in front of me, unable to resist one last look over his shoulder.

Down a hallway, we pass an elderly man in a funereal black three-piece suit and tie (maybe they really did hire security), seated outside a door. The man ignores us, head down, engrossed in a magazine, like he's waiting for someone to come out, rather than waiting to be invited to go in.

Silver guides us past him and into a brightly lit conference room dominated by a glossy dark wood table surrounded by high-back leather chairs. People stand as we enter, and Clay leads us through a series of greetings and small talk with each member of the Paws Unlimited advisory board.

For the record, I am awful at remembering the names of people I've just been introduced to, and the first person surging forward is no exception. This woman, somehow insisting on an awkward, overly familiar hug, looks totally miscast for a leading role in a nonprofit charitable organization. She's too young, late twenties tops, a pretty pale redhead with freckles and unquestionably false eyelashes, sporting way too much cleavage and what can only be described as a sparkling boulder weighing down her left hand.

"And you must be the famous Jasper Blunt," she says, letting me catch the hint of a drawl, delighted to take Jasper's hand in a formal shake.

I want to believe she's *not* a trophy wife. I want to believe she's a highly successful entrepreneur with a love of dogs and a determination to be philanthropic. Even so, I can't help but think about Miss Scarlet in Jasper's board game Clue.

Another name gets fired my way, but it flies right past, and I'm caught in a fierce double-hander greeting from a man who looks like he just got back from somewhere tropical based on the intensity of his tan. It makes his teeth pop. A small diamond stud twinkles in his left ear, and the stringy bolo tie was a mistake, but what strikes me is the way he will not be hurried in his encounter with Jasper.

"Whose colors are those?" he asks, seemingly engrossed by the backstory regarding Jasper's Argentinean soccer shirt.

The weakest and meekest greeting comes from a tiny Hispanic woman—I know the last name ended in "chez," but that's
all I got—with a pair of glasses dangling around her neck on a
gold chain like a piece of jewelry. She wears her jet-black hair
straight and long, the part in the middle so precise it forms a
thick white line splicing her scalp into two, like a surgical scar.
Unlike the others, she maintains her distance, offering a perfunctory nod and a polite but antsy smile, as if sad or pained to
see us, and I wonder if she's having second thoughts. Perhaps
she's been caught up in the excitement of uniting Emily Smart
with Whistler, but now, with my boy standing in front of her,
she's realizing how this new merger requires a painful breakup.
What if she regrets having to tear Jasper away from the dog he
loves?

The last person to say hello is also the slowest. With a practiced hand leaning heavily into a wooden cane, a woman who
must be pushing ninety negotiates the corner of the table and
lurches toward me. She wears a charcoal gray suit, the cut no-
nonsense, like a Catholic girl's school principal, the collar of her
blouse high and frilly, no jewelry, her white hair cut short and
simple. Her head and neck crane forward and duck down from
her shoulders, her cheeks sucked flat against bone. But it's her
eyes that demand attention. Forget rheumy, bloodshot, or milky
with mature cataracts: for all the wrinkles and liver spots, her
eyes are a vivid, sparkly green that telegraph all anyone needs to
know—ignore the frail exterior, for inside here I am very much
alive.

"And last but certainly not least, this is Alice McClennon."

McClennon. Now that is a name I remember. That was Whistler's sponsor on the plaque in the lobby.

I make to shake but Alice's right hand tightens on the cane, forcing me to alter my flight path, faking a smile, and veering into an unscripted hair adjustment.

Alice smiles back and replies with a crisp, single nod—approval or disdain, it's impossible to tell. Rarely have I felt so scrutinized.

"And this is Kate's son. This is Jasper."

Clay has pushed Jasper forward, and Jasper is so close to Alice McClennon he has to strain his head back to meet her eyes. It's not helping that Jasper is gawping. She's probably the oldest person he's ever met.

"Thank you, young man," says Alice.

My hypnotized son only manages to mouth, "You're welcome."

"Why don't you two have a seat?" says Silver. "This won't take long."

Jasper and I are seated before Ms. McClennon has flopped back down in her chair at the far end of the room. Perhaps she's purposefully isolated herself from the others.

I drop my hands below the table ledge so no one can see I'm checking my watch. In four more minutes Jasper needs hooking up to another antibiotic.

"It's hard to know where to begin," says Silver, "but let me start with some marvelous news. Before you arrived this morning, this board unanimously agreed to cover all your expenses for bringing Whistler home."

He pauses, perhaps waiting for me to interject with "That won't be necessary," while my attention is on Jasper, the way he winced at the word *home*. Nobody seems to notice.

"In this handout"—Clayton Silver slides a copy to both Jasper and me—"we've laid out the program for tomorrow's graduation ceremony. You'll see that we get going around ten and we'd like to be done by twelve, twelve-fifteen at the very latest."

Jasper leans my way and whispers one word: "Flight."

"That may be a problem," I say, "our flight back to Boston is out of Dallas. Leaving at twelve might be cutting it a little close. With the drive."

Miss Scarlet turns to Tan-Man and mouths "Dallas?" wrinkling her perfect nose, and like that, I'm on edge, the old me on the defensive, ready to lecture her on the challenges of coordinating medications and flight schedules, prepared to squash her high school mean girl attitude before she can add, "What kind of loser flies out of Dallas?" But instead of blowing a gasket, I hesitate, recognize the lurch inside, and wait long enough to let it settle back down as her question transforms from a bitchy— yes, of course I take my sugar daddy's Learjet for granted— accusation, to one of honest surprise, reflecting the abundance of more convenient airports nearby.

Tan-Man—Ian? Ethan?—eases forward in his seat, consulting his own copy of the program. "I don't foresee a problem. As long as Congressman Jessup doesn't run over, we should be good. If needs be, we can always push up our presentation to Jasper and go straight from there to Whistler."

Clayton Silver glances around for other opinions and I notice how his first port of call is Alice McClennon. He's rewarded with a slow blink of assent and, as best as I can tell, that's the only "yes" that matters.

"Perhaps, Kate, Jasper, I might share a little backstory so you can better—"

"I'm sorry to interrupt, Mr. Silver, but would you and the rest of the board mind if I set up Jasper's antibiotic treatment? We can go somewhere private if you'd prefer."

"If it's fine by you, Jasper, it's fine by us," says Alice McClennon.

Nods of agreement all round, but I'm impressed by the way the old woman consulted directly with my son, and not me.

Jasper rolls up his sleeve, exposes his PICC line, and we hook up. Sensing he's not the least bit self-conscious, I dare to let the Eclipse ball sit on the table for everyone to see. This is good.

"Sorry, Mr. Silver, you were saying."

"Yes. Right. I wanted to be totally honest with both of you. Our annual graduation of service dogs is our biggest event of the year. It's uplifting, inspirational, and hugely emotional. Everyone partnering with a dog gets the opportunity to share their story, to talk about what it means for them to have this canine companion in their life. Actually being here, witnessing these bonds, well . . . I thought it would be helpful. I hoped it might, I don't know . . . ease your concerns . . . confirm that you were doing the right thing."

"Trust me," says Miss Scarlet, "do not wear mascara unless it's waterproof."

Tan-Man agrees. "Never a dry eye in the house."

Alice McClennon looks as though she begs to differ, and perhaps her colleague with the melanin addiction should get a grip.

"The timing with Whistler, finding him when we did, it couldn't have been better. But it's not entirely coincidental. What I mean is we plan this event months in advance, and we are constantly looking for new angles to attract media attention."

"It's a huge fundraising opportunity," whispers the Hispanic woman, almost grimacing with the awkwardness of discussing money.

"Whistler is like a soldier missing in action," says Silver. "To us he's a legend, an enigma, an unsung hero, vanishing in a twister, his partner tragically killed. This time of year I always try to put feelers out, check in with rescue groups, just to be sure, never thinking that from a distance of two thousand miles away he'd turn up. What were the chances? It was like winning the Powerball."

He's speaking directly to Jasper now, but my mind is back with the Hispanic woman. *It's a huge fundraising opportunity.* Is she trying to guilt me into *not* taking the reward? I need to clarify; this isn't about the money. It's about getting Jasper another dog because he can't have the dog he wants.

"See," says Tan-Man, elbows on table, hands clasped together, edging closer, "not only do we get to donate a seizure alert dog to a young girl in desperate need of assistance, we also get to celebrate the return of a service dog given up for dead. TV and print media covered the Beaver Creek tornado tragedy for days. It was national news. How often do they get to come full circle with a success story after a disaster of this magnitude? It's a win-win situation for everyone concerned."

There's a second when I catch myself, prepared to bite my tongue, but the injustice refuses to be ignored. Is this the moment to make my final plea? And how far do I go? Unmasking the vulnerable version of me may win more sympathy, but Jasper still expects his mom to be a rock. Best to strike a balance. Give a little. Less of a crack, more of a bend.

"Actually, that's not true," I say, feeling the heads going back, the synchronized recoil from my dissent. "My son is the loser and, arguably, so is the dog at the center of your story. Oh, I totally get it, and we're on board with a uniquely talented dog helping a uniquely receptive person in need. But don't tell me it's a win-win. It doesn't make it any easier to bear, not least for my son."

"My apologies," says Tan-Man, hand on heart, playing the gesture like a measure of sincerity, "and just to be clear, the reward we intend to present to Jasper is meant purely as a show of our gratitude for Whistler's return. It in no way constitutes a . . . well . . ."

"Bribe? Incentive? Sweetener?" I offer. "It's okay. I wish we weren't here to collect a check, but we are. We need the money. Yes, I'm an animal doctor, but I'm a single mom. I work in a nonprofit animal shelter that's struggling to survive and I'd love to tell you the money will come in handy to buy a new car, or take Jasper on a cruise, or pay for his first year of college. But I need it to help us move apartments, to a place where we can have a dog, because that's what I promised my son."

A moment of silence follows, and I don't care if it's uncomfortable.

Unfortunately my son does. "When does Emily get to meet Whistler?" he asks.

"It's going to happen at the graduation itself," says Silver. "It's not how we normally do it, but a number of producers from the TV networks suggested that it might be a nice touch."

"I'm sorry," I interject, "but Terri mentioned you have a center where dogs and partners get to know each other, see if it works out. It sounded like it takes a while. What if Emily and Whistler are not a match?"

Silver consults with other board members, but I notice how Alice McClennon keeps her eyes cast down.

"Sadly, Kate, if this doesn't work out for Emily, there are a dozen other Emilys in need of his service as a seizure alert dog."

Of course there are, I think, and once again it's an effort to tamp down the frustration I've felt ever since Silver insisted we bring him back. Time to try a different approach.

"But what about Whistler's injuries? I mean, not putting too fine a point on it, he was . . ." I want to say tortured, not least for dramatic effect, but I don't want to frighten Jasper. "Abused, his muzzle taped shut to stop him barking."

Jasper startles, genuinely appalled, and though I probably should have warned him in advance, the fact that he might burst into tears has definitely got their attention.

"I've examined the dog's throat. His vocal cords appear perfectly healthy. I think he is simply *afraid* to bark. I'm sure we'll never know what monster did this to Whistler, but the physical scars he bears are perhaps only a small part of what continues to haunt him. Imagine the psychological turmoil necessary to make a dog hold back his bark. What else is going on in this poor dog's head? And he's been out of training for years. What if he's forgotten his purpose for being here, his ability to predict a seizure? Surely that would allow him a chance to retire without the need to work?"

"You're asking questions I cannot answer," says Silver. "But what I will say is this: if nothing else, having Whistler back gives us a fantastic opportunity to raise awareness of the importance of service dogs, on a national level. The demand for these special companions has never been greater. If our organization gets to partner more dogs with more people in need, thanks to Whistler's return, it will have been more than worth it."

"You make his return sound like a publicity stunt."

I think about that article I saw in the newspaper—a timely piece of advertising—as Silver sighs and twists uncomfortably in his seat.

"Sorry," I say, "that was unfair. Normally I wouldn't be so invested. But this is my son. And for whatever reason, he's fallen in love with this dog. What I want to say, to all of you, is if Whistler doesn't make the grade, if he can't work, refuses to work, has forgotten how to work, please, please think about my son. He and I will gladly come back any time and give Whistler the best retirement any working dog could ever wish for."

Miss Scarlet and Tan-Man nod in unison, the Hispanic

woman refuses to meet my eyes, while Alice McClennon can't stop staring at Jasper. Silver takes a moment to deliberate, a finger and thumb smoothing down his mustache.

"If it ever becomes necessary, I'm sure this board"—he opens both palms wide, the preacher turning to his congregation—"will give your offer our most serious consideration."

But in that moment, to my way of thinking, his polite smile telegraphs, "I'm just humoring you," no less insensitive than turning to Jasper and saying, "Don't hold your breath."

56

Jasper

I KIND OF switched off after Mom finally fessed up about how Whistler got his zebra scars because it made me really sad and then really mad, like I wished I could find whoever did it and duct tape their mouth shut to see how they liked it.

Mom was scary serious, even making her voice tremble, and it was cool the way the room went dead silent when she was saying those nice things about Whistler. More proof that she really loves him.

Cowboy Clay kept talking about the graduation and where we had to go and what time we had to be there and something about speaking to reporters about how we found Whistler and, blah, blah, blah, on and on he went. I just wanted to know what was up with Whistler. Did he think I'd just walked away, like peace out and gone? Was he upstairs with Terri failing his tests? Was part of my sadness his sadness?

The next thing I know, Mom says we're done, I'm waving my

Eclipse ball to everyone as we leave, and we're out in the parking lot headed for the Tahoe, feeling all wrong, because our three-some is back to a twosome.

"Dr. Blunt, Dr. Blunt." It's the guy from outside the conference room, the one in a black suit like someone died. He's way too old to be running. Maybe Cowboy Clay sent him to say, "We've changed our mind. You can keep Whistler after all."

"Dr. Blunt." The guy can barely catch his breath. Welcome to my world. "Mrs. McClennon wonders if you and your son would care to join her for lunch."

Mom and I turn back to see the oldest woman I've ever met, rocking on her cane, heading our way.

"She's most insistent," says the man, looking worried, like he's afraid that we will say no, like she might kill him if we say no.

Mom consults her watch and then me. "We've still got another couple of hours before check-in. It's up to you."

I shrug. "So long as it's not seafood," I say to the man.

He smiles. His front tooth is chipped, which only makes me think of Whistler again. "Thank you," he says, waving at the old woman. "I'll get the car. Be right back."

He disappears as the *clack-clack-clack* of the cane gets closer and closer.

"So glad Stephen caught you," says Mrs. McClennon. She's carrying a small handbag in her other hand—a bit like the Queen of England. "I would have invited you earlier but I didn't want to attract attention in front of the others. It's only a ten-minute drive so you can leave your car here and Stephen can run you back, or, if it suits you better, follow in your vehicle."

"We'll follow," says Mom, as a loud "Whoa" gets away from me when this really fancy car rounds the corner and glides into place beside us. It's massive and long, shiny dark blue, and there's this great big silver angel statue hanging off the front.

Stephen hops out and rushes around to open the passenger door. It takes a while for Mrs. McClennon to climb into the back seat, but once inside she says, "Would Jasper like a ride in a Rolls-Royce?"

"That would be brilliant," I say, waiting, but not wanting to wait, for Mom to say no. But she doesn't. Mom smiles, then mouths, "Go on."

I drop my antibiotic ball into the pocket of my sweats, about to climb in, when Mom leans forward and whispers, "Be yourself," giving me the serious eyes and a quick little nod like I should understand before jogging off to the Tahoe. I don't get it. *Be yourself.* Who else would I be? What's she trying to say?

I take the seat opposite and across from Mrs. McClennon— because I can—with my back to Stephen behind the steering wheel. She makes a show of putting on her seat belt, hitching up her brows like I'd best do the same or we're not going anywhere. When Mom lines up the Tahoe behind us and flashes her lights, off we go.

I probably should say something nice about the soft seats, or the drinks cabinet, or the fancy adjustable footrest, but the window glass is tinted so dark that people on the outside will probably think I'm famous, so I pretend to be cool. Then I start to worry that facing backward may not have been a good idea. What if I get carsick and throw up in her lap?

Mrs. McClennon presses a button and something buzzes behind my head. It's a long glass wall powering up to the ceiling, separating Stephen in front, from us in the back—way cool.

"He's a wonderful assistant, but he loves to listen in for gossip," she says. I nod in a no-worries kind of way. Then I wonder if she thinks I'm agreeing, like everyone has a servant so I know exactly what she means.

"What's with . . . ?" She points to the ball rolling around on the seat beside me. I stuff it back in my pocket and tell her a bit about antibiotics and CF. It's weird, telling the oldest woman I've ever met how hard it is to stay alive, but she seems really interested.

"I'd never know you were sick, aside from the, um—"

"Eclipse. That's the thing about CF; the bad stuff is deep down where you can't see it. A bit like an iceberg."

Mrs. McClennon seems confused but she must have seen *Titanic*. Maybe she was even on it.

"Do kids with CF get seizures?"

I like where she's going with this and then it hits me. I bet Mom thought this ride might turn into an interview about me keeping Whistler. That's why I have to be myself.

"Maybe," I say, because of course, I've done some serious research on the subject. "A lot of CF patients get diabetes and when that happens the sugar in your blood can go low and sometimes that can cause seizures, so in answer to your question, kind of."

Mrs. McClennon leans in close, crinkles up her wrinkles, and asks, "Do you get afraid?"

Wow. Tough question.

"Only if it gets hard to breathe, and usually a hit on my puffer bails me out."

She rocks back in her seat but keeps her eyes on me like I might steal something. No wonder Stephen is frightened of her.

"I think you are very brave."

I shake my head. "People have to *choose* to be brave, *decide* to be brave, and I don't have a choice. So I'm not brave, I'm just a kid with CF."

This time I get a tiny smile. Much better.

"You have friends, at school?"

"A few," I say, hoping kids on the soccer team count.

"Healthy children, children living without restrictions, without a care in the world?"

I nod and slowly she raises her chin—at this distance I notice it is powdery and covered in fine fuzzy hairs.

"Don't you get jealous? I know I would. Having to work so hard, just to stay alive, and them getting a free pass?"

"It's not my fault. It's not theirs. It's all I've ever known. And anyway, they may look normal, but what's normal? When Mom and me go to the hospital, I look around and realize I don't have it so bad. Lots of kids have it much worse. Lots of parents have it much worse, like if their child dies in a car crash, or gets kidnapped, or does drugs, or ends up in prison."

Mrs. McClennon almost smiles again, but then she catches Stephen checking her out in the rearview mirror. She presses a button next to her armrest, keeps it pressed down and says, "Dr. Blunt still in hot pursuit?"

A tiny voice says, "Yes, ma'am."

She lets go and returns her hand to her lap. I stare at her hands. I stare at the hands of all old people, at the popped up veins and the creases and the spots because I'm probably not going to grow up to have hands like that.

"That stuff about taping Whistler's mouth shut makes me so angry," I say. "And not just 'cause it must have hurt, but because he wouldn't have known what he did wrong."

She gives me a grown-up stare—slight head tilt, narrow eyes—the one when they want to know what you're really thinking. "You two are close?"

Big nod. "Very."

She looks surprised, like she's not sure she believes me. "Maybe he's changed after all these years."

"Wait. You knew Whistler from before he went missing?"

"Certainly. My late husband, Donald, gave Whistler his name."

Whoa. Of course. The plaque for retired names in the lobby. D. H. McClennon. *D* is for Donald. This is huge.

"What was Whistler like back then? What made your husband pick him? Was he difficult to train? No. Couldn't have been. Whistler's way too clever. But did he get his name from the guy who painted his mom? Did he live with . . . ?"

She pats the air between us like I need to calm down. "My Donald loved all dogs; pedigree, mutt, big, small, didn't matter. I imagine something special about Whistler caught his attention, but he never said what. When Donald came back from the war, dogs played a big part in his version of solace. Being the heir to an oil fortune may have helped turn Paws Unlimited into a reality, but his passion for helping others discover the joys of canine companionship has kept it alive."

Two things: Alice McClennon's eyes get sad when she mentions her husband; second, which war is she talking about?

"But Mr. McClennon gave Whistler his name?"

"That's right. Oh, it's a gimmick, paying to name a dog in training, a way to give more money, but it always gave Donald a personal connection to both the animal and the person they went on to help. More often than not he'd pick from his favorite artists, especially those from the nineteenth century—Manet, Monet, Matisse, Munch—"

"And James Abbott McNeil Whistler."

She flashes me big "smarty-pants" eyes and I blush. I could tell her I only know because of the biker guy who rescued us when the Fiat broke down.

"Do you think he'll be able to work as a service dog again?" I ask.

"Why not?"

"Because he might have forgotten how to warn someone they're about to seizure?"

She smoothes down her skirt and hums, like she's thinking. "I do recall Donald saying something about Whistler being a particularly difficult dog to place."

My "What?" comes out as more of a scream than a question.

"At Paws Unlimited we pride ourselves on the fit, selecting precisely the right dog for the right client. I'm led to believe no dog was more challenging than Whistler. And the problem wasn't the clients. They loved him. It was whether Whistler loved them back, whether he wanted to work for them. Clayton always makes sure his big donors get regular updates regarding dogs they've sponsored, and I can't tell you how many times Whistler kept changing partners. That's why it never made sense, the whole Beaver Creek tornado tragedy. I mean, it seemed like Whistler had finally clicked with poor Mr. Wallace. So why did the dog disappear? Why wasn't he by his master's side?"

"Maybe he was trapped, or injured, or went to crime scene B." I can tell she's impressed by my knowledge of stranger danger.

"Possibly," she says, "but if Whistler was truly bonded to his partner, wouldn't his natural response be to try to find him?"

I think about this and imagine the Antarctica scar, the ratty chewed ear, and the droopy eyelid and wonder: If he had all these injuries and I was his partner, would he try to look for me?

"He's wandered around a lot since living on the Cape." I tell her about him running away from different owners, and then I tell her about when we were in the hospital and Whistler remembered his way back to our apartment.

"What else have you two been up to?" She makes it sound like I might be in trouble, and for a second I stutter and mumble about stuff like slow licks and how Whistler likes to rest his chin on your lap and drool, but then I think about the way Mom is in the hospital, going on and on to all the doctors and nurses about my disease, like she can't stop, and suddenly that's how I get, telling Mrs. McClennon about hide-and-seek with Cousin Tawd and how we got into the soccer playoffs and, without me thinking about it, I kind of slow down and forget my words, because this Whistler talk is making me sad and Mrs. McClennon is right—I need to be brave.

She creaks forward and pats my knee. "From what you've told me, despite everything that poor dog went through, the essence of Whistler, everything that you have come to . . . appreciate . . . appears to be just the same as before. Unchanged, resilient, and intact."

Mrs. McClennon talks to me like she thinks I'm a lot brighter than I really am. Perhaps I should remind her that I'm only eleven.

For the first time on this ride her eyes drift off mine, go all shiny, and then, from nowhere, she begins to smile. "Sorry," she says, reaching in her pocket for a white handkerchief, dabbing at her right eye, "I always get a little sentimental in this car."

I ask, "Why?" to be polite, and because I'm pretty sure she's going to tell me anyway.

"Oh, Donald loved his Rolls. Loved his classic cars; always the classics. Insisted Stephen take them out for a regular spin."

Here we go. This kind of thing happens whenever I talk to Burt back at the shelter. Old people love to blab about a time before cell phones and the Internet, when no one was rude, and there was no gluten-free food, and rock and roll hadn't been invented.

"It was what you were saying about Whistler, the way it reminded me of the night Donald and I first met, nineteen forty-nine, a charity ball at the Hotel Lawrence in downtown Dallas. It was love at first sight."

"Exactly," I want to scream—but I don't. That's exactly what happened when I first met Whistler, only now I can't have him anymore.

The car slows and we make a sharp turn. Outside the tinted glass, a sign slips by, and I catch the words *country club*.

"Mrs. McClennon, can I ask you a question about Mr. Mc-Clennon?"

"Go on."

"Because . . . with Whistler . . . well . . . ever since he found me, these big ideas have been popping into my head . . . like I'm smarter, like I can see stuff different, and it all makes sense suddenly. I swear they're not my ideas, so I'm guessing they have to come from Whistler. I know, that sounds kind of weird and I don't want to freak you out, but I wonder if Mr. McClennon ever said that he and Whistler could, like, know what the other was thinking, just know, without words, like a special way of communicating."

From her expression I'm guessing she thinks the train to crazy town has left the station.

"It's just . . . my sinuses are totally messed up, so I can't smell properly and one of my meds is making me deaf, but—and this might be the biggest 'but' ever—it's like I've swapped my crappy senses for one completely new and awesome sense—being able to feel what Whistler feels, deep inside, knowing exactly what he would say out loud if he could."

Mrs. McClennon grins a big false-toothed grin. "I know exactly what you mean."

"You do?" I say.

"Of course. Oh, I don't know whether my late husband did

that sort of thing with Whistler, or any other dog for that matter, but I certainly experienced exactly that sort of thing with Donald himself."

"Really?"

"Definitely. And this ability to know what another person or an animal is feeling, it's got a name."

This is brilliant. So much better than psycho dog-speak.

"Yes," she says, "it's called love."

57

Kate

His eyes flutter, speech slurs, and try as he might, my beautiful boy succumbs to sleep, still mumbling something about you know who.

What with the driving and last night's camping adventure I'm just as beat but it's not even eight. One more dose of poison to deliver before I can crash.

Of course I'm biased, but if Mrs. McClennon's motive for lunch was to find out whether Jasper and Whistler were compatible, then how could she not be impressed? My son ignored the dark stuffy setting, the country club staff fawning over a Texas blue blood, the absence of a kids menu, and gave her his all. It scares me the way the elderly mesmerize him, the way he studies them, like I can see him wondering what it would be like, this phase of life beyond his reach. He melted every time she asked him about Whistler, like he and the mutt were more than just allies, like they could finish each other's sentences.

Back in the real world of the Holiday Inn Express, Jasper's disappointment at not being able to order room service was off-set by an attraction with far greater appeal—a Jacuzzi.

"Promise I won't go in above my belly button."

I've always railed against these bubbling vats of bacteria, but in this new spirit of showing Jasper a good time, I cave, and watch in delight as the pale skinny kid, with a Ziploc bag and rolls of Saran Wrap distorting his upper arm, lowers himself into a blue-green cauldron. Besides, having surreptitiously snagged a copy of the *Lincoln Peak Tribune* from the front desk, it's a perfect distraction while I finally read the article that's been bugging me all day.

"'Emily will receive a dog that not only loves her uncondi-tionally, but can also, potentially, save her life,' says Clayton Sil-ver, in charge of tomorrow's ceremony. 'Graduating our class of service dogs is always special, and emotional, but uniting Emily with Whistler promises to take the event to a whole new level.'"

I have to put the paper down. This may be nothing more than a promotional teaser, Silver's attempt to draw a big and generous crowd, but it doubles down on his conviction that Whistler is destined to be with a girl the dog has never met, and pried apart from a boy he already loves. How on earth can I keep Whistler and my son together? For all Alice McClennon's deep apprecia-tion of their bond, she gave no hint of changing course, of choos-ing Jasper over Emily, leaving me with a sense that, despite her clout, her hands were already tied. Having read the story, and with tomorrow's graduation upon us, perhaps it's time to bag my attempts at reason and polite appeal. I'll try to keep Jasper out of this, but, unlike him, I've got nothing to lose. Clearly, in order to keep Whistler, I'm going to have to fight ugly.

After a shower—to wash off the Jacuzzi's primordial ooze—and brushing his teeth before bed, Jasper is sitting cross-legged on the floor, straight-backed, in what looks like a yoga pose.

"What's going on?"

"Try this," he says. "Get down on the floor, sit like me, and see if you can get up without using your hands."

I comply but fail miserably, while my son transitions from sitting to standing in one fluid, effortless motion.

"I'm impressed," I say.

"I read online that if you can do it, you're going to live for a long time."

"And what if you can't?"

He scrunches his eyes and twists his lips into an unsaid "Sucks to be you," so I chase him into bed.

But thoughts about my imminent mortality must still be swirling inside his head. "What's going to happen to me if something happens to you?"

And once again, as easy as that, Jasper knocks the wind out of me.

I think about who would take care of him. Not his father, even if it was over my dead body. Gwen? Mom and Dad?

"Nothing's going to happen to me."

"But how do you know?"

"Because," I say, sitting on the bed beside him, "I made a promise."

"To who? When? I don't remember."

"Not to you. To Baby Jasper. When you were first diagnosed with CF I swore an oath to the two-year-old version of you, promising I'd always be there, no matter what. Can't believe you've forgotten already."

"Mom." Jasper squirms under the cover and I want time to stop, for him to never get one second older, one second sicker than he is right now.

He adjusts his pillows, turns on his side, and I tuck him in.

"Whistler doesn't want to be there. I can tell."

"Jasper, when I was your age, my parents shipped me off to a camp up in Maine every summer. Each time I started out homesick and hating it. Eight weeks later I cried because I didn't want to leave. It's perfectly normal to be upset by change, but Whistler will be fine. He'll adapt. He's probably ready to settle down."

"But what if he doesn't?"

"If he doesn't, I'll remind your new best friend Alice McClennon who's got first dibs."

He's asleep before my lips even leave his cheek. I don't think he's coughed all day. I should hook him up to this toxic juice forever. This is the glimpse of what might be possible, our temporary cure, sucking me back into a world of promise and second chances. It's irresistible, intoxicating, and it will break my heart, this calm before the next storm. Can I run with it, milk it for all it's worth while it lasts?

This strange, sterile hotel room unsettles me and the lack of our ugly mutt isn't helping, the big dog leaving a big hole. I flash to our meeting with Terri the trainer, the way she sees something remarkable in this creature, and now I realize that Whistler's talent is not limited to intercepting an electrical storm brewing inside a child's head. It's far less complex but more far-reaching. How else to explain the way I notice his absence, this dog who performs his magic with nothing more than his presence?

Whistler is the gift. The dog is the gift, having an effect on everyone he meets. He can make you smile and make you swear, he can change your perspective and harden your resolve, he can make you bristle or smooth out the rough edges. For all his specialized training, he's a dog who provokes a response, forcing you out of your comfort zone. In other words, like a wise little boy insisted, Whistler makes you live. Not bigger, not smaller, just more.

Aware and a little uncomfortable with this new, introspective version of me, I crack open my laptop, click on the Outlook icon, open Martha's latest email—"No need to rush back," and "Tell me you've thought of a long-term solution to keep the shelter afloat"—and think, why not, picking up my phone.

Martha starts out surprised and awkward, but she quickly evolves from monosyllables to waxing lyrical about the shelter's imminent insolvency.

"Whatever happens," I say, "we would have sunk long ago, if not for you."

Silence, and I wonder if she's about to unload on me, for getting distracted, for leaving her in the lurch, for putting family first. But then she hits me with, "He's lucky. You're such a good mom."

And even though her voice is shockingly, unnervingly meek, it's a jolt, so unexpected and yet so personal, making it all the more potent and persuasive.

You're such a good mom. When was the last time I paid Gwen or my mother this compliment?

Then my mind backpedals, sees past the flattery, and settles on that word again, *lucky*. Back in the hospital, speaking to Martha, I heard an adjective that made me flinch, my previous disposition primed to interpret sarcasm or hostility. Not anymore. Martha wasn't referring to Whistler. She wasn't being mean-spirited. She probably said something like, "Hope Jasper realizes how lucky he is." A throwaway line, wanting a son to appreciate his doting mother. Nothing more. From time to time I've bristled at Martha because I've chosen to see an employee who, by preferring animals to people, by being curt and imperious to the volunteers, might harbor an unspoken resentment toward my son. Now I see how mistaken I've been and, more importantly, how detached. That's why the question I ask is wrong, is not me, doesn't sound the least bit like me, yet I ask it all the same.

"Martha, what are you doing for Thanksgiving?"

It's away from me, this awkward invitation, followed by the nervous joke about my dysfunctional family, the promise that she'd be doing Jasper and me a favor, the confession regarding my lack of culinary talent.

The empty static between us makes me think she's hunting for an excuse, trying it on for size in her head. I'm about to give her an out, suggest she's probably already got plans when Martha jumps in with a quick "Sure," and "Let me know what to bring." Ten seconds later she's gone, as if hanging up will stop her from changing her mind.

Back to reality, endless emails, and one from Katrina

Goddard-Brown featuring a red exclamation point that, in part, reads, "Having not received a reply to the contrary, I propose we meet at the shelter the day of your return, no later than eleven." Wait a minute. KGB wants to visit the shelter? A face-to-face meeting? I re-read her last half-dozen emails—cranky, but nothing more than her usual corporate coldness. Surely, if she wanted to fire me or close the place she'd have laid the groundwork?

Something must be seriously wrong with me if I can find a positive spin on being able to keep my job. Thanks, Whistler. Perhaps I should take advantage of my psychological reboot—because God knows how long it will last—and exploit this mind-set with two other phone calls I've been putting off for way too long. And so what if they think I've grazed my way through the contents of our minibar.

First up, my sister, Gwen. We do the usual pleasantries, a superficial catch-up and synopsis of the trip, and then I get down to it.

"When were you going to tell me, about the drinking?"

The phone line falls silent.

"Gwen, you still there?"

"There never seemed to be a right time, what with everything you go through," she says, her words syncopated and cautious.

I flinch, realizing I've made a mistake. Just as I feared, everything comes back to my son's incurable disease.

"Please, don't blame Jasper."

"It's not Jasper, not really," she says. "It's just . . . it feels wrong to unload. If I'm being honest, sometimes it's like you're mad at me."

Ordinarily, a line like this would prove overwhelming, Gwen's premonition of anger becoming a reality. Since when was *my* pain and *my* fear for Jasper about her? But this time is different. Why? Because on some twisted level, she's right. I'm mad as hell. Mad at Jasper's lot, my lot, and the unfairness of it all, convinced that we suffer and everyone else gets off scot-free.

"Talk to me," I say, and slowly, cautiously, she sets free her tale of loneliness, marital insecurity, and fear for the future. It's a simple tale, a universal tale, a tale that could be told by any mother anywhere, regardless of their children's health.

"I've known a couple of friends with cancer," says Gwen, "and I can't imagine what they go through but . . . and I know this sounds bad, but sometimes I swear you and Jasper have it worse."

"What are you talking about?"

She hesitates, but still steps into the minefield. "Look, don't hate me for saying this, but, like, for lots of cancers there's either a cure, remission, or you're dead. It's horrible, but it's true. When friends and family hear you've got cancer they rally around, they root for you, cook meals, fundraise, shave their heads, visit you in the hospital, because they are fighting for a cause with some kind of a resolution, and hopefully a good one, that's within reach. CF is different. CF just keeps going with no end in sight."

I want to stop her right there. I don't care what type you're talking about, cancer is never a picnic; and when it comes to CF, there is an end in sight—one that won't fly in Hollywood.

"After a while we give up, take the easy option, checking in because we feel we have to. Not venting my crap seems like the least I can do."

Gwen's totally fooled me, but to some extent she's not that different from me. I don't share because if you care enough, I don't want to let you down and I can't "get over it" because there is no getting over it. Droning on and on about the bad stuff will render you speechless, lost for words, and as strange as it might sound, I'm left with a perverse sense of guilt for being such a downer. Easier to zip it, back off, and curl up into a ball, hope no one notices.

"But Gwen, you *know* my situation. How was I supposed to know you had a problem?"

"What are you talking about?" says Gwen. "No one lets anyone know."

She's probably right. Who can tell what lies behind the forced smiles, the lofty aspirations, and the humble brags? Since when did incurable lung disease hurt more than paraplegia, than leukemia, than the loss of a parent, than an unpaid mortgage, than a failed marriage, than the craving for another glass of wine? My pain is not greater than your pain. It's just different. What matters is how we choose to handle it and try to push through. I wish I had the answer, directions to the easiest path forward. If my son is to be believed, I should tell Gwen to toss a dog into the mix, any dog, and let him lead the way.

"I can come off as impatient and intolerant," I say, "and bitter and a pain in the ass, but I promise not to hide so much from you, so long as you promise not to hide so much from me."

She sucks down a deep breath. "Deal," she says, and by the time we hang up I feel better—which is not the same as deluded.

If Jasper's health were declining, my head might be in a different place.

That was the easy call.

The time difference shouldn't be an issue. My mother the night owl, not constrained by my father's early-morning tee time, picks up on the first ring.

"Hello, dear, how's your road trip going?"

I latch onto her alertness and the way she sounds unconcerned. For a second I dwell on the possibility of cynicism, that she wanted to ask, "How's your ill-advised road trip going?" as if jonesing for a disaster story. But what if years of single-parenting a sick kid have rendered me overly sensitive?

"Great. Jasper's loving it." I glimpse the boy in the bed, the boy asleep on his back and say, "In fact, he's the reason I decided to call."

She waits a beat—maybe out of fear, maybe out of confusion—before asking, "Is everything alright?"

"Everything's fine. I just want you to know . . . it's just . . . sometimes I don't appreciate how hard it must be for you, being a grandmother to a CF kid born out of wedlock, and it's my fault I don't let you in, it's my fault I hide and sugarcoat and avoid and try to be normal, but I want you to know that Jasper needs you. We both need you. He's just a little boy who wants a little life, whatever that life may be. I am who I am because of him. He may have shaped me, but he loves being part of a family, and like any kid with only one parent, that makes his grandparents very special."

There's a huge pause and, for a while, all I hear is the gentle hiss of her breathing, and I can't believe she didn't cut me off, or change the direction of the conversation, but then the rhythm of her breathing shifts, replaced by the ragged sound of air chopped apart by crying.

"Oh, Mom, don't get upset."

"You kids were . . . easy . . . healthy . . . sometimes I . . . sometimes I don't know what to do. I mean I know I get . . ."

I wait for "impatient, self-absorbed, bitchy."

". . . frustrated . . . but I'm not being judgmental . . . okay, I am . . . but not about you."

"You've lost me, Mom."

She hesitates, as if searching for the words that need to be said, the proverbial air that needs to be cleared.

"You said 'out of wedlock,' as if marriage were some kind of solution or salvation, but look at your sister—fancy clothes, fancy house, never wanting for money, and perfectly miserable. And look at your father and me."

"You two have done okay. What's it been, forty . . ."

"Forty-four years."

"There you go."

"Kate, come on, your father and I live in the same house but we're roommates at best. Have been forever."

I can't argue the point.

"There's something I've been meaning to share with you, something I've spent the better part of my life trying to forget. And don't worry, by today's standards it's no big deal, and I never thought you knowing would be in any way helpful, but . . .

these past few years . . . you and I have . . . you know . . . well, we've drifted apart, haven't we?"

After a lifetime of avoidance, and Mom's gift for sweeping unsavory or awkward topics under the carpet, pure panic begins to build inside me.

"The thing is, I envy you. Not your situation, of course not, but I am jealous of your strength."

"Thanks, I guess."

"Seeing what you go through with Jasper, and how you handle it, makes me feel less than, like I should have done better."

"Mom, you did a perfectly fine job of raising three—"

"Your brother, Bob, was conceived three months *before* your father and I got married."

It's out like a burst of gunfire and no less shocking.

"What? But . . . Bob was born March eighth. Your anniversary is . . . some time in May?"

"We chose May. We were actually married the end of August. Look, everyone remembers birthdays. Only two people—if you're lucky—remember a wedding anniversary. Our parents are dead, what few friends that attended the wedding have moved on. The secret was safe."

Shock catches its breath as anger kicks in.

"What the hell, Mom? Why drop this bombshell now and not twelve years ago when it might have helped, when I was going through the exact same crisis?"

"But it wasn't the exact same," she says, sounding defensive. "Back then there was more of a stigma to being a single mom . . . and it wasn't as if Simon, whatever his name is, was prepared to

marry you." She pauses. "And anyway, it had to be your decision. What if you had regrets and blamed me if I swayed you
one way or the other? No, Kate, a decision that big had to be
yours alone."

I want to scream or say something I'll regret. Even if she's
right, why share now and not six months, a year, five years ago?
Have I shut her out that much? How long has she been biding
her time, waiting for my attitude to soften? Tonight, did she
pick up on a change in my tone and jump on the chance to tell?
Don't tell me I have to thank the ugly mutt again. Or does she
recognize a breaking point, forcing her to use the card she hoped
never to play? I wonder if Bob knows? Perhaps I'll have to share
with his wife, the next time she badgers me over my lack of a
boyfriend.

"The thing is, Kate, I envy the way your choices have not been
defined by a man. You were—you are—your own person. And
sometimes . . ."

She begins to cry again.

"Seeing your strength . . . the way you juggle everything . . .
you make it look easy, and it can be a reminder of my own decisions, fill me with regret, especially when your father's being a
pain in the ass over something as stupid as beef tenderloin."

I laugh, and it's sincere, and in that instant I think, if only
Mom had shared earlier, how close we could have been, two
mothers united by a secret to which we can both relate.

"I do pray for you and Jasper," says Mom. "Every day. It may
not seem like much, but it makes me feel better for trying, and
in some small way, I hope it makes him feel better. You know

you only have to ask if you need anything. Oh, and your father may gripe and make excuses, but I think it's only because he's afraid—afraid of being hurt, and . . . you know . . . afraid of losing a grandson."

My state of mind is far from Zen, so I rein in the desire to jump all over this head-in-the-sand philosophy. A mental note suffices—better the pain of loss than the pain of hardening your heart.

I let her know how much I appreciate her honesty, promise we'll talk more when we're home, and put a tirade of ugly questions on hold. Hanging up, it's still too early to tell whether or not I like this new version of me.

In theory, the last thing on my to-do list should be the easiest. Even so, it takes a force of will to fire up my complimentary single-serve coffee maker with the chipped carafe, brew the elixir of the desiccated magic bean, and drink from a polystyrene cup. Yes, I may be a coffee snob, but this is about trading a copacetic fix for something I've been meaning to deep-six for some time.

Adequately caffeinated to stay awake for his final treatment, I rifle my pocketbook and find the container of faux-Advil. Part of the label has sloughed off and the plastic container is scored and gnarled from canine bite marks. Okay, I get the message, visit the bathroom, and toss what remains of the Adderall into the trash.

58

Jasper

"Mom, I look like a total plonker."

She's got me in this shirt and tie and blazer combo and the collar is tight and scratchy at my neck and if anyone from school could see me now they'd be wetting themselves.

"You look great," calls Mom from the bedroom, without even looking. "Besides, it's all you've got, so make do."

My bathroom mirror image grunts and sulks as I take a brush to a sticky-up clump of hair when I notice something in the trash. I pick it up, shake, and it rattles.

"You know this bottle of Advil's not empty," I say.

"Don't worry," says Mom, "I meant to throw it away."

"But there are still lots of pills inside."

"It's okay, Jasper. I'm switching to Tylenol."

The bottle has barely hit the bottom of the can when I hear, "Come on. Grab your suitcase. We're late."

The Paws Unlimited Annual Graduation is held at a big fancy Marriott, and even though the lobby is full of signs directing us to Ballroom A, it's easier for Mom and me to follow the trail of people, some of them with Labradors in vests.

"There'd best be time to say a proper goodbye to Whistler."

"There will," says Mom. "Relax. And smile if I take some pictures. Let me worry about making our flight home."

I wasn't worried. Now I am.

We slow because there's a noisy crowd stuffed into a wide hallway. People in Paws Unlimited sweatshirts are everywhere, smiling, giving out brochures and programs, and trying to find clever ways to get at your time and money (Mom and I do the same thing for the shelter, so we know all the tricks). Tables sell T-shirts and mugs and leashes and fridge magnets, and there's a line for a silent auction, but my attention, because of my height, focuses on the four-legged guests. I've spied mainly Labs (every color), a couple of German shepherds, one standard poodle, a little black terrier, and a doodle (guess someone has a fur allergy). There are squeals, shrieks, laughs, and shouts, and every single dog is behaving perfectly, seated or lying down, totally cool, like they are not impressed by the fuss. The one dog that matters the most is the one dog that's missing.

"I don't see him."

"He's here somewhere," says Mom, accepting a program from a girl with a grill of green braces. "Look. There you are." Right at the very bottom it says, "Special Presentation: Jasper Blunt, Emily Smart, and Whistler."

I pretend smile. How come it's not Jasper Blunt and Whistler and then Emily Smart? How come I've lost him already?

"Kate. Jasper. Thought you might not make it." It's Cowboy Clay, spiffed up in a suit, cheeks on fire, clutching his chest. I hope he's not about to have a heart attack.

"This is going to be great," says Clay. "Our videographer will record everything, so forget about your cell phones. We'll mail you a disk, even though you're not really graduating." He makes it sound like this is a big deal. "The TV crews are set up in the front, and if it's okay with your mom, I'll let the reporters know you've arrived."

"But Mr. Silver, where's Whistler?"

"What? Oh, he's probably with Terri. She'll grab you when it's your turn to bring him out. Now don't be surprised if we invite you to say a few words, something short and sweet, after we've presented the check and before you hand over the dog. There'll be some photos and—"

"You haven't forgotten that we need to be out of here by twelve fifteen at the latest, if we're going to make our flight."

"Don't you worry," says Cowboy Clay, patting Mom's arm—I can tell she hates that. He's acting like a bad TV game show host, jacked up and over-friendly. "I run a tight ship. It'll be like the *Golden Globes* out there." He mimics lassoing a neck and yanking it in. "Keep things tickin' along. Look, there's Emily Smart with her parents."

The thought of having to make a speech goes straight to my belly and I almost dry heave. There's barely time to follow the direction of his pointy finger when the receptionist with the sparkly white teeth pops up and whispers something in his ear.

"Sorry, got to go." He leans closer to Mom and pretend whispers, "Mrs. McClennon is getting restless. Catch you both before you head off." And with that he's gone.

59

Kate

BEFORE I TURN to face my enemy, I pray the Smart family offers me signs of arrogance, contempt, or some other blatant character flaw that might assuage my shame for begging to keep Whistler. I mean there's no good way to deprive a sick child of a dog that will change their life, to look Emily in the face and say, "The deal's off. You're going to have to pry Whistler's leash from my cold dying hand." Right now, fighting ugly feels like the world is watching me on grainy closed-circuit TV footage as I steal from an epilepsy foundation charity box.

Maybe I'd stand a chance if I could loathe Mrs. Smart for the skills of her plastic surgeon, or the dedication of her personal trainer to sculpt her body. Or loathe Mr. Smart for being so Ryan Gosling handsome, or for holding his wife's hand. Yes, ease my burden by being rich and entitled, greasing palms to get a service dog in order to silence a spoiled daughter who already has a stable full of ponies.

Alternatively I'll take poverty, unprotected sex, and the possibility of a bribe. If the Smart clan is big enough to field their own soccer team then maybe they'll be strapped for cash, receptive to trading Whistler for the twenty-five-grand reward. Better still, what if Mr. Smart is a brawny, chain-smoking redhead and the family's obsessed with playing golf?

But even from a distance Mrs. Smart disappoints, her ballet flats telling me she's more than comfortable with her diminutive height, while her Sunday best floral dress and straight shoulder length blond hair declare an uncomplicated modesty. A good foot taller and broader, Mr. Smart sports an open-necked plaid shirt, his girth providing ample cover for the young girl hiding behind him. Emily towers above her mom, which surprises me, until I notice her four-inch heels, the shortness of her skirt, the eyeliner, lipstick, and scrupulous spirals in her hair. Clearly, this is special. This is her big day.

"We should say hello," I tell Jasper, heading their way before he can reply, before I can change my mind.

"Mrs. Smart? I'm Kate Blunt, and this is my son, Jasper. We thought we'd say hell—"

Mrs. Smart steps forward, grasps me by the upper arms, and lays into me with eyes tempered by years of anguish over her daughter's illness.

"Oh—My—God. We've prayed for this day, haven't we, Jeff?"

Jeff Smart nods, he's actually tearing up, and I can't help but notice his wife's only concession to jewelry—a small gold crucifix on a thin gold chain around her neck.

"Words cannot express how your . . . your sacrifice . . . is our glimmer of hope for a future we thought Emily would never have. You and your son will always be in our prayers. Always."

And now, I witness the broken look of an exhausted parent beginning to fade, Mrs. Smart daring to exude relief and an inner peace, before sweeping me up in a hug that feels more like a Heimlich maneuver.

It's all I can do to keep the breathy expletive inside as I glance down at Jasper and realize my plan to fight ugly is totally screwed.

60

Jasper

MOM'S SO EMBARRASSING, thinking no one notices her "secret" eye jerk in the direction of Emily Smart—she's only twelve but she's got boobs and wears makeup—like I'm supposed to go over and say hi. Fortunately, this woman in a really tight bright red dress pushes past me, says she's a reporter from a TV station, and shoves one of those Dictaphone things into Mr. and Mrs. Smart's face.

"We'll leave you to it," says Mom, pulling me away before I can ask why the reporter's not interviewing me about the best dog in the world.

"You think Whistler's going to be okay? In his new home?"

Mom doesn't answer, so I'm guessing she's not convinced.

"Ladies and gentlemen, we'd like to start so please take your seats."

It's Miss Scarlet from the board meeting—the really pretty

one with the nice accent (neither Mom nor I could remember her name)—making the announcement with a microphone.

"But I thought that reporter might—"

"You can catch her later," says Mom, the two of us drifting with the tide of people.

The man with the tan—his name was definitely Ian—stops us to say, "Let me show you to your seats," apologizing to people left and right as he nudges and pushes me and Mom through the swarming crowd. "They're reserved, way up front. Very special."

We enter the ballroom. It's massive, full of thousands of people taking their seats, well, maybe not thousands, but a lot. A walkway splits the room into two halves and down at the front photographers and TV crews play with their equipment. On a stage sit empty chairs in a row—five on one side, a dozen or so on the other—and there are stairs and ramps and a rail so anybody can get up in front of the audience. Two big screens, movie theater big, fill the entire back wall. One features live video of nothing but the podium and a microphone on a stand; the other, smiling photos of service dogs and their partners fading in and out on a loop.

"Here you go," says Ian, after he's led us to the very end of the far, far right on the first row. I want to ask if the seats come with binoculars or a Segway, but then he gives me a hug and says, "In case I don't catch you later, I just wanted you to know, you're a very special young man."

"Very special?" I say to Mom, as soon as Ian has disappeared. "Like these seats?"

"No, this is good, especially if we need to make a quick getaway. Look, there's your new best friend."

Alice McClennon hobbles with her cane onto the far side of the stage and takes the first of the five empty seats nearest to the front row. The other four chairs fill up with Ian, Miss Scarlet, the shy little Hispanic woman, and one left empty as Cowboy Clay heads to the podium to a round of applause.

Where is he? Where is Terri? And why would I want to make a quick getaway?

"Welcome to this our thirty-fourth annual . . ."

Instantly I switch off, fidget in my seat, and check out the room. The nearest service dog is the doodle, sitting up straight, locked on Cowboy Clay like it's part of her job description. When I scan about the rest of the room, it looks like all the dogs are listening. No yips, yaps, growls, or whines. Or maybe they're just being polite.

I smile when I finally spot a troublemaker, a big chocolate Lab at full stretch, yawning before trying to distract a nearby German shepherd. This chocolate Lab must be the class clown, soft-mouthing his way along the length of the shepherd's bushy tail like a toothless baby on a cob of corn. The shepherd tail flicks and swishes away, and the Lab sighs. I try to reach out, thinking he's distracted and may be receptive. Nothing. I try the doodle because she's closest. Nothing. I try Whistler again, my best shot, but it's hopeless. Are they all working and won't let me in? Or have I already started to lose it?

". . . but before we present the certificates and allow each of you to share what it means to have your new canine partner, it is my great pleasure to introduce our keynote . . ."

"I'm scared," I whisper to Mom.

"What do you mean?"

"About making a speech in front of this many people."

She squeezes my shoulder. "Just say what you feel."

I think about this, and I think about never seeing Whistler again after today and my brain jumps to me being in the hospital, when they are putting in another IV line and the nurse in a yellow mask gets in my face to say, "The worst part is nearly over," and I sweat and scrunch my eyes and grit my teeth and tense up waiting for the badness to end. Only this feeling right now, this is ten times worse.

Some old guy has grabbed this cordless mic and starts pacing the stage and I try to listen but it's so boring, stuff about laws he's written to help the disabled and everything he does for war veterans, and on and on about how wonderful he is, even though his perfect hair-free suit probably means he doesn't have a dog of his own.

I open my copy of the program. This is the congressman, and after him there's a list of about twenty names of people and dogs, with me way down at the bottom, the very last item.

Mom's not great at doing subtle and I catch her checking her watch every ten minutes. I don't understand why I have to sit here when I could be with him. And I thought Terri was nice. Then I wonder if she thinks a quick goodbye might be easier for him, not me.

I check out Alice McClennon on the stage and she's looking

my way. She smiles and nods. Is she trying to tell me something? I hope she's had a chance to meet Whistler before he goes again.

Then I notice Miss Scarlet raising her eyebrows, pointing to someone in the audience, and giving a scuba diver's okay signal (not that I'll ever be able to scuba dive) and realize it's Emily Smart, sitting with her parents, off to my left and one row back. Maybe Miss Scarlet is worried because Emily can't stop fidgeting and smiling and doing that hand-flapping thing in front of her face, like she's trying to cool off and calm down. Maybe she's really excited to meet Whistler, which makes me feel glad and sad at the same time, but then Emily catches me staring and blushes, which makes me blush too. Fortunately, everyone starts to clap and Cowboy Clay is on his feet, shaking hands with Congressman Snooze-fest.

Mom groans, and says, "They're already way behind schedule."

"When's my next IV?"

"Forty-five minutes, at twelve."

"Isn't that when we need to be out of here?"

"Close enough. Even then it's going to be tight."

I pat Mom's hand. She has no problem when I'm doing the patting. "Maybe not many people will want to speak."

That was the stupidest thing I've said all day. Everyone wants to speak. And you know why? Because the stuff they have to say about their dogs is incredible.

There's this ripped guy in a dope desert combat uniform and he's got this little black Lab called Drama by his side, and she's totally into him and protective and he's so happy he's crying, telling everyone how he's got PTSD and how he used to get scared going out but now with this dog he finally feels safe. When he goes home and says the word *perimeter*, Drama knows to go around every door in the house and make sure it is locked and secure and if he's out and someone comes walking toward him, Drama will rush forward and block the way, like the ultimate fullback to a quarterback (not that I pay much attention to the American version of football).

This is only the first graduate, and already most of the audience is in tears.

Next up is a woman on crutches, struggling up the ramp but determined to do it without help. Balancing with a hand on the podium, she takes the mic and talks about losing both her legs in an accident and feeling like her life was over and how she worried that no one would ever love her again. "I was wrong," she says, asking her yellow Lab named Kaylee for a kiss, and getting one straight away. She tells us how this dog will fetch her legs for her in the morning, can tell left from right, and if, at night, she pretend shivers, Kaylee will go get her a blanket to keep warm.

The room is laughing and ooing and ahhing and there are more tears and all I can think about is him, wherever he is, afraid that, even though he has to be close by, I can't feel him anymore.

One by one the graduates walk or stagger or roll onto the stage and each and every one of them tells a story that makes my heart happy and sad and ache.

"We need to start your next IV."

"Here?"

"Sure," says Mom. "You're in good company."

I take off my blazer, roll up my sleeve, and Mom grabs the stuff from her pocketbook and hooks me up. Only the doodle checks me out, like she might want to help.

With the last graduate whizzing up the ramp in his wheelchair, thanks to a German shepherd as big as a pony, a voice whispers in my ear. "Come with me."

It's Terri. Finally. But before I can ask, "Where have you been?" she's halfway to a sliding door I hadn't noticed in the corner of the room.

Mom jerks her chin for me to follow, and when I squeeze through the gap—it's really a sliding wall that leads into an empty and slightly smaller Ballroom B next door—there he is.

"Whistler."

His tail is in voice-activated mode, cranked up to eleven on the crazy scale, and I squat down for slow licks, his final taste of my salty cheeks. He's had a bath, he's wearing a brand-new Paws Unlimited vest, and Terri has obviously tried her best to get creative with his fur, bizarre comb-overs hiding some of the smaller scars.

"You doing okay?" she asks, over another wave of applause next door.

I nod, not taking my eyes off him, not taking my hands off him.

"Back in a minute," she says, and I don't know where she goes, but she gives me his leash, hooked up to the Gentle Leader, a little too snug across his zebra scars.

"Here," I say, working my fingers under the nylon band, scratching with my nubby nails. Whistler goes floppy.

"And so to our final presentation of the morning."

Through the gap I get a side-on view of Cowboy Clay, back at the podium, laying out a piece of paper like he doesn't want to flub his lines. Two big guys down in front mess with their TV cameras and a photographer gets his camera up to his face.

"I'm sure most of you remember the tragic events that played out in Beaver Creek, Oklahoma, some four years ago, and how personal that was to our Paws Unlimited family. The dogs in this room represent the best of the best, with only a small percentage of the dogs we train reaching the required standards to graduate as a certified service dog. So you can imagine . . ."

Terri's back, pulling me up and onto my feet saying, "At last."

"What time is it?" I whisper.

"Twelve twenty."

My antibiotic is still going, but the ball has shrunk small enough to fit inside the breast pocket of my shirt, the line running to my arm, a bit like Grandpa's old-fashioned pocket watch. Seems like every measure of time is running out.

". . . claiming not only the life of Christopher Wallace, but leaving us bereft at the disappearance of his beloved canine partner, Whistler."

Up pops a photo on the big screen, probably Mr. Wallace and what looks like Whistler before the tornado messed with his body. Mr. Wallace seems kind of old and feeble and not what I was expecting if he was the one teaching Whistler how to swim and play soccer. Then the image changes and I see it's his missing poster, with the before version of Whistler smiling at the camera, with teeth and a normal eyelid and a whole right ear, and suddenly I wonder if Emily Smart has any idea what her new canine companion looks like now.

This might be my last chance, and so, down on my knees, Whistler and I press heads together and I open my eyes, see his two brown eyes merge into one, him looking at me, me looking at him and for a few seconds, as if he were speaking inside my head, I know we are both asking the exact same question—*why?*

I hear my name, his name, and then there's a roar, like the sound of soccer fans at Man United or Arsenal when the home team scores a goal.

Terri pats me on the back and says, "Okay Jasper, you're up."

61

Kate

THROUGH A MIXTURE of zoning out, force of will, and refusing to get sucked in, I nearly make it. Nearly.

Each graduate takes the mic, shares a heart-wrenching but ultimately inspirational story, and I manage to keep it together. And then, last but not least, Army Staff Sergeant Bobby Trask rolls onto the stage with a huge German shepherd called Maverick.

"Now I have a job. An actual paying job, because Mav's there to help me stock shelves, bag groceries, round up shopping carts in the parking lot."

Trask—big guy, neat goatee, Popeye forearms—leans forward in his chair and surveys the audience, Maverick spellbound, hanging on every word.

"It may not sound like much. But, to me, it's everything."

And in a moment of weakness, I let him in, and it's not the way he says it, because I can tell Sergeant Trask doesn't want my sympathy. And it has nothing to do with the fact that he's dressed like a biker—grungy sleeveless denim vest, American flag bandana on his head—and I'm still wracked with guilt for my reaction to the Hells Angel on our journey. Sure, the humility and grace of the handsome and formidable sentinel by his side isn't helping me hold back the tears, but in the end it is the message that Trask conveys. More than loyalty and service, more than comfort, confidence, independence, and assurance, this selfless creature has given a man with disability the power to change his life, the power of ability. Best of all—and what has me blubbering like a fool—it is the smallness of what this dog has done for Trask, compared to the magnitude of how it makes him feel.

I blow my nose. Through blurry vision, I see my watch says 12:20. So much for Clay Silver working his magic as the slick and expeditious MC. Instead of wrapping up, he's milking this last order of business, taking every opportunity to pluck at the heartstrings as if with every tear he might earn another dollar for the cause. The TV reporter—stuffed inside a bright red cocktail dress and wearing a mask of thick, gaudy makeup—can't stop smiling as Silver delivers one emotionally charged sound byte after another.

"As most of you know, more often than not, the names of our dogs are chosen by generous donors. These can be special names; the names of loved ones no longer with us, the names of fallen heroes, names that carry weight, meaning, and legacy. And sometimes, for those dogs that serve with distinction, and as a tribute, the name is retired, to be forever associated by this organization with that one special animal."

A big black mutt of a dog appears on the screen with a man

by his side and only when Clay Silver tells me do I see that this used to be the Whistler I have come to know.

I glance over my shoulder at the Smart family. A smiling Mrs. Smart gives her daughter a nudge, but there's no need. My evil alter ego may have hoped that Emily had no idea what Whistler *looked* like, let alone *looks* like now, unable to hide her disappointment, no, better still, her slack-jawed recoil. But I catch myself, because all I see is a wide-eyed young girl, bursting with excitement, about to pop like a champagne cork. Emily Smart is one more perfect example of a child with a hidden disability. Truth is, she wouldn't qualify for a seizure alert dog unless she really deserved or needed one. No, time's up. I need to accept our fate, to run, never look back, and, once again, prepare to nurse Jasper through another bout of pain.

"Losing Whistler became personal, for everyone at Paws Unlimited. It was the not knowing, to have him vanish without a trace, this selfless hero dog, missing in action."

Okay, Silver is now officially out of control. He might have plagiarized this speech from a Hallmark movie of the week; though, judging by the rapt audience, I may be the only person in the room grappling with her vomiting control center.

"We tried everything, explored every avenue, left no stone unturned in our quest to find this dog or, at the very least, recover his body."

The bright-toothed receptionist has appeared in the central aisle, waving for the Smart family to follow her over to the far left-hand side of the stage.

"Even a generous reward for Whistler's safe return went unclaimed."

Silver can't help himself, glancing over at Alice McClennon, and I realize, of course, she's the one behind the $25,000 check. It's exactly what her late husband, Donald, would have done and she'll do anything to keep his spirit alive.

". . . and especially at this time of year, graduating another class of dogs, I'm reminded of him." He thumbs over his shoulder at the screen. "And every year, albeit in vain, I feel the need to reach out to police, animal control, shelters, and dog rescue groups, just in case there's the chance that . . ."

Stephen, Mrs. McClennon's chauffeur, still on his way to a funeral, creeps onto the stage carrying one of those ridiculous oversized checks, as Alice McClennon maneuvers her cane and gets to her feet.

". . . from a group going by the name Panhandle Canine Railroad. After all this time, Whistler, our remarkable and rare seizure alert dog, turns up nearly two thousand miles away, in a shelter on Cape Cod, Massachusetts."

There's a sporty "Yeah" from the back, a smattering of applause, and I wonder how he's doing, my boy on the other side of the gap, my boy saying goodbye when he only just said hello, my boy who knows their time together has finally run out.

"Of course, we'll never know the truth, but if truth is written in scars, Whistler's survival is a story of determination and the will to find a way home."

I didn't think Silver would go there, and maybe he was on

the fence, but probably, sensing the empathy of his audience, he pulls the pin and tosses out the ultimate incendiary suggestion, dropping the word *torture* as he describes those zebra stripes across Whistler's muzzle, wrapping up, a quaver in his voice as he says, "permanently silencing his voice, but not his spirit."

Gasps break out around me and even Trask, our seen-it-all war veteran, appears stunned.

Twelve twenty-seven. Totally screwed.

"I know Jasper has become very attached to Whistler. And I can tell you, with absolute certainty, this remarkable young man has a generous heart, because, by bringing Whistler more than halfway across this great country of ours, he has placed a desire to help others far above helping himself. Jasper fights his own health battles every day and we know he'd choose Whistler over any financial reward, but hopefully this check will go a long way toward getting him a pertinent service dog of his own."

Around me eyes narrow. It must have been the word *pertinent*, the way it sounded odd, some probably thinking, *Did he mean permanent?* while others wonder, *What's wrong with this kid?*

"Ladies and gentlemen, it's been four years, five months, and seventeen days since he went missing, but he's finally home. Please join me in giving a warm welcome to Jasper Blunt and, at long last, Whistler."

The crowd explodes, most people up and on their feet. It could be the relief of Silver being silenced, and it could be the sight of a wounded canine warrior returning home, but I like to think that some of it is for Jasper, that the small boy holding his head high, shoulders back, and chin up—just like we practiced—can feel what

I'm feeling and sense their collective gratitude. I want him to soak it up, to let it sink in. I hope that it will be enough. But as I take them in, dog and boy side by side, partners for one last time, their final walk in perfect synch, the leash redundant, I wonder, *Is this it for me too?* If he never graduates, if he never marries, is this my one and only chance to glow as a proud mother in a room full of strangers?

When he checks in, smiling his timid crooked smile, his eyes pleading, "Am I doing okay?," it's all I can do to nod and hold back my tears until they pass.

Once on the stage, Jasper clings to Whistler's leash, the dog seated at his side, while Silver and Alice McClennon move in with the massive check. The videographer and two photographers take their cue, and now a very different-looking Whistler is up on one side of the screens, the transition from before to after striking, a grim "reveal," inciting more muttering and raised eyebrows among the crowd. Flashes pop as Alice McClennon, Silver, and Jasper smile for the photographers, cries of "Whistler, Whistler" ignored as we, the audience, see how the dog on the screen only has eyes for a certain young man.

"And now," says Silver into the podium microphone, "we'd like to invite Jasper to say a few words."

Silver adjusts the standing mic so it's low enough for Jasper's lips, and my breathing stalls as my son steps forward, still unwilling or unable to let go of the leash, and I think, *Come on, baby boy, come on. Shock them with something magical. Show them you two are one.*

Awkward empty seconds pass before my precious angel, riding the courage of a deep inhalation, finally finds his voice and declares, "Whistler is not a good dog."

62

Jasper

"Whistler is not a good dog."

I stand there, pretending to be afraid, staring into the crowd, waiting until I see people whispering to one another, worrying that I'm too nervous or I've forgotten what to say next, which is, of course, exactly what I wanted them to do.

"Because . . . because . . . Whistler is the best dog ever."

Forget Mr. Boa Constrictor, Happy Fourth of July fireworks explode in my stomach and without needing to check in, I can tell Whistler thought that was funny.

"Well . . . thank you, Jasper," says Cowboy Clay, not sure if I'm done but firing up the crowd with applause, just in case. "If it's okay, we'll have you stay put a moment longer for our pre-sentation."

I spy Mom on her feet, really obvious, shaking her head, tapping her watch like we've got to go, right now, and I'm guessing Cowboy Clay sees her but totally ignores her. We're going to miss our flight, that monster check will never fit in my hand luggage, and now I don't have a dog.

". . . so it seems only appropriate that you be the one to introduce Whistler to his next *potential* partner."

I should have stolen some EMLA cream from the hospital. It's this white sticky local anesthetic they rub on your skin before they shove a big IV into your vein, and it never works, but right now, if I smeared enough of it over my heart, maybe it might help things go slightly numb.

"Let's give a warm Paws Unlimited welcome to Emily Smart and her family."

There's applause and it's okay, it's up there, but it's nowhere near as wicked as the applause for Whistler and me.

As they walk across the stage, Cowboy Clay nudges me forward and somehow the leash moves from my hand to Emily's, Mr. and Mrs. Smart lapping up the flash of the cameras, as Cowboy Clay puts one hand on my shoulder and sweeps his other toward my mom like I'm no longer needed.

"Hurry," hisses Mom, already on her way down the right side, making me run.

"But what about the check?"

I've left it on the stage.

"They'll mail it," she says, not waiting for me to catch up or ask how it will ever squeeze into a mailbox. "We've got to go."

"But my antibiotic's done."

"I'll unhook you in the car," she snaps and by now we're at the back, the ballroom doors flung wide open, Mom still refusing to slow down until I scream, "But it's not fair."

This does the trick. Mom freezes like a bad boy on a TV cop show and even though her head looks like it is about to explode, most people in the last row prefer to watch Whistler and Emily Smart.

Close enough to speak in a whisper I say, "It's not fair because I never chose to have CF and I know you never chose to give it to me and that's because lots of things in life come without a choice. But Whistler picked me, for a reason, and for the first time having this disease made sense. He even made it feel worth it."

She sighs, her eyes go sad, and she dips down to my height—a move that says, *Time for a serious conversation.* "Sometimes choice makes life difficult. Sometimes we choose wrong. Just look at me and your father."

"No, you don't get it. Whistler could have gone anywhere, could have stayed in lots of other nice homes, but he didn't. I never offered him more fun, more love, more walks, more soccer, or more food, but I can help him say what needs to be said."

She reaches out to take my hand. "C'mon. We'll talk about this on the ride."

"No, listen," I say, breaking free. "It's like Whistler knows the answers to all the tough questions, because they're not meant to be a secret, and it's driving him crazy, wanting to give them away and not being able to. That's why he found me; to help him unlock what's been trapped inside for way too long. And even though I want him to be my dog, he's not meant to be just mine, he's meant to be shared, with people who need his help, like people who are sad, or scared, or lonely. And people like you,

Mom. People who've forgotten how to really live, because, in some ways, Whistler never really chose me. *He chose you.*"

She drops my hand like it's on fire, her mouth making a perfect O—definitely more stunned than mad—and I take one last look over my shoulder, but a few people are on their feet, blocking my view of the big screens and I can't see anything and I realize that this is it. This is how it ends. No final eye contact, no final wave goodbye, not even a pretend smile to try and fool him that I'm okay and I promised myself I'm not going to cry, I'm not going to cry, I'm not going to cry.

I begin to cry.

And then I hear it—a strange, scratchy, honking sound, starting out quiet and far off, but getting louder and louder, a bit like a goose on final approach, coming in for a landing.

"Oh my God." Mom's tall enough to see, and I don't know what it is but she's spooked.

"What?"

But she won't answer or can't answer as the croaky screams get faster and faster and closer and closer and that's when I see it, see him, pounding toward me, ears flapping in the breeze, lips jiggling, strands of drool stringing off his chin. It's Whistler, leash flying behind him like a kite string, charging up the central aisle, full-throttle, pedal to the metal, and that dry, painful, un-dogly noise is all that's left of his bark.

Whistler is barking.

Whistler is barking his head off.

He's barking his head off for me.

63

Kate

IT'S HARD TO imagine, getting your voice back after living in monastic silence: no wonder Whistler sounds like an adolescent choirboy, repressed vocal cords ready to break. But this action, this gesture, is about so much more than the mechanics of sound. It must have taken an extraordinary force of will. How many times when he was trapped in a hell he couldn't escape must this dog have forgotten the rule, that barking was forbidden, until he learned not to make a mistake? How many times must this dog have wanted to bark but been afraid? Yet he never did, he never dared, until now. Whistler waited for our departure, and in choosing this particular moment above all others to override his years of voiceless suffering, his actions seem as clear as any words, a last ditch declaration: "Given what I stand to lose, this is more than worth the risk."

If only my son had shared what he just said to me with the

rest of the room. His unnerving, impassioned insight, felt like a verbal stun grenade and I'm still reeling as barking Whistler doesn't so much greet as attack. He plows into Jasper, the two rolling on the carpet, a continuum of smiles and saliva, until the mutt pins the kid and celebrates by pretending Jasper's face is covered in ice cream.

For a few seconds I'm as confused as the rest of the audience, most of them on their feet, the videographer and one of the camera crew fast enough to catch the whole spectacle, with plenty of cell phones for backup just in case.

On one of the big screens the Smart family appears decimated. Mr. Smart gawps, Mrs. Smart looks trapped in a moment of shock, trying to process the indignity and the loss, while Emily's eyes betray panic, darting between her mom and the runaway dog, as if this turn of events might be her fault.

Then either the podium mic or the standing mic picks up on Alice McClennon berating Silver under her breath. "I agree, but everyone in this room heard what I heard, a supposedly mute dog barking for the first time in years. Something made him do it. And it wasn't any of us."

More than ruffled by this unscheduled detour from the program, Clayton Silver appears lost, both for words and about what to do next.

"Use your eyes, Clayton," says Alice, gesturing to the screen behind her, at the mob watching Jasper, and a yipping Whistler locked in another round of Greco-Roman wrestling. "That dog does not want to be parted from that boy."

"Damn right," says a familiar voice, and the rest of the crowd turns to see Army Staff Sergeant Trask, Maverick by his side, once more rolling forward to snatch back the mic.

"Come on, man." The staff sergeant appears to be speaking directly to Silver. "You said it yourself. This dog has been abused, forced not to bark. What kind of a crazy psycho mind game is that? Telling a dog not to bark is like me telling you not to eat. It's messed up."

Jasper and Whistler are back on their feet, listening in, and the masses part enough for everyone to see the stage.

"I don't know this kid, but I do know what we all saw." Trask wheels back half a turn and spins to face Emily Smart. "I'm sorry young lady, I really am, but I hope you see it too because, from where I sit, this dog found his voice and made his choice."

Over to my left a band of similar-looking biker guys get on board, hollering their support, whooping it up, and I find myself checking them out, as if I might discover my knight in shining leather, the guy who rescued us from the broken-down Fiat. He's not there.

"I'm tellin' you, dogs are no different than you and me. It may seem hard to find love, but when you finally fall, it's easy. Right, Mary Beth?"

There's a high-pitched screech from the same corner of the room as the bikers. I guess Mary Beth agrees.

"Meet the right one, and nothing else matters. You just know."

A smile shapes Alice McClennon's lips, bursting into life, and as she initiates a hearty round of applause, the rest of the audience joins in. Only the Smarts and Silver abstain, Silver politely trying to pry the microphone from Sergeant Trask's hand.

"Thank you, Sergeant Trask, and I know I speak for the entire board when I say how much we've enjoyed working with you and learning about your unique take on dogs . . ." I'm not sure if Silver meant that to sound condescending but into the hush he nervously adds, "however I'm not sure how a dog can really know which partner he or she wants to choose."

Clayton Silver turns to the Smarts for support but gets nothing in return.

Trask flicks his head, ever so slightly, and Maverick snags back the microphone, Silver checking his fingers to make sure they are all there.

"Sometimes," says Trask, "the *how* doesn't matter. Sometimes you just have to let it go and embrace the *why*. Whatever the reason, there's no denying the fact that this dog Whistler barked because he wants to be with that boy."

Trask hands back the mic and Clayton Silver eyes the Smart family, and Mrs. Smart in particular. In fairness, Silver appears torn, miserable in this role as arbitrator, harried and forced to choose. Perhaps sensing this, Mrs. Smart steps forward, raises a hand as a shield against the stage lights, and, addressing the back of the ballroom, shouts, "Please, I need to ask Dr. Blunt a question?"

The crowd grumbles and murmurs and then the cordless mic passes like a baton in a relay race from the front to the back and into my hand. One of the cameramen must have me in his focus because there I am on the screen behind the stage.

"Dr. Blunt," says Mrs. Smart, leaning into her own mic, "as the mother of a sick child, given what we've all just seen and heard from Whistler, tell me straight, if you were in my shoes, would you still want to keep this dog?"

I almost laugh, staring at Jasper and Whistler as the two of them stare back at me, bracing for what might happen next, identical expressions on their faces, their eyes aligned like a dotted trail on a map that leads from anticipation to hope and back again. Haven't I earned the right to speak out, to be selfish for Jasper's sake? The room holds its collective breath, waiting for my answer. This is it. This is my chance.

"Of course I'd want to keep the dog," I say. "Definitely. Without question or hesitation."

The audience braces for the "but," but as much as I want to, I can't deliver. Mrs. Smart knows I get it. We may be fighting different foes, but when it comes to our children, we'll fight to the death.

The cameraman spins, zooms into Mrs. Smart's face so everyone can witness the heartache welling in her eyes. I can't tell if I gave her the green light to go ahead and keep Whistler or whether my honesty has made her think twice, convinced her that we are good people, and that Jasper truly deserves to keep his dog.

For an awkward moment, some sections of the audience groan and grumble, as if disappointed by my response, while everyone on stage appears to have forgotten their lines.

Clayton Silver scurries forward to regain control of the mic. "Look, it's obvious a lot of you want to see Jasper and Whistler together, but it's not that simple. I guarantee we will certainly do our best and I promise to find an amicable resolution."

He finishes with a flourish of prepared pleasantries and, as hotel staff hover in the wings—we're told the room's booked for a wedding at three—people begin heading for the exit.

FIFTEEN MINUTES LATER and we're still waiting for this amicable resolution. Silver, Mr. and Mrs. Smart, and Terri the trainer huddle near the stage. The advisory board, including Alice McClennon, are gathered at the ballroom entrance, while Jasper with Whistler and Emily Smart hover in the aisle a few steps away, rival factions maintaining a safe distance from one another. The various camps appear to be in a holding pattern, the only person desperate for a decision being the reporter in the red dress, her one-sided call to her station loud enough for everyone to hear how she'd love to put a bow on a fabulous feel-good story for this evening's local news.

I check the current time on my phone—no chance of making our flight—and I'm about to turn it off when I notice the number three next to the envelope icon on my email. I should check my inbox, put out a fire at work, appease KGB, but something makes my thumb scroll to the drafts, to a certain letter hanging in electronic limbo, a note to one Dr. Holden Patterson, harmless but bursting with the potential to start something new. Blame the dog or the boy? What do I have to lose? I hit send.

Alice McClennon breaks away from her pack and dodders my way.

"How's it going?" I ask, my eyes flicking to the rest of the board. Has Alice been sent on a diplomatic mission to break the bad news?

"Oh, they're a pushover. Never should have made you come all this way, but I'm so glad you did, so glad I had a chance to meet your son and see the two of them together."

This endorsement is huge but it's still not enough.

"So what's going on up front?"

Down by the stage Silver gestures with open palms and hands on heart, while Mrs. Smart is all flustered hair adjustments and harried finger-pointing.

"That's Clayton trying to save face. Terri's the one we need to worry about. She'll be focused on one thing and one thing only—what's best for Whistler. Someone's got to advocate for the dog in this equation, especially when you've put so much training and effort into an animal. Her opinion carries a lot of weight."

What's best for Whistler.

As if on cue, the dog lets loose another creaky, dry bark—like he can't stop trying it out and needs to get it just right. I look over as Jasper, unzipping the pocket on Whistler's service vest, pulls out a piece of paper, grinning ear to ear before glancing my way and giving me a big thumbs-up.

"People like Terri spend a lot of time trying to match the right dog with the right person," says Alice. "She won't do any better than those two."

I follow her gaze to the little man lost inside an oversized blazer and the mutt who can't take his eyes off him.

"They're an odd couple," I say.

"Not at all," says Alice, taking them in. "Just different shades of beautiful."

And she's right, and I see it, how this beautiful boy and this beautiful dog are perfectly matched, why they fit, and click, and make perfect sense together. Jasper, my angel, showing the world a normal-looking boy, damaged and ravaged on the inside, and Whistler, his gifts hidden, waiting to be unlocked, his scarred and twisted body on permanent display.

"You believe him?" she asks. "What he says about the dog filling his head with ideas and feelings?"

"What I believe doesn't matter," I say, "because what's right in front of my eyes is definitely pretty magical." And for a second, little more than a slow blink, I let myself go to that future I crave but dare not imagine. In my dreams someone calls, or it's on the news, or I read about it online, and at first I can't believe it, can't get my head around it until I reach for my new reality, this inconceivable freedom, crumpling to the floor as the weight of everything he endures leaves my body and every hope for a future takes its place. The cure is all I think about and all I dare not think about. It is always out there, on the horizon, this state of permanent levity. Today there is no newsflash, no medical breakthrough, but even so, the possibility that a boy and a dog can share a future together is pretty special. I open my eyes. I'm still smiling. Not *the* cure, but *a* cure. Like every dog, Whistler is a healer, a cure on a leash, the perfect remedy for a better now, and in this moment, the way it makes me feel will do just fine.

My phone vibrates, signaling an incoming text. Normally I'd

ignore it, but I press the messages icon, instantly giddy and gob-smacked by what I see.

Hi Kate,
This is Holden. Your email just made my day.

A little gray bubble tells me he's typing more.

"Everything okay?" asks Alice.

"Oh, yes . . . great . . . really good."

Reluctantly I slip the phone in my pocket as it buzzes over and over again.

"You notice the reporter?"

"Hard not to," I say.

"I'm glad she stuck around," says Alice. "If Clayton won't let you keep the dog we'll tell him you'll give her an interview."

Well, well, feisty Mrs. McClennon, letting me catch a flash of a mischievous, much younger woman having fun. Didn't see that coming.

"Don't worry," she says, "I'll find the perfect dog for Emily. Promise."

I smile, reassured by her conviction, her certainty, trying not to dwell on how seizure alert dogs are like hen's teeth. Alice lays her hand on my arm and adds, "Everything happens for a reason."

It's another one of those mindless nails on chalkboard inanities that, not so long ago, would have had me lashing out. Instead I let it sail right past, banal, and powerless, and reply, "Especially if Whistler is the reason why."

Approval dances in Alice McClennon's sparkly green eyes. "Almost forgot," she says, producing an unmarked envelope.

"If that's what I think it is, we won't be needing it. This was never about the money. This was always about the dog."

She hesitates, the check floating between us, and for an uncomfortable second I wonder if she knows that our eleventh-hour attempt to keep the mutt still hangs in the balance. But then I think of the shelter back home, of making it right, of open not limited, of no more day-fourteen dogs. Can I silence the KGB by discovering the best prospect ever?

"Mrs. McClennon, what if I told you I could use the money after all?"

64

Jasper

THERE ARE LITTLE pockets on Whistler's service dog vest and inside I find three incredibly useful items:

1. Poop bags.

2. A Ziploc containing miniature Milk-Bones for treats.

3. A certificate confirming that Whistler is a fully qualified service dog.

This last item is a big deal. Now Mr. Crabtree—the Apartment Nazi—will have to let Whistler stay with us. I look up and see Mom with Mrs. McClennon and they're checking me out. I give her a thumbs-up, shake the certificate, and put it carefully back.

Mr. and Mrs. Smart are in a huddle with Cowboy Clay and Terri. Emily has been left out, wandering the aisle, working her cell phone. A head butt behind my knee tells me I should bail her out.

"Hi, I'm Jasper Blunt."

Emily's eyes are really red and puffy from crying, but they still manage to convey a confused "Yeah, I know," without saying a word. Close up, I see that, like her mom, she wears a gold cross on a gold chain around her neck.

"Look, I think you need Whistler, for the . . . seizure thing . . . so he should definitely stay with you because—"

"It's okay," she says, rocking side to side. "I heard that trainer person tell my dad she's not a hundred percent sure if he can still work as an alert dog, like Whistler's been through so much he might need a service dog of his own."

I feel terrible but I have to believe Terri knows best.

"Two years on a waiting list, and still no dog. I know it's bad to say this but sometimes I think it would be better to be blind or deaf because seizure alert dogs are so rare."

A sarcastic "Yeah, right" pops into my head, but it doesn't belong to me. Whistler pretends to be innocent, and at first I think he's saying, "Who chooses *not* to see or hear?" but then I realize he's talking about seizure dogs. Of course they're not rare. I bet lots of dogs tune in before seizures happen. Dogs send the memo. We humans just need to learn how to read it. And I know the perfect teacher to give Emily her first lesson.

"What's so funny?"

Her question takes me by surprise until I realize I'm grinning like an idiot. What if this is *why* I got this life. What if I'm meant to be a dog translator when I grow up?

"Do you believe in miracles?" I ask.

Emily's nose wrinkle says "no" but I keep going.

"Okay, how about believing that things happen for a reason, that you were meant to be here today, and so was I, and so was Whistler." I figured that by wearing the cross she might be cool with something amazing and impossible to explain, but she leans away from me.

"What's wrong with you?"

Is she referring to what I just said or my general health?

"I have a thing called CF. It's this lung disease. You're born with it."

"That sucks."

"Sometimes."

"But if you got your disease for a reason, then what's the reason?"

I smile. "You saw what I saw. A dog who couldn't speak decided to speak again."

"Wait. You think that because you have a lung disease you made that happen?"

I'm not good at cool, especially around girls, but I shrug my shoulders.

"So you really love this dog?"

Now I know she's not convinced, trying to embarrass me with the four-letter L-word reserved for Mom and Whistler, and only when no one else is around.

"He's okay," I say, and then I feel the thump of a zebra-snout on my thigh, a snappy *hey, I heard that* bark, and catch the sparkle in Whistler's good eye, wanting me to come clean. "Yeah, he's the best."

"And you really think they'll let you keep him?"

"Definitely," I say, trying not to hesitate, trying not to look worried.

It's Emily Smart's turn to shrug. "You're probably right," she says, handing me her phone. "Can't imagine they won't give him to you now."

I see that she's on YouTube.

"You're already trending. Someone must have downloaded a cell phone video of when Whistler decided he didn't want you to go. Twenty minutes and you're already up to ten thousand views. You're about to be famous."

There's a red "play" arrow on top of an image of Whistler about to slow-lick my face and I press it and even though it's blurry and jerky it's the coolest video I've ever seen. But then I read the tag for the clip—*Boy helps dog find his voice*—and I think, that's not right, it's the other way round, Whistler's the one who helped *me* find his voice, and it's not an actual voice, or talking, or proper words, and you can only find something if it's been lost in the first place and this inner dog voice has always been there; we humans just have to be smart enough to listen.

But then Whistler reaches out and reaches in, staring up at me and through me with his magical forever stare and instantly I feel like when I'm in the hospital and Dr. Dan listens to my lungs, scrunching up his eyes and taking his time before saying, "Much better," and suddenly I can breathe and everything goes calm and unwinds and I realize I've got more—more time, more life, more to learn, and finally, at last, more Whistler. And then the dog with the droopy eyelid and the ratty ear and the Antarctica scar blinks and tilts his head and I hear "Wow, what took you so long to get it," and instead of Fourth of July fireworks I'm getting the biggest shock-and-awe explosions ever.

So I hand back Emily's phone, knowing only one word will do to sum up exactly how I feel. Ms. Sexton would be pleased. Best adjective for the best dog ever.

"Brilliant."

Epilogue

In the end, just three things matter: How well we have
lived. How well we have loved. How well we have
learned to let go.

—Jack Kornfield

Dr. Jasper Blunt

SARGE AND I take the stairs, as usual. My practice is on the third
floor and it's a haul, but thanks to the lung transplant, I take
pride every time, the twinge from the long pale scar that splits
my breastbone a reminder of just how lucky I am.

The dog by my side is a mutt—a lot of Lab, a splash of shepherd, a dash of Doberman. Sarge's name has nothing to do with
the armed forces: it's short for Sargent, as in John Singer, the
famous artist. He's young, only two years old, and although he
and I get on great, we both know I'm not the one. It's obvious
he's ready for bigger things.

The waiting room is packed, people and dogs, a potpourri of

age and breed. Behind the reception desk sits Denise—petite, bespectacled, guru of digital records.

"Your first case is in room three," she says, handing me an electronic tablet which displays the relevant clinical, biochemical, diagnostic, and therapeutic information for each visit. I scroll, smile, hand it back, and Sarge leads the way to my office.

"Half a dozen confirmed for Sunday, already," Denise calls after me.

Confused, I stop and turn around.

"Father's day. Remember? Forecast says it's going to be a perfect day for the beach."

"Right," I say. How could I forget the third Sunday in June, my annual excuse for raising a middle finger to absentee fathers everywhere?

Please, don't overthink my intention. This is not a sacrifice. It's not noble or heroic, penance or restitution. I just want kids who grew up like me to know they're not alone, that *not* celebrating a male parent is okay. Hopefully, for this one afternoon, a few frazzled, selfless moms get to forget and catch their breath. Besides, who wouldn't take any excuse to visit the best beach on the Cape?

While I dress the part—old-fashioned white coat, stethoscope scarf (nostalgia never goes out of style)—I can't help but think about that one time I met him, my father, Simon Swift, though the word *met* is not entirely accurate.

It was Mom's twenty-five-year Vet School reunion and she insisted I join her.

"They'll all be bragging about what they've been up to for the last quarter century," she said. "That's why I want my greatest achievement to be my date."

And so we spent a fun weekend in London, culminating in a black-tie affair at a swanky hotel. He wasn't supposed to be there—Mom kept checking the RSVPs online—but late into the night, across the room, she spied a man staring in our direction.

"Oh my God," said Mom, grabbing me by my hand, dragging me toward the bar while I stared back, wanting to make sure he saw where we were headed.

I ordered shots of tequila while we formulated a plan. I ordered two more, while Mom swore up and down that "he never looked that bad when they were dating." I was barely listening. The father I had never known was somewhere in this heaving mob, and from that look on his face—confusion to recognition to fear—he knew exactly who I was.

"Don't you want to speak to him?" asked Mom, already slurring her syllables. "Aren't you curious? Aren't there questions? Things you want to say?"

There I was, opportunity had finally knocked, loud and clear, yet I didn't hesitate. "No. It doesn't matter if I'm across a room or across the pond, he's always known where to find me. He's had a lifetime to make his position clear—selfish, weak, and without conscience. Now it's my turn to make a far more powerful statement that he will never forget."

"And what's that?"

I smiled, met her eyes, and said, "My mother is the only father I will ever need."

Mom kissed me on the cheek and I told her how much I loved her and we never saw him again.

"GOOD MORNING, SORRY to keep you waiting."

Mark and Sally Saunders get to their feet to say hello and I introduce Sarge. They're in their early forties—of similar height and weight, pallor, and freckle count; the two of them make a point of attending every appointment together. Their five-year-old daughter, Kaitlin, engrossed in a classic game of Operation, delivers a "can't you see I'm busy" finger wave from the floor on the other side of the room. Her Boxer pit mix, Toasty—because her fur's the color of charred bread, obviously—has no such reservations, leaping over like an Olympic triple jumper, full tail transformed into a rider's crop, whipping back and forth, normal canine decorum abandoned. I was expecting happy, delighted, or at the very least, satisfied. I check in with Sarge to make sure I'm not mistaken but he agrees; Toasty's got one emotion on her mind—*anxiety*.

"Bobby back in school?" I ask. Bobby is Kaitlin's ten-year-old brother and he's usually here.

"He's in the waiting room, doing homework," says Mark, and the flat tone, the absence of any further explanation, only heightens my sense that something is not right.

I take a seat and Sarge joins me, curling up at my feet, alert and ready to begin.

"So, no seizures for the last three months?" I ask, knowing the answer but wanting to gush over the achievement.

"Yep," says Mark, "things have been going well in that department."

"What about close calls?"

Sally has her fingers clamped under her thighs like a flight attendant readying herself for a bumpy landing.

"Twice she made us get her pills but there was never any panic. We gave them to her and she was fine."

"Great. And I saw her weight is up. Is she sleeping through the night?"

Husband and wife consult before synchronizing their nods. Definitely holding something back.

"And what about playdates, social interactions?"

"Better," says Mark, "but—"

"Fine," says Sally, as though shutting him up rather than finishing his sentence for him. "She went to her first birthday party last week."

"Brilliant," I say—old habits die hard.

I kneel on the floor next to Kaitlin.

"Mind if I join you?" I ask Kaitlin, reaching over to the board and failing dismally to extract the funny bone without setting off the buzzer, to her squeals of delight.

I time my moment to ask, "Do you love Toasty?"

She nods but her focus remains on Cavity Sam and his broken heart.

"And what's her special signal?"

"Head butt," says Kaitlin without thinking, reaching out a hand for reassurance, Toasty shuffling close for confirmation.

"And you're working on those exercises we talked about last time?"

I earn a silent nod that evolves into a little girl full body wiggle.

Once upon a time everyone thought that the ability to detect seizures was based on sensitivity to subtle behavioral changes, distinct shifts in smells or body chemicals. Like predicting earthquakes for a seismologist. Science can do all the brain scans and electrical tests it wants, but I still believe a much younger version of me put it best: "When you sleep in a room with a fan, you wake up when the fan is turned off." When the normal background noise inside your brain goes silent or changes because of a pending seizure, it's going to get your attention—so long as you are listening.

Toasty checks in with me as Kaitlin concentrates on the spare ribs. Experience has made this connection faster, more accurate, but most of all more nuanced. Direct communication—language—can be a barrier, it gets in the way, it can trap and tangle, be open to interpretation. This is real, genuine, unambiguous. No agenda, no head games, no lies.

Within seconds I feel a mixture of sad, lonely, and neglected. Where is Toasty getting this from, and why?

Kaitlin flinches again, giggling at the sound of the buzzer.

"I'm just going to step outside the door with your mom and dad, if that's okay? This is my friend Sarge, and he'd like to say hello."

Sarge moves into position, sliding his head under her hand, demanding to be petted.

We slide out into the corridor, with a view into the waiting room but far enough away for a private conversation. I leave the door slightly ajar. Sometimes I do this to get a better read on the adults. Sometimes I do this to allow the dog to get a better read on the situation without distractions and interference from other humans.

"Maybe I'm wrong," I say, "but having Toasty around seems to be working well."

I get a synchronized "yeah," before Sally looks past me and spies her son, giving him a "five more minutes" hand sign. Even from this range I catch the theatrical sigh, the slumped shoulders of the kid cradling an open laptop.

"It's only been a couple of months and we're batting a one hundred percent alert rate."

More nods, but Sally has her lips clenched vice grip tight.

"So what's making Kaitlin so sad?"

For a moment neither of them talk, eyes peering through the gap, watching their daughter trying to teach Sarge and Toasty the difference between an Adam's Apple and a Charley Horse.

"She won't tell us," says Mark, "but sometimes I find her crying at night, saying she's sorry or that it is all her fault."

"We've done everything to let her know that there is no blame," says Sally, "but she doesn't seem to get it. I can tell her I love her no matter what till I'm blue in the face."

Sarge comes trotting out of the room, sits at my feet, and stares up at me, absolutely no expression on his face. I imagine my face mirrors his, until it hits me, like I finally get the punch line to a joke that the dog no longer finds funny. His messages always get through, but they are often incredibly frustrating and cryptic when you least need them to be. I register the sensation percolating through my brain, akin to the thrill of solving a difficult problem or placing the last piece in the puzzle, pure satisfaction mixed with the relief of no longer being stumped. The trouble is that's all I get. Sarge isn't sharing the solution.

"Dr. Blunt?"

"Sorry," I say, "so aside from a lack of seizures has anything else changed at home?"

Mark and Sally make the usual mistake, hunting for something earth-shattering—divorce, death of a grandparent, loss of a job.

"Small stuff. Little things."

"Bobby quit violin lessons," says Sally. "Said he was bored. But he's doing amazing in school. Best grades he's ever gotten on his last report."

I glance inside to check on Kaitlin. She's still engrossed in the board game. I glance down at Sarge, but he's gone, no longer at my feet.

". . . seems pleased, like that's a good thing."

I come back, Sally still talking. That's when I notice Sarge, on the other side of the waiting room, cozying up to Bobby, the laptop abandoned, the boy's body language transformed, leaning forward and down, engaged, petting, nuzzling, and laughing. Bobby doesn't notice me looking, but Sarge does. For a full three seconds the dog glances my way, not just in my vague direction, but aiming right inside me, a direct hit. And this time, instead of an indecipherable scrawl, this message is delivered in indisputable block capitals.

". . . says it's common to change friends in this grade."

"I'm sorry," I say. "I just realized what I've been missing."

Sally inhales, deep and slow, not like someone bracing for an unpleasant truth, more like someone outraged by my incompetence.

"I should have seen this months ago," I say. "It's classic, probably started out as jealousy for attention, perfectly normal, but I'm betting there were flashes of anger or resentment, hardly surprising given this new, pervasive, and permanent risk of what might happen every time you're out in public as a family. Other kids, classmates this age, can be brutal. It's a testament to your parenting that there's been a transition to guilt and frustration for feeling this way. Almost certainly Toasty tuned in first. But Kaitlin wasn't far behind. Bobby's acting out, quitting music lessons, desperately trying to overachieve in school, it's a cry for help, but it's a cry for help with a perfect solution."

Neither of them speak, bracing for my revelation.

"You need another dog," I say. "Your family needs another dog."

A shrill sound, caught between a laugh and a scream, catches in Mrs. Saunder's throat.

"No, no way," says Mark, straightening up, "we're not dog people. Never were. Okay, Toasty makes sense, but one's enough. Another dog is the last thing we need."

"Look, Dr. Blunt," says Sally, "we like you, we do, but you're a child psychologist. You're not a veterinarian."

"Please," I say, "it's not for you, or your daughter. It's for Bobby."

I jerk my chin toward the waiting room, hoping they see what I see, a boy who has been hiding from the pain, a boy who wants to be resilient, but he's afraid for his little sister's future. Mr. and Mrs. Saunders are not at fault. They are the parents of a child with a chronic disease, struggling to cope while rebalancing their future. Standing beside me, they ache with the realization that their firstborn might have felt less than, or worse still, forgotten.

"Bobby knows you are there for him. But for all the other times, here's a chance for him to confide, share, and vent with a friend guaranteed to listen and, better still, understand. I think Sarge has just found himself a new home."

Mark curls his arm around his wife's shoulder as she begins to shudder and cry.

"But this is *your* dog," she says.

Inside I cringe, the ownership concept awkward. Part of me wants to say, "If he is mine, does that make me his?"

"He's just a kid," says Mark. "Who wouldn't love a dog wanting to say hello? But what happens when his water bowl is empty, or it's midnight and the dog wants to go out to pee?"

"I'm not worried," I say, "because finding the right dog isn't that difficult. None of us have to make the decision."

I let the statement hang there, relishing the pause, clouds of confusion gathering in their eyes.

"Dogs choose us, not the other way round. Trust me, Sarge knows what he's doing."

The awakening written across their faces stays with me until they leave and once more I am alone, left to wonder if life is nothing but a series of collisions and near misses, the path we take, and the one we wish we had. Choosing regret or sorrow over saying goodbye to Sarge would be all about me. Choosing to plaster a grin on my face would be all about Sarge. Burt, the old volunteer from Mom's shelter, put it best, "There's a simple reason why a dog's life is so short—dogs give us lots of chances to find the perfect match."

Everything goes back to Whistler and what he taught me; the way you fall in love with a dog, and then spend the next ten to fifteen years afraid to say goodbye. That's why it is best to let them lead and for us to follow. How many times can you recall the tiniest, most inconsequential detail about an animal in your life—how they slept in a particular band of sunlight; their preference for round, not bone-shaped, kibble; the way they could never pee on a walk of less than a quarter of a mile—yet, so often, the telling details of a human life go unnoticed and are instantly forgotten? By banking the small stuff, it will be there forever, on speed dial in our brain, primed to remember, guaranteed to make us feel better when we don't want to feel alone.

When I was thirteen, still volunteering at Mom's shelter after school, still obsessed with teaching her everything Whistler needed to share, I remember her asking me if I was afraid, knowing how old and frail Whistler had become.

"When you cry about losing a dog," I told her, "it means the dog did its job. It means the dog made a connection. You got him. He got you. The bond could involve one person. It could be a million. The number doesn't matter. A dog is proof you don't need an opposable thumb to grab and keep hold."

Before seeing my next case, I reach into my back pocket, snag my phone, and dial. In this line of work, there's no one better at finding me another four-legged solution to every human flaw.

"Hi, Holden. Yeah, me too. Doing great. You sure it's okay to use your place again this Sunday? Positive? Well, thank you. No, the kids always love it. Absolutely. Watching their faces when they first catch sight of your beach never gets old. Yes, that'd be fun. But don't let me keep you. Is Mom there?"

And then she gets on the phone and, to my delight, says what she always says:

"I had a feeling you'd call."

Acknowledgments

Any mistakes about living with, or caring for, a patient with cystic fibrosis are mine alone. No CF journey is the same. It was never my intent to instill fear, but at the same time, I don't want to understate the challenge facing any parent of a child given this diagnosis. My best hope is for awareness, education, and a new perspective on a positive path forward.

Similarly, any mistakes about animal shelters, service dogs, and service dog training programs are mine alone. I am in awe of what these folks do and their ability to change people's lives for the better. In particular, I'm grateful to Dr. Terri Bright and Dr. Cynthia Barker Cox for their insight, and I apologize if my writing fails to ring true.

I may possess some of the personal and professional credentials vital to this book's authenticity, but make no mistake, my agent, Jeff Kleinman, made it happen. Jeff was there when this book was little more than a vague concept, an awkward elevator pitch, and, recognizing its potential, worked tirelessly over many years to help me get the story and its message just so. Many thanks to Jeff, and also thanks to Christine Pride and Jamie Chambliss, for their savvy and constructive feedback regarding the early drafts.

This is my first book with William Morrow and I'm indebted to an amazing team—Amelia Wood, Andrew Gibeley, Jennifer Hart, Yeon Kim, Elsie Lyons, Liate Stehlik—and the immense editorial talents of Lyssa Keusch. Lyssa, thanks for making me look a whole lot better on paper than I could ever deserve. Likewise, many thanks to Lyssa's son, Xander Lee, who helped me find the authentic voice of an eleven-year-old boy. Jasper's lexicon wouldn't be complete without "half past not happening."

Jessica Kensky, Patrick Downes, and, how could I forget, their service dog, Rescue, contributed an honest, raw, and compelling insight into living with and moving forward from a totally different form of debilitating, life-altering event. They have taught me a lot about service dogs but, more importantly, about resilience, bravery, and a fierce determination to make a difference.

Finally, none of this would have been possible without the support and love of my family—Emily, Whitney, Andrew, and, always keeping me honest, my grandson, Henry. If I'm lucky, in reading this book you found a line that resonated, that made you read it twice, that made a personal connection to you, have no doubt that it either came from, or was directly inspired by, my wife, Kathy. Dedicating this book to a woman so fiercely devoted, selfless, and driven was the only no-brainer part of this entire writing project.

About the author

2 Meet Nick Trout

About the book

3 Behind the Book
12 Reading Group Guide

Insights,
Interviews
& More...

Meet Nick Trout

Deborah Feingold

NICK TROUT works full-time as a staff surgeon at the prestigious Angell Animal Medical Center in Boston. He is the author of five previous books, including the *New York Times* bestseller *Tell Me Where It Hurts*, and his writing has been translated into sixteen different languages. He lives in Massachusetts with his wife, Kathy; their daughter, Emily; their adopted labradoodle, Thai; and Emily's service dog, a black Labrador named Bella. ❧

Behind the Book

The "write what you know" adage
narrowed my options. Having worked
as a veterinarian for the past thirty years
I hope I know a little something about
dogs. As a father, I'd like to think I
know a little something about parenting.
And, sadly, thanks to a roll of the dice,
Powerball odds, and an invisible defect
in my DNA, I've been forced to know
a little something about an incurable
genetic disease called cystic fibrosis,
or CF.

Perhaps it was inevitable, bundling
this accumulated knowledge into a
not-so-neat little package and using
fiction for a cathartic outpouring of
emotions, but the insight and honesty
I have tried to capture in *The Wonder
of Lost Causes* is only made possible by
fate and the path it's led me down for
this past quarter century.

Like most veterinarians, I strive
to connect with pet owners, to earn
their trust and confidence in the spoken
and unspoken interaction that is bedside
manner. Being English, and not calling
the United States home until I was
twenty-six, I imagine my dry British
reserve—firm handshake, over-awkward
hug, steely upper lip, emotions on
lockdown—turned some pet parents
off (though the accent remains an
irrationally useful tool for adding a
little heft and gravitas to many a
statement). If so, that all changed
with my daughter's diagnosis. ▶

Behind the Book *(continued)*

Emily was born during the second year of my surgical residency training (less than ideal for a father routinely putting in a seventy- to eighty-hour workweek), but it wasn't until the age of two that her constant struggles with coughs, colds, sinus infections, and abdominal pains got packaged into a diagnosis no parent wants to contemplate, let alone receive. Emily had CF. My wife, Kathy, and I were unsuspecting, asymptomatic carriers of mutated genetic material. Neither of us had any family history of the disease. In the Caucasian population there is a one in twenty-three chance of being a carrier. Pretty long odds, getting longer when you think Kathy and I found each other from across the Atlantic Ocean. Add in the one in four chance of our offspring carrying an abnormal gene from each of us and, well, maybe not lottery-winning odds but remarkable all the same.

Here's what you need to know about CF. Thanks to a defect in a busy little protein that sits on cell membranes, vital, slick, lubricating mucus in our lungs and guts and liver and pancreas transforms into a sticky-as-molasses gunk that plugs everything up. Nowhere is that more problematic than in the lungs, leading to chronic, catastrophic chest infections. Because this occurs deep within the body, CF patients can totally fool you, prompting a plethora of variations on "but you look fine to me." Fine, but here's the thing—there is no cure for CF. Half of all CF patients will not live to see forty. For many, it's a battle for every breath, a life riddled with constant care, constant hospitalizations, and constant dreams of what it would be like to be as normal on the inside as they look on the outside.

Emily's diagnosis remains the ultimate turning point in my life, a before and after moment that literally dropped me to my knees when I received the news. CF is a relentless, omnipresent enemy creating a bottomless crevasse into which I fell and continue to fall to this day. When Emily is sick, hooked up to oxygen, crying from the pain of relentless coughing, unable to catch her breath, I am an angry father, railing against the unfairness and my impotence to make her well, weighed down by unshakable depression and isolation because no one gets her suffering and the impact it has on her parents. When Emily is well, I ride the unsurpassable high of reprieve, of a lost levity, of disproportionate gratitude for a glimmer of normalcy. During these good times, Kathy and I can regroup, convince ourselves we can still handle this, renew our determination to keep Emily in the fight, all the while bracing for the next time. This is the conceit of CF, the way it allows you these glimpses, the tease of possibility, and even though this taste of what might have been possible sometimes feels worse than if you ever had it at all, I'm eternally grateful for what I have. There are far worse diseases, far shorter lives, far greater pains as a ▶

parent. I am incredibly lucky. Catch me on a bad day and it will take me longer to answer, but I wouldn't trade this sadness, frustration, joy, and pride in my child for anything. I may be the parent, but she is the lesson and her life constantly shows me how much I needed to learn.

It's also possible that, in small ways, Emily's diagnosis has made me a better veterinarian. At least I hope so. Back in 2010, in a book called *Love Is the Best Medicine*, I wrote, "Through my daughter, I came to find a renewed empathy for my clients, the 'pet parents' whose fear of losing a loved one is no less heartfelt than mine. Sometimes I think this lesson helps me connect with people in ways that would have been unattainable before Emily." We reciprocate the outpouring of unconditional love from our pets knowing that, in our lifetime, we must face a future without them, a state painfully familiar to any CF parent living with fear of loss and the permanent ache of anticipatory grief.

Emily has always been an animal lover—goats, chipmunks, cats, elephants—but she is especially fond of dogs. In the book *Ever By My Side* I wrote about her request when she was eight years old, during a visit to the intensive care unit of Boston's Children Hospital. It was around 2 a.m. and, totally caught off guard, she asked me if she could have a yellow Labrador.

At that moment in time, in that precise situation, watching your daughter being poked and prodded, with tubes and cables running in and out of her body, frightened about how her body will react, I defy most parents not to be vulnerable to a child's wish, no matter what it is.

"Of course," I said. "Once we get out of the hospital, we'll get you a dog."

What is it with children? Even soused with medication, at an ungodly hour, she still managed to spot the discrepancy.

"Not just a dog," she said. "A yellow Labrador."

"Sorry," I said. "Yellow Labrador."

"Promise?"

"I promise," I said, kissed her on the forehead, and melted as she smiled.

I kept my promise (there's no reneging on a promise made in a hospital) and Emily shared the next eight years of her life with Meg, her yellow Lab, but as Emily ages, her disease has doubled down, and given the increasing frequency and length of her hospital visits, we began to look into the possibility of a different kind of canine companionship for her.

It was 2012, and I was invited to give the commencement address to a graduating class of service dogs and their partners with the National Education for Assistance Dog Services (NEADS) program. I spoke for my allotted seven minutes, striving for a little humor and pathos, but as soon as each handler took the mic and their opportunity to convey how much having their dog has changed their lives, my ►

speech became irrelevant and prosaic compared to the stories being shared. For two hours I smiled, laughed out loud, and cried until my cheeks dried stiff, as, one by one, these brave folks walked, hopped, and wheeled onto the stage eager for an opportunity to say thank you and share what this chance meant to them. As for the dogs, the creatures were impeccably behaved— mainly sleeping and yawning—and I came away from the event in awe of what they do, as well as emotionally exhausted.

In part, Emily's bouts of cystic arthritis (another little gift affecting 5 to 10 percent of CF kids) and periodic reliance on a wheelchair started to make us think about the practicalities of a service dog. But, for me, it was her isolation and loneliness, every time she went into the hospital, that sealed the deal. Not so long ago, CF patients might share a hospital room, an oxygen mask, go to summer camps together, allowed to be among kids fighting the same fight. It was uplifting, unifying, the camaraderie among patients and parents, and it was also a disaster waiting to happen until the medical profession realized that sharing their experiences also resulted in sharing bacteria guaranteed to shorten their lives. As a result, whenever Emily is hospitalized, normally to receive top-shelf, kick-ass intravenous antibiotics, she is alone, sentenced to a stay of anywhere from two to six weeks. She cannot leave the room. Doctors and nurses gown up, glove up, and often mask up, fueling her impersonal isolation. The Internet and social media help, but, as almost anyone can attest, Facebook and Instagram can be a double-edged sword, offering connectivity while pointing out that your normal is not as good as your friends'.

Enter Bella, an eighteen-month-old, highly trained, highly attentive, female black Labrador. Those savvy folks at NEADS interviewed Emily, considered the specifics of her disability, the requirements of a dog, and, after months of deliberation, specifically chose Bella to fit the bill. It's like Match.com for service dog and partner. It's a big deal and it's uncanny how time and time again they get it absolutely spot on. Of course Bella can do all the cool stuff—turn on lights, open the fridge, pick up your cell phone if you drop it, bark for help—but in Emily's world, Bella is also about the intangibles, the small stuff, the easy silences, the goofy, funny simplicity of sharing time and space. Arguably Bella's greatest achievement is the way doctors and nurses have recognized her contribution to Emily's wellness. This dog, like most dogs, has infected those around her with a warmth and recognition of how a canine philosophy that pares down what matters most to the basics has reach, longevity, and power.

As you can see, the elements for a story about a child with CF, making ▶

a connection to a dog, while his troubled parent searches for direction and life's meaning, was not such a stretch of the imagination. Yet there was one important piece of the plot that, once more, Emily helped me work out. It centers around a phrase guaranteed to annoy anyone caught up in a fight against chronic disease: "Everything happens for a reason." Believe me, it's not helpful and it's right up there with "God only hands it out to those who can handle it," but I thought, *What if I look at this inanity from a child's perspective?* A vital antibiotic has robbed Emily of 50 percent of her hearing, another has numbed sensation in her fingertips. Multiple sinus surgeries have quashed her sense of smell. Medications necessary to keep my daughter alive are gnawing away at her senses, and this reality got me to thinking. If I were a kid with CF, searching for a "why," couldn't I believe that this was all part of a bigger plan, a trade-off with the universe, and losing one sense was okay, so long as something bigger and better and more wonderful took its place, especially if that something wonderful was communicating with dogs.

So there it is, the "write what you know" adage making perfect sense. It may be personal to me, but at the end of the day, it doesn't have to be cystic fibrosis. If you are in the throes of chronic disease yourself, or you are a parent, a sibling, a family member, or a friend of someone who is, the message remains the same. It could be autism, PTSD, diabetes, epilepsy, cerebral palsy, Down syndrome, muscular dystrophy, cancer, the list goes on and on, but this book is about the struggle, the quest for hope, and, in this case, how an unlikely dog might just be what you need to get through and lead you to the other side. I hope you get it, because as you read, I believe you'll see what matters most to me—I get it too. ∿

Reading Group Guide

1. Kate quotes data from an American Animal Hospital Association Survey that asked, "What percentage of pet owners believe they know what their pet is saying?" Does the answer 97 percent come as a surprise? Why do you think almost all of us believe we share some form of unspoken communication with our pets?

2. Over the past two decades, there has been an explosion in the growth of pet rescue groups. What do you think has changed in our society to make adopting a shelter dog feel so right?

3. How do you feel about Kate's argument against having a family dog? Would you take your pet to a veterinarian who does not own a cat or a dog?

4. Before reading *The Wonder of Lost Causes*, had you ever heard of cystic fibrosis? Were you surprised that an estimated ten million Americans are unknowing, asymptomatic carriers?

5. Kate gets frustrated at always playing the bad cop when it comes to tough parenting decisions and, in the eyes of her family, not having a partner to back her up. Does this perspective on raising a child as a single parent ring true?

6. Does Kate's illicit use of Adderall make you think less of her or, given her circumstances, would you, like her, do whatever it takes to survive as a mom of a sick child?

7. Have you ever attended a school sporting event, watched the other parents, and noted the various cliques and parenting styles of those around you? If you are being honest, into which category would you put yourself? The Gossips? The Blasé? The Revered? Or a totally different one?

8. How do you feel about Kate's perception of what it is to be "normal"? Do you have friends caring for sick or aging parents, kids with disabilities, with autism, cerebral palsy, or Down syndrome? If so, how do you engage them? How do you relate to the challenges they face as parents?

9. Fake service dogs have become a thorny issue, not least for the commercial airlines. How do you feel about pet owners claiming their pet to be a therapy dog to ensure a seat next to them in the cabin? Do you feel there should be greater regulation/accountability of service dogs?

10. Family gatherings can be stressful at the best of times. Does your extended family back off or rally around in times of need? ▶

Reading Group Guide *(continued)*

11. When Gwen calls in the night, trying to set her sister up on a blind date, she says, "I just want my sister to have what I have." Do you experience sibling rivalry? Is competition harmful or helpful to such relationships?

12. Mr. Crabtree, the so-called Apartment Nazi, claims to love dogs, but can't think about having a dog in his life. He worries about who will look after a dog if he dies. This is a real concern for so many older pet owners who desperately need the companionship but fear for the animal's future in their aftermath. A whole new area of adoption has sprung up in the United Kingdom, where loving homes are guaranteed for older animals if their owner dies. How do you feel about this program?

13. When Kate meets another CF mom in the hospital, this stranger discusses the moment her life changed—the diagnosis of her child with cystic fibrosis. How did her description make you feel?

14. Cystic fibrosis, epilepsy, PTSD, and various forms of autism can be thought of as "hidden" disabilities, the disease having its effect on the inside, creating the appearance of "normal" on the outside. Have you ever found yourself wondering why a completely normal-looking

individual parked in a handicap spot, or didn't give up a seat on a bus or a train?

15. Kate's sister, Gwen, talks about the challenge of offering long-term family support with a disease like CF given the decades of care involved. To Kate's disapproval, Gwen compares and contrasts CF with cancer. What did you think about her conclusions?

16. Jasper loves the way that Whistler, through his actions, wants to squeeze everything he can out of life. How do you feel about this canine philosophy?

17. Service dogs can prove to be incredibly popular and helpful in elderly care facilities, hospitals, and schools. Have you ever witnessed what they can do and, if so, do you believe in the "power of dog"?

18. In the scene where Kate's rental car breaks down, a knight in shining armor in the form of a grungy biker proves that you shouldn't judge a book by its cover. Have you ever found yourself in a similar situation, being judgmental and regretting it?

19. If you have ever picked up a dog from a shelter, a pet store, or a breeder, did you notice the way specific creatures grab your attention? Do you think Jasper is ▶

correct in stating, "Dogs choose us, not the other way around"?

20. Social media can be both a blessing and a curse for those with CF. Because the disease creates so much isolation it can provide an invaluable source of connectivity to other CF patients, yet it can also be a direct window into everything they are missing out on in life. How do you feel about social media in this context? ⌒ﾟ

Discover great authors, exclusive offers, and more at hc.com.